JUDGEMENT

EDIE BAYLIS

Boldwood

First published in Great Britain in 2023 by Boldwood Books Ltd.

Copyright © Edie Baylis, 2023

Cover Photography: iStock

A CIP catalogue record for this book is available from the British Library.

Paperback ISBN 978-1-80280-196-5

Large Print ISBN 978-1-80280-197-2

Hardback ISBN 978-1-80280-195-8

Ebook ISBN 978-1-80280-199-6

Kindle ISBN 978-1-80280-198-9

Audio CD ISBN 978-1-80280-190-3

MP3 CD ISBN 978-1-80280-191-0

Digital audio download ISBN 978-1-80280-192-7

Boldwood Books Ltd
23 Bowerdean Street
London SW6 3TN
www.boldwoodbooks.com

For Anneliese x

PROLOGUE
JUNE 1996

Leaving Carlos Garcia on the bed, Marina Devlin swung her leg over the well-muscled torso of the man she'd just milked dry and pulled her baby doll negligee around her.

She walked to the floor-to-ceiling balcony and looked down from her beachside villa onto the azure expanse of the Mediterranean Sea, a smile playing on her lips.

The sheer material draped around her nakedness showcased her perfect figure; it meant Carlos was unable to take his eyes off her, like he'd been unable to do since their paths had crossed only three days after arriving, which was gratifying.

It had been almost three months now since Marina had escaped the miserable drizzling Birmingham weather. Almost twelve whole weeks away from that cursed shithole of a city which had brought nothing but trouble. This period away had bought plenty of time to move on with her life in unreserved luxury without having a bunch of losers out for her blood.

It also meant it was almost three months since she'd last clapped eyes on Samantha – that sister of hers who had been given everything on a bloody plate. Despite this, she had in no way devi-ated from her original mission. Why would she?

Marina smirked with satisfaction. She may have made the call to bide her time, but that didn't mean she had forgotten her aim.

And the end result remained firmly at the top of her to-do list.

She *would* get control of Samantha's casino and the rest of the business along with it. She'd have all the money it raked in, plus she'd take the kudos that came with it.

Lovely.

The whole thing could be run remotely from Marbella. It would be easy.

Marina's smirk grew wider because as well as all that, the best bit would be once she'd made sure her grasping bitch of a sister was aware she'd got the lot and there was fuck all she could do about it, she would be deleted.

Permanently.

Since she'd upped sticks it hadn't been difficult to keep track of goings on back in Birmingham. There was usually frequent coverage in the press about Samantha, being as her nemesis of a sister had manufactured herself into the city's self-professed darling. Marbella being a tourist destination heavily populated with Brits made it easy for Marina to get her hands on English newspapers to keep up with what was going on back home. Sure, sometimes the news was a day behind by the time the newspapers rolled up, but who cared?

'Marina...' Carlos's strongly accented voice murmured. 'Come back to bed, *bella*. I have nowhere to be until later, so we may as well use our time wisely, no?'

Allowing her negligee to slip from her shoulder giving a better view of the globes of her breasts, Marina smiled at the man in her bed. 'I guess I can spare another hour...' *If she had to...*

She moved back across the marble floor of the villa's bedroom to Carlos.

Carlos hadn't been part of the plan. But it wasn't a complete drudge. With his finely chiselled Mediterranean looks and fantastic physique, he wasn't unpleasant to look at. It was the fact he was loaded and held a renowned position in the music industry that was the incentive.

His standing and money weren't necessary. She had enough of both of her own – certainly enough to purchase an elite and popular beachfront bar, as well as an equally fine four-bedroom villa within two days of touching down.

She was sure exchanging a percentage of her red-hot cash for something physical – something that would remain *hers*, was the way to go. And she'd been right.

But that wasn't to say there were no plans to attain a large stake in Carlos's fortune down the road. He was already generous with his money, which of course meant more for her, but once she'd completely reeled him in, she could go one better. Although keeping him interested may be dull, it wasn't offensive. Forfeiting anything in order to get by these days wasn't required, but ensuring he became obsessed with her, was. But one thing at a time.

Feeling Carlos grab her hips, Marina upped her pace.

Much to her surprise, she was enjoying Marbella life. She'd expected the place to be filled with tons of skanky Brits on cheap package deals paid for by their giros. It *was*, but luckily, thanks to choosing her initial movements wisely and purchasing a business and property frequented by what could only be described as the elite and well-connected, she rubbed shoulders with very few of the great unwashed.

And there were no plans to change that.

That was, of course, until the time came to finish what she'd started.

And that would happen.

Just not yet.

When exactly, she wasn't sure, but she'd know when the time was right.

In the interim, she'd continue just the way she was – revelling in the luxuriant and prosperous niche she'd created for herself.

It seemed a shame to remove herself from this situation for even a short period of time, but it had to happen.

It wasn't Samantha Reynold's money that she was after.

It was a lot more than that.

Marina's mouth flattened into a hard line as, like always, the image of her sister filled her veins with poison.

No, she didn't want Samantha's money. She wanted her *life*. And nothing would be complete until that had been done, whatever attaining it involved.

This time, the bitch would not outsmart her.

And that was a promise.

1

JULY 1996

Seb Stoker straightened up from where he'd been leaning over the large table in the banqueting suite at the hotel he and Sam had chosen for their wedding reception, admitting he was impressed.

Stone flagged floors, arrays of armour along the candle-lit corridors and majestic wood panelling offered the epitome of mediaeval luxury. It symbolised their union – beauty, elegance and power.

He'd been so busy admiring the scenery, he hadn't taken too much notice of the seating plan, but if Sam was happy with it, that was just fine.

Keeping the reception more intimate with only a hundred guests ensured they wouldn't be awash with hangers-on or blaggers who'd shoehorned an invite. He and Sam would create a beautiful day where they weren't exhibits. They'd already put up with that for too long.

He entwined his fingers in Sam's, barely able to contain his enthusiasm for the day when he could slip the wedding band on her slender finger. Raising her hand to his mouth, he trailed his lips over her soft skin. 'You're happy with the seating plan?'

Sam beamed with delight. 'More than ever. And this place! I'm convinced it's more beautiful than when we booked it!'

The wedding coordinator hovering in the background shimmered with pride. 'I'm very pleased everything is to your satisfaction. Anything else you require, then don't hesitate to let me know.' She tossed her perfectly styled hair over her shoulder with aplomb. 'We'll ensure everything you desire for your special day is met.'

Seb returned the woman's smile. 'Thank you.' Regardless of her intentions, she couldn't provide *everything* he desired. Only Sam could do that.

Without thinking, his hand moved down over Sam's belly, a wave of love and amazement washing over him as his fingers followed the slight curve of her once washboard stomach.

Giving Seb a knowing look, Sam allowed him to steer her from the magnificent room which would soon be theirs to use and smiled, knowing the next time they entered this building, it would be to become man and wife.

Moving through the huge stone entrance, she squinted against the bright sunlight and feasted her eyes on the beautiful grounds.

Seb placed his arm around Sam's shoulders and bent to kiss her as she gazed wistfully over the ornamental lake at the end of the stone pathway. 'How much longer before I can formally announce you have made me the happiest man in the universe?' he murmured, the gradual changing of Sam's body never failing to enthral him.

'A few more weeks. I know it's hard, but we agreed doing things this way was what we wanted.'

'That's not the only thing that's hard!' Seb grinned, his eyes twinkling mischievously as he enveloped Sam in his arms.

Sam snuggled against Seb contentedly. They'd thought it safer to save the announcement of her pregnancy until she passed the three-month mark. To be extra vigilant, they'd taken that one step further and decided to wait until three and a half months had passed before making the announcement. But after eleven weeks of bursting with excitement and the need to share their good news, a further three weeks on top seemed an *age* away.

This decision was made doubly difficult by including her mother and Gloria in the blanket ban. Having two mothers, thanks to Linda being Sam's biological and Gloria, her adoptive, made her doubly eager to speak with them of her excitement as well as her fears. But absolutely *no one* could know until the agreed time.

Call it superstition or perhaps not wanting to tempt fate, but keeping the news under wraps for now was something both her and Seb had jointly agreed on, but she was certain people had begun to speculate whether the patter of tiny feet was on the horizon.

Both Seb and herself had struggled concealing their general contentment and pleasure, but had so far passed their happiness off as relief over the burden of Tom Bedworth and the threat from the Rosses no longer being an issue as being behind it. Now those two had been removed, thanks to Seb torching that Portakabin in Wolverhampton containing both Potter Ross and Bedworth, meant the risk from the pair of them was now finally gone.

It was that, along with stepping away from the riskier sides of their businesses, like they'd planned, that easily explained their joy to everyone else.

Thankfully, this decision to alter their mode of business hadn't affected their popularity or diluted the hold they commanded on Birmingham either. Cutting back on their coke and gun dealings to concentrate mainly on the casinos, whilst keeping the extortion and money laundering going as the side arms to keep their fingers in the pies, had proved a good choice.

The standing and reputation in the city of their two firms

hadn't faltered. Their platinum reputations were better than ever, ensuring no incoming chancers risked playing their hand. And due to the immense cash injection the heist had brought, the influx of money once needed to keep their firms ticking over was no longer necessary. The casinos held their own and were more than profitable, so they were in the best position ever.

And with the wedding next week and a baby on the way, everything was perfect.

Sam gazed out in awe over the grounds once again and sighed in contentment. It was a beautiful venue and this gorgeous man would soon be her husband.

Seb watched Sam, knowing he'd never tire of looking at her unassuming and natural beauty. *Ever.*

He'd never been so proud as when Sam told him she was pregnant. He didn't think anything could make him happier, short of the day they got to meet their child six long months from now.

The wedding was something else he'd longed for. When his casino, the Royal Peacock, was torched and his capital stolen, there had been a time when he'd genuinely feared he'd have to postpone marrying the woman he loved. Then with the onslaught of issues arising from Tom Bedworth and the Ross firm from Wolverhampton, to name but a few, his prospects had become limited in being able to happily offer his name to Sam.

Being unable to provide her with what he deemed a decent life was a no-do and he'd been adamant the wedding could not go ahead until he was back in an acceptable place.

Thankfully, he'd got there. The bonus of shortly becoming a father was the ultimate gift. 'Do you think your wedding dress will last another week?' he asked, his eyes dancing with amusement.

'I bloody well hope so!' Sam grinned, glancing at her belly. 'I hardly show, so providing this baby doesn't have a huge growth spurt over the next few days, I'll be fine. Luckily, the dress isn't skin-tight otherwise I'd be in trouble!'

'Well, *I* can see there's a baby in there! *My* baby.' Seb tilted Sam's head up to his and pressed his lips to hers. 'I didn't think I'd ever be this happy.'

Sam beamed widely. *Nor did she.* She was blessed in so many ways. 'You might not be quite so happy when I say I want you to go out and grab me more of those Pringles on the way back. The sour cream and chives ones.'

Seb laughed, his green eyes sparkling. 'That's not a problem! I'd do anything for you, Princess. Nothing could ever make me unhappy!' He raised an eyebrow. 'But don't get too complacent about your dress fitting by next week if you keep eating Pringles at the rate you have been!'

Sam returned Seb's laugh, her eyes shining with joy. 'Ah well, that's the risk I'll have to take because I insist on having them!'

'Mr Stoker?'

Seb spun around expecting to find the hotel manager, but on seeing a reporter, his eyes narrowed. They'd taken great pains to keep the details of the venue as low key as possible, not wanting the location known to anyone, apart from the invited guests. Sam was especially adamant about this, along with the finer details of what would be involved at the venue of their choice to be kept a secret, so to be a surprise for those invited. 'What the fuck do you want? This is private.'

The reporter held up his hands. 'I'm here covering an architecture exhibition the hotel has on tomorrow and I happened to spot you.' His eyes gleamed with the prospect of a scoop. The *Birmingham Mail* had been speculating for *weeks* about the exact venue and details of the upcoming nuptials of Seb Stoker and Samantha Reynold, but had failed. If he could get the story over the *Mail*, he'd score brownie points with his gaffer at the *Coventry Echo*.

'How are you doing today, Miss Reynold?' he pressed, moving towards Sam. 'You look beautiful. I take it this is where your wedding reception will be held? Mind if I just take a quick snap of...'

'Look, mate,' Seb hissed, hastily blocking the reporter's route. 'This is a private matter, so regardless of why you're here, we don't give authority for pictures or an...'

'But if I could just have one with you and Miss Re...' Stumbling as he scrambled to get a clear view, the reporter lurched forward.

Seb broke the man's fall in the nick of time before he crashed into Sam. Pulling the reporter up by the scruff of the neck, he yanked the terrified man close to his face. 'You almost smashed into her, you stupid fucking fool!' he roared, his green eyes fired with rage. 'Do not go near her now or *ever*! Do you understand me?'

The reporter grappled fruitlessly with the hands around his throat. 'I'm sorry. I-I didn't mean... I...'

Sam touched Seb's arm. 'Leave him and forget it. There's no harm done.'

'This bloody idiot would have fallen into you had I not stopped it!' Seb raged. Sam could have been hurt. The *baby* could have been hurt. Icy fear combined with rage built. 'No photographs now or ever!' He made a show of staring at the lanyard pass hanging around the reporter's neck. 'So, John Salter from the *Coventry Echo* – do I make myself clear?'

The man nodded as much as possible with his head in a vice. 'Okay, okay... I...'

Holding the man at arms' length, Seb ended the conversation with a headbutt, leaving the reporter to crumple to the floor. 'Keep the fuck away from my family!'

Grabbing Sam's hand, he steered her away. 'Cheeky bastard!'

Sam smiled pleasantly at the woman staring through a hotel

window at the man groaning on the floor. 'You didn't have to go over the top!' she hissed out of the corner of her mouth.

'I did!' Seb countered. Stopping, he pulled Sam close. 'You're my life. And now with the baby, you're doubly precious, if that's possible. No one is ever going to *think* about laying hands on either of you. That's a promise!'

Returning Seb's kiss, Sam inwardly smiled. God forbid they had a daughter. She didn't hold much hope of the poor girl having boyfriends down the line that would successfully pass Seb's suitability test.

Overprotective Seb may be, but there were a lot worse things to be than that.

* * *

Sitting in the back reception room of Gloria's beautiful home in Edgbaston, Linda sipped her tea and watched birds fighting for space in the stone birdbath on the patio edge.

Past this, near the end of the first part of the landscaped garden, Linda smiled at the area Gloria had insisted on being specially created for her two youngest children.

That this woman had taken in her kids at Sam's request when Linda had been first kidnapped by Tom Bedworth was more than enough for someone who had already been good enough to adopt her firstborn daughter to do. Then in addition, Gloria giving Linda a place to stay when she had been released from the rehabilitation clinic was a further sacrifice which could never be repaid.

Despite any of that, Gloria *insisted* the children have a proper play area – one which was theirs and theirs alone. For God's sake, the woman had already given the kids a climbing frame and a place to build dens in within *days* of them arriving, and now to have this massive area full of fantastic equipment and a tree house was beyond kindness.

Much to Linda's eternal shame, in the dump of a flat she'd dragged those kids up in, she'd never made the effort to take them anywhere to run around, let their hair down and be children. She doubted whether they'd even *seen* a decent expanse of grass that wasn't crappy Astroturf littered with dog-ends, old cans and used needles.

The worst thing was that Linda couldn't actually remember one way or the other.

But there had been other things taking precedence back then. Things like alcohol, drugs and her never-ending guilt over her many failures.

An acceptable excuse?

Not even slightly, but true all the same.

But those days were done now. She was clean and free from the people and things which had plagued her. She would never revisit that side of life again and would still be slap bang in the middle of that mess if it wasn't for Sam and, of course, Seb. Not forgetting Gloria.

Without all of those people offering their faith and kindness, she'd still be in the state she'd always been. Or, if Tom Bedworth had anything to do with it, dead.

Linda shuddered, before shaking away thoughts of the man responsible for setting her life on the downward spiral she'd found herself in. Now Tom was no longer on the planet, she could breathe easy and enjoy her life whilst making up, as much as possible, what she'd ruined for her children.

Linda watched a pair of goldfinches land on the birdbath, their distinctive black and gold plumage and bright red faces never failing to captivate her.

Staying at Gloria's was only supposed to be temporary. She'd planned to stay only for a few weeks until she'd adjusted to life outside of the clinic and got herself sorted. Money to buy a nice little place of her own wasn't an issue – Sam had already insisted she would cover that, but now after almost four months here, Linda knew she should start looking for somewhere else for her, Tayquan and Shondra.

She would sorely miss Gloria, this wonderful house and the local area which had warmly welcomed her. She'd miss all of it. It would also be upsetting uprooting the kids from school. They'd settled amazingly well over the past six months, considering their unstable prior existence.

However, Linda couldn't outstay her welcome or take advantage. She owed Gloria enough as it was.

Opening the local paper, she turned to the property section and began flicking through the local estate agents' listings, hoping something suitable was available to enable them to remain within the local area.

'I thought I'd join you for a cup of tea.' Gloria glided into the sunny room, her face falling on seeing what Linda was looking at.

Linda nodded to the paper. 'I'm just seeing what's about. I promise you'll have your home back to yourself soon,' she said, hiding her misery at the prospect.

Sitting down in front of the French windows, Gloria placed her cup of tea on the occasional table. 'I realise you must want your own space, rather than being cooped up here with me.'

Linda laughed – a *genuine* laugh – one she had now become used to when previously laughing had been invariably fake. 'You've got to be joking! Cooped up? This place is bigger than a palace!' Her face then became serious. 'You've been more than good enough to put up with us for so long, Gloria. I realise it can't have been easy.'

'Actually, I was hoping you might consider remaining permanently,' Gloria said quietly. 'I've enjoyed children being around again, not to mention your company. It's been lonely since Samantha's father, I mean, Len, died. When Tayquan and Shondra and then you came along, it gave me a reason to bother again.' She smiled sadly. 'Although of course, I completely understand you'd rather be on your own with your children. It's silly of me to think you'd want to remain here forever.'

Linda's mouth fell open. 'Are you serious? The *last* thing I want to do is leave! I thought th...'

'I'd *love* you to remain here!' Gloria smiled.

'You're not just saying that?' Linda gibbered, her previous paranoia peeping through. 'You're not saying it because you feel you should or...'

'Linda! I'd hardly offer someone a permanent place in my home unless I meant it.' She shook her head. 'I've come to regard you as a friend, not just my daughter's biological mother. I love those children like they are my own – the same as I did with Samantha, so what do you say?'

Without knowing whether it was the done thing or not, Linda jumped from her chair, almost knocking the cups of tea from the table in her haste, and threw her arms around Gloria. Planting a kiss on the woman's cheek, she beamed widely. 'Thank you so much! I'm over the bloody moon! I can't tell you how much this means to me. I was dreading having to leave!'

'That's sorted then!' Gloria clapped her hands together, the fear of impending loneliness dissipating. 'Now, let's talk about what we'll wear for Sam's wedding. As mothers of the bride, we need to look our best, don't we?'

Linda laughed with joy, unable to believe that her life had got this good.

But one thing was missing and it had played on her mind more and frequently over the last couple of months.

Vera.

Not having contact with her best friend and comrade in arms bothered her immensely. None more so than now everything was sorted and her life was genuinely good.

The awkwardness resulting from when Linda had disappeared had taken its toll with Sam and Vera. During the time she'd been held prisoner in the attic of Tom Bedworth's seedy brothel, the contact between her daughter and best friend had dwindled to nothing. For whatever reason, it had not been reinstated and the longer it continued, the more difficult it became.

Sam hadn't gone into too much detail when Linda had asked – and she'd asked several times. All she knew was that it was something along the lines of Vera feeling Sam wasn't doing enough to look for her mother, believing Sam had accepted the reasons on that note Tom had forced Linda to write before her disappearance: that she'd abandoned her children in favour of drugs.

Or maybe the breakdown in contact was because Sam felt *Vera* didn't want to know what the real truth was?

Of course, Linda knew there had only been two options that could be the truth: she'd abandoned her two youngest kids in the pursuit of oblivion, like she'd done to all her children at various points in the past. Or, like promised, she'd turned the corner on all of that, meaning something dreadful had happened.

Linda shuddered. Tom Bedworth taking her to keep her prisoner and drugged in his attic counted as the latter of those two options by miles, but perhaps the concept of her having fallen off the wagon was not only more likely, but less *final* than being dead? Maybe that's why Sam or Vera had believed that to be the case at first?

Linda chewed her lip. Whichever one of them had initially thought that, she didn't know. Either way, she couldn't blame them. She knew for sure that Seb had believed she'd abandoned her kids in favour of drugs, which had hurt, but again – it was hardly surprising. After all, she hadn't been particularly trustworthy in the past, had she?

Still, Vera had been a huge part of Linda's life for a very long time. The woman had helped her immeasurably over the years and was the sister she'd never had. It was time to bridge the forced gap in their friendship.

2

Tom Bedworth picked up the remains of his cheese and onion roll in the Red Admiral public house. The bread was stale and the cheese tasted like Potter had made it from the mould culture growing around the sink in the dosshole they now called home.

'Home' was a bad use of words. Tom hadn't had a proper home for as long as he could remember. Come to think of it, he was unsure whether he'd *ever* really had one at all. But one thing was for certain – where he was stuck at the moment was definitely not home and never would be.

He glared at the depressing shape of Potter Ross, taking up almost an entire wooden settle seat with his massive bulk opposite.

Pub settle seat capacity = 3 × normal people = 1 × Potter Ross.

Tom's nose wrinkled up with the smell from his lunch combined with the vision of Potter.

It was a daily battle keeping Potter focused on what they were doing. This difficulty level changed from day to day. Sometimes the man seemed normal in his capacity to hold a standard conversation and half-rational thought process. Other times, the bloke was as loo-lah as he'd first been when his brother had been killed, making it impossible to get a word of sense out of him.

Tom's thick brows knitted to make a dark furry line which overtook his entire face.

In many respects it was more palatable when Potter was threatening, trying to rob him and generally being a violent, vindictive wanker than this zoid-like specimen, who believed he had frequent conversations with the dead Mark Ross.

Quite frankly, Tom was never quite sure whether Potter was talking out of his arse or not. It was hard going. It also meant that 99 per cent of the time, working this shit out, foreseeing their next plan of action and deciding what to do, lay on *his* shoulders alone.

He'd get more input from a waxwork than this loony fat bastard!

'You getting another round in?'

Tom glanced up in irritation. Potter had barely said a word all day, yet now he'd spoken, he might have known it would concern another beer. No doubt *he'd* be expected to stump up for that again… 'You haven't finished that one yet.' He nodded to the chipped pint glass which was still half full.

'It's flat,' Potter mumbled.

'What makes you think a fresh pint won't be?' Tom snapped. The beer in here tasted like piss, but what exactly was expected from this shithole? Even if they had the money, it wasn't like there were many decent places they could go to at the moment. Especially in Telford.

At least it hadn't been difficult getting Potter to leave Wolverhampton. Despite the man's dubious lucidity and lack of comprehension of what was going on around him, coming to the agreement they couldn't remain in or around Wolverhampton was met without argument.

Tom had thought Potter would have a tantrum when he'd

stressed they needed to walk away from his firm and the city, but there had been little resistance.

Whilst all the residents of Wolverhampton, what was left of Potter's firm, the police and most importantly, the bastard Stokers, all believed the pair of them had been charred to a crisp when Stoker and his arsewipe brother had torched that Portakabin and most of Potter's yard, it was vital that belief stood fast.

They might be stuck in a dump in the back end of Telford, but as far as the rest of the world was concerned, they were ash.

A smile formed on Tom's raddled face. Being ash in the minds of everyone who'd been after him meant one thing and one thing alone – no one would expect it when he rose like a phoenix and finally took what he was owed.

That he'd almost been there – no, *had* been there, was gutting. He'd been in receipt of more than half the money swiped from the Stokers' casino and he'd got out of goddamned Birmingham too. If only he hadn't pushed his luck...

He scowled. If he hadn't been forced to hang around longer than necessary waiting for a fake passport to escape this crappy country once and for all, then none of this would have happened. Conversely, if he'd just kept his head down and waited, rather than pretending to be on side with Potter, then it *would* have all been done and dusted by now regardless of the passports.

All that he'd achieved by trying to filch more brass was losing the lot and worse – now he was lumbered with this fat cunt for the foreseeable.

Tom's eyes narrowed as Potter pushed his now empty pint glass over the sticky table towards him. Without fail – come what may, *this* time he would land enough of a payout to fund him for eternity.

But one of the worst insults, short of sharing a flat, as well as a bathroom with Potter Ross for the *second* time, was seeing that picture of Linda in the paper a couple of months ago.

That had got his goat even more than the remains of Potter's bowels stuck around the toilet bowl on a daily basis.

He'd left that old bitch of an ex for dead. Linda had been a fucking corpse, yet there she was again in the paper, looking better than ever. Yep, somehow she'd come back from the dead and aligned herself back within the throng of their daughter's wealth and success. She'd got Seb Stoker on side too...

The whole thing made Tom want to shove his own tongue down the back of his throat and choke himself. The only light at the end of the tunnel and stopping him from jumping head first into the nearest canal out of sheer frustration was that now everyone thought him dead, he could bide his time unhindered and anonymously, rather than waiting for a bullet from Stoker's gun with his name on it entering the back of his skull.

Tom resentfully snatched up Potter's empty glass and made his way to the bar. He'd been systematically watching and waiting for the time to reap the overdue payment with added interest. And that time was almost upon him.

He glanced over his shoulder at Potter slumped in the far corner and shuddered at the glistening trail of saliva hanging from the man's slack mouth.

The time to end this for good couldn't come soon enough.

* * *

Andrew Stoker leaned back in his huge leather chair and allowed his eyes to roam his desk. Unlike Seb, he'd opted for a modern look for his surroundings within the Royal Peacock. The sleek lines of the pale wood of his desk and the matching cabinets spanning the wall were a contrast to the old-world charm of Seb's office.

He shrugged. Seb wanted to keep the head office the same as it had always been – like their father, Mal Stoker, had back in the day. Seb had opted for an exact replica of the statuesque mahogany desk with green leather inlay. The dark wooden cabinets housing the drinks and crystal decanter were the same too. *Everything* was the same – even down to the office lighting.

Andrew understood that. Both he and his twin brother Neil respected Seb's wish. That office had been the one they'd been brought up around and where their father masterminded the plans, clinched the deals and undertook the initial hard graft to put their family, their firm and the Royal Peacock on the map.

When the Peacock burnt down, Seb was adamant it should be rebuilt to be as much of a carbon copy as possible. It was what they all knew and associated with the firm's success and fortune.

And it *had* been rebuilt and decorated in the same meticulous way – even the same colour scheme had been reinstated, but with the difference that the place was now fully modernised. The gaming rooms housed up to date lighting systems, there were brand new gleaming bars and all the restaurants had been upgraded. There was a wider range of materials to choose from compared to what had been originally available, but in essence it looked similar to how it always had, which was what everybody wanted.

Apart from Andrew's office. That, he would not back down on. And that was the only good thing the arson attack had achieved. He now had his *own* office, rather than sharing one with Neil. Not that it made much difference.

Andrew looked up as Neil entered the room. Despite the intrusion, his rugged face pulled into a smile. 'What's up, bruv?'

'Not a lot,' Neil grinned. 'Everything's running perfectly, as always.' He plonked himself down in the chair opposite and looked at his brother like the reflection in a mirror.

'I want to talk to you about the flat,' Andrew said. The large apartment above the Peacock, previously reserved for Seb, had also benefited from a substantial upgrade to its fittings and furnishings during the rebuild. And *he* wanted use of it.

'What about it?' Neil frowned, half expecting what would come next. As head of the firm since their father had retired, Seb got first dibs on the flat, like he got first dibs on everything, but he'd hardly used the place since buying a house with Sam.

'I'd like to move in. It's useful having one of us on site full time.' Andrew cocked an eyebrow. 'And it's not like Seb will live there now, is it?'

Neil pursed his lips. 'No, but you're not head of the firm, *he* is, so it's his call. Besides, I have as much right to it as you!'

Andrew steepled his fingers under his chin. 'Hmm, but I'm six minutes older than you, therefore *I* take precedence. It's not like you've settled down with a bird so...'

'What and you have? Have a day off! Just because I'm the better looking one out of the two of us and got more birds on tap, doesn't mean shag all when it comes to property rights!'

Andrew laughed. He and Neil had always been competitive – sometimes to detrimental costs, but not any more. Their relationship, as well as that with Seb, was now better than it had ever been.

But he wasn't about to mention the woman he'd recently met to Neil, or anyone. He hadn't expected the connection he felt with her. This was partly down to the fact that she clearly didn't have a clue who he was, which was a refreshing change, but it was also early days. Things could amount to nothing. But as it stood, his feelings were more than a passing fancy. Still, he wasn't giving anyone the opportunity to rib him. He'd been part of the stick Seb had received when he became involved with Sam and Andrew knew his brothers wouldn't pass up the chance to take the piss. And *that* he was not handing them on a plate!

Pulling a coin from his pocket, he focused back to Neil. 'You want the flat? I'll toss you for it!'

Neil lit a cigarette and shoved the packet across the desk. 'Nah, I'm only joking. I'm happy where I am, so I won't fight you for it.'

'Good job. You'd lose...' Andrew winked, only to receive a heavy gold lighter thrown in his general direction.

He grinned at his brother. Things were good.

Despite his initial fear Seb's insistence to pull back with certain sides of the firm's dealings would dilute their standing, he need not have worried. The word of their success in the Rosses' downfall, plus the removal of the flourishing trade of grooming young girls to work in less than salubrious city clubs, courtesy of Bedworth, had spread like wildfire.

Not only were the city folk grateful, but it reminded everyone that the Stokers and Reynolds were not to be trifled with, should anyone start thinking otherwise.

This knowledge also meant other random firms thinking they may chance staking a claim in England's second city decided it was a pointless and very dangerous idea.

But Andrew had learnt one very important thing from all that had occurred in the not too recent past – *never assume anything.*

Comfortable and trouble free they might be, but none of them could become complacent. They'd been in this game too long for that.

No one was untouchable.

But at this point in time, the firm was doing well, the casino was making a mint, their staff, as well as the family were happy and on a personal level, there may be a glimmer of a future with a woman. All in all, so far, so good.

Thinking back to the vacant apartment, Andrew nodded decisively – probably more to himself than Neil. 'I'll broach the subject with Seb later.'

'Broach what with Seb?' Strolling into Andrew's office, Seb chucked a pile of paperwork on the desk. 'Here's the rotas for the enforcers.' He pulled up a chair and looked between his brothers. 'So, what did you want to speak to me about?'

'I want to move into the upstairs apartment,' Andrew said confidently. 'After all, you've no need for it now.' But *he* might if things progressed the way he hoped.

Seb put to use one of his sterner expressions before breaking into a wide grin. 'Not a problem. It's all yours!' He slapped his brother on the back. 'Got you there, didn't I? You thought I was going to refuse!'

Andrew wanted to scowl, but couldn't help but return the grin. 'You bastard!'

'I could still change my mind, so don't push your luck...' Seb laughed as he got to his feet. 'Right! Unless there's anything else you need me for, I'm off. I've got a meeting with Baker shortly. It's about time I caught up with that toerag to make sure everything's in order.'

'Enjoy yourself!' Neil winked as his eldest brother left the office. Spending time with the detective inspector they had in their pocket was never an enjoyable pastime.

3

Vera stood at the window of her third-floor flat and gazed absentmindedly out across the skyline. Not a lot to see, short of further blocks of flats and a chimney belching smoke from one of the factories in the distance.

She steadied her rattling teacup on the kitchen work surface as a freight train rumbled past, the vibrations sending her crockery all of a clatter.

The noise of the Lickey Incline and its busy railway traffic didn't bother her. After a few days of living here, she hadn't really noticed it and she'd been here aeons now. But going anywhere these days seldom happened. Not anywhere different, anyway.

Vera frowned. Despite having trained herself some time ago not to allow herself to dwell on what *other* things were missing from her life, Vera found her eyes, as well as her thoughts moving to the flat she could see further along the walkway. The flat which had once belonged to her best friend, Linda.

By all accounts that friend had forgotten her roots – at least as far as she could deduce. As much as Vera prided herself on being tough as old boots, with skin thicker than a six-month-old gammon, Linda not bothering to get in touch hurt like buggery.

Vera sniffed loudly to remind herself that she no longer cared.

All of that she'd now put to bed. She'd got over it because after spending months convinced her bestest friend of all time must be dead, she'd cried enough tears to fill the cut at Stourport and enough was enough.

Putting her life on hold waiting for news that Linda Matthews had been found alive, well and safe had not happened, and so she'd had to accept that her friend was no more. She also realised she may never truly discover what had happened to the woman she'd always looked upon as a sister. Someone she'd loved to pieces and would have done *anything* for.

For months on end she'd got up each morning and walked along the walkway to Linda's flat and waited, listening. She'd hoped to hear a small hint from within which might signify her friend's return during the night. But each day proved disappointing. Linda never returned to her home to pick up where they'd left off. They'd never been able to go down the Hen and Chicks for a few jars like they always had; putting the world to rights and sharing their woes.

And it didn't look like they ever would again, so Vera had eventually started to accept that Linda was definitely dead.

Until she'd seen it...

Her lips formed a tight line as she snatched her cigarettes off the Formica worksurface. Bending down, she risked her newly dyed hair by lighting one on the gas hob and took a deep drag, aware her fingers were trembling.

They weren't trembling from fear or upset, but with *anger* because Linda Matthews wasn't dead at all.

Three months ago Vera was glancing through the *Evening Mail* when she'd seen the photo of Linda with Sam and Seb Stoker in the newly opened Royal Peacock.

Even though she didn't want to recall the moment when it hit her that the person she classed as a dear friend hadn't given enough of a shit about her to let her know she was okay, it materialised in her brain regardless. She could still remember the exact wording of that newspaper article as clear in her mind as if she'd read it three seconds ago:

JOY AT REOPENING OF CITY CASINO

The Royal Peacock opened its doors to the public tonight after the terrible arson attack in February completely destroyed it.

Pictured below at yesterday's pre-opening night is proud owner Sebastian Stoker, his fiancée Samantha Reynold and soon to be mother-in-law, Linda Matthews…

Vera hadn't needed to read any more. What she'd seen had told her all she'd needed to know.

Linda had looked a million dollars – much better than she *ever* had. She certainly wasn't the drug-addled wretch everyone had assumed her to be after her disappearance.

Attending the pre-opening night for the Peacock also spoke volumes. It meant that Sam had been in touch with Linda for some time – if not all along, yet Sam hadn't once bothered letting Vera know of Linda's safe return.

Vera's face creased into a frown, the lines deeper than ever these days.

All that time she'd been going out of her mind and trawling the streets of her own volition, asking around to see if Linda could be located. She'd done it faithfully, being as everyone else seemed to have given up on the woman as a bad job, yet it had all been for nothing. The whole time, Linda had been living it up in luxury with her daughter!

Even though Vera had vowed never to shed another tear over the woman who had so easily turned her back, the fresh burn stung her eyes.

For Christ's sake, she'd even ensured Linda's kids had gone to a good home. She didn't have to drag them across Brum to Sam's casino, then on to the woman's house who had brought Sam up, but she had, hadn't she?

No, she could have just phoned social services and been done with it. And she bloody would have had she not given a toss about those two little kids.

Vera violently stubbed her cigarette out in the saucer of her teacup, wondering why she still cared.

The sad thing was, she knew deep down that if Linda returned to her old flat this minute with a vaguely plausible explanation for not coming to see her sooner, then she'd accept it, like a twat.

Why? Because she loved Linda and missed her like crazy. She'd do *anything* to have her back. She'd forgive all the hurt like it had never happened.

But that wasn't going to happen either. This was set in stone the minute the council assigned Linda's flat, which had sat empty for several months, to someone else. This had come to light one morning a month and a half ago when on her daily sojourn down the walkway, Vera had heard singing coming from Linda's place.

Heart thudding like a drum, she'd pressed herself against the door, all thoughts of the lack of contact falling by the wayside. *Her friend was back and that was all that mattered!*

She'd hammered on the door, her excitement overtaking everything. But when the door had opened she could have cried.

She might have actually cried, she couldn't remember.

All she knew was that the person who opened the door wasn't Linda.

Suddenly hearing movement outside, Vera glanced through the yellowing net curtains of her kitchen and returned the wave from the woman passing the window.

That was who now resided in Linda's old flat – a young bird by the name of Sophie.

Grinning, Vera cranked open the leaky Crittall window. 'You up for a couple down the Chicks tonight, bab?' she shouted.

'I can if it's early doors, but then I've got to shoot off for a while.' Sophie smiled, the haunted look on her face gradually reducing each day.

Vera cocked an eyebrow. 'And are you going to enlighten me as to where you're off to tonight?'

'Maybe... maybe not,' Sophie giggled. 'I'll catch you later, V.'

Shaking her head, Vera shut the window. Linda wasn't coming back. It was clear the woman wanted nothing more to do with her old life and whether she liked it or not, she just had to live with it.

* * *

'How are your parents, Seb?' DI Baker attempted friendly conversation, even though it was a mere formality and they both knew it. 'Still cruising the world, are they? They've been off seeing the sights for so long, they'll run out of places soon!'

Hearing the man chuckle, Seb bit back the urge to tell Baker to fuck off. The dozy old fart wasn't being sarcastic, it was just the blundering buffoon's way of being friendly, but it never ceased to grate on his tits, regardless.

Seb wished the man would get to the point if there was one, rather than drone on with mindless niceties. 'They're still at sea.' He forced himself to smile. 'I've lost track of where they are.'

He hadn't, but he didn't want this conversation dragging on longer than necessary. He could never be friends with a copper, so didn't quite see why Baker pretended otherwise. Keeping the man on side was for necessity only.

Considering the screw-ups this overgrown twat had managed on more than one occasion over the last year or so which could have dropped him in the shit – correction, *had* dropped him in the shit – the man wasn't exactly useful. The only real use DI Baker had was providing a way to launder a bit of money out of the company on his fees.

Aside from that, there were no real redeeming qualities to their relationship, but Seb figured it never hurt to have at least *one* contact in the force, even if that contact wasn't much use.

'I take it Mal and Judith will be returning to see you get married next week?' Baker asked, his beady eyes weighing up the percentage of receiving an invite. 'It would be nice to see them both again.'

Baker frowned. Where the Stokers were concerned he knew he wasn't flavour of the month – *year* even – but if he could drag out their arrangement a few more months, he could comfortably retire and put it all behind him.

But getting invited to Seb and Sam's wedding would cheer his missus up no end. She could don her glad rags, as no doubt the wedding would be somewhere exquisite. But he needed to keep Stoker on side, so it was a case of how he broached this *next* subject...

Baker eyed Seb warily, the twitch under his left eye gaining pace. 'So, your parents? Will they be returning for your wed...'

'Cut to the chase for once, Baker, for fuck's sake!' Seb growled. 'You called this meet, so does that mean I'm about to be hauled over the coals for something I haven't done again?'

He folded his arms over his wide chest, watching Baker scrabble around for the right thing to say.

Oh, Baker knew what he was doing, Seb thought. The man wanted a wedding invite, but that wasn't happening. The last thing he wanted was the cops in attendance. And no, he didn't know whether his parents would make it. They knew it was happening and when and promised they'd be in touch, but he'd yet to hear from them.

It would be disappointing if they missed it, but marrying Sam was the most important thing in the world and he wasn't postponing that for anyone – his parents included.

He fixed his eyes on the exceedingly nervous detective inspector. Seb wanted to know the score and would get to the point himself if this muppet didn't. 'So, tell me... Am I being investigated about the Ross firm's fire in Wolverhampton?' He arched an eyebrow. 'I've heard the word on the street is that it was *me* behind the deaths of that fat fuck, Potter Ross and that cunt, Tom Bedworth, but for the record, I strongly refute those allegations!' He smiled coldly. 'People talk and I let them get on with it. I have far more important things going on in my life to care about tittle tattle.'

The fact that what was being said was true, was irrelevant...

Baker forced himself to laugh. He'd aimed for it to come out like one of those jovial belly laughs from people who had a good camaraderie together. Unfortunately, it sounded like someone had stamped on his balls. 'You're not a suspect! Why would you be? From our side, you've never been a consideration.'

Okay, so he'd had to lose a ton of circumstantial evidence and witness statements in order to make sure it remained that way, but he'd managed it. And although Baker didn't know it for certain, he had strong suspicions Seb Stoker *was* behind the torching of that

Portakabin and along with it, the boss of the Ross firm and that two-bit piece of crap, Bedworth.

Truth be known, he was glad they were off the scene – Bedworth especially. It was less hassle and paperwork for his men to deal with. But whether Seb had done it or was behind it or not, he'd keep those thoughts to himself. He owed the Stokers for his past fuck-ups. 'We aren't fazed when losers like them happen to shuffle off this mortal coil, so you won't hear anything on that subject from us.'

Seb's smile didn't reflect in his eyes. 'Hmm, just trying to remember how many times you've said that before, only for you fuckers to turn up on my doorstep and arrest me.'

Baker shook his head. 'It won't happen this time.' The general attitude of the force where the Stokers were concerned now was to give them a wide berth. It was common knowledge Seb and his brothers were choosing to lean in a more 'above board' direction, so there was no point upsetting the applecart. He for one wasn't willing to rock the boat and cut his extra income off.

'Right then! If that's all there is to report.' Seb stood up and slapped Baker on the back a little bit too hard. 'Keep me up to date with any concerns and our arrangement can continue. Now, must dash as I've got a wedding to finalise.'

Baker opened his mouth, but Seb had already left the room before he could say anything, realising with a heavy heart that he still hadn't been invited to the wedding everyone wanted to go to, and by the looks of it, never would.

4

Sniffing the maroon liquid in the crystal-clear jug, Marina took her time inspecting the freshly made sangria, enjoying the young and attractive bartender nervously hanging on a thread waiting for her verdict.

Making a concerted effort to separate each thick slice of orange, she swirled her pink-nailed finger into the drink and checked the pieces of fruit matched the exact number she'd specified.

It was also imperative there were no less than whole perfect circular slices of fruit. And definitely *no* loose pips.

Personally, she couldn't give a toss if the fruit in this shit was as mangled as fuck, or scraped from a pig's trough, but she liked keeping this lot on their toes. It was good practice reminding those who she paid wages to that they could be easily replaced if their service and standards were not up to par. She especially liked playing this game with the nice-looking young men in her employment. That and the handful of women she felt she must employ to keep the male clientele of her establishment happy with eye-candy.

Definitely a no-touch rule here though.

Not that her beachfront bar was that kind of establishment. Far from it. The Casa del Océano was the crème de la crème in only allowing entry to discernible people of Marbella. No riff raff here. And the private marina, like her namesake, offered a sectioned-off, private seafront included as a benefit of membership to her exclusive watering hole – one of many perks her rich and influential customers enjoyed.

Fuck you, Samantha Reynold. Others have the nous how to run a red-hot, luxurious gaff too, Marina thought.

But hers had the added bonus of being located in a beautiful sun-drenched part of the world, dripping with money, cool people and kudos – unlike the smut-lined streets of Birmingham, where the inhabitants thought pie and chips was à la carte.

Sniggering at the stark contrast, Marina's hand lingered far too long on the tanned wrist of the bartender as he poured her usual tester glass of his freshly prepared sangria, aware she hadn't yet uttered a word as to whether today he'd passed her standards.

Marina ran her tongue slowly along her bottom lip, knowing the young man was avidly watching her with a combination of awe, nerves and lust.

Because everybody did.

With a self-satisfied smile, Marina took a leisurely sip of the sangria and allowed the delicious-tasting wine cocktail to float around the inside of her mouth. Swallowing, she pouted her fuchsia lips and tossed her long blonde hair over her shoulder. She raised her heavily lashed eyes to meet those of the hovering young man. 'Hmm... acceptable, I guess...' she muttered airily.

Getting to her feet on her patent Louboutins, she stretched over the bar and straightened the man's bow tie. 'Don't forget to pay extra attention that your tie is straight...' She pointedly looked at the man's chest and pretended to read the gilt name badge. '...

Anton.' Her mouth curled into a lazy half smile. 'Appearances are everything, are they not? You know I only ever allow the best and most perfect to work here.' She fluttered her eyelashes. 'Now prepare me a fresh jug, please.'

'Si, Senora. Will Senor Garcia be in this afternoon? I prepare drinks for him too?'

'Yes, yes. He'll be in, so prepare them if you wish.' Marina waved the bartender away and let the breeze from the azure ocean, floating through the windowless opening to the golden beach in front, wash over her.

This was the life. As was the attention of all these grateful fawning bastards.

She felt her eyes narrow before purposely relaxing them. Not wanting to risk letting her mask slip in public, Marina fished her Dior shades from her clutch bag and put them on. Her eyes had a habit of revealing her true thoughts when she was busy thinking and sunglasses were the way to go to refrain from revealing any hints of what might be going through her mind.

An immaculately dressed woman with plaited auburn hair and a pristine white blouse tottered over and held out a silver tray loaded with a selection of English newspapers.

'Gracias.' Marina pointed to the table next to her. 'Put them down there.'

She watched the smartly dressed waitress deposit the newspapers and make a graceful retreat. All perfectly trained like obedient puppies, this lot, Marina thought, secure in the knowledge of what money and status commanded.

She wouldn't rush to look through the papers. She never did. It didn't pay to look like she was pining for Old Blighty or worse, that she wanted to know anything that might be going on back in that shit hole.

Because she didn't. She couldn't give a rat's arse what was

happening back in England. She worried about it as much as
syphilis, so it was sensible to maintain the belief that ordering the
newspapers was purely for the benefit of the guests. Not that there
were many British members. In fact, off the top of her head, she
could think of five or six of them. A couple of old duffers with a
shed load of cash; a retired judge and his wife, who she swore were
perverts of some description, and another couple – where the
husband in particular, thanks to his trade, was necessary for the
plans she had in the pipeline.

The majority of her members were local. *Real* people of *real*
importance. People like Carlos Garcia with money and status.
Proper people, running *proper* organisations – not two-bit trolls, like
her sister or that collection of inbred Stoker bastards.

Yeah, everyone thought her providing every possible thing
anyone might want – including the English papers – was good. Not
only did she get the national papers, but she got the local rags from
across the country too. One from up north, London – all of that
tosh. And of course, the Midlands…

The Midlands ones were the only ones *she* was interested in.
Well, Birmingham, mainly.

One person and one person only was the subject of the articles
Marina was interested in reading.

And on that note, it had been worryingly quiet.

Still, Marina thought, stretching her long legs out onto the
opposite stool. She had all the time in the world to wait.

'Hey you!' Sam ruffled Tayquan's curly dark hair and playfully
tapped him on the arm. 'How's things, little bruv? Where's your
sister?'

Sam's young half-brother grinned up at her with his endearing gappy-toothed smile. 'I'm good. Shondra's round at a friend's house tonight. Do you want to see the new play area Auntie Gloria's bought for us?'

Sam smiled warmly at the little boy, thinking how much he'd come out of his shell in the short time since living in a stable loving environment for the first time.

He'd excelled further once Linda joined the household and Sam thanked her lucky stars once again for Gloria having such a big heart to not only take on her young brother and sister, but also for giving Linda stability after leaving the rehabilitation clinic. It had worked wonders for them all. 'Show me in a bit after I've seen your mum and Gloria.'

Tayquan grinned. 'Okay. Auntie Gloria's in there.' He pointed to the sitting room, then ran off towards the garden.

'Don't stay out there too long!' Sam called. 'It'll be dark soon.' She rolled her eyes, realising she was acting like a mother hen already. Her hand gently caressed the slight bump that only she and Seb were party to.

'Samantha!' Gloria appeared in the hallway. 'I thought I heard your voice.'

'I just thought I'd pop over to see you and erm... Linda.' Sam kissed Gloria on the cheek, always finding it awkward knowing how to refer to Gloria and Linda when they were together. In her eyes, they were both 'mum'.

Gloria grabbed Sam's hand and led her into the sitting room. 'Come and sit down. Me and Linda have been busy discussing what to wear to your wedding,' she enthused. 'And before you ask, we're not telling!'

Sam laughed, glad things were back on an even keel with the woman that until last year she'd believed to be her real mother. Finally putting aside the hurt and confusion over not being told the truth had been aided by Gloria's insistence on helping with

Linda and the children. The wedding had also brought everyone closer, yet Gloria and Linda had developed a surprising bond – something else she was glad about. It was such a relief Linda had finally broken the cycle of the ruinous ways her past had lumbered her with.

She smiled to herself. Everyone was putting the past behind them. Her and Seb's decision to move in different directions with the businesses only cemented the fact that their lives were now heading on a completely different path. One she was both happy and excited about.

The only thing still prodding in the back of her mind was not knowing what happened to Marina – the half-sister who despised her enough to kill her and scheme so hard to try and wreck her and Seb's relationship and business. But Linda was adamant her other daughter had returned to London with her tail between her legs and wouldn't risk showing her face again, aware the extent of her deception was known and the feared Stoker firm were out for her blood.

In a perfect world, Sam would have liked a sister close in age to her, but that wasn't feasible. Whether she liked it or not, Marina was warped and twisted. It could never have worked.

'I'm ever so pleased she's accepted, but how do you feel about it?'

Sam looked up, horribly aware she hadn't listened to a word Gloria had said. 'Erm... sorry... What did you say?'

'Samantha!' Gloria teased. 'Is this wedding melting your brain? Or is there something else turning it to mush that you haven't mentioned?'

Seeing Gloria's eyes pointedly rest on her belly, Sam coloured, but managed to deflect the conversation elsewhere. She beamed with delight as Gloria animatedly filled her in about Linda agreeing to live in this house with the kids on a permanent basis.

This change of plan was better than she could have wished for. Long-term stability for Linda and the kids, as well as an end to Gloria's crippling loneliness was a winner all round. 'It's a wonderful idea! I'm very glad.'

'As am I,' Gloria agreed.

'Where is Linda?' Sam craned her neck past Gloria to look through the patio windows. 'Is she out in the garden with Tayquan? I didn't realise. Maybe I should ha...'

'She's not out there.' Gloria's brow creased with a slight frown. 'She's gone out. I... erm... I wasn't sure whether to say anything, but I'm uncomfortable about it and could do with your take on it.'

Sam felt the first spark of worry creep in. 'Uncomfortable? What do you mean? Where has she gone?'

Gloria leant forward, wringing her hands. 'Well, I... I don't want to sound like I'm being judgemental, but...'

'Just tell me what's worrying you,' Sam said, trying not to snap, but having previously felt so secure about Linda's new life and how she'd settled on the straight and narrow, Gloria's anxiety was ringing alarm bells. Had Gloria got a reason to think Linda would repeat the history everyone had worked so hard to keep her away from?

'After talking about the wedding earlier, Linda went quiet,' Gloria continued, her hands still frantically wringing together. 'I pressed her as to what the matter was and she admitted she wanted to get back in touch with her friend. You know, that woman – the... the one who accompanied you when you bought Tayquan and Shondra here?'

Sam sat back in surprise. 'Vera?'

Gloria nodded. 'Yes, that's her. Vera.' She stared at her hands like they weren't part of her body. 'I mean, I know they were friends and all that, but I... I don't know... I'm worried that if Linda gets back in contact, then...'

'You're saying you think she'll go back down the road she was on before?'

Gloria nodded, apologetic for even contemplating such a thing. 'I have no wish to cast aspersions about Vera. She seemed a nice person, but... you know... it *could* happen if...'

'Vera didn't take drugs!' Sam cried. In fact Vera was extremely against them. That subject was half the reason why she and Vera had lost contact. Or rather because *she* hadn't made the effort to keep Vera abreast of the situation.

It had been difficult. Vera didn't share Sam's opinion that Linda had abandoned Tayquan and Shondra in favour of drugs, like that note had suggested. Much to Sam's shame, it *had* been something she'd come to believe plausible after a while – something Vera vehemently disagreed with.

Sam chewed her lip. In reality, she should have known better, but so many things had been up in the air during that time, she hadn't known what to think. But she *should* have put things straight with Vera. She should have made the effort to go and see her and that she hadn't, weighed heavily.

Gloria studied Sam. Having bought her up from a baby, she knew her adoptive daughter well enough to read the signs. 'I understand why you didn't go out of your way to maintain contact. It was a reminder of all the bad things that happened to Linda, wasn't it?'

Sam nodded guiltily. 'I guess so and as time went on, it became harder to make contact. Vera's a feisty one and as much as I hate to admit it, I had other things to worry about. But I should have made time. She's Linda's best friend.'

Gloria pursed her lips. 'But the fact remains the same, Samantha. Vera belongs to Linda's "old" life and if she returns to her old haunts, she might become tempted.'

'Maybe,' Sam sighed. 'But I think she would be okay. Besides, what right do we have to stop her getting back in contact with her friend?'

'I hope you're right,' Gloria sniffed, a little put out that Sam didn't share her concern. 'Because I think that's where Linda's gone tonight.'

And if she was completely honest, there was a prodding in the back of Gloria's mind, nagging her that if Linda got back in contact with the woman who had always been her best friend, then where did that leave *her*?

Call it right, wrong or indifferent, but she wanted to keep Linda's friendship. She wasn't lonely any more, but if this friendship with Vera was reinstated, then she might lose her.

5

Sophie sipped her pint and grinned at Vera. She hadn't expected to make friends. She hadn't expected *any* of the things that had happened over the last month. She certainly hadn't expected to remain in Birmingham.

Coming to this city was supposed to be a short-term thing, but things had changed. A lot.

Her, more than anything.

For a start, if someone had asked her whether she'd enjoy sitting in a crummy old dump of a boozer with a woman old enough to be her mother, she'd have laughed.

But that was before everything had happened. Before all the things she once believed important, she'd realised with a short, sharp shock, were not. Before she'd almost lost her life and spent every day since waiting for further comeback.

She hadn't thought she'd ever breathe easy again or dreamt she'd wake up in the morning excited about what lay ahead. She hadn't thought she'd be comfortable going anywhere or socialising ever again. She certainly hadn't thought she would consider getting involved with another man. Or rather, *hoping* to. Yet all of those things were starting to happen. And, dare she say it, she felt that maybe, just *maybe*, there was a chink of hope left after all.

Sophie was the first to admit she wasn't the brightest button, but she wasn't so stupid to open her gob and discuss what she *did* know and what had happened.

She took one of the offered cigarettes. 'Cheers, V.'

'Right! That's it!' Vera cried, adopting a mock-stern voice. 'I can't bear it any longer. Even old Ned over there is getting suspicious!'

Sophie's head spun towards the bar in the Hen and Chicks and stared wide-eyed at the man Vera had referred to before realising her new friend was pulling her leg. She reminded herself to chill out. Acting nervous and defensive was good for no one. If nothing else, *that* would cause suspicion.

But how she'd love to tell Vera everything. It would be a relief to unburden herself. If she ever trusted anyone again, it would be Vera, but she'd made the decision never to discuss anything about her previous life with anyone – and that still stood.

'Did you not hear me, girl?' Vera cajoled. 'I'm still waiting... All I know is that *someone* has helped to take that haunted look off your mug these past few weeks and I'm pretty certain it ain't Ned!'

Sophie spat a mouthful of flat lager onto the table, unable to hold back her laughter. 'Not much to say really, V.'

'Oh, give over!' Vera flapped her hand. 'This is the fourth or fifth time you've buggered off "somewhere" halfway through the evening. Why are you being so cagey?' Her eyes glinted mischievously. 'It's got to be a bloke, otherwise you wouldn't have that look about you. Good in the sack, is he?' Her eyes suddenly narrowed. ''Ere, he ain't married, is he? Don't play that game, girl. It always ends in tears and I don't want you getting hurt.'

And she didn't. Call it a strange twist of fate and yet another reason to back up Vera's theory that life worked in mysterious ways. Linda may no longer want anything to do with her, but the universe had brought *this* woman into her life instead. Not as Linda's replacement – no one could ever be that, but someone to share time with; to look after and almost mother, in a way...

'He's not married.' Sophie felt unable to meet Vera's eyes. *At least she didn't think he was.* She hoped not, but she knew little about him. She preferred it that way. Asking no questions meant less reason for him to ask *her* any. And that's the way it had to be.

'And I'm not being cagey.' This time Sophie met Vera's inquisitive gaze. 'I don't want to tempt fate by talking too much about anything yet, if you know what I mean?'

Vera smiled knowingly. 'Yes... It means you like this man a lot!'

Sophie knew her cheeks had flushed close to the colour of her lipstick, but she couldn't help it. It was true. Against her will she'd found herself really liking this man and although the prospect was exhilarating, it scared her to death. She'd promised not to get involved with anyone again and yet, within a matter of months, here she was falling faster for someone than was remotely comfortable.

Because of her spiralling feelings, this person could have the power to ruin her, should she not keep a lid on it, so the longer she could keep him at arms' length, the less chance there was of that happening.

That was the plan, anyhow.

Sophie glanced at the clock on the wall sitting at a strange angle. Tilting her head, she worked out it was time she made a move. Nerves jangled like they always did each time she pictured the man she was shortly meeting.

Necking the remains of her pint, she got to her feet and kissed Vera on the cheek. 'I'm off now, so I'll see you in the morning.'

Vera's lips pursed. *Scuppered again and still none the wiser. Oh well. Give it time.* She plastered on a smile. 'Have a good night then, love. I won't stay much longer myself now, so if you want to pop round later, then feel free. Failing that, I'll see you tomorrow.'

Returning Sophie's wave as she left the Hen and Chicks, Vera stared at the remains of her pint, wondering whether to have one more before returning to the flat.

It didn't matter – another drink wouldn't remove the similarities between Linda and Sophie.

Vera snatched up her cigarettes and lit one.

When she'd first introduced herself to Sophie, it had been like a blast from the past. The day she'd met Linda in the coffee shop all those years ago when the wench had been but sixteen years old, she'd been immediately drawn to the subdued girl with the weight of the world on her shoulders and had felt compelled to take her under her wing.

Okay, so Sophie wasn't sixteen and hadn't been looking to go on the game like Linda had, but they shared the same haunted expression; the eyes which had seen things they shouldn't; the things in their mind they'd prefer to forget, and the hurt and betrayal that wouldn't resolve. They shared that look behind the eyes that only fear could bring.

Sophie had all the traits. And so, like with Linda, Vera was drawn like a moth to a flame. Sophie reminded her so much of Linda and immediately clicking with the girl only confirmed that fate had brought them together.

Vera's hand closed around her pint and she flicked the wet beer mat stuck to the bottom of the glass in irritation.

But try as she might, Sophie remained a closed book when it came to her past and what had brought her to Northfield. From her accent, it was obvious she wasn't a Brummie. Sophie was a southerner if she'd ever heard one, but despite all the avenues she'd tried, Vera had not been able to get the girl to open up.

Of course, she didn't want to force Sophie's hand. What right did she have? All she could hope for was that in time Sophie trusted her enough to share the real story of the darkness behind her eyes – the darkness that was gradually lifting.

Vera hoped that perhaps some of the disappearing hurt might be courtesy of their friendship, but suspected it to be more along the lines of this new 'mystery man'.

She dearly hoped this guy wasn't a wanker, like most men seemed to be.

Grinding her cigarette out in the ashtray, Vera finished the dregs of her lager and prepared to make the short walk back to her flat.

* * *

It didn't take Vera long to get back to the flats, aided by the chippy being closed. Bloody Greeks! They'd probably all fucked off to a family wedding. Didn't their celebrations bang on for bloody days? Sod anyone wanting sausage and chips!

What the fuck would she do now? She had sod all in the freezer and an equally paltry offering in the cupboard.

Vera paused halfway up the stairwell to the third floor. Maybe she should have gone back to the Chicks? At least she could have blagged a bag of crisps or pork scratchings. It was Monday, so the darts team was in tonight and the Chicks always knocked up a few plates of sarnies for them. She could have pinched a couple and no one would have noticed.

Nah, she'd head home and find a tin of soup or something knocking around.

Shaking her head, she continued up the stairwell, stepping over the huddled figure of a glue sniffer sprawled on the bottom step.

Turning onto the third floor, Vera continued, her eyes half on the figure of a woman moving away further up the walkway.

Who was that? Maybe another newbie? Wasn't the flat two doors up from Sophie's empty now? No, it couldn't be for this woman. She wore far too posh clobber to live around here.

Shrugging, Vera carried on, her eyes still focused on the back of the woman in the distance. It was something about the way the woman walked which caught her eye and jogged her memory.

The woman moved in the same way as...

Vera stopped dead, yards from her own front door.

Fuck. It couldn't be!

The urge to call out the name burnt on her tongue, but she held fire. She'd done that several times in the past, only to look like an utter loon when a complete stranger turned to eye her with irritation.

But Vera didn't need to call out a name, because the sense of recognition was reciprocated by the other woman too because she turned around.

'I knew it had to be you! Only *you* have shoes with one heel that clacks louder than the other!'

Dropping her handbag to the floor, Vera raced towards Linda. They crashed into each other halfway along the walkway and enveloped each other in a hug, tears pouring down their cheeks.

6

'You're two fucking minutes late,' Amber Davis muttered as Tina Smith skulked in for the morning shift. 'You make a habit of scraping in by the skin of your teeth and you'll lose this job, girl. Do you understand?'

Tina nodded. 'Sorry. The bus was late. I'll catch an earlier one from now on.'

'Make sure you do,' Amber snarled, flouncing off.

Tina refrained from meeting Alan's look. He knew *exactly* what she was thinking: that Amber Davis was a jumped-up, sad cow who thought herself a boss at NASA, rather than the deputy shift manager at a Wimpy branch inside Birmingham Airport.

But she'd keep her gob shut and her head down.

Making sure no loose tendrils of hair had escaped from the elastic band of her ponytail, Tina wedged the uncomfortable cap on her head and quickly buttoned up the sides of the ugly tabard that formed her uniform.

Yeah, a job at a burger joint was a far sight removed from her previous jobs, but she was lucky. She was *damn* lucky actually, and she should remember that, rather than ballsing up the chance of the new life she was building for herself.

One which didn't involve being murdered.

Tina smiled at Alan as she cranked up the deep fat fryer and made a start on wiping down the stainless steel before getting the first load of fries underway.

Alan was a good laugh. He'd showed her the ropes when she'd first started and went out of his way to cover for her if she happened to be a few minutes late, which seemed to be happening more and more frequently, thanks to the bus. He made no secret of wanting to take her out for a drink, but it wasn't something she was interested in. Not after Dan. Not after *any* of that. She wanted nothing distracting her from what she was now set on doing.

The last thing she wanted was to lose this job. Poxy as it may be, it was a steppingstone.

But one thing was for certain and that was she would not go back down the road of her previous line of work. It was a miracle that she'd lived through it. Or survived the aftermath...

And to think not so many months ago she'd had the chance of escaping that life. If she had, then she'd now be somewhere the other side of the world with a man who had really cared about her.

Tina's fingers clenched tightly around the bleach-covered J-cloth. *Don't think about Dan or the past*, she reprimanded herself. *You know it will do you no good.*

But no matter how much she didn't want to think about Dan, his memory still pushed into her mind most days and certainly every night. Along with the vivid image of finding his body butchered and mutilated like an animal in the hallway of her house that night after doing Samantha Reynold a favour.

Tina's mouth formed a thin line. How pleased she'd been to think that she, Tina Smith, was of use to someone like Sam Reynold. That was until she discovered that to do Sam's bidding and get justice for her own murdered mother, she'd be dropping the man she loved in the shit.

And by fuck, had she done that! The night she'd returned from telling the police it was that bastard, Bedworth, behind the murder of her mother and half the other outstanding crimes in Brum was the night her betrayal had somehow reached the man himself.

Tina felt tears of sadness and rage brewing behind her eyes. She pulled her cap lower.

Yeah, Bedworth had come to kill Dan. He'd have killed her too, had she been there...

It *had* to be Bedworth. Who else would have done that and then taken the money that her and Dan planned to leave with?

And that was why she'd had to go.

In hindsight, she should have remained under Sam's protection, rather than throwing that lovely flat and the job at the casino back in her face. She should have believed Sam when she'd said Bedworth would be dealt with.

Instead, she'd robbed a float from the till and done a runner. She'd only done it because she'd been terrified. Utterly terrified – both of Bedworth *and* of the Stokers.

Tina knew the Stokers hated her and didn't trust her, so she couldn't stay there, she just *couldn't*.

But every day since she'd felt guilty about Sam, who had been so kind in her hour of need. Okay, so she'd only taken four hundred quid. She could have swiped all the money from the till, but she hadn't. She'd just taken enough to get out of the city centre and find somewhere to stay for a while. But she should have stuck firm. She should have listened because not long after, she'd seen the paper. Bedworth had been torched in that Wolverhampton fire.

And Tina knew the Stokers must have been behind the man's demise, just like Sam had promised.

How she'd yearned to rustle up the courage to contact Sam

ever since, but she'd never managed it. Now it was better to let things lie. For all she knew, Sam and the Stokers could still be mad with her. She doubted whether people like that forgot or forgave anything.

But Bedworth was dead and that was the only thing that mattered.

Now having swung this job at the airport, things were looking up. Every day she chatted more and more to other airport staff, getting especially friendly with some of the air hostesses.

She could do a job like that if she got the chance and where better than to eventually get the option, but at an airport?

Start low and aim high. Burger shop now – air hostess later.

That way she'd have a decent job, see the world and escape the foul memories of her previous life.

And she'd work her arse off until that opening materialised because eventually one would. It *had* to.

This morning Potter was in one of his more lucid frames of mind which made Tom think it worth running ideas past him whilst he had the chance.

He focused on Potter studying the racing form in the paper and pretended it was normal for him to be doing something which required a modicum of concentration, rather than staring at the wall, dribbling like a pointless fool, like he did half the time. Oh yes, he'd keep up the act that having a standard conversation with the man wasn't a rare occurrence and just hoped it lasted, rather than being a fleeting blip.

'Anything decent on today?' Tom asked, toying with the idea of having a bit of a flutter himself.

Tom knew Potter had a vested interest in a couple of dogs at

Hall Green. And from what he'd said in the past, it was long overdue that the mangy fuckers brought a reward for the money he'd ploughed into decent dog trainers. But, considering, like him, Potter was supposed to be dead, payment for the greyhounds' upkeep would have fallen by the wayside, like a lot of things, meaning they'd no longer be welcome in the owners' area at the track. That was an utter shit, but then it wasn't like they could risk going to Brum.

That aside, there was sod all stopping him from recouping a few quid via a bet, was there?

'There ain't any decent ones running today,' Potter mumbled, not bothering to glance up. 'Looking at the form of this lot, I reckon half of them have three fucking legs!'

Tom frowned. 'Is Champion Star not running today? Or what about Pegasus Peg?'

Potter shook his head. 'Nah, neither of them, whoever they are, but with shit names like that, they've probably been put down out of pity!'

Tom rolled his eyes. Could Potter not recall that *he'd* chosen the names for those greyhounds himself? Probably not, but he wouldn't bother mentioning it. He resented telling Potter *anything*. He always had. The only reason he was stuck here with the mental toad was because he was out of fucking options. And the sooner he had options, the sooner he could get away from the mad bastard.

Which reminded him. 'I think we should put together some viable ideas on how to move forward with our plan.'

This time Potter looked up from the paper. He placed his pen on the kitchen table. 'I've been thinking that myself. Actually, I'm getting pissed off with you ignoring the subject. We haven't got time to sit around just because you can't be arsed!'

Tom's hands clenched into fists out of sight of Potter's beady eyes. *What? He couldn't be arsed?*

Forcing himself to swallow the unjust insult, he jumped straight into the subject. 'Well, let's look at the facts: we've been clear of both Wolverhampton and Brum for three months; everyone thinks we're dead and no one in Telford knows us. We've been in contact with no one, so I reckon we're in a safe position to strike.'

Getting into the swing, he leant on the table Potter dwarfed with his bulk. The table was small by anyone's standards, but next to *him*, it looked the size of a shoebox. 'Our main aim is to replenish funds an...'

'Get revenge for Mark's murder, along with the fucking insult, you mean?' Potter interrupted, his eyes shining with malice. 'Mark won't accept anything else but retribution for his death.'

Tom glared at Potter, disappointment brewing. *Couldn't they just have one realistic discussion?* This bollocks about conversations with the dead brother had started already? That did not bode well. Still, he'd have to humour the bloody idiot if he wanted to get anywhere and hope things didn't further deteriorate.

'I hear what you're saying, but isn't taking the money the Stokers stole back from me and for pulling that heist on our cocaine the most pressing things?' Tom asked. 'When the Stokers realise it's us behind it and that we're not dead after all will be most satisfying.'

He could already imagine the snarl on Seb Stoker's face as it dawned on him there wasn't a thing he could do. *It was beautiful.* 'By the time they can act we'll be long gone with the money.'

If Potter wanted to stick around, that was his call, but *he* would be on the next plane and never darken the borders of this shitforsaken dump of a country ever again.

'Bedworth,' Potter snarled. 'Have you forgotten that I found my own brother's head in a drum of washing powder, courtesy of those cunts? Because *I* haven't. So, no, the money won't be enough!' He slammed his meaty fist on the cheap table. 'I've promised Mark it would be like for like revenge and that is what we'll be doing. Yeah, I want the money, but more importantly, I want one of their lives!'

Tom flinched at the worrying splintering sound Potter's fist made on the kitchen table. No, he hadn't forgotten about Mark Ross's head. That was because it hadn't happened like Potter remembered it. The fat bastard hadn't found Mark's fucking head, *he* had. And what was this shite about wanting retaliation for Mark's life? Potter had hated his brother and treated the guy like crap. Why now pretend the man was an important member of his family? *Short fucking memory, this prick*, Tom thought. *Or rather, a selective one...*

His eyes tracked up to Potter, hearing the tell-tale humming coming out of his fleshy mouth. *Oh no, he was on one again. He knew this would happen. For fuck's sake! Quick, pull him back to Planet Earth.* 'Okay, I completely understand. Then that's what we'll do. Revenge and money.' *Just say it, Tom. It doesn't have to amount to anything when the time comes.*

The last thing he wanted to do was lurk around longer than necessary, but he did have an idea – one which had formed some time ago and now, if he played his cards right, would satisfy Potter's demand – at least on the surface. What it would *definitely* do was guarantee the money.

'Did you hear me?' Tom said loudly, waving his hand in front of Potter's face. 'I said, we'll go for revenge *and* the money.'

Potter grabbed Tom's wrist and twisted his hand away from his face. 'I'm not deaf or mad! I heard you, so get your fucking hand out of my bastard face before I snap it off!'

Wincing, Tom rubbed his throbbing wrist. *Keep calm, keep calm, Tom.* 'Okay, so here's my idea...' He grinned hopefully, not liking the creepy look in Potter's eyes. It put him off every time. 'I suggest we kidnap Samantha Reynold. Stoker will pay through the teeth to get her back.' He sat back all pleased with himself and waited for Potter's congratulations on his foresight.

'You want to kidnap and kill your own daughter?' Potter raised his eyebrows, enjoying the shock on Tom's face. 'Didn't realise I knew that, did you? Contrary to whatever you think, Bedworth, I remember. It was what you said when you saw the picture in the paper of the Peacock's reopening.'

Tom acted like his previous slip-up didn't matter. *Actually, it didn't.* 'It makes no difference to me if Sam's my daughter or not.' Family loyalty should have dictated the little bitch should never have treated him like a cunt in the first place. Yet another rogue gene she'd inherited from her slag of a mother. 'I owe Sam no favours and certainly possess no urge to protect her.' He eyed Potter slyly. 'If we're getting revenge, then I want mine to be aimed at her, as well as Stoker.'

But unlike Potter, he didn't want to risk getting had by Stoker in order to achieve that, so the quicker they blackmailed him, got the money and fucked off, the better. If it just so happened that Sam paid the ultimate price, then so be it. As far as he was concerned, money was worth a thousand times more than her, so the green stuff took precedence any day. He wouldn't mention that bit though.

'If that's the way you feel about your own flesh and blood, then who am I to judge?' Potter clapped his hands together. 'Fine! I'm happy to go with Sam Reynold being the trade-off.'

The fucking hypocrite, Tom seethed. Like Potter gave a shit about his own.

Potter eyed Tom suspiciously. 'When are we going to kidnap and kill the bitch then?'

'I'm working that out now,' Tom said confidently. 'There are a couple of available options.' *No, there wasn't.* He might have had this idea for a while, but hadn't yet figured out when they'd have a clear opportunity to strike.

But he *would*. The only issue was how to cover up this major flaw in his plan in the interim.

Tom glanced up, waiting for Potter to throw the next question at him, but for once he was overjoyed to find the man muttering to the blank wall as he started another in-depth conversation with his dead brother.

Sitting back, Tom grinned. That was bloody good timing. All he had to do now was tidy up the loose ends and they'd be good to go. Even if his brain fried under the strain, before the week was out he'd think of a way to take that cow from under Stoker's nose.

7

Feeling like all his Christmases had come at once, Andrew found his hand playing with a long tress of blonde hair belonging to the sleeping woman.

Never could he remember wanting to touch a woman's hair, short of grabbing it during a frantic shagging session or to pull a troublesome bitch out of the way if the need arose.

But Sophie was different...

He found himself swallowing a smile. For fuck's sake, he wasn't entirely convinced her locks were even real! Her hair looked too shiny to be kosher, but he didn't have the first clue how to tell the difference whether it was those extension things some birds wore, or not. It never mattered as he didn't usually go out of his way to spend time with chicks who possessed certain 'attributes'.

Thanks to his situation, he'd been surrounded by birds with silicone tits, lips full of filler, fake nails and plastic hair his whole adult life. And although happy to partake in the goods on offer in the casinos and clubs, the kind of woman donning that get-up, he earmarked for gratification purposes only.

The fact that these women also tended to own the additional

traits of lack of brain power, along with a homing device to a stacked wallet, may be a sweeping presumption – Andrew knew the main reason these birds threw themselves at him was because of his name and what it may bring.

Sophie may have many of those physical attributes, but unless she was an Oscar-winning actress, which he very much doubted, she didn't have a blind clue who he was. And along with liking everything about her – more than he thought possible – was the other major factor in thinking that she *could* be one to keep.

And he liked that unfamiliar prospect.

Leaning over Sophie's prone body, he reached for his cigarettes from the bedside table and lit one. Sophie did not stir, short of an endearing little moan as she turned over, still sleeping soundly.

Staring at the lashes fanning her cheek, Andrew's chest swelled with possibility.

What was the matter with him? Could a chick have captured his heart?

It was beginning to look that way. It wasn't as scary as he'd first thought. At least, not yet. How it would pan out down the line might be a different story and not one he wanted to think about right now.

At this precise moment, he was too much in a state of rose-tinted bliss to allow thoughts about *that* to poison his budding happiness.

Andrew blew out a thin line of smoke and rubbed his fingers across the overnight growth of stubble on his chin, trying to remember what had possessed him to first go off the beaten track for a drink a couple of months ago?

Going out of town a couple of nights a week hadn't been to hook up with a woman! If anything, that achieved nothing but complicating matters, so it was the furthest thing from his mind.

He frowned. It was more to do with taking a leaf out of Gary's book. His youngest brother, God rest him, had done just that. Something Andrew would always remember.

Before Gary was murdered, he'd taken to drinking in pubs where few knew of him or his infamous family. When questioned, Gary had explained his wish was to be anonymous – to be someone other than a Stoker for a short while.

Andrew scowled with a mixture of sadness and guilt from how he'd pooh-poohed Gary's reasoning and called him a stupid cunt, amongst other choice insults at the time. He'd thought him an absolute prick because going somewhere where no one knew him had worked to Gary's detriment – to *all* of their detriment. Befriending someone he believed not to know him, had set them up and eventually resulted in his death, not to mention all the other things it spawned.

Yet now Andrew was doing exactly the same thing...

The difference was, Sophie genuinely didn't have a clue who he was and neither did anyone else around here.

The pub in Hopwood just over the border into Worcestershire was far enough away for his face not to be widely known. He certainly wasn't the first person anyone here would expect in their local boozer, even if they half-recognised him. So far it had all been good.

Now having met up with Sophie here the last few weeks – the first *whole* night they'd spent together had not been a disappointment. *Far from it!*

The prospect of shortly leaving to go back to the casino, even though he now had his own apartment there, was depressing and he wished he could stay here forever.

Clearly, staying in a room above a pub in Hopwood was not an option, but last night had cemented one thing in his mind... He would shortly have to come clean about who he really was and hope to hell it didn't scare Sophie off.

'How long have you been awake?' Sophie asked, her sleepy voice making Andrew hard on cue.

'A while,' Andrew murmured. Stubbing his cigarette out in the ashtray, he turned onto his side to face her. 'Did you sleep okay?'

'The best in a long time,' Sophie said, drowning in the green of this man's eyes. She'd been nervous about staying overnight with him. Not because they would sleep together. She'd slept with more men than she could keep count of, but nervous because she worried how it would make her *feel*.

Not in body, but in mind.

She'd been right to harbour those concerns because aside from every pleasurable nerve ending in her body singing its heart out, it had confirmed what she'd been dreading and could no longer reasonably deny. *Or stop.*

She'd fallen for this guy like a lead weight. She'd done the exact opposite of what she'd sworn not to. Now *everything* was on the line.

'Hey, what's the matter?' Andrew asked, his fingers hungrily trailing up Sophie's inner thigh to the place where he longed to bury himself into again. Concern glimmered. Did she regret spending the night with him? Was she looking for an excuse to leave?

His fingers froze, his raging erection at risk of deflating.

'Nothing's the matter.' Sophie guided Andrew's hand back on course. 'I just wish we could stay here longer. I had a really nice time, Andy.'

Taking Sophie's mouth, Andrew hoped his passionate kiss would translate that he felt the same.

It was strange to be called 'Andy'. He'd never been referred to as that, by his mates, nor his brothers. Not even his parents. But on introducing himself to Sophie the first night, that's what he'd called himself.

He had no idea why. Perhaps to disassociate himself from 'Andrew Stoker'. Whilst he was in Hopwood in a pub where no one did a double take and Sophie didn't know him from Adam, he was 'Andy Waterford'. Andrew Stoker didn't exist. But he would have to soon and he was dreading it.

For now though and for a while longer, he'd be Andy.

* * *

Sam hid her inkling of knowing what was behind Linda's excitement. She didn't want her mother being aware of Gloria's worries. Neither did she want Linda to know they'd been discussing the probability of her being tempted back to her old life.

Hearing the unbridled joy and excitement as Linda babbled away down the phone about the night she'd spent catching up with Vera, Sam was glad she'd kept up the illusion of ignorance. She'd have hated putting a dampener on her mother's happiness.

But she'd been somewhat surprised to hear Linda had stayed over at Vera's last night and spent half the day today with her.

Sam knew Vera well enough to assume there would have been animosity for the lack of contact, but it appeared that had been already mended. 'It's fantastic news, Mum,' she enthused. 'But didn't Vera ask why you hadn't been in touch?'

'I'm not going to say there weren't cross words,' Linda admitted. 'Vera was hurt that neither of us got in contact. She felt abandoned. Do you know she spent months looking for me, presuming me dead?'

As did I, Sam thought, remaining silent.

'It was only when she saw that photo of us in the paper at the Peacock's reopening night that she realised otherwise and it boiled her piss,' Linda continued. 'She shouted a lot, but understood in the end, especially when I told her where I was all that time.'

'I don't suppose she's too happy with me,' Sam mumbled guiltily. 'There was no excuse why *I* didn't get in contact.'

To Sam's surprise, Linda laughed. 'You could say that, but she admitted she could have come to see you too, but didn't. She's too much of a proud, stubborn old bitch for that – her words... But it's sorted now. Fuck me, Sam, it's like no time has passed. We've picked back up where we left off. Now, that's proper friendship for you!'

'Isn't it just!' Sam agreed, hoping the burgeoning worry wasn't noticeable in her voice. It was a good job Linda was down the other end of the line rather than in the room, otherwise she'd have spotted her concern straight away.

It was 'picking up where they left off' which nagged in the base of her brain. Gloria's warning rushed to the forefront of Sam's mind and glowed like a neon light the second Linda said they'd gone down the Hen and Chicks for a lunchtime pint. She hoped her mother hadn't picked up *exactly* where she'd left off...

There was also something else to consider too.

'What will you do about your living arrangements now? What about Gloria and the kids? You've only just accepted the offer to live there permanently. The kids are settled an...'

'Whoa!' Linda cried. 'I never said nothing about moving back to Northfield! Christ, Sam, it took all my power to walk up that shitty stairwell again. Short of Vera, that place only holds nightmares for me and it's not something I want to revisit or repeat! Me and the kids are staying exactly where we are. We're settled and I love Gloria to bits, so no, I'm not going back to where I came from. The only thing that's changed is that Vera's back in my life and I'm over the fucking moon about that!'

Linda must have heard Sam's sharp exhalation of relief

because her frown could almost be felt down the line. 'You thought I'd go back to my old ways, didn't you?' she snapped, insulted. 'Give me some credit! Vera can be in my life without it meaning that!'

Sam looked skyward in desperation. 'I'm sorry. I didn't want it to come across like that. I'm truly glad you've patched things up with Vera. I will do likewise.'

The clumsy affront forgotten, Linda cackled with mirth. 'Vera all but pissed her kecks when I told her how Tom met his end. She laughed for a good ten minutes straight! She'd seen it in the papers, like everyone else, but didn't believe it. Now she does!'

Sam couldn't help but chuckle, able to imagine her mother and Vera slating their nemesis.

'V's also over the moon about you and Seb getting hitched,' Linda continued. 'She knew it was coming, but there's been no reports as to exactly when, so she's well chuffed for you, bab.'

'Aw, that's nice,' Sam said, guilt flowing harder for cutting Vera out of the loop.

'And,' Linda added, 'although I haven't said anything, I know she'd be chuffed to receive an invite...'

'Of course!' Sam cried. 'It would be a pleasure for Vera to come to the wedding. I don't know why I didn't think of that myself. I'll get an invite posted straight away.'

'Nah, don't worry. There's only a few days left, so I'll tell her the details when I see her later on or tomorrow.'

Finishing the call, Sam put the phone down feeling a lot better.

Hearing Linda so adamant about there not being a chance of being tempted back into her old ways was a huge relief. Gloria would also be relieved. She'd also be glad to hear that Linda had no intention of moving out because Sam had the sneaky suspicion *that* fuelled at least a part of Gloria's concerns. Vera coming to the wedding would be the final piece in the jigsaw to smooth over all past issues and start a clean slate. It couldn't be better.

Apart from one thing. Since Gloria had mentioned Vera was back on the scene it had reminded Sam of one more piece of the jigsaw that remained unsolved – Tina, the girl who had become embroiled in the nightmare with the one-handed man found murdered in the hallway.

And if Sam was correct in her theory, this man had been butchered by Tom Bedworth in order to recoup the money he'd stolen from Seb in partnership with Bedworth.

Sam frowned. The only reason Tina had fled after being offered protection was because she feared Bedworth would come for *her*. Tina being a target was because she'd forced the girl to tell the police what she knew of the despicable man's actions in the first place, she was sure of it.

It was all right for Seb saying she couldn't be responsible for every waif and stray, but Sam couldn't help but feel responsible for Tina's predicament. And now only God knew where she was.

Sam chewed her lip. If she could find out that Tina was aware Bedworth was definitely dead and know the girl could go about her life in peace, then from *her* side, she'd feel better about her part in the whole thing.

But she had no clue where Tina had gone.

She'd looked for her occasionally over the last couple of months, making sure to keep her ear to the ground, but there had been no word; no hint of Tina's existence, so there had been little choice but to reluctantly accept that Seb was right. She had to forget about it.

But Sam could at least put things right with Vera. And that she was more determined than ever to do.

Looking up at the tap at her office door, Sam watched her second in command, Kevin Stanton, enter. 'I haven't forgotten a meeting, have I?'

Gloria had been correct last night about that too. Her brain *did* appear to be turning to mush. 'Baby-brain' they called it, so the doctor said. *That* she would have to nip in the bud.

'No, no meetings.' Kevin moved his big frame across the Violet Orchid's main office and placed a copy of a newspaper on Sam's desk. 'Thought you might want to see this, though you're not going to like it...'

Sam glanced at the paper. The *Coventry Echo*?

Sensing Sam's confusion, Kevin leant over and thumbed through the paper to page seven, his thick finger tapping on an article.

Sam saw the majestic frontage of where she would be marrying Seb at the weekend and her eyes darted to the accompanying story:

COOMBE ABBEY TO HOST GLAMOROUS COUPLE'S WEDDING DAY

Our reporter stumbled across two famous Birmingham faces when attending an exhibition at Coombe Abbey Hotel this week.

Although the exact location of Seb Stoker and Samantha Reynold's wedding has been kept strictly under wraps, we at the *Coventry Echo* are delighted to share where both the wedding and the reception for Birmingham's favourite casino owners will be held this Saturday.

The reporter, John Salter, chatted to Seb and Samantha as they finalised Saturday's arrangements...

'The cheeky bastard!' Sam cried. Kevin was 100 per cent correct when he said she wouldn't like this. *She didn't.*

And Seb would hit the roof.

* * *

'Where have you been?' Seb raised an eyebrow when his brother sauntered into his office. 'I've been trying to get hold of you all morning.' He thoughtfully inspected his fingernails. 'I know you've now moved into the apartment upstairs, but the runner I sent said there was no answer.'

Andrew dropped into the chair opposite Seb's desk. 'Didn't realise you're now my mother...'

A slow grin spread across Seb's face. 'You've got a woman, haven't you?'

To his horror, Andrew felt heat rush to his cheeks. 'Just because I stayed out last night means fuck all! Plus, I don't have to disclose to you where I go in my spare time!'

Seb laughed amiably. 'No, you don't, but I know you, Andrew, and you're acting strange. You've never been the sort to keep your conquests under wraps, so by that alone, I'm guessing this bird may just be one that you like...'

Andrew shrugged. 'Nothing new there. I like women! Who doesn't?'

'Yeah, but you're being too defensive, therefore I know I'm right! Come on? Who is she?'

'You've summoned me to your office to grill me about this?' Feeling trapped, Andrew rose from the chair. He didn't want to tell Seb about Sophie. Neil would find out and then he'd never hear the end of it. They'd all want to meet her and before *that* could happen, he needed to level with her about who he really was.

Seb frowned. Something had got Andrew's knickers in a twist. He must have it bad for this woman, whoever she was, but he wouldn't push it. 'Actually, where you've been is not why I wanted to speak to you.' He nodded to the vacated chair, indicating Andrew should sit back down.

Andrew reluctantly obeyed the silent order, worry prickling. 'Has something happened?' Just when he'd thought things were running perfectly...

'Nothing's happened,' Seb said hastily. 'I just wanted to speak to you whilst Neil isn't here.'

Andrew raised an eyebrow. 'Right, so...?'

'I want you to be my best man,' Seb smiled. 'So, how about it?'

A wide grin spread over Andrew's face. He jumped up, enthusiastically shaking Seb's hand. 'Yeah! Yeah, course I will. I'm honoured. Thanks, bruv!' If there was a chance of him being as happy and content with a woman like Seb was with Sam, there was even more reason to stick with his instincts about Sophie.

Watching Seb's relationship blossom and stance on life change since being with Sam had made Andrew contemplate his own life more than once over the past few months. Even though he'd never considered it an option for any of them, Seb had proved there *was* a woman out there perfect for each man. One who accepted the life and ticked every single box and the thought of settling down at some point had for the first time begun to seem a plausible, yet still unlikely option.

But what were the chances of *him* finding a woman like Sam was to Seb?

But with the way he felt about Sophie, perhaps he had? Perhaps, in addition to the firm, he could have a life and be genuinely happy?

Grinning, Andrew sat back in the chair, glowing with pride. 'I'm well chuffed you've asked me, I really am.'

Seb smiled. 'Good. I can't think of anyone else I'd want. Especially as I believe you're now tasting the power of what it's like to really want someone.' Seeing the immediate defensiveness rush back behind his brother's eyes, he held his hands up. 'You'll level with me as and when you're ready, so enough said.'

Anyway, *Seb* could hardly berate Andrew for keeping his cards close to his chest where matters of the heart were concerned. He hadn't levelled with anyone about his feelings for Sam for a long time. And then there was the secret growing inside Sam they hadn't yet shared with anyone. Andrew would tell him about this woman of his when the time was right.

Andrew deserved the same happiness that he had been lucky enough to find.

Seb glanced at his desk phone as its shrill ringing interrupted his thoughts. He snatched up the receiver. 'Yes? What? No, I've told you countless times, I'm not doing any stories or discussing th... What? You fucking *what*?'

Andrew tensed as his brother's face formed that particular expression he wore on hearing something which made him livid. His brows knitted as Seb continued to listen to the voice down the other end of the line.

'I have nothing further to say on the matter, now leave me be!' Seb slammed the receiver down in its cradle, his face like thunder. 'That was the *Birmingham Mail*.'

'For fuck's sake!' Andrew rolled his eyes. 'How many more times do you have to spell it out that you're not giving them info about the wedding? Why can't they underst...'

'It's more than that!' Seb spat. 'That cunt from the *Coventry Echo* – the one I told you about the other day? He's only gone and run a fucking story despite me half strangling the bastard! Now the whole world knows we're getting married at Coombe Abbey!'

'Shit!' Andrew hissed. Now the day would be hampered by a deluge of press and gatecrashers – just what Seb and Sam had been desperate to avoid.

8

Sophie's heart lurched with the frantic hammering of her front door. All the efforts of pushing away the thoughts that people could still be out there looking for her and maybe had finally located her, avalanching.

She'd been stupid remaining so close to where the trouble had been. Stupid to think it wouldn't catch up with her. She'd really begun to believe, now months had passed, that it was over. That nothing would rear up and ruin the glimmer of possibility that she might be able to get on with her life unhindered.

Yet now it was happening…

Finding herself scrambling underneath the kitchen table, Sophie's whole body shook with fear. *This table wouldn't protect her from that woman or…*

The door's banging increased in intensity and the tears seeped from Sophie's eyes. She'd had such a wonderful night and morning with Andy, but now she'd never know whether they had a future. Whether they might have been able to…

'Sophie? You in there, girl?'

Sophie's breath flew from her lungs. *Vera. It was Vera!*

Scrabbling off the floor, she pulled herself to her feet and hastened to the front door, her legs like jelly. Her shaking fingers struggled to turn the round knob of the lock.

'Where the bloody hell have you been?' Vera exclaimed, her face a picture of excitement. 'Oh my God, I've had the most fantastic night! I came round earlier to tell you but y...'

Stopping dead at the tears on Sophie's pale face, Vera pushed into the hallway and grabbed the girl's shaking shoulders. 'Dear God! Whatever's the matter?' All manner of horrible scenarios flashed through her mind. 'What the fuck has happened? Has someone attacked you? Has...?'

'No! Nothing like that!' Sophie gasped, struggling to normalise her breathing. 'I just thought... I...'

Frowning, Vera steered Sophie into the tiny kitchen and settled her down at the table. Taking the other chair, she grabbed the girl's trembling hands. 'Hadn't you better tell me what the fuck is going on? Is this to do with that mystery man of yours?' Her face morphed into a snarl. 'If he's laid a finger on you or if...'

'No! He's done nothing! It's just...' Sophie faltered. She couldn't tell Vera what bothered her, what haunted her and what she was terrified would catch up with her. But one thing was clear – she was in no way as comfortable with what she'd run from as she believed herself to be. This reaction had proved that.

'Sophie,' Vera pressed. 'Something has clearly happened and I think you should tell me what it is. I might be able to help if y...'

'You can't help!' Sophie blurted. 'Please don't ask me anything else. I can't discuss it. Or rather, I *won't*.' She fanned her face with her hands. 'I'm all right. I just had a wobble and panicked.'

Vera suddenly felt horribly guilty. 'It was me banging on the door, wasn't it? You thought I was someone else?' Seeing Sophie's small nod, she squeezed her hand. 'I'm so sorry, love. I'm like a bull in a china shop when I've got news. I take it someone's looking for you? Someone you don't *want* looking for you?'

Sophie shrugged, her nervous state making her look younger than her years. 'I don't know whether there is or not. I talked myself into thinking I'd been forgotten about, but then when the door...'

Vera knew better than to push further. Whatever had happened to Sophie in the past had affected her greatly, but forcing her to talk about something she was not ready to share would not help. She would extract it from the girl eventually and then see what she could do about it. In the meantime, she needed to put the poor wench on an even keel and bring this down.

'I don't know what you have or haven't done or who you're worried about,' she said firmly. 'I won't keep on at you about it, but what I *will* tell you is that I'm not a stranger to shit or the sort of people behind it, so when I say that if whoever you're bothered about hasn't come for you yet, then they're not likely to.' Vera forced herself to smile. 'The chances are they're already in the ground, okay? Besides,' she winked, 'they have to get past *me* first and I'm not going to let that happen!'

Sophie sagged with relief for not being pressed on her past and to have an ally in Vera. 'Thank you,' she whispered.

Vera could have wept at the smallness of Sophie's voice. These bastards, whoever they were, had a lot to answer for. She didn't need to know the ins and outs. She was long enough in the tooth to know a decent girl when she saw one. She'd love to get her hands on whoever had put the fear of God into this little thing. But that, she suspected, would have to wait. All she could do was sit tight and hope Sophie opened up before whatever tortured her succeeded in completely breaking her.

Putting on a brave smile, Sophie tried to look eager. She was lucky she had Vera on side. Knowing someone had her back made a difference. If it should all kick off, she doubted whether Vera's presence would prove much of an impediment, but that wasn't the point. 'You said you had a fantastic night? Are you going to tell me about it?'

'Ah, that doesn't matter.' Vera waved Sophie's question away. 'I'm more bothered about *you*.'

'No, really. Like I said, I'm all right. I just had a bit of a panic, but I'm fine now.' Sophie grabbed Vera's hands. 'Please tell me your news. It will cheer me up.'

'Okay then.' Vera smiled and prepared to tell Sophie all about the brilliant and unexpected reunion with her friend of old.

And since receiving the call from Linda not long ago about what Sam had said, Vera might have just thought of the perfect idea to *really* cheer this girl up and give her something to look forward to, as well as take her mind off whatever was bothering her so much because she was sure Linda would take to the girl as much as she had.

* * *

'You look amazing, Miss Reynold,' the dressmaker gushed, admiring Sam in the dress she'd spent so long getting just right. 'You really do look a picture. Your new husband's jaw will drop to the floor when he sees you wearing this.'

Sam turned to the other side to look at her reflection in the floor-to-ceiling mirror. It really was a stunning dress. She loved everything about it. 'It's beautiful. You've done a fantastic job!'

She'd breathed a quiet sigh of relief when the zip and satin-covered buttons fastened without too much effort, glad she'd stuck with her instinct not to have the dress made to her exact original measurements. Although her figure hadn't yet changed dramatically, her waist had thickened a little and when standing in her underwear, although slight, there was now a visible bump of pregnancy. Dressmakers were trained to spot slight changes, but if this woman had spotted anything, she was too professional to comment. Sam also knew speculation over this, along with details of the dress were safe, hence why it had taken so long to carefully select the right dressmaker for the job.

Far too many people would jump at the chance to leak information or to sneak photos, let alone a suspected pregnancy. Sam pushed away her irritation. It wasn't a case of being paranoid. She'd experienced more than enough episodes of her personal business being splashed about for every Tom, Dick and Harry to see in the past. The consequences it brought weren't easily forgotten and she'd had it up to her neck with people.

The most recent incident over the article in the *Coventry Echo* had underlined it loud and clear that people would queue up to use any snippet of her and Seb's or the firms' dealings to grant them a payout of one kind or another.

It drove her mad. That reporter being so stupid to press ahead with printing details of their wedding venue despite the stark warning Seb had issued was sheer foolishness. This was further backed up by Seb's mood when he'd returned last night telling her about the call he'd received from the *Mail*.

She hadn't even had a chance to gently break what she'd seen in the paper to him before the *Mail* had jumped on the bandwagon. She dreaded to think what was planned for that *Coventry Echo* bloke now.

Although she too had been angry, and still was, Sam had tried her best to play it down to calm the situation. She didn't want Seb reacting in a way to stop Saturday going off without a hitch.

Sam's heart did a small flutter. *Saturday.* It was now Wednesday – only three more days before she would finally be Mrs Stoker.

Her face split into a huge smile. She couldn't wait. Nothing could be more important.

On the big scale of things, that newspaper article was annoying and had half-ruined the surprise she'd planned as to how the day would pan out for their chosen guests, but it wasn't the end of the world.

Turning her attention back to the mirror, Sam giggled. 'I can't stop admiring myself. I'm so very pleased.'

The dressmaker returned Sam's smile. 'Shall we try your veil? I've hand stitched all the Swarovski crystals in place like you requested, but I need to check they're in the correct position to catch the light.'

'I'm sure they will be,' Sam replied, her eyes lighting up with excitement as the gossamer-like material, shimmering with a thousand rainbows, was pulled from the box on the side.

Saturday would be the best day of her life. The only thing set to top it would be meeting her much longed for baby.

* * *

Vera had been spot on, like usual when it came to matters such as this, Linda thought, smiling once again at the big-busted blonde sitting on the sofa.

It had been strange entering the flat which had once been hers. It had been even stranger going into the kitchen and blanking the image of that pile of cocaine Tom Bedworth had lifted from their own daughter and stashed under the floorboards in the far corner. It had been equally difficult seeing the table she'd been forced to sit at and write that note stating she was abandoning her youngest children – the note which not only had nearly cost Linda her life, but the one which had also caused her to almost lose her family, as well as her best friend.

Then there was the lino covering the floor she'd lain on after taking the final beating of many at the hands of the man she'd once loved. It was still the same as it had been that day – the day she'd been convinced was her last.

Instead, it had been the start of an indescribably long period of what nightmares were made of: being kept prisoner in the attic of a seedy brothel and jacked up with Tom's dirty drugs.

She shuddered involuntarily.

That side of things was done now – long gone. She was no longer that person and never again would be.

The man who had done all of those things to her was dead and could no longer trouble her, so there was no need to let the horrible memories haunt her. And neither should this flat. It was bricks and mortar. It no longer belonged to her and did not, like any of the other pieces of shit associated with the nightmare of her previous life, have any power over her any more. It could be seen as it was: a home for this young woman who, Linda thought, with a twinge of pity, had the look behind those big blue eyes of hers which mirrored similarities of a past she was desperate to rid herself of.

Vera was right on that too. Sophie possessed some of the same hallmarks she herself had done and therefore it would be a pleasure to help the girl if she could.

Plus, Vera's idea on how to do that, Linda thoroughly agreed with. It was just what the doctor ordered to give the wench a boost. But, Linda reminded herself of the other important point Vera made, she'd have to make sure to tone down the importance of what was being offered.

If Sophie knew the ins and outs of whose wedding she was being invited to and that just about everybody in Birmingham and half the surrounding areas would gladly butcher each other for the chance of one of those coveted gold invitations, then the girl would freak out. That would defeat the object.

'So, what do you think? Are you busy on Saturday or would you like to come as Vera's guest?' Linda asked chirpily.

'Well... I... It's so kind of you to ask me, but I don't know the bride and groom. Wouldn't it be rude of me to just turn up like some kind of gatecrasher?' Sophie looked from Linda to Vera with worry.

'Bollocks to that!' Vera laughed. 'You'd be coming as my plus one. Look – how many plus ones at weddings know the bride, groom or either? Not many, I can tell you! But I know both of 'em.'

'Besides, it's *my* daughter who's getting married,' Linda added proudly. 'So there's no need to be nervous. Anyone who is mine or Vera's friends are my daughter's friends.'

Sophie's pulse increased with excitement. 'Really? Well, if you're sure?' *Oh, this was fantastic!* Apparently, the wedding was being held in a right swish hotel out of town too. It would be lovely going somewhere decent, with nice people. To be genuinely invited somewhere so special had all but erased the memories of yesterday's panicky meltdown.

Vera was right. Things would have happened by now if they were going to, so she must grab her life back. Having women like Vera and her lovely friend, Linda, on side made that a real possibility.

Sophie understood why Vera was so over the moon about being back into contact with her oldest and best friend. Linda was lovely – a real gem. She may wear expensive, posh clothes, but she was as down to earth as the rest of them and she dearly hoped she would see as much of Linda as she did Vera.

Maybe one day, she'd accompany Andy to an event or take him as *her* plus one...

Sophie glowed with hope. Perhaps, at some point down the

line, she'd be inviting Linda, Vera and Linda's daughter to her and Andy's wedding...? She swallowed a giggle. Now she really was running away with herself. She looked at Vera and then Linda, the smile dropping from her face. 'Wait a minute... What would I wear?'

Sophie glanced down at her short skirt and rather revealing tight crop top, feeling not for the first time that the look she'd once felt happy with only brought back memories of a life she wanted to leave behind. 'I haven't got anything really nice or suitable for a posh do.'

'Don't you worry your pretty little head about that, chick.' Linda patted Sophie's hand. 'If you think I've had such nice clobber as what I'm wearing now for long, then you'd be mistaken. We'll sort you something out, won't we, V?'

'We certainly will!' Vera agreed, flashing Linda a grateful smile, keenly remembering the time she'd half-inched those posh frocks from Rackhams for her and Linda the first time they'd set foot in the Violet Orchid.

Now the whole thing had come full circle. It was time to pass on their good fortune. She'd known Linda would warm to Sophie. A night out at a fancy place would be just what the girl needed to get her out of the doldrums and realise there was more to her life than worrying about what had gone on in the past.

Surely it would bolster Sophie's confidence to be at the wedding of Sam and Seb Stoker? Sophie *must* have heard of them – everybody had – it was the wedding of the year! But she'd done the right thing making sure Linda didn't let the details slip. It would only make the girl more nervous.

Now this way she'd get the best surprise *ever* on Saturday.

9

'Tell me again where this place is?' Potter asked for what seemed like the fortieth time.

Tom pushed the newspaper across the table in front of Potter. He'd already told him over and over since seeing the story. How long would it take the thick bastard to remember what he said? It was driving him nuts. 'Here!' he snapped, his finger prodding the article. 'Like I keep telling you, it's at Coombe Abbey.'

'Where the fuck's that?' Potter muttered, reading the article yet again.

'Coventry,' Tom mumbled. 'Well, not central Coventry. It's to the east – the opposite side and furthest from Birmingham.' Unlikely they'd bump into many Brummies there unless they went to the wedding itself and that wouldn't be happening.

'Looks a bloody posh place,' Potter grumbled. 'Bet they do nice food and stuff.'

Tom stared at the man in front of him. *Food and stuff?* What the fuck? Was that all this prat thought about? This was the perfect solution for getting a cast-iron way to lift his daughter without stepping foot in Birmingham. It was an excellent opportunity and all this idiot could bang on about was food?

As usual, luck was falling on Tom's side and, like he'd promised, he'd found a way to tie up the loose ends of his plan within schedule. *Well, sort of...*

'How will we get in there without anyone recognising us? I don't know whether this lot are familiar with what you look like, but the Stokers know what *I* look like, so I'll be spotted right away.' Potter looked up suddenly, his eyes gleaming with possibility. 'But if we storm in and shoot the whole lot of them up in one go, that would work! I'll suggest that to Mark later on and see what he thinks.'

Tom sighed. *How? Via a fucking Ouija board?* He clenched his teeth. This nut-nut stuff with Mark was grating on his rug and he didn't know how much more he could stand. 'We won't be going anywhere near the bloody place. How will we get the fucking money if we gun them down?'

'I want revenge, Bedworth,' Potter snarled, his eyes flipping back to the shiny manic look he wore more often than not. 'I've already said I don't care about the money. I promised Mark th...'

'Yeah, I know, you promised Mark. And you'll get that,' Tom lied. 'But we're doing this together. Trust me, the best way to cause Stoker the most agony is by taking his wife.'

And *he'd* have the money if Potter didn't want it. If the fat fuck then fancied a shoot-off with Stoker after that, that was his prerogative, but quite frankly, Tom would be happy with the money. If the rest of them shot each other to fuck in the aftermath whilst he was at 36,000 feet, then that was an extra bonus.

'You're definitely killing the bird then, even though she's your kin?' Potter checked, his eyes narrowing. He'd never trusted Bedworth and still didn't, but he was having this *his* way and more besides.

'Yeah, course I am. Sam Reynold ain't my kin. Maybe biologically speaking, but that's the extent of it.'

'Are you sure she's even yours?' Potter frowned. 'She's a tasty-looking bird and you're an ugly fuck.'

'Who knows...' Tom sighed. 'She's probably nothing to do with me, but I don't give a shit either way.' Except Sam *was* his daughter, he knew that. Back in the day before she'd changed, Linda had been more frigid than a fucking iceberg, so the chance of anyone else getting between her legs was an improbability. He'd only managed it once before she'd got herself up the duff.

Jesus, how that not particularly pleasurable two minutes of his life had served to haunt him.

But now at last, after all this bloody nightmare and everything he'd given up, he'd be getting his payout for his contribution.

'With a face like Sam Reynold I reckon I'd enjoy putting her to use before we kill her,' Potter grinned, his tongue running over his lips as his large hand grabbed his own crotch.

'Do you have to fucking grope yourself in front of me?' Tom spat. Imagining Potter rutting on someone made him feel nothing but queasy. 'Do what you like after we've got the money, but I personally don't want to see your cock!'

'Yeah,' Potter said, his mind conjuring up all sorts of interesting things he could do with a hottie like Samantha Reynold. 'I'm going to enjoy this in more ways than one.' Suddenly, he frowned. 'Hang on. If we're not going to the wedding, how the fuck will we snatch her?'

'At the airport, of course,' Tom said smugly. 'They'll be going on honeymoon. All we've got to do is wait and when they leave the hotel, we'll follow. The airport will be busy. We'll easily blend in and get our chance there.'

Potter remained silent for a moment thinking and then spoke.

'Where exactly? Where in the airport are we going to snatch her and then where do we take her?'

'I'll tell you once you've quit playing with yourself. I can't concentrate whilst you're doing that!' Tom snapped. That would hopefully give him chance to think about that bit. With any luck, Potter would have zoned off down his loop by that point and be too busy talking to the dead to remember to ask anything else for a while.

* * *

Marina felt her nipples pucker into tight little buds as Carlos stripped his crisp white shirt off and carelessly tossed it on the pile of clothes on the floor.

Catching her watching, his dark eyes sparkled with pride, believing her interest was down to his bronzed and muscular physique.

Allowing him to believe whatever he wanted, Marina languished in the chaise longue, taking her time to cross one shapely ankle over the other and kept her knowledgeable smile remaining where it should be. *Hidden.*

Only the gentle parting of her pumped-up lips remained purposely poised, just the way she knew Carlos liked it – exactly how she formed her mouth when she wrapped them around his hard length.

Except this time she wouldn't be doing that. Not right now, anyway. She had more interesting things to think about – like how she would kill her sister...

The concept of murderous rage always turned her on. When she'd killed Dan and hacked him to death, it had been the one and only time that bastard had ever succeeded in making her wet. Her dream man was someone who thought along the same lines as her. *They'd be like Bonnie and Clyde.*

If Carlos was capable of beating or killing someone, that would make her day. If that were the case, maybe he could offer her more than the money from his successful business?

Carlos, the stupid prick, thought her acting like a dog on heat was all to do with him...

But it wasn't like that, was it? The music industry was the music industry. Not *her* kind of excitement. But if it did? If he...

That wouldn't happen – not unless he had a change in direction. Maybe she should point out this fact? Perhaps he'd be more interesting if she explained that anyone with the power over life and death had a certain effect on her. It always did and always would.

Lowering her lashes, Marina swung her long legs off the chaise longue, allowing her pink floaty skirt to remain hitched mid-thigh for longer than necessary. She could already see the extent of Carlos's desire straining against his black trousers.

Sliding off the chaise longue completely, Marina glided over to Carlos, busy watching her with fire burning in his dark eyes.

'*Dios, bella!*' Carlos panted, his large hands reaching to grab Marina's buttocks. 'You don't know what you do to me. You drive me crazy!'

Licking her lips, Marina pulled away from Carlos. 'Go and shower, then you can tell me about your day.'

Carlos faltered, perplexed. 'Not a lot to tell you, *bella*.'

What a surprise, Marina thought as she strutted across the room. 'Go and shower, then,' she said with a flick of her hair. Now she'd had her daily dose of reinforcement that Carlos was gagging for her, he could do one.

With a shrug of irritation, Carlos strode off into the en suite bathroom, shutting the door loudly behind him.

Marina rolled her eyes in annoyance and flicked through the latest copies of the newspapers which had arrived earlier. Rearranging her skirt, she kicked off her heels and tucked her legs underneath her as she thumbed through the pages.

Normal dreary bollocks from the collection of dreary miserable Midlands cities... More shite at the steel works; a pay dispute at the Leyland; a bust train track... *Wow! How fucking exciting!*

Rolling her eyes for the second time, Marina was just about to sling the newspapers to one side, when she caught sight of something. She normally wouldn't have even bothered taking a second look, but there was something about the photograph that made her read further.

She squinted at the palatial building:

CAT OUT OF THE BAG FOR SECRET WEDDING VENUE

Following up on the unexpected story in the *Coventry Echo*, we at the *Birmingham Mail* can confirm the wedding of Sebastian Stoker and Samantha Reynold is to be held at the beautiful Coombe Abbey Hotel in Coventry this coming Saturday.

It is believed the nuptials and reception will take place in the renowned mediaeval banqueting suite the hotel is famed for.

The *Mail* endeavours to bring readers pictures of the day itself and pride themselves on their long-standing relationship with Seb Stoker, granting us official pictures of this year's most special occasion...

Marina didn't even realise her wine glass had slipped through her fingers to smash on the marble tiles.

'What was that noise? Are you all right?' Carlos rushed out of the bathroom.

'Yeah, yeah, I'm fine,' Marina muttered. She was more than all right because it had finally happened...

The time had come. Her bitch of a sister had stupidly opened the window of opportunity for the wheels to be put in motion for the finale.

This was what she'd been waiting for.

'It's time,' she mumbled.

'What is? What is time?' Carlos frowned, crossing the room. 'You're acting odd, *bella*. I don't like it when you act odd. It... how do you say it? It unnerves me!'

Marina realised she was speaking out loud and Carlos was in front of her. Now wasn't the time to draw unwarranted suspicion or questions. No one else needed to know the details. But one thing was for sure – time was of the essence.

Flicking on her stellar smile and making sure her cleavage was nicely visible, Marina reached for Carlos's hand and guided it tantalisingly close to the top of her thigh. 'Do you fancy a quick trip over to England? Perhaps tomorrow. Or Friday at the latest?' she purred, hoping she'd remembered rightly that he had a new signing at the end of this week. The last thing she wanted was *him* accompanying her, but she had to maintain the act.

10

'Off out again?' Neil studied his twin brother as he loped down the stairs from his new apartment.

'No law on that is there?' Andrew shrugged. 'There's nothing going on tonight that needs me here, is there? Or are you saying you can't handle it on your own?'

'Oh, fuck off!' Neil snapped. Having a laugh was one thing, but certain things wore thin after so long and this was one of them.

Seb wasn't about either – it was all wedding preparations this and wedding preparations that. Now it was all about the *Echo* blowing the cover on the wedding venue. Yeah, it was annoying, but it hardly warranted this end of the bloody world stuff.

Neil frowned. All things considered, the only person here who wasn't having nights off left right and centre or interested in weddings was *him*. 'Am I the only fucker working here any more or what?'

The grin fell from Andrew's face realising his brother was being serious. He paused at the bottom of the stairs. 'What's the problem? Are you seriously begrudging me the odd night out?'

Neil shrugged, embarrassed by his stroppy comment. 'Well, no... It's just... Oh, it doesn't matter.'

A bashful smile formed on Andrew's face as he put two and two together. *He should have realised.* Seb should have told Neil of his decision before he heard about it from anyone else. Or maybe *he* should have mentioned it, rather than letting Neil find out from some of the others but he'd been so chuffed about being asked, he hadn't thought too much of the implications when he'd blurted it out to his enforcers.

'Hey, come on. It wasn't personal. It's only because I'm a bit more serious than you. Seb would dread the speech if you did it!'

Neil frowned. 'What are you talking about? What's the speech got to do wi...'

'The wedding speech,' Andrew shrugged, his foot already on the first step down leading to the reception. He didn't want to keep Sophie waiting. After tonight it was unlikely he'd get chance to see her much if Seb and Sam being on honeymoon meant he had to take on extra tasks.

'The wedding?' Neil repeated. 'Nah, it's not that. Well, maybe it is a bit... It's all anyone's going on about and... Oh, I'm just on one. Ignore me!'

Andrew grinned. 'Good! I thought for a minute that you'd had a hissy fit that I'm best man and you're not. I know how competitive you are.'

Neil tried to mask his shock and forced a smile. 'No, of course not!'

Andrew studied his brother. 'Shit. You didn't know, did you? Sorry, mate. I thought that was what had got the bee in your bonnet.'

'What?' Neil cried. 'Don't be silly. Of course I knew. Everyone does.' He waved his hand dismissively. 'It's fine. Don't flatter yourself!' Grinning, he turned on his heels. 'Enjoy your night out with your mystery bird!'

Knowing his face was burning, Neil traipsed into the casino, aware Andrew's eyes remained burning into his back long after he could no longer see him.

Humiliation stung.

He knew he was being irrational. If Seb wanted Andrew as his best man, rather than him, that was his call. And if Andrew wanted a night off to slope off with this woman he knew was on the scene, then that was his prerogative.

Did he really resent either of his brothers being happy?

Neil's mouth curled at the edges as he felt around his inside pocket for his cigarettes.

No, of course he didn't resent them being happy. He'd learnt enough in the past to know that harbouring resentment for family only brokered problems that could prove devastating. No one wanted to make that mistake again.

So why the fuck was he feeling so shitty and, if truth be known, resentful and bloody hurt?

Stomping around the back of the bar, Neil ignored the bartender and helped himself to a large whisky. Downing it in one, he slammed the empty glass on the pristine shiny bar, wiping off the splashes of spirit with the sleeve of his jacket.

Neil stared around the opulent interior of the Peacock's casino. He'd been content with everything and everybody not long ago, so why the sudden change?

He frowned as the truth dawned. Because he was jealous, that's why. *Fucking jealous.* He felt excluded.

It was a bitter revelation and one that left a nasty taste in his mouth. The issue was *him* and he had to nip this in the bud. He refused to drown in pathetic jealousy because his brothers had their own lives.

The hard truth was, the concept scared him. Neil didn't want to be the only one without a life. Their lives had always revolved around the firm. Everything else was a bolt-on.

But Seb had had a life in addition to the firm for some time and that hadn't detracted from his loyalties.

Now it looked like Andrew was also breaking away to have a separate life, so where did that leave him?

* * *

'You won't get any grief for this, will you?' Tina nervously glanced around as Penny beckoned her behind the British Airways check-in desk.

Penny's hazel eyes lit up. 'The desk is closed for the day now. There's no more flights until tomorrow and I'm off shift, so I'm not doing anything wrong.'

Tina grinned. *Neither was she.* She'd finished her shift at Wimpy hours ago, but in no rush to go back to the poky single room she rented in Brownhills, she hung around the airport longer than necessary most nights. It gave her something to do other than dwell on what she'd lost, whilst keeping sight of what she *could* be doing if she tried hard enough. That, and if a sliver of luck fell her way.

And why shouldn't it? She wasn't a bad person. Not really. Sure, she'd done plenty of things in the past that she'd rather not broadcast, but she had no intention of doing that.

Of course, there was always the nagging fear that a punter from the Aurora or the Sunset Boulevard might one day come through the airport and recognise her, but then again, would any of those men really want to announce that they'd paid to sleep with some two-bit hooker from a back-street dump?

Besides, most of the people who frequented the places *she'd* worked at never got as far as an airport, let alone on a plane, so she didn't know what she was worrying about.

Tina swallowed the lump in her throat that appeared every time she thought of what she'd previously done. A hooker and a stripper. Not great for the old CV.

She jutted out her chin with determination. There were a lot worse things she could have done – like being a murderer or a pimp, like that bastard, Bedworth.

She shuddered in revulsion at the thought of that man, still glad every single day that he was no longer on this earth.

'You all right?' Penny asked, noticing Tina's shaking shoulders.

'What?' Tina's head jerked around. 'Yeah, I'm just a bit cold, that's all.'

Penny smiled. 'You get used to the air conditioning.'

Tina returned Penny's smile. If Penny knew exactly how much time she spent hanging around this airport watching the world go by, then her sanity would most probably be questioned. But she liked guessing where people were heading. It was all pie in the sky. None of it got her any further to actually getting a job doing something interesting, or one to take her away from here.

'Where have you been today?' Tina knew she was asking loads of questions, but she hadn't the first clue about how this worked. And she'd need to if she was going to attempt to get a job.

'Portugal. Just a short hop. Tomorrow I'm on the Marbella run and then probably Portugal again,' Penny said, like country-hopping was a standard practice.

But it *was* standard practice for her, Tina thought, her spirits dropping like a stone. It was insane thinking it plausible to get a job as an air hostess. Didn't they have to be stunningly pretty, well-spoken and have tons of qualifications? She didn't possess any of those things.

'If you like, I'll show you the...' Penny frowned. 'What's the matter?'

Tina picked at her fingers. 'I'll never get a job doing anything like you. I haven't got any GCSEs, so it's stupid. *I'm* stupid.'

'What nonsense! You've been working, haven't you? You already work at the airport and...'

'Yes, but not doing what *you're* doing,' Tina mumbled. Plus she'd lied in order to get the job at the Wimpy. It was unlikely somewhere like British Airways would omit checking references and qualifications.

'The first thing to do is get a job with BA doing *something*,' Penny said. 'And you don't need tons of qualifications to be an air hostess because you get training.'

Tina's mood brightened. 'So what do you suggest I do first?'

Penny smiled awkwardly. 'I was thinking perhaps a cleaner?'

Tina's heart sunk again. *Cleaner?* Not exactly the jump up the ladder she'd hoped for. But then again, if she could get a job – *any* job with one of the airlines, then it was another foot in the door.

'Tell you what,' Penny said conspiringly. 'I know a guy in HR. I'll find out what jobs are going at the moment and what the requirements are and then we'll go from there.'

Tina's heart beat faster. 'Couldn't you just introduce me to him or...'

'Well, I could...' Penny winked. 'Oh, sod it! I didn't want to get your hopes up, but put it this way, I'm pretty confident I can get you a job.'

Tina's mouth fell open. 'Really? How?'

'Because the guy in HR happens to be my boyfriend,' Penny laughed. 'Grab your coat. He's picking me up in five minutes, so come with us for a drink. I'll get you out of serving burgers sooner than you think!'

* * *

'Sorry I'm late,' Sophie cried as she dashed into the pub at Hopwood, her relief at spotting Andy palpable. She was late and not just by a few minutes. She was a bloody *hour* late and was terrified he'd given up and left.

As Andy stood from the table at her arrival, Sophie flung herself into his arms, aware that she was acting like it was her last night on earth, but she didn't care. It was how she felt about Andy Waterford.

All she knew was that she was crazy and madly in love with this man and missing a second of his presence crushed the air from her lungs.

She sighed with pleasure as his lips crushed onto hers. She could drink the taste of him. He was divine – just *beautiful*.

'I was starting to think you'd stood me up.' Andrew pulled back from Sophie, his finger softly grazing her cheek. As usual she looked stunning. *More* than stunning. 'I've got you a drink.' He nodded to the glass of wine on the table and indicated for her to take a seat.

Flushing happily at the gentlemanly behaviour, Sophie was walking on air, but she must control herself. She didn't want to come over like a bunny boiler. 'I wasn't going to stand you up,' she gibbered. 'I would never do that.' She fiddled with the clasp of her bag, searching for something to say that didn't make her sound like a crazy loon. 'How's your day been?'

Andrew smiled. How had his day been? All the better for seeing her. 'Not much happened. How about you?'

How he'd love to share how chuffed he was to be his brother's best man. He'd love it even more if he could ask Sophie to accompany him to the wedding.

He frowned. Maybe he could? Maybe now was *exactly* the right time to lay his cards on the table and fess up about who he was? But what if she freaked out? What if she went batshit and told him to piss off and that she didn't want anything to do with him? What if she didn't want to be involved with someone whose family were infamous for instilling fear and chaos into anyone who crossed them?

She must have heard of the Stokers, even if she didn't know what they looked like. It was only a matter of time before she came across a photo somewhere and put two and two together. Or someone else said something...

Andrew was surprised he'd kept things under wraps for this long. He was living on borrowed time which had to end somewhere, so surely it would be better coming from him, rather than her finding out? Now that really would look bad.

His teeth cut into his bottom lip. But what if he told her and she walked away? This was Seb's special weekend and if Sophie binned him off, he'd be a shit best man. He couldn't risk anything marring his brother's big day.

Andrew stared at Sophie. No – he *should* tell her. She liked him as much as he liked her, he was sure of it.

'You're not cross then?' Sophie asked, her big eyes wide.

Andrew blinked in surprise. 'Cross? What about?'

Sophie pursed her lips. 'I didn't think you were listening. I was explaining that my friend came round with a dress and I didn't realise the time. I really am sorry.' Not as sorry as she was that Andy wouldn't see her in the beautiful gown. 'I've been invited to a do at the weekend and...'

Watching Andrew's face fall, Sophie stopped. *Shit.* Had she arranged to see him this weekend? She hadn't, had she? What if he thought she wasn't interested? How she'd love to invite him to this posh do as her plus one. But that wasn't her clout to have and even if she could, it might come across as too heavy.

Panic fluttered and thanks to her trembling fingers, she knocked her wine over.

Andrew jumped from the seat. Snatching a beer towel from the bar, he mopped up the wine before it tracked onto either of their clothes.

'Oh God! I'm sorry,' Sophie blathered, tears forming. She was ruining everything. *Everything!*

'Don't stress, it's fine,' Andrew smiled, turning to the bar to shout up a replacement drink. Well, that made his decision easy. If Sophie was busy this weekend, then she couldn't come to the wedding anyway. He'd wait until afterwards. It had been a silly idea anyway. Dropping that bombshell and expecting her to face his entire family, along with hordes of fucking press that would undoubtedly be present, was a tad too much. He'd decide on a better time to tell her.

Nodding his thanks to the barman, he placed the new glass of wine down in front of Sophie. Picking up her hand and finding it trembling, he frowned and pressed his lips to her soft skin. 'Don't knock this one over!' he winked, trying to allay her embarrassment. She didn't need to be nervous with him. As far as he was concerned, she was perfect. 'Are you going somewhere nice this weekend?'

'Yes, my friend has invited me as her plus one. It's a posh do, apparently...' Sophie squirmed with embarrassment. 'I'm a bit nervous.'

'You'll be the most gorgeous one there!' Andrew grinned, meaning every single word and relieved this 'friend' was of the female variety.

The next do he went to, Sophie would be on *his* arm as his plus one.

'So, you were going to tell me about your day,' Sophie

enthused, gingerly sipping from her wine. 'I don't even know what you do for a job! How ridiculous is that?'

Andrew laughed hollowly, reality pulling him back to earth. 'It's not very exciting,' he lied. 'I'm sort of involved in the pub trade.'

The sooner the truth was out the better. His feelings had gone too far and he needed to do something about it.

11

Seeing the article in the *Birmingham Mail* about Sam and Seb Stoker's wedding this weekend had knocked Tina for six.

When she'd got in last night, a little bit tipsy, but over the moon with what had materialised over drinks with Penny, she hadn't thought anything had the power to put her on a downer.

But seeing that article had brought Tina's feelings of guilt and worry back to the forefront.

It also rubbed her face in just how far removed her life was from Sam Reynold's.

Thanks to this, she hadn't slept very well, but the cold light of day enabled her to look at things afresh.

Staring in the mirror at the airport staff toilets, Tina straightened her hair and inhaled deeply. *No more Wimpy uniform for her!*

She glanced down at the uniform she now sported. Okay, so a cleaner's uniform wasn't much better than the Wimpy one, but now she, Tina Smith, was working for British Airways.

What a difference twenty-four hours made.

Tina pinched her cheeks to infuse a bit of colour into her tired, pale face and smiled brightly at her reflection.

She was now one step closer to achieving her aim of a career to be proud of. Maybe then she'd have the balls to face Sam Reynold and let her know what that four hundred quid she'd pinched had helped achieve.

And Amber's face when Tina had strutted in with her Wimpy uniform stuffed into a carrier bag, giving notice of her leaving with immediate effect, was priceless. Yes, Amber may have threatened her, saying that she couldn't just 'leave' and that she 'had to work out her notice', but she'd walked out the door regardless, like she'd planned.

Tina pulled her new British Airways tabard down over her jeans and proudly smoothed it down.

Thanks to Penny, she'd been fast-tracked into this new job. Her fella had even blagged the hoops with clearance and she was now working airside.

It may not seem a huge step up to many, but cleaning planes and being behind the scenes was the right direction for *her*. It was closer to the career of her dreams, along with a ticket out of here.

Tina snatched up her cleaning bucket with all the required items and headed to the room to receive her first brief and instructions.

The prospect of hoovering up peanuts and cleaning kids' sick off the seats had never been more exciting.

* * *

Tom pulled his coat lapels higher around his neck and confidently walked out of the terminal building. He probably hadn't needed that overcoat from the charity shop. It was equally unlikely he needed black-rimmed glasses either, but it paid to cover all eventualities.

If, by any slight chance someone happened to be in the airport who could recognise him from the past, it was unlikely they'd give him a second glance. Looking like *this*, they wouldn't class him as being the same bloke to be seen anywhere without his trademark leather jacket or who hadn't ever worn specs in his life. On top of that, no one would expect to spot a man widely known to have died three months ago either, would they?

He looked like anyone else who happened to be moving through an airport. And, as expected, no one had given him the time of day.

But Potter was a different story...

Tom briskly headed back towards the car park. This particular one was seldom frequented by security on the lookout – that's why he'd parked here – but he hoped Potter had remained where he'd left him – in the passenger seat of the Ford Escort van he'd got on a good deal from that bloke down the chippy.

The van was old, unassuming, and in no way connected to him and never had been. Neither would it be. And it ran. *Just about...*

As long as it kept going long enough for the next few days, that was all that was required.

Actually, the van was pretty much *everything* they required. It had enough space for him and Potter in the cab, that's if he glossed over putting up with Potter's fleshy thigh spreading across his side, forcing him to brush against it every time he changed gear. But most importantly, it had enough space in the back to shove his darling daughter when they grabbed her so he could collect his money.

As he approached the van, Tom frowned. *Where the fuck was Potter?*

His face morphed into a grimace. *He knew it.* He knew the fat fuck couldn't cope with obeying the very simple order of, 'Stay where you are.'

Christ, it wasn't difficult. The man had one job – one fucking job and he'd screwed it up.

Tom's eyes darted around. *Where the hell had he gone?* 'Please tell me he hasn't wandered into the terminal,' he muttered out loud, panic brewing.

Potter was recognisable. With his grossly overweight frame and strangely misshapen head, he was the sort that people did a double take at, even if they hadn't seen him before.

Shit. He should have made the prick wear a disguise too, but he'd seemed compos mentis this morning and Tom thought Potter understood the importance of staying put until he returned. He'd only been gone half an hour, for fuck's sake.

Oh God, there he was...

Breaking into a run, Tom darted towards a tall wire fence where Potter stood along with a group of other people armed with cameras and notebooks.

Fuck – he was talking to them. Shit, shit, shit!

Approaching, Tom grabbed Potter's arm. 'What the fuck are you doing?' he hissed. 'Go back to the van!'

'You've missed some right good take-offs!' Potter beamed, his face lit with more expression than Tom had seen in months. 'Dave here was just saying that the Boeing 757-500 has just come in from Lyon and...'

'Shut up and move!' Tom pulled Potter in the opposite direction from the approaching grinning man armed with a notebook that he could only assume was 'Dave'. 'Get back to the fucking van!'

Jesus Christ. Now he knew without doubt Potter was truly beyond help. Acting like a plane spotter? Was there no end to this torture?

Pulling a now protesting Potter with him, Tom wanted to

scream. 'What else did you bloody say? You didn't introduce your-self or say anything you shouldn't have, did you?'

Potter snatched his arm from Tom's grip. 'No, I didn't!' he barked. 'I ain't stupid. I was just watching the fucking planes because I like them.'

Overtaking Tom at a speed which belied his frame, Potter yanked open the van door and clambered inside. 'Well? What did you deduce? Being as you interrupted what I was doing, I hope you've got something cast iron to tell me.'

Jumping into the driver's seat, Tom swallowed his annoyance. 'I've worked out where I reckon they'll park.' Starting the van, Tom ignored the slightly worrying groan and clanking the engine made for ten seconds each time it fired and manoeuvred out of the car park. 'It'll be this one here.'

He nodded towards the entrance to the long-stay car park. 'We'll tail them here. Stoker will have to deposit his keys at that cabin over there, so that's when we'll strike and grab Samantha.'

'What happens if they get dropped off by one of their lackeys or a taxi?' Potter asked, chewing his fingernails thoughtfully.

Tom blinked. *He hadn't thought of that.* 'Nah, Stoker will take one of his own motors. They'll leave the reception alone to go on honeymoon. They won't want anyone else accompanying them. That's how it's done.'

Potter studied Tom curiously. 'Not everyone goes on honey-moon straight from the reception.'

'*They* will,' Tom spat. *He hoped so, anyway.* Was Potter trying to catch him out or have a dig? How the fuck would he know the ins and outs of weddings? It wasn't like he'd ever got married. He'd rather fucking die.

'Okay, so let's assume you're right and Stoker drives himself.' Potter steepled his pudgy fingers under his chin. 'What happens if the Reynold bird accompanies him to drop the keys off? How will we snatch her from under his nose then?'

Tom felt himself shaking with rage. Potter wasn't supposed to over-analyse stuff. He wasn't usually in a fit state of mind to think to that degree, so why was he extra lucid today, just when he didn't need him to be?

He'd only just put together this bloody plan. He hadn't thrashed out all the what-ifs, yet Potter was back to his old ways of making him look a cunt. But as much as he resented admitting it, the man had a point. All of these things *were* feasible.

Fuck.

Perspiration beaded on the back of Tom's neck. He needed to plan for all eventualities... He'd think of ways around things, should he need them, like he usually did. He just needed a clear head to do that, but how the hell did he achieve that with Potter throwing a spanner in the works with every single bastard suggestion?

Resisting the urge to push Potter into the tempting-looking puddle outside the passenger seat door and scream that if he had any better ideas, then he was more than welcome to share them, Tom instead forced himself to smile. 'You worry too much. Trust me on this. I know how men like Stoker's minds work in situations such as these. He'll drive and Samantha will remain in one place whilst the keys are deposited. The twat is too much of a control freak to allow anyone else to do anything and Samantha is a lazy bitch, so won't move her arse anywhere she doesn't have to.'

Potter continued staring at Tom dubiously. 'I hope you're right, otherwise this won't work.' His eyes narrowed menacingly. 'And it *has* to work, Bedworth, because I'm having that slut's life in revenge for Mark losing his.'

He clicked his fingers four times, his head jerking in unison in a strange rhythm. 'I ran your plan past Mark last night when I spoke to him and that's what he wants.'

Tom nodded, like this was normal. It showed jumping to conclusions believing Potter had regained a sane way of thinking was wrong. The man was still as fubared as they came.

He grimaced, wondering why he'd allowed Potter's stupid comments to make him doubt his plan. It was good and just needed fine tuning to be tip top.

Best of all, he'd got wind of someone who could arrange a dodgy passport and in a few days from now, he'd be out of here.

12

Strutting down the road in tall white stilettos and a floaty sarong, Marina knew the deep tan on her body was accentuated by the light colour of her loose dress. She also knew the sheer material allowed just enough of a hint to let people know all she had on underneath was a turquoise bikini.

The deep greeny-blue colour of this particular bikini reflected the gorgeous colour of the ocean she saw every day. Bikinis and loose floaty cover-ups, only expensive ones of course, were the standard dress code around here, regardless of whether someone was on the beach or not.

She fitted into this lifestyle like a made-to-measure glove.

Her hand moved to her Gucci clutch bag. No expense spared with accessories either. *And why the hell not?* She'd damn well earned the money she now possessed and soon she would have even more of it.

And not before time.

It hadn't been difficult to source a ticket to England. The old cow at the travel agents had fallen over herself when she'd walked in, demanding a first-class ticket.

Her eyes narrowed. Even though she hadn't wanted him to, she'd fully expected Carlos to be gutted that he had other commitments that he couldn't change, but she'd been wrong.

Of course, she didn't *want* him to accompany her, but she had expected a reaction other than, *'I'm too busy, bella.'*

And she was livid about that. It meant Carlos hadn't quite crossed the line of being obsessed with her. She'd thought she'd nailed it, what with his inability to keep his hands off her, but clearly he wasn't 100 per cent under her control yet. Something that would have to be addressed if she wanted to get her fingers into his business. But she was buggered if she was going down the road of upping the ante with sexual favours. That only happened on *her* terms. Attractive as Carlos was, she'd only utilise such actions when *she* felt like it.

For now this 'excursion' took priority.

Marina's pink glossy lips pouted in frustration. Her fingers traced the outline of her plane ticket in the small back compartment of her bag. Pablo Ruiz Picasso to Birmingham International on Friday, 16 July. *Tomorrow.*

Just in time.

She flounced through the open doors of her beachfront bar and clicked her fingers at the barman, who scrambled to prepare a drink.

A tight sneer inched at the corner of her mouth. It wasn't like *he* wouldn't obey her every desire, was it? Maybe she should have ploughed her interest into someone like him who would be more grateful for her attention?

No, that was stupid. What prospects did a bloody barman have? Certainly not in the league of running a lucrative business such as Carlos Garcia's.

His firm would be the next step of her plan to up her game, which she'd put into motion the minute she returned.

The next time she stepped off the plane back at Malaga, she'd have even more collateral than now.

Sitting back in a large chair overlooking the private jetty, Marina watched one of her members' yachts set ready to sail, a collection of resident bronzed trophy women lounging on the deck.

Stupid bitches.

They might keep that man's interest whilst they were being paraded around; displayed like dolls and opening their legs on cue, but *she* was in a whole different league.

Never again would she be pawed by a greasy loser in a shitty strip club to get what she wanted. Because now she'd got everything perfectly worked out.

As the barman gingerly approached with her drink and laid a scalloped gold coaster on the glass tabletop to the side of her, Marina looked up. 'Prepare Mr Cooper's usual drink please. I'm expecting him shortly.' She gave the young man a disparaging once-over. 'And straighten your tie!'

Robin Cooper would arrive any minute. The shit-boring old English ex-pat wouldn't usually warrant a second thought, but recalling his trade, he'd become vital...

Called to a meeting about a sudden opening for a business proposition and listing what she required to put it in motion, he'd bitten her hand off.

Of course, nothing would come from this fabricated opportunity, but that was irrelevant. The man had what was required and therefore she was having it.

Her mouth twitched with the beginnings of a smile, seeing Robin Cooper approach the Casa del Océano.

* * *

Robin Cooper couldn't help but envisage how much money he stood to make if this deal pulled off. Admittedly, it was an odd choice of samples to request – especially one in particular, but these sort of deals seldom, if *ever* came up. To get this, would mean an extremely lucrative sideline that could be run from the luxury of his villa.

He glanced auspiciously around the office at the rear of the Casa del Océano. It was sparkling – exactly what he'd expect from someone like Marina Devlin. It was widely known that this fellow Englishwoman was loaded and from good stock. That's what everyone said, anyway.

And that she had the capacity to purchase this elite and renowned bar, along with the luxurious beachfront villa she also owned, spoke volumes.

It could also be seen by just looking at her that she was worth millions, so was undoubtedly successful. Judging by the selection of clientele who were members here, *everybody* couldn't be wrong, so with all those factors to consider, this opportunity she presented *must* be worth speculating on.

The time spent in the pharmaceutical trade made Robin well accustomed to how the industry worked. He'd thought his idea of using half his retirement fund to set up a small company manufacturing drugs and tools for the medical trade in Spain was a wise choice. Unfortunately, in the eight years since embarking on this, it had proved vastly less fruitful than he'd envisaged.

But getting regular orders in for components for medicines, as well as ad-hoc requirements for test samples for an established UK company would put him on the map, not to mention remove the need to sell his villa, which was on the cards if things didn't change.

But he did need to know a bit more. 'So, Miss Devlin, can you tell me about this company interested in having a supplier from Spain?' he asked. 'Is it one you were involved with back in the UK?'

Marina wore her best and most reassuring smile: one which had yet to fail getting her exactly what she wanted. 'No, it's nothing to do with me. It's my brother. He's worked within the pharmaceutical industry all of his life and has recently become chair of the board of directors of this company.'

She traced a long-nailed finger slowly along the edge of her glass-topped desk, then opened a drawer. Extracting a leather folder, she placed it down and clasped her hands together on top of it. 'Before I go any further, did you bring the requested samples?'

'Yes.' Robin glanced down at the metal case at his feet. 'But I...'

'Good, otherwise there isn't any point in this conversation,' Marina said briskly. *Thank fuck for that!* 'In that case, could I ask you to sign this before we continue?'

Opening the folder, she fished out a sheet of paper and pushed it across the desk, along with a gold pen containing an inset diamond.

'What is it?' Robin peered at the small type in front of him, strongly regretting not bringing his specs.

'It's a non-disclosure agreement. If I am to tell you more, then I'll need you to sign.'

Robin nodded. There wouldn't be a non-disclosure agreement if whatever was being offered wasn't kosher. This was standard practice in the pharmaceutical world – especially with things of high importance or secrecy.

His sense of self-grandeur fizzled as he scrawled his name in the relevant space on the document.

Marina smiled serenely as she placed the document back in the leather folder. *Stupid twat. That would go straight in the shredder.* 'Thank you. Okay, so the contract is for you to potentially supply a company called Ether Laboratories with a regular order of the chemicals in the requested samples.' She raised an eyebrow. 'You may have heard of them?'

Robin sat back astounded. *Heard of Ether Laboratories?* Of course he'd heard of them. Everyone in the industry had heard of Ether Laboratories! They were one of, if not the most prestigious, sought after and well-renowned pharmaceutical firms. They undertook all manner of contracts for very special clients and her brother was on the board there? 'Yes, I've heard of them...'

'Good. Well, if you're successful and the quality of your product is acceptable, the contract will initially be for one year, with the aim of that becoming a ten-year contract, with an increasing amount of goods in each subsequent order.'

Robin nodded avidly. *Ten years?* 'What amount of orders are we talking about here?'

Marina tapped her gold pen on the table. 'From what my brother has said, the company initially wants a thousand units at varying dilutions. This first order is relatively small. Call it a test batch.'

Robin nodded. *That would still bring a tidy sum.* 'But what about the, erm... the special test sample? It's a very unusual, not to mention, risky thing to request.'

'That's a one-off for a special project in association with a very important organisation conducting top-secret experiments.' Marina smiled knowingly. 'I'm sure you can guess what I'm talking about? But that's not something I can possibly discuss further.'

She almost laughed at the expression on Robin's face. He looked like he'd come in his pants over that one. *God, she was good at this.*

Robin could barely believe his luck. *Jesus Christ!* It had to be the MOD or the Secret Service or something really important. He'd end up with a decoration from the Queen for his part in helping the country at this rate!

'Your payment for this special one-off sample,' Marina's eyes tracked to Robin's metal case at his feet, 'will bring you $4 million. You will of course not receive payment until the validity of it is checked and proves to be usable.'

That would get him, the silly cunt. Not that he'd ever see a penny because for a start, the contract didn't exist and neither did her brother any longer. *Shame...*

Robin Cooper almost choked. *This was fabulous.* 'I hope your brother finds everything to his satisfaction, Miss Devlin,' he said, beaming widely. 'But this *must* be transported extremely carefully, as I'm sure you appreciate.'

Marina's gaze moved pointedly to the metal case on the floor. 'If you're happy with what we've discussed, then...'

'Oh, of course!' Robin scrambled to retrieve the case from the floor and carefully deposited it on the desk. 'You won't forget what I said about making sure this is carefully transported?'

'I'm well aware it holds risks, Mr Cooper,' Marina said, extending her manicured hand to shake his.

It was sad really. There he was, all pleased, thinking he was finally making something out of his pointless waste of a life, when in reality, Robin Cooper would have to meet an unfortunate accident as soon as she returned from England.

He'd done his part in what was needed and she didn't want him opening his gob or asking questions, let alone expecting money, the silly bastard.

13

'What a nice surprise!' Sam exclaimed as Seb folded her into his big arms. 'I didn't expect to see you until tonight.'

Dropping to his haunches, Seb kissed Sam's belly. 'I couldn't resist popping in to see you both.'

Sam beamed with happiness. *See you both.* What a strange, yet lovely thought that was. And it was true. There *was* now two of them in one.

She involuntarily found her hand moving to rest on the slight bump, the mere reference to having Seb's child inside her causing her heart to flutter with both love and excitement. It wouldn't be long before she'd feel the baby kicking and by that point, everyone would know about their impending arrival.

She couldn't wait.

She'd never felt more beautiful or relaxed and she was positively radiant and glowing with happiness. She couldn't thank her lucky stars enough for having this very special man in her life. And now she was about to become a mother. It was an amazing and exciting prospect.

Apart from the question that still remained unanswered – the other half of her biological parents, was the only thing still outstanding. And that, she could only get from Linda.

Standing back up to his full height, Seb found himself running his hands over Sam's changing body. 'God, I love you, soon-to-be Mrs Stoker. I also wanted to tell you I might be late back tonight. Besides,' he winked, 'it was a good excuse to come and see you!'

He jerked his head towards the blinds over the glass panel of Sam's office. 'Fancy shutting those and having a quickie?' He pulled her against him once more.

'You won't be back until late?' Sam asked, disappointment brewing. She'd been hoping for a night where they could talk about the future. It was something they'd been doing a lot of lately and she loved the passion with which Seb was committed to how their lives would go. But if he wasn't going to be back until late, maybe she should use the time to go and see Linda. 'Where are you off to?'

'Oh, just tying up a few loose ends before we jet off on Sunday. I want to spend the whole two weeks away with you without being interrupted with thoughts of things back home. Or worse, bloody phone calls!'

Sam grimaced. That was the last thing she wanted too, but she was confident things would run happily during their absence. From her side, Kevin and her staff had things in their capable hands.

'There's a couple of drops left to do which will happen whilst we're gone. They're the last ones in finalising our agreement with the Irish and then that part of the business will be all but dormant,' Seb said.

'And you're sure it's going to be okay for me to fly?' Sam asked, a flicker of worry resurfacing. The Maldives was a place she'd always dreamed of going to and this would be the first holiday she'd ever been on with Seb, but they'd booked this honeymoon before she'd fallen pregnant.

It was also the first holiday she'd had in *any* respect for years, being as her life had consisted only of work, work and more work. It also would be the only break away she and Seb would get as a couple before the baby arrived. There was little chance of her being comfortable going on holiday without her child after he or she was born. 'The Maldives is a long-haul flight and isn't that risky during pregnancy?'

Seb rolled his eyes. 'Stop worrying, Princess. We've checked with the doctor. Several times, if I correctly recall!' he laughed. 'The doc said you're more than fine to fly, so there will be no problems.'

He pulled Sam into his arms once again. 'I've already told you. Nothing bad will happen to you or the baby. I won't let it! So stop bloody worrying!'

And that's exactly why he was doing what he was doing tonight. And it had nothing to do with tying up loose ends. Not in the way he'd made out, anyway.

Seb frowned, glad whilst Sam was pressed against his chest she couldn't see his face.

As much as he'd tried, he couldn't release the injustice that wanker from the *Coventry Echo* had fuelled by marring the wedding plans. Oh yes, Sam had played it down, saying it wasn't important on the big scale of things and maybe it wasn't.

But it was to *him*. That shithead had purposely gone against what he'd instructed, hence causing unnecessary stress and upheaval for Sam. He knew how important it was for her to have privacy on their special day, that's why they'd gone to great lengths to keep things about the venue under wraps.

Now this scrote had taken it upon himself to ruin that. And by doing so, he'd upset Sam. Seb didn't like it when *anyone* upset

Sam. Even less in her current condition – that, to him, made her more priceless than a Ming vase. More priceless than *anything*.

He found himself holding Sam tighter, the real fear nagging away inside him deep down, relentless, even if he made a good job of outwardly concealing it from her and everyone else.

His jaw clenched with pent-up rage. The same way it did any time the woman he loved more than anything in the world was at risk or upset. And none more so than the fear he'd experienced the other day.

And this anger had increased daily since that business with the reporter.

And it wasn't just about the reporter stabbing them in the back and spilling the beans like the silly cunt he was. It was about the image that had haunted him since. Despite his best efforts to not even *think* about it, let alone envisage it, the hideous picture constantly pushed into his mind and it fired the very fear of God into his soul.

The tell-tale burn of cold nausea brewed in the pit of his stomach.

Seeing that reporter crashing towards Sam, Seb had thought his heart might stop. Yes, he'd immediately stopped there being an impact, but he couldn't remove the thought that there *could* have been. If he hadn't been there and that man had fallen into Sam, knocking her to the ground...

Bile rose as the illogical image appeared in his mind's eye. It wouldn't go away: Sam lying on the floor hurt and bleeding; the life inside her – his child, ebbing away. He'd been frozen with pain and impotent, for once in his life, to stop something from happening. He'd failed to prevent it. And no amount of revenge could ever put that right.

This haunted him on a constant spiral and the prospect kept him awake every night since.

Any fear – real or imagined, that ever got stuck on repeat, he took to be an omen. And that frightened him more than anything.

Sam and this baby were his whole life and the thought of... Seb shuddered. *That* was why he would deal with that reporter. Yes, he knew it may be irrational doling out punishment for something that hadn't happened, but it had been far too close for comfort and something that he couldn't stop thinking of until the person who had caused this all-consuming panic to snowball had been dealt with.

And there was only one way to do that.

* * *

'What did you think of the dress?' Linda asked, stubbing out her cigarette in Vera's ashtray. 'I bet you look a million dollars in it!'

Sophie's cheeks flushed pink as she looked at Vera and then Linda. 'I don't know whether I could ever look a million dollars, but I certainly felt it!' She clasped her hands together. 'I can't wait to wear it! Thanks so much, both of you!'

Vera flapped away the gratitude. 'Don't even think about thanking us. It was our pleasure, wasn't it, Lin?'

'Definitely!' Linda grinned. 'We're all going to look fab. I just hope I don't fall over. The heels Gloria has talked me into wearing are a tad higher than I'm used to. I don't want to land flat on me mush now, do I?'

'Yeah, your dress up around your arse is a great look!' Vera cackled with laughter. 'If only you didn't have such fucking flat feet!'

'Says her!' Linda retorted, rolling her eyes in mock offence.

Sophie giggled, loving the rapport these two women had. They were so easy going and fun to be around. She couldn't wait for Saturday and for this wedding. The only thing missing was Andy.

Still, she hoped there would be time for that soon. But as he'd mentioned he'd got quite a lot coming up with work over the next couple of weeks, she hoped he'd find time for her.

Her face fell. She'd have loved to stay overnight with him again last night, but he'd been unable to. Something about an early meeting this morning. But they had arranged a quick meet-up tomorrow.

She'd broken another one of her rules not to ask questions, so he wouldn't expect likewise, but she'd gone ahead anyway. Now she'd admitted to herself that she'd fallen for the man hook, line and sinker, she accepted that at some point she'd have to offer up more details about herself. Even so, there was only so much she could reveal...

'Hey up! She's off on one again! Off with the fairies!'

Sophie looked up, aware that Vera was referring to her. 'What? I...'

'It's this mystery bloke,' Vera said, winking at Linda. 'She's crazy for the fella. It's sending her doolally, yet she insists on keeping him under wraps.'

'She doesn't want you getting your claws into him, I expect!' Linda laughed, nudging Sophie in the ribs. 'Nah, I'm only joking. Seriously though, who is this fellow of yours, Sophie? Is he real?'

Sophie squirmed. Maybe it was time to tell her new friends about her little bit of happiness? What hurt could it do? 'He's most definitely real.' Her eyes shone brightly. 'He's gorgeous and treats me like a lady.'

'I should think so too!' Linda cried. 'Never think of yourself as anything less, my girl.'

Sophie smiled weakly. If only she could. But thanks to Andy, she was slowly beginning to.

'Come on then. What's lover-boy's name?' Vera pressed, fuelled to see a crack opening in Sophie's well-protected armour.

'Andy.' Sophie blushed harder. 'Andy Waterford.'

'Never heard of him, but then I don't know everybody!' Vera laughed. 'How old is he and what does he do for a living?'

'Oh, erm... he's in his early thirties and works in the pub industry,' Sophie said, getting flustered.

'Jesus, V!' Linda cried. 'This ain't the Spanish Inquisition. Leave the poor girl alone. Can't you see you're embarrassing her. She's in love – anyone can see that!'

Sophie coloured again, this time deeper. *Was it that obvious?* But she was glad Linda had intervened because although she knew Andy worked in the pub trade, she didn't know exactly how old he was. Nor did she care.

'Shame we can't meet the gorgeous Andy at the wedding...' Vera said, raising her eyebrows at Linda.

'You're right, V! Why didn't I think of that! Invite him!' Linda squealed excitedly. 'Go on, bring him!'

Sophie went hot. She was being offered the chance to bring Andy as her plus one like she'd dreamed of? But she couldn't. She was damned if she would blow this by being too eager. 'No. It's still early days.'

'You could have fooled me,' Linda winked. 'Seems like you're flat up to your neck where feelings are concerned about this man.'

'More reason not to scare him off then,' Sophie retorted.

'Christ, if you scare him off by inviting him to a fucking wedding, then he ain't the right man, babe!' Vera added, determined to put a face to the name of the man who had given her new friend renewed hope. *She wanted to shake his bloody hand!*

'Anyway, he's busy this weekend, but thanks for the offer,' Sophie said. *That was true as well.* Andy had said he had something to do on Saturday. She didn't know what and neither had she asked.

'We'll just have to be patient in meeting this wonderful man of yours then,' Linda said, getting to her feet. 'I'll have to love and leave you now as my daughter said she might pop around tonight. Her fella's on a late one, so I suspect she wants to drive me up the wall with last-minute wedding worries.'

In reality, if Sam was panicking with last-minute jitters, then that was what Linda was there for.

Bending down, she kissed Sophie and then Vera on the cheek. 'If I don't see you before, I'll see you both on Saturday at the wedding.'

14

─────────

'I'm really pleased with your work today, Tina,' Ruth Goldstore said, smiling as Tina rinsed out her cleaning equipment. 'You've picked up everything so quickly!' She lowered her voice. 'A lot quicker than anyone else ever has, so you'll be the perfect asset to our team. How did you find your first day?'

Tina beamed with pride. 'I never thought I'd enjoy cleaning so much, Mrs Goldstore. All this plane lark is completely new to me, but I'm finding it fascinating!'

And surprisingly, it *was*. The people she worked with were great too. The rest of the cleaning staff on her shift had welcomed her with open arms – no cliques, backstabbing or closing ranks on the 'New Girl'. They'd accepted her into the fold and she'd got on with everybody like a house on fire.

All the air hostesses in their pristine skirt suit uniforms and patterned neckerchiefs had smiled and spoken to her too. And when the pilot acknowledged her with a smile and a 'hello' as he'd left the cockpit, she'd almost fainted!

Being inside that huge empty plane was something she'd never imagined to be doing either. She'd never even been *in* a plane before.

They'd scrambled to get on board once the passengers had disembarked. Even the place being covered in half-eaten food and rubbish hadn't put Tina off. Neither had the checklist as long as her arm she'd had to adhere to – a very *thorough* checklist. Even the hideously short time slot they had to get things sparkling and looking brand new hadn't deterred her. Shovelling up the countless amounts of rubbish and random discarded things, Tina had questioned whether any of the passengers would dream of being so slovenly at home.

Yes, she was beginning to sound like her mother, but it was *true*.

Tina suppressed her giggle, tinged with sadness at the thought of her mom, Amelia. Even though her mother wouldn't have outwardly said it, or if she had, it would have taken her *ages* to admit, believing one of her daughters was going above her station by working for an airline, Amelia would have been as proud as punch how Tina had turned her life around.

Tina smiled widely at her boss. 'What time do I start tomorrow? I can come in earlier if you need me to? I'm eager to do my best.'

Ruth put her hands on her hips and laughed happily. 'I hope you don't lose this eagerness when the initial few days are over!'

Tina shook her head resolutely. 'I won't, I'm sure of it, Mrs Goldstore!'

'I've put you down for the twelve to eight shift tomorrow.' Ruth nodded towards the door. 'Now get yourself home and have a well-deserved drink.'

Tina grinned so widely, she felt her face may split. 'I will.'

Yep. She was going to like it here.

* * *

Seb listened carefully to the address Andrew reeled off down the mobile phone and mentally committed it to memory.

He knew where the place was, but he'd wanted to check the best and quickest route using as few main roads as possible. His brother was the best when it came to analysing routes. This ability had been very useful in the past and would prove to be now, too.

Okay, so there was a bigger risk factor involved originating from this prick's workplace, but there wasn't time to stake out drinking holes or find less obvious places to wait for a suitable opportunity to strike. This had to be dealt with immediately otherwise he would implode.

'Yep, got it. Cheers,' Seb said. He'd already reached the outskirts of Coventry and having pulled over to await Andrew's call, it wouldn't take long once he got back on the road. All being well, he'd be back early enough to spend the last part of the evening with Sam.

Then, and providing things went to plan, he'd sleep soundly for the first time in days. And that he could sorely do with because he was knackered.

'I need you to remain at the apartment tonight in case I require the use of your ablutions,' Seb said, firing the engine of one of the motors they kept for instances such as this. 'Sorry if that buggers up your plans, but it can't be helped. Yep... okay. We'll talk about the rest later.'

Grimacing as the gears crunched as he started the engine and slipped into gear, Seb tried not to let the scraping noise set his teeth on edge. A Ford Granada wasn't his usual style of motor, but it was nondescript, worked okay and most importantly, had no link to any of *them*.

The host of cars and vans they had with swappable reg plates were worth their weight in gold. Keeping them parked in varying locations within a wide radius of the city enabled them to always be reachable fast, which was beneficial, as well as keeping them away from premises associated with the firm.

Ending the call, Seb threw his mobile onto the passenger seat and pulled out of the layby on the A45. Off at the next slip road, then round the back way. A few more turnings after that and he'd reach the destination.

He hoped the intel on this guy's movements and timings was correct.

They'd better be. He hadn't got time to piss about or hang around longer than needs be. To undertake this himself was risky enough, but necessary in order to throw his mind off the looping spiral of unwanted thoughts.

Glancing through the gloom, Seb slammed on his brakes and swerved around a corner.

Coming to a stop, Seb put the Granada in reverse and backed into the alleyway Andrew had suggested. He glanced around. It was perfect. On route to the car park around the corner, his target would walk past here to reach his own motor.

And that was *exactly* what Seb was waiting for.

Grab, drive, do the deed, then away – job done.

There was no need to drag it out. This wasn't a normal situation, so his usual way of working did not apply.

He pulled his gun from his inside pocket and stared at it within the gloom of the dark alley. He could get one ready for firing blindfolded he'd done it so many times.

Checking it was ready to go, Seb shoved the gun back into position and quickly got out of the car.

Striding a few yards to the mouth of the alley, Seb pulled his lapels higher around his neck, the breeze surprisingly cold for a

July evening. With his head down, he leant casually against the damp brickwork, pretending to look at his mobile phone.

Unobtrusive, that was him... And he'd remain that same way until the time was right.

Which should, if his calculations were correct, be any time now...

Seeing the person he was waiting patiently for coming directly down the road towards him out of the corner of his eye, Seb's lips twitched with the beginnings of a smirk.

Without looking up, he garnered enough information about his surroundings from his peripheral vision to know that, aside from the man approaching, the street was deserted.

Like he'd foreseen, this wanker had left after everyone else, desperate to be the one with the most important piece of whatever bullshit he was working on, more than any of his colleagues.

And it was good the man was predictable because no one else could be dragged into this.

As his target drew level, Seb's arm shot out and locked around the man's forearm, pulling him into the shadows at the mouth of the alley. Taken off guard at this unexpected disturbance, the man's expression fast turned from shock into pure unadulterated fear as his eyes accustomed to the darkness of the alley.

'Mr Stoker!' John Salter gasped. 'What brings you h...'

'Get into the car!' Seb dragged John Salter further down the alley and closer to the Granada.

'Mr Stoker, I...' Now this man was in front of him, John Salter's hands moved to cover his face and his head from the expected onslaught. 'I'm sorry if I caused problems... I know you said th...' His eyes widened as Seb pulled a gun from underneath his jacket as casually as he would a mobile phone or a wallet.

'Jesus!' John yelped, his eyes automatically darting around. His shoes slipped on the wet alley floor as he attempted to make a run for it, even though the chance of succeeding was slim. However, his wish to run was immediately quelled when the barrel of a gun pressed into the side of his neck.

'I said, get in the car,' Seb repeated, his other hand now on the back of John Salter's neck as he frogmarched him towards the Granada.

'Please! Can't we just discuss this?' John blathered. 'There's no need for things to get nasty.' His words fell on deaf ears as he found himself thrown in the passenger seat.

15

'I wasn't sure whether you'd come round tonight or not, but I made sure I was back just in case.' Linda poured Sam a cold glass of mineral water, like she'd requested. 'You don't fancy a wine to quell any last-minute wedding nerves?'

Sam fidgeted but found it easy to deflect the question. 'I had a couple earlier and I've got a meeting first thing tomorrow, so I'll pass.'

Having always had a penchant for a few wines of an evening, not doing so was unusual, but Sam felt the excuse was believable. She'd be glad when the secret about the baby was out in the open so she could stop being furtive.

'Seb ended up working late, then?' Linda eyed Sam suspiciously. Something was bothering her daughter, she could sense it. She hoped Seb wasn't up to anything to cause problems. Sam should have the perfect day on Saturday. 'Is there a problem?'

'Problem?' Sam glanced at her mother over the top of the tall glass. 'No. Seb's tying up a few loose ends with outstanding deliveries before we leave, that's all.'

'Two whole weeks away, you lucky cow!' Linda grinned. 'The Maldives too! That place looks too perfect to exist in the brochures!'

Sam laughed good naturedly. 'I hope it exists, being as we're flying there!'

But there *was* a problem. Something which had played on Sam's mind ever since discovering her parents, as she'd known them, weren't her *real* parents.

Although she'd asked when first meeting Linda, her mother's reaction had been so bad, she hadn't pressed it. Then, what with Linda's disappearance and rehab, there hadn't been a suitable time to revisit the subject since.

But being pregnant had brought the question to the forefront of Sam's mind more and more over the last couple of months and knowing the answer had become all-consuming.

'By the way, V's bringing the girl who moved into my old flat to your wedding as her plus one. That's okay, isn't it? She's a sweet girl. She reminds me a little of myself at her age,' Linda said.

'Yes, of course,' Sam answered, her mind distracted by the burning question she had to ask. 'Is Gloria about? Or the kids?' She didn't want to broach this subject only for someone to interrupt the delicate conversation.

Linda swigged from her glass of cider. 'Gloria's off getting her hair done ready for Saturday. I've told her there's still two days to go, but she was insistent. The hairdresser agreed to a special late-night appointment just for her.' She winked. 'I'm not having mine done until Saturday morning. It cuts down the chance of a fucking bird shitting on my head before I even get to the bloody wedding! As for the kids – they're in bed. They'd better be anyway, as it's getting late.'

Watching Sam, Linda stopped babbling. Her glass paused

between the table and her mouth. 'Something *is* bothering you, isn't it?' Placing her drink down, she folded her arms. 'If it's not Seb, then what is it? Tell me, Sam! My job is to be here for you – even if it's taken me bloody years!' Worry prickled. 'You are still getting married? Nothing's happened between you and Seb to make y...'

'We're still getting married!' Sam exclaimed. There was nothing in this world that would make her cancel becoming Seb's wife. 'I just need to ask you something.'

The hairs on the back of Linda's neck tingled. *Whatever this was, it sounded ominous.* 'Go on...' she said with trepidation.

Sam couldn't stop her fingers from twisting together. Not much made her nervous these days, but *this* did.

She knew Linda had been young when Sam had been born, but what if she was the product of something dreadful? What if her real father was a rapist?

Sam felt sick to the core. How would she feel being a by-product of *that*? But she had to ask. Not knowing who she was had become more important than ever now a new life grew inside her.

'Sam?' Linda frowned, her fear increasing as she reached for her daughter's hand. 'Please tell me what's wrong. Ask me anything and I'll try my God's honest best to give you an answer.'

'I want to know who my father is,' Sam blurted. 'My *real* father...'

Linda's mouth opened and then shut again. *Her father?* She'd told Sam to ask what she liked, but not that. How could she answer *that*?

It was the one thing she'd desperately tried to shield Sam from. It was why she'd upset the applecart and not told the police her side of the story about her imprisonment at the hands of Tom Bedworth. Had she spoken out, it would have saved the angst over the untrue allegations of Seb being behind the murder of that woman in the cupboard, amongst other things. If she'd done what was requested then time wouldn't have been wasted looking for Tina to speak instead.

The reason Linda had kept schtum hadn't been because she wouldn't tell the police about Bedworth. She'd have done *anything* to ensure Seb wasn't imprisoned for something he had no part in. But speaking out would have made the police dig further into her connection with Bedworth and it would only have been a matter of time before Sam discovered the truth: that the horrific excuse of a creature was her father.

And that was not something Sam would get over. *Ever.*

To allow her daughter to live with the knowledge that she shared that beast's DNA was impossible. Because of her, Sam had already been through enough and there was no way she would allow one more thing from the choices she'd made in the past to further hurt her beautiful firstborn child.

Whatever the personal cost, she'd remained steadfast, promising herself that Sam would remain shielded from that hideous revelation. It would achieve nothing, apart from unrelenting pain and damage.

'Mum?' Sam pressed, aware of Linda's silence. 'I know I've asked before and you wouldn't say. I respected that, but I really do need to know, so can you please tell me?'

Linda wrung her hands together. *This was a nightmare.*

'I want to start married life and our new way of running the businesses with nothing left hanging,' Sam explained, a hint of pleading in her voice. Seeing the conflicting emotions on Linda's face, her heart sank like a stone. 'You were young, I know that. B-but was I...? Did he... Did he force you?'

'No!' Linda said hastily. Stupidly, she'd willingly given herself to Tom Bedworth and regardless of anything else, she couldn't say otherwise, even though doing so would give her a justifiable reason for not mentioning his name. *She had to think, think, think. And quickly.* 'I wasn't forced. I...'

'Do you know who he is?' Sam gingerly asked, aware how awful her question sounded. 'I mean no disrespect. You know I don't think badly of you. You were honest enough to tell me that you... what you used to do for money, so if that's what it is, I won't judge, I promise.'

Linda swallowed the lump bigger than a breezeblock wedged in her throat. Yes, she'd progressed into selling herself, but not back when she'd fallen pregnant with Sam. She'd loved Tom. *Loved* him. He was the only man she'd ever been with at that point and she'd believed his lies when he'd said they'd get married. *How little she'd known...*

'He's dead.' Linda's eyes brimmed with tears at the hurt her choices had caused. 'He died some time ago. I'm sorry, love.'

It was true Tom was dead and Linda wasn't sorry at all. In fact, she'd never been gladder of anything.

Bedworth was dead because Sam's husband-to-be had killed him – not that Seb or Sam knew the truth of Tom's blood tie connection and okay, she hadn't been completely honest about the 'some time ago' bit, unless three months counted? *Still, it was the truth...*

'Dead?' Sam gasped. She hadn't known what to expect, but it wasn't *that*. This knowledge opened another line of worry – something she needed to think about. 'What did he die of? A disease? What?'

If her real father had died from a genetic condition, then she could be carrying a rogue gene – something to pass to her baby...

Her blood pressure spiralled and she found herself digging her nails into the plush arm of the upholstered chair to steady herself.

'Sam!' Linda rushed to kneel in front of her daughter. 'You've gone deathly pale! Look, I don't know the exact ins and outs of why he died, but it was an accident from what I heard, not an illness.'

Yeah, an accident with petrol and matches. How she hoped the bastard had suffered. 'I'm sorry that I can't tell you more. I hadn't seen him for years.' Until he'd returned, that was...

Sam inhaled deeply, fighting to control her escalating panic. 'Tell me his name. I want a name for my father.'

'I...' Linda froze. Now she'd have to lie. Wait! Maybe there was a way she could do this?

'Mum?'

Linda took a deep breath. 'His name was Vaughan. Thomas Vaughan.'

'Thomas Vaughan,' Sam repeated. 'What did he look like?'

Linda sighed. She had to end this. Vaughan was Tom's middle name, so it wasn't a lie. Not completely.

It wasn't the entire truth either, but *that* would remain hidden. 'Dark hair, medium build. Look, this is difficult. He abandoned me and well, you know what happened after that. He's dead, but you now have a name, so can we please leave it there?'

Despite promising not to, tears spilled from Linda's eyes. Tom Bedworth continued to haunt her from beyond the grave. He'd done enough damage. She didn't want to think about him any more. She'd been as truthful as possible without destroying her daughter's soul and that was the best she could do.

'Okay,' Sam nodded. 'Thanks for telling me.' Linda was right, she now knew her real father's name, but could never meet him because he was dead. From what she'd been told, she probably wouldn't want to meet someone who felt it acceptable abandoning a pregnant young girl. She had the only answer she could ever get now and it would have to do.

It was more than she'd possessed an hour ago. Maybe Linda

would tell her the whole story one day when she was fully recovered. Perhaps she'd never know? Either way, she had to let this be.

'Where are we going? You could at least tell me where you're taking me. We've been driving for ages.' John Salter's voice was high-pitched – squeaky even.

There was a high chance they hadn't been driving for ages at all, but it *felt* like it. Every second in the car he'd been forced into at gunpoint, whilst in the company of Seb Stoker, felt like a year. The man's silence made things even worse, if that was possible?

He'd tried his best to keep tabs on where they were heading, but his concentration was not up to its usual standards. They were still in Coventry – on the outskirts, but he didn't recognise this area at all. The country roads and surrounding fields all looked the same in the dark of the evening.

He wanted to get out of the car and leg it, but it was impossible. Stoker had locked the doors.

John's heart rate reached an alarming level. He wanted to gibber in fear; scream – *something* to get a reaction. Why wasn't Stoker responding to anything he said? He was just driving, staring ahead at the road that led to nowhere, his face frozen into a manic expression.

John didn't even know where that gun was, apart from no longer jammed in his neck.

He'd only run a story in the paper, for God's sake! It wasn't like he'd burnt Stoker's casino down like that last lot had. Everyone would know of the wedding venue on Saturday, so what difference did a couple of days make in the grand scheme of things?

John opened his mouth to say something that might get

through to this psycho in order to reason with him, but then shut it promptly when the Granada swerved off the road and bumped down a short lane.

Fuck! Where were they now?

His eyes darted around in the gloom, making out dense foliage. It was only when he heard the car door slam, did he realise Seb Stoker had got out. Panic surged as the boot opened and then shut.

Was he being left here, miles from civilisation?

John tugged feverishly at his door handle. He had to get out.

It was locked again. Shit.

He spun around in the seat. *Where had Stoker gone?*

His questions were quickly answered as the passenger door flew open. His stomach lurched into his mouth.

'Out!'

John had little choice but to obey, his eyes centring on the gun which had reappeared back in Seb's hand. A torch in his other hand lit up an area several metres away.

'Over there.' Seb jerked his head and pushed the barrel of the gun into John's ribs.

Staggering from the car, John squinted in the unexpected bright light, finding himself propelled towards a patch of hedging, his legs working independently of what his brain wanted. 'Whatever you think I've done, I can make amends. You're getting married on Saturday, Mr Stoker and...'

'Yes, I am, aren't I?' Seb stated, his voice dripping with venom. 'Get on that. On your knees.' He kicked the back of John's legs, causing him to hit the deck like a badly built card stack.

Landing on his hands and knees, John felt vinyl or canvas underneath his fingers. His brow furrowed in confusion, until he realised what it was...

It was a tarpaulin. A fucking tarpaulin spread on the floor!

Christl Stoker wasn't going to... wasn't going to...? 'Wait!' he squawked. 'Whatever you're thinking of doing, you...'

'Shut the fuck up!' Seb spat. 'I said *kneel*, not crouch on all fours like a fucking animal!'

John struggled to push himself to his knees, his shoes scraping against the tarpaulin. With a lot of effort, he manoeuvred into the instructed position and looked up at the menacing figure of Seb Stoker looming above, the green of his eyes glinting in the torch-light. 'I...'

'Goodbye, Mr Salter,' Seb said calmly. *There was nothing else to say.*

John tried once again to think of something to say to reason with this man. Surely Stoker wouldn't do something to jeopardise his own wedding at this stage in the day?

But as he watched the gun being cocked, the barrel still less than three feet away, all John could manage was a faint mewling noise from between his teeth.

There was a split-second flash of bright light as the bullet left the barrel. Then there was nothing, apart from darkness.

* * *

Seb calmly accelerated along the road, the carefully wrapped tarpaulin safely secured in the Granada's boot.

He'd deposit this motor somewhere convenient before torching it and then he'd hasten back to the Peacock.

Even if someone stumbled across the car before it burnt out completely, by the time the fire engines extinguished the blaze, Salter would be a blackened, burnt shell of cinders.

Even if the police bothered employing forensics and discovered the singular bullet hole through Salter's temple, it couldn't be traced back to a gun *he* possessed.

The police were welcome to check his stash of firearms. All of his weapons were licensed and kept in cabinets, as per the rules. And they still were. To link him to one with no serial number and the batch of ammo used was impossible. Weapons for jobs such as *this* were taken from a different collection. A collection well and truly off radar.

Besides, this gun would shortly be out of his hands and all traces suitably disposed of, like the tarp and its contents would shortly be...

Relief cascaded, the burden of the troublesome image of Sam's demise already lifting. With John Salter's removal, the omen was deleted.

Certain things that some may call superstitious were adhered to in his family as well as the business. *This* being one of them.

That omen behind the reoccurring image had to be removed, otherwise it would come true.

Now, Seb smiled, it wouldn't.

Pulling onto an open stretch of the A45, he stamped on the accelerator and the Granada shot up the road.

Dump this motor, do the required business to it and then get Andrew to pick him up and take him back to the apartment. He'd have a quick shower, then he'd be back home before he knew it.

He glanced down at his trousers. From what he could see in the dim light, there weren't any leftovers from the Salter incident. But then, it wasn't like he'd employed his standard tactics, which invariably became messy.

Seb grinned savagely. There had been no need to torture the man, despite how nice it would have been. He'd just needed him gone.

Now the job was done.

Opening the window a notch, Seb sparked up a cigarette and

continued driving, glad to see the skyline of Birmingham appearing in the distance.

Once he'd offloaded this car and his brother had collected him, he'd find a petrol station with a Spar. What better to take home but some of those sour cream and chive Pringles Sam was obsessed with.

He'd buy every single tube he could find if it made Sam happy.

16

Waking up, Tom winced as the pounding of his head steamrollered into being priority number one. Turning over on the sofa, he didn't get a chance to put his hands out to cushion his fall before hitting the deck.

Feeling even more pain, this time to his face and left eye, Tom groaned loudly, sickened to see that he'd landed on Potter's foot.

Getting a close-up view of a fungal-infected toenail made Tom's guts roil. Great! A mouldy fucking toenail stuck in his eyeball. He'd probably lose his sight now.

Pulling himself into a sitting position, Tom rubbed his throbbing eye and glared at the sprawled figure of Potter on the living room carpet, lying amongst the remains of a kebab. The horrible guttural noise escaping from his slack mouth, he could only presume was some kind of snore.

Snatching a half-full can of Tennent's Super from the coffee table, Tom took a swig, scowling at the warm flat liquid and then paused to peer into the can.

Had someone put fag ash in this?

He rubbed his hand over his stubbly face. This was getting

beyond a joke. There was only so long he could live with this fuck-turd. It had already gone past the point that any sane person could endure without experiencing permanent mental injury.

However, getting pissed as a way of making it through the evening had helped refraining from bludgeoning Potter to death.

Tom scowled. He shouldn't have got so wasted, but after finally getting Potter back from the airport, he'd then had to endure a four-hour conversation the fat retard was having with a dead person.

No wonder he'd got hammered.

Hearing an excruciatingly loud fart – the sort that sounded like it may have made a mess, Tom stared at the shifting bulk on the floor. 'Are you getting up or what?' he barked.

He hadn't got the patience to be pleasant this morning. If his plan didn't work, then there was no choice but to kill the man and walk away from this whole state of affairs. What an utter shitheap his life had ended up.

Again...

Receiving no response, apart from more offensive piglike snorting as Potter went back to sleep, Tom got to his feet.

Cramming a cigarette in his mouth, he lit it, then held his hand out so the match slipped through his fingers to fall on Potter's cheek. He hoped it may burn a hole in the twat's face. Anything to grant a smidgen of amusement to this offensive living arrangement.

But no. The match fizzled out. Even that hadn't achieved the desired effect.

Tom angrily dragged on his cigarette. *Would anything he did ever work?*

He jutted his chin out in determination. He needed to snap himself out of this bullshit. He hadn't come this far and put up with this bollocks just to lose all hope at last knockings.

No. Fucking. Way.

It was a good job Potter was still asleep because a) it meant he didn't have to listen to his insane ramblings, and b) he could go out alone and unhindered to collect the passport.

Tom may have got pissed as a rat last night, but he hadn't forgotten *that*. Collecting the passport was numero uno of importance today. Something he was doing *without* Potter.

Tom squinted at the plastic clock on the mantlepiece. He was already dressed. He even still had his fucking shoes on, so there was little point having a shower. No one would notice if he didn't wash for a bleeding week around here. In Telford, people would think that overkill.

He'd go now. He'd be early, but it didn't matter.

Stomping across to the unit designed to hold a TV and videos but which had neither, Tom pulled the sticky drawer knob and fished out a wad of what remained of his money. It was fast diminishing to nothing. He didn't even have enough left to justify buying coke any more.

Thanks to the bastard Stokers and his poxy daughter, he'd been reduced to fuck all once again.

Yeah, it was all right for them, swanning around and getting married at some posh bloody mediaeval turrety place with Samantha thinking herself Rapunzel, but their fairy tale would soon be over...

Tom stared at the wad of money in his hand, then shoved it into his pocket, tugging at the zip which always stuck.

It drove him mad. *Everything* was driving him mad.

This bloke had best come through with this bastard passport, otherwise he didn't know what he'd do. But what he *was* sure of was that pair of clowns would sorely wish they hadn't splurged out for a honeymoon they'd never see.

Stomping across the room, Tom stepped over Potter, resisting driving his boot into the man's guts. He'd only lose his shoe in all the fucking fat and with the state of his dwindling finances, he couldn't afford to shell out for another pair.

Taking a quick last glance, Tom snatched the van keys from the sideboard and slipped out of the door. Locking it behind him, he pulled the handle, double checking it was locked.

He wasn't stupid. He'd taken both sets of keys for this shit-hole – Potter's *and* his. When or *if* that turd ever woke up and realised he was on his own, he wouldn't get far if he tried to get out.

No, the mental toad could wait until he got back and with any luck, by that time, he'd have calmed down enough to think clearly and brace himself for the test run on the route planned for tomorrow.

Because this plan was going to work. It had to.

* * *

'I can't wait to show you off on the beach in a bikini.' Seb wrapped his arms around Sam. 'Just think – two whole weeks of not watching what we say and you not picking clothes to make sure you don't give things away.' He moved his hands to rest on her little bump. 'Everyone on that beach will be able to see there's a baby in there. And he's *mine!*'

Sam laughed. 'Or she. It may be a girl...'

'Girl or boy, I don't care!' Seb turned Sam around and kissed her. 'One more day before you're Mrs Stoker. In fact,' he glanced at his watch, 'it's less than that now.'

The good night's sleep he'd had, finally free of that bloody dream, had done him the world of good. Now he was in the best frame of mind *ever* and fully able to concentrate on the weekend he'd waited so long for.

'You didn't say how it went last night.' Sam straightened the knot of Seb's tie. 'You were too intent on ravishing me!'

'Are you complaining?' Seb winked, one eyebrow raised.

'I don't seem to be, do I?' Sam laughed, smiling down at the swell of her belly. And she wasn't complaining. Not even *slightly*. 'The last-minute checks on the drops? All set and good to go?'

Seb faltered. *Drops? Ah, yes – the Irish. He'd said about the Irish...* 'Yep. All in hand. Everything's sorted and will be just fine.'

It most definitely would now.

Last night, Andrew had come up trumps. Quickly showering in the apartment, his brother had taken the gun used to dispatch Salter, promising to get rid so he could go straight off back to Sam.

Seb had been more than grateful. He hated being away from Sam – even more so now. And he wasn't upsetting her by telling her what he'd done to Salter. She'd only worry that it might come back on him. It wouldn't. Like DI Baker had made clear, the force wasn't concerned with their dealings now the gameplan had changed.

In all truth, Seb also didn't want to admit how much this omen of doom had bothered him. Sam would either laugh, saying it absurd nonsense, or worse, become convinced that something bad would *indeed* happen to her and the baby, even though by doing what he'd done, the chance of that had been neutralised.

But there was another thing which had come to light that Seb *did* need to mention. And it wasn't likely she would be overly impressed about it. But there would be no bad feeling within his family again – especially not this weekend.

'It appears I've put my foot in it with Neil,' he muttered sheepishly. 'In retrospect, I should have told him I'd asked Andrew to be my best man, rather than him finding out...'

Turning around, Sam fixed Seb with one of her stares. 'Oh Seb! Seriously? You didn't say anything? Why?' The grief and resentment in the past between the brothers had almost ripped the family apart. That could not happen again under any circumstances. 'How do you think that looked to Neil?'

'I know, I know!' Seb raised his hands submissively. 'Guilty as charged. It wasn't purposeful. I'll straighten it out. Andrew was probably exaggerating over how hurt he reckoned Neil was.'

Sam pursed her lips. *That she doubted.* 'Make sure you put it right.'

'Yes, ma'am!' Seb mock-saluted, ducking out of the way as Sam pretended to slap him.

'I found out something interesting last night,' Sam said, aware she'd yet to mention *her* news. 'I know who my father is...'

Seb stopped in his tracks. 'What? Linda told you? I thought she wouldn't discuss it?'

Sam shrugged. 'I had to give it one last attempt. I want no loose ends now we're starting a new and different chapter in our lives.' She smiled guiltily. 'I actually put a lot of pressure on her, but I *had* to know.'

'Don't keep me in suspense!' Seb cried. 'Who is he and where is he? Do you want to meet him or...'

'He's dead,' Sam said quietly. 'A while ago, apparently. Some kind of accident. Thomas Vaughan is his name.' Saying the name of the man she now knew to be her father felt strange. *Really* strange.

Seb whistled through his teeth. 'Ah shit, Sam. I'm sorry.'

Sam shrugged. 'Don't be. After him abandoning Linda, I'm not sure I'd rush to meet him even if I had the chance. I have his name now, so that's the end of it and the chapter can be closed.'

Seb frowned. 'Thomas Vaughan? I haven't heard of the surname. Local lad, was he?'

'No idea,' Sam said. And that was the point. She knew nothing. Just a name: the name of a dead man who had fathered her, then walked away. And by what she'd been told in the past, a man who had been low enough to sell his own child. Not the sort of person she had time for, father or not.

Seb studied Sam. Would she really be satisfied with just a name? 'I can put things in motion to do some digging? See what other info can be dragged up about this Vaughan bloke?' He raised his eyebrows. 'It might give you more answers?'

Sam shook her head. 'Please don't. I've no need to know anything else.' Sitting down, she thought for a moment before speaking again. 'You know what he did to Linda and how he profited from selling me, so I want to let things be. All I want now is to concentrate on us and *our* family.'

Seb grinned. Pulling Sam from the chair, he gently swung her around in his arms. 'Then that's what you will have. By the way, are you still staying at Gloria's tonight?'

'Of course,' Sam giggled. 'It's traditional.'

'Bloody stupid, if you ask me,' Seb said. 'But because I can't bear being here without you, I'll stay with Andrew. I'll probably end up working, but it will pass the time.'

'Maybe he's arranged strippers for you,' Sam laughed.

'Andrew's not dim enough to think any woman could possibly outshine you!'

'Top marks for responding with the correct answer!' Sam laughed, tilting her face up to Seb's lips.

17

Gloria sipped her breakfast tea, watching Linda across the table. 'Is everything okay? You've been very quiet and out of sorts. Do you not feel well?'

Linda pushed her toast around the plate, unable to face eating it. No matter how much tea she drank, her mouth remained dry. She suspected it would remain so, whilst the burning question Sam had put to her last night revolved around her head like a turntable with no off switch.

Her night's sleep had been haunted with that question: '*Who is my real father?*'

And as much as Linda loved Gloria to bits, she couldn't unburden herself from the quandary she found herself in. She'd never told anybody. Not even Vera.

Although she'd told Sam the *partial* truth, it had still been doctored. That didn't sit very well, but there had been no alternative. Sam must be protected at all costs. It didn't make things more palatable, but Linda would have to live with that.

Whatever happened, she had to pull herself together. Painting on a smile, Linda looked up. 'I'm just tired. It's all the last-minute wedding things running through my head. You know what it's like.'

Suddenly remembering where Gloria went last night, Linda made a point of examining her friend's hair. It was a good excuse to get off this subject. 'Your hair looks a treat! I hope my barnet turns out as well tomorrow otherwise I'll be forced to wear a bag on my head!'

She laughed in an attempt to act normal. In reality, her hairstyle was the very least of her worries, but she couldn't let Tom Bedworth interfere with her life any more than he already had. He was dead, goddamn it. It was over. *Remember that, Lin*, she told herself.

'Aw, rubbish, you'll look amazing!' Gloria patted her coiffured hair with pride. 'But thanks. I'm pleased how it's turned out.' She then sat forward. 'I'm so excited for tomorrow! In our day, weddings were only ever at churches or registry offices, not at posh hotels! It's all very fancy.'

'Isn't it just,' Linda agreed. She clearly remembered her wedding to Mickey Devlin, if she could call it such.

She shuddered inwardly. She'd waddled into the registry office, eight months pregnant with her son, Grant, wearing a horrible blue smock. It had been the only thing to fit which wasn't stained or peppered with holes. *That* was the extent of her wedding dress.

Not that Mickey had looked much better. Turning up half an hour late, he'd been half-cut and stinking of rum. The overlarge suit he'd cadged off a bloke down the boozer who'd recently been to court hadn't helped. Neither did Mickey's version of putting in the carnation she'd given him for his buttonhole. It wouldn't have taken him much effort to do it properly, rather than sticking it to his lapel with fucking Sellotape, would it?

Linda sighed. At that moment, she should have realised how married life to Mickey would turn out. That, and because the only other guests attending were two witnesses they'd grabbed off the street. They'd even had to buy them bloody drinks afterwards in the pub, as a means of payment.

She'd known deep down it would never work. But she'd *wanted* it to. After Tom's devastating abandonment which had led to having her firstborn adopted, Linda had been desperate for security. Someone to love. A *proper* family.

Linda shook her head in disbelief at her own stupidness for even going through with the marriage. And for her self-pity that cascaded over her right now in waves. Her son, Grant, was now dead and Marina was a psycho who had fucked off out of her life, thank God. But at least she'd got Sam back.

Shoving the thought of Tom, Mickey and her disastrous previous life from her mind, Linda pulled herself together for the second time. 'Right, the plan is a car will arrive to take us together as mothers of the bride.'

Gloria nodded. 'And Vera? Will she be coming with us?'

'No. Vera and her friend are coming to the reception afterwards. They could have come to the wedding – they're more than welcome, but because Vera hasn't seen Sam since my disappearance, she doesn't want to make things awkward. She'll come after the ceremony when there's more people. That way she can have a quiet word with Sam and they can smooth things over.'

'I know how much Vera thinks of Sam, so it must be difficult for her not to witness the actual ceremony,' Gloria said.

Linda shrugged. 'That's Vera for you. Honest and good to the core, that one. She's doing the best thing.'

Gloria frowned. 'I do hope Seb and Sam won't be deluged with hordes of those awful press, now that dreadful reporter has announced the venue to the world.'

'Yeah, I know.' Linda snorted in derision. 'I'm sure Seb has it

under control. I can't see him allowing the day to be spoilt or for
Sam to be upset. He's a good 'un, that one.'

And wasn't he just. Linda trusted Seb Stoker implicitly to ensure
her daughter remained all right.

'I can't believe I was worrying to start with about Sam's involvement with Seb! I'm so glad I was wrong,' Gloria admitted. 'I
wonder if we'll be blessed with grandchildren anytime soon?'

'Hopefully,' Linda grinned.

'Actually, I half thought Sam might already be expecting,'
Gloria continued. 'She seems different lately, but I can't put my
finger on it.'

'Nah,' Linda laughed. 'She'd be too excited about it not to have
told us by now if she was up the duff!'

'I still don't see why you had to lock me in there!' Potter muttered
as he glared through the Escort van's dirty windscreen.

Tom ignored Potter. He didn't have to explain himself. *And
neither would he.* It was fairly obvious to anyone with half a bloody
brain why the stupid bastard was locked in the flat in the first
place. *Because the fat wanker couldn't be trusted.*

As the few remaining marbles Potter possessed rolled out of his
neanderthal skull on a regular basis, he'd become a major liability.
One that Tom could not risk. Had he not locked the door, he could
have returned to find the muppet amiably chatting to that woman
with the extra set of teeth on the floor below. As it was, that old bat
had a penchant for whipping out her notebook each time anyone
in the entire block of flats farted, let alone left the building, nosy
bitch that she was.

Plus, Potter was so mangled half the time, Tom wouldn't put it
past him to tell the old crone everything they'd done, who they

were lying low from and what they had planned. The crazy freak might even go so far as handing her the bloody Stokers' phone numbers as well, suggesting she let them know in advance...

Of course, conveniently, Potter would have zilch memory about doing any of those things...

That, or he'd invite some of the local tramps to live with them, convinced Mark had returned from the dead in a different body.

Tom changed gear, glaring as he had to grope Potter's leg to shove the stick into fourth, sure the fat prick was leaning further across his side on purpose.

But neither Potter's snotty grumbles, nor his fat fucking leg could remove the good mood Tom was now in.

Taking his hand from the wheel, he patted the pocket of his jacket where his new passport and mobile phone were safely stashed. His way out of this drum finally accomplished.

About fucking time!

He'd have gladly paid four times more than what he'd handed over for the privilege. Well, not gladly – even a grand was steep in his opinion, but he'd still have done it if needs be. Now he was sorted. Just the last part of the plan to pull off and then he could disappear, happy in the knowledge he'd be leaving for the final time.

'Have you planned where we'll hold this daughter of yours once we've got her?' Potter asked, having accepted there would be no forthcoming explanation for his earlier incarceration. 'I'm buggered if I'm killing her straight away! Like I said, I want my fun before I rip her tits off and kill the bitch. *And* I'm filming it. I want Stoker to see exactly what happens to his little wifey at the end.'

Tom winced at Potter's stained teeth as he grinned savagely. 'We'll rent a shitty hotel room,' he muttered. He didn't intend staying there long. Only as long as it took for Stoker to deliver the money.

Unbeknown to Potter, this morning he'd booked three nights in the worst, most grotty B&B he could find. The place was perfect: the landlady was as deaf as a post and the other 'guests' were so off their trolleys they wouldn't notice if a nuclear bomb dropped on their fucking heads. It was exactly the sort of place he'd been looking for. That was where Potter would stay with Sam.

It wasn't like *he* was hanging around the same place. In addition he'd booked another place for himself. A *decent* place. That's where *he'd* bide his time in and wait until Stoker came good with the readies.

Whatever happened to dear little Samantha or Potter after that was of no concern to him. He'd be long gone.

'Isn't renting a hotel room risky?' Potter asked. 'She'll be with us for several weeks and we don't want any interruptions.'

Tom rolled his eyes. There was no chance he'd be staying *days*, let alone weeks, but he'd let Potter think otherwise. 'Do you have any suggestions, being as you think mine are so crap?'

'Why don't we rent a house? A detached, somewhere out of the way. We wouldn't get disturbed and there would be no one to hear the screams.' Just the thought of causing pain to someone Stoker loved made Potter feel warm inside. 'I could ask around the local and see if anyone knows of anywhere short notice.'

'What, like today?' Tom snapped. There was only so long he could humour this ludicrous bullshit. 'Why don't we explain what we want the house for whilst we're at it? Or how about we apply to an estate agent? That way, they'd have our names too. Top idea that!'

Potter snarled, but didn't bother adding anything further to the conversation.

'Ah, here we are.' Tom swung into the sweeping driveway and glanced at the dashboard clock. 'That took an hour and a half.'

He mentally calculated what time they would need to leave

Telford tomorrow to arrive here in time. They'd wait, hidden, but with a view of cars arriving and leaving to ensure they were ready to tail Stoker's motor the minute the newlyweds left for the airport.

It would undoubtedly be a long wait. Best-case scenario – a few hours, or maybe not even until the next morning, but *he'd* be there – ready for as long as needed.

'Is this it?' Potter crunched down to look at the view. 'Fucking hell! It's like a castle! But what's all this?' He waved his tree trunk arm in the direction of hordes of staff festooning the long driveway with ribbons, flowers and lights.

'That, I suspect, is part of the wedding preparations,' Tom spat through his clenched teeth. And weren't they going all out to have the perfect 'look at me' wedding, the jumped-up bastards?

This alone depleted his mood further. How dare that greedy slut of a daughter capitalise on what she'd done? And Stoker – the black-haired, dago-looking wanker who thought himself so fucking clever?

His blood silently boiled within his rapidly furring arteries. Stoker wouldn't be so cocky soon. Oh no, he'd shit his kecks once his new bride went AWOL.

18

Catching her breath, Tina hurried to the coffee machine. Fishing change from the pocket in her tabard, she fed it into the slot and tapped her foot impatiently as the machine clanked a plastic cup into place.

The drink would be rancid. Machine coffee always was, but she hadn't time to head to the staff room or cafeteria to make herself a proper cup. Half of her break had already passed and it wasn't long before the next plane her team was due to clean landed.

Tina gingerly lifted the squashy cup from the holder and sipped the scorching liquid, wincing as sourness flooded her tastebuds.

It was her own fault. If she hadn't used up most of her break tidying her cleaning caddy, she'd have had enough time to fetch a decent brew. But she was adamant to do everything in her power to be the best worker Mrs Goldstore ever had. A glowing recommendation and reference could never be a waste of time when applying for a hostie position.

But Tina also *wanted* to be meticulous. For the first time she had a job which didn't make her sick to her stomach, plus she liked the people she worked with. What could be better than that?

Tina rushed to swig down the hot coffee. If she got a few minutes she wanted to pick some of the ground staffs' brains. Perhaps even catch one of the check-in girls if she spotted one of them going on a break. She needed to use every opportunity to learn as much as possible about how the airport and airlines worked. That would give her an advantage over others wanting a job, even if they were better qualified and prettier than her.

She stared up the open corridor to the bustle of the arrivals hall. So many people coming and going. It was so exciting.

'Hey! I was hoping to see you!' Penny rushed towards Tina. 'I've just got in from Portugal and wanted to see how you were getting on.'

Tina swung around at Penny's voice. She beamed widely. 'It's great! I love it! I just wanted to thank you for getting me in here. It's a dream come true!'

Penny raised an eyebrow, somewhat dubious that anyone could possibly find cleaning a 'dream come true'. 'You're welcome. I'm pleased you're getting on well.' She waved a sheet of paper. 'I suppose I'd better get this to Operations!'

Tina moved closer, her interest piqued. 'Is that from the plane you've just come in on? I think that's the one we're scheduled to clean next.'

Penny smiled at Tina's obvious enthusiasm. 'Yes, it is. We landed five minutes ago.'

'I figured it's in my interest to learn as much as I can if I want to eventually do what you do,' Tina grinned. Then a horrible thought occurred. 'Shit. Is the plane ready for cleaning?'

She chucked her half-drunk coffee in the bin next to the machine, scowling as some splashed on her tabard. She didn't want to be late. She knew she shouldn't have stopped for a bloody drink.

'Relax!' Penny laughed. 'Not all of the passengers are off yet and there's always a few stragglers. Then they've got to get their bags. You know the turnaround is an hour and a half before the next lot get on anyway, so don't stress.'

'Thank God for that!' Tina gasped, staring at the sheet of paper in Penny's hand. 'How do you know whether everybody's off and whose bags are whose?'

Penny nodded to a column on the manifest. 'See this? These are the passengers who boarded. And this,' she pointed to another column, 'shows which ones have bags in the hold. When the dolly brings the bags round, ground staff make sure none have gone adrift. Then they go on the conveyor belt in the baggage hall ready for pickup.'

'What happens to the paperwork?'

Penny shrugged. 'I either give it to Operations or put it in the tray in our crew room.'

Tina scanned the list of names and strange markings on the passenger manifest. *It was all very complicated.* 'But how do they know if...' Stopping, she frowned as a name on the list jumped out at her.

Stoker!

That name always sent the fear of God through her. Even more so not knowing if they were after her still, not only wanting revenge for stealing from Sam Reynold, but also because Tina had hidden her knowledge of Dan's involvement with the robbery of the Stokers' safes. They must have half of the heavies in Birmingham keeping watch for her.

'Hey, what's up?' Penny frowned. 'It's pretty straightforward once you understand how it works, so why have you gone as white as a sheet?'

Tina couldn't pull her eyes from the Stoker surname. It wasn't Seb or his brothers. None of them were called *Malcolm*. Seb's brothers were Neil and Andrew, she was sure of it, so who was this? And there was another one – *Judith*.

Suddenly aware of Penny's scrutiny, Tina forced herself to laugh off her angst. 'Oh, I'm just terrified of the stuff I need to learn.'

Penny started explaining something else and Tina wanted to listen, but instead she remained focused on those names on the list.

Malcolm and Judith Stoker. They were the parents. She remembered now. She'd seen that name several times in the past within the papers. Mal Stoker had been the boss of the Stoker firm and casino before retiring.

And then there was the article she'd read about him stepping down from the business to spend time travelling the world with his wife.

It *had* to be them. It made perfect sense why they'd be back. The paper said the wedding was tomorrow and it was normal for parents to see their son get married.

Tina's eyes darted to the opening of the corridor leading to the arrivals hall, sure her face must be tinged with green.

They'd come through there once they'd collected their luggage, but *she* had to pass through there to reach the gate where the plane waited to be cleaned too.

Fuck.

If the parents had just landed, then surely Seb or one of the brothers would be collecting them?

Tina felt faint as her pulse soared just thinking about it. If they saw her, they'd recognise her. They all knew what she looked like.

Christ!

'Tina? Are you listening?' Penny said. 'If you're not, then I won't bot...'

'I was! I was just taking in what you said,' Tina blathered, smiling weakly. 'I'm not intelligent like you and can only process one thing at a time!' She tried to laugh, but it came out like a squeak.

The Stokers could probably even *see* her from where she was standing right now if they happened to look. People like that possessed an uncanny ability to sense people they were after.

Tina used the wall to support her steadily shaking legs.

Fuck. Fuck. Fuck.

How would she get through there without being spotted?

Penny gave Tina an odd look. 'I'd better go. I'll explain this again later, if you like?'

'That would be good. Thanks.' Tina watched Penny totter off in her stilettos out into the arrivals hall, not a care in the world.

But how would *she* do that?

All but hyperventilating, Tina willed herself to calm down.

Wasn't she slightly overreacting here? She couldn't be *that* important to the likes of the Stokers, could she?

Maybe. Maybe not.

Think about it realistically, she reasoned. If they wanted you that much, they'd have found you by now.

Although she'd gone to great efforts by not returning to the house she used to live in – the one *they* were aware of and where Dan had been found, she was still relatively local. It was the other side of the city and right over in Brownhills, but still...

No, this was silly. If the Stokers were hellbent on finding her and killing her, they'd have done so.

Taking a deep breath, Tina skittered out into the arrivals hall to make her way down to her next job.

Regardless of her bravado, she kept her head down and moved

as rapidly as possible. There was no point asking for trouble, even if there was only a small chance her original panic was warranted.

* * *

'I'm still not sure this is a good idea,' Potter grumbled, uncomfortable in the cap Tom had forced him to wear. 'You said the other day I'm very recognisable, so why couldn't I stay in the van, like before?'

'Because you didn't stay in the bloody van, if you remember?' Tom hissed, striding confidently into the arrivals terminal at Birmingham International with Potter trailing behind him like a bad smell. 'Anyway, after last time, I realised it's so busy, no one bats an eyelid!'

Besides, they wouldn't be here long. 'All I want to do is check to see if I can get a hint as to where Stoker and Sam might be flying to because that way, we'll get a rough idea what time they'll leave the reception.' Therefore he'd be able to mentally brace himself beforehand how long he'd be stuck cooped up with this retard.

Potter stopped to study a selection of overpriced baguettes in a café window, only to be tugged away.

'We haven't got time for that!' Tom snapped, his temper fraying further. 'I need to look at...' Stopping dead, he barely felt it when Potter slammed into his back. His eyes focused on the woman moving across the other side of the terminal.

He squinted and craned his neck around the masses of people walking in front of and around him obstructing his view. *Bollocks. He'd lost sight of her.*

'What are you doing?' Potter griped. 'You just said we didn't have time to stop, yet you've...'

'I thought I recognised someone,' Tom mumbled, carrying on towards the information boards.

Potter glanced around worriedly. 'Who?'

'No one important. It wasn't who I thought.' Tom could have sworn from the glimpse he'd got of that bird it had been that rancid bitch from the Aurora. Too many of those young chicks looked the fucking same.

His eyes narrowed.

He'd worked out ages ago that Tina would have legged it the minute the Aurora closed. Or more likely, the minute she'd realised her tramp of a mother was dead and crammed in the wardrobe.

Being as he suspected Tina to be the cow responsible for helping that raddled cunt, Linda, escape from the attic, she'd have made it her priority to get as far away as possible from anywhere *he* might be. Because Tina would have known if she hadn't, he'd have found her.

She was more likely dead by now anyway. Grasping, mercenary slags like her invariably copped it in the end from the wrath of one of their disgruntled, ripped off punters.

A shit quality blowjob had probably been the tart's final nail in the coffin.

Tom couldn't help but snigger. What a fitting way for the slut to have met her end.

'What the fuck are you laughing at?' Potter growled. 'A second ago you looked like you'd just seen the Horsemen of the Apocalypse, but now you're laughing? What's wrong with you, Bedworth? Are you mad or something?'

Tom slowly turned to face Potter in disbelief. Was *he* mad? Potter was asking him if *he* was the one with the sanity issue?

Taking Tom's silence as agreement over his lapsed state of mind, Potter continued. 'I worry whether you're capable of pulling this off tomorrow at all! For a start, planes departing on a day other than today won't be shown on the fucking board. Even if they were, departures aren't shown in the bastard arrivals hall!'

Tom dug his teeth into his tongue. It hurt, but it was meant to. He required something immediate to stop him from knocking Potter to the ground and kicking the life out of him right here, right now. Doing that in front of hundreds of witnesses was not an especially good idea. But it still galled having the glaring fact about the arrivals hall shoved in his face. Because that meant Potter was right.

Turning on his heels, Tom silently seethed as he made his way to the exit, for once not caring if Potter followed or not.

Living with this fat gimp and putting up with stupid madness all the time was beginning to affect his *own* concentration.

Now he'd been reduced to seeing people who had disappeared months ago and on top of that, ballsing up with which building he was looking in. This was all Potter's fucking fault.

He had to concentrate. Too much was riding on getting things right tomorrow for stupid mistakes to happen.

19

Marina slipped the remaining few bits of her luggage into the suitcase. Considering she wasn't planning on staying in England long, she didn't need so much stuff, but it made sense to account for all eventualities. Furthermore, she needed a certain amount in order to pack out the case properly.

Making sure the special lining was in place, Marina stared at the meticulously hidden compartment, satisfied it was invisible. The lining of this specialist case she had sourced ensured nothing could be detected in any scanner, and was ideal for this particular task. Due to her standing in this town, there wasn't much she couldn't source. No one thought to question her as she could make life most difficult, as well as embarrassing for people if she revoked their memberships or sullied their reputations.

Besides, anyone and everyone fell over themselves to offer whatever she required.

Of course, it would be a thousand times more preferable to take hand luggage only. It would mean no faffing around waiting for bags to come off, but hand luggage was checked and she didn't want to be copped with *that* in her case.

Turning as Carlos exited her bathroom, her lips formed a well-orchestrated pout. 'I'm disappointed you're not accompanying me, babe,' she purred, thinking the exact opposite.

'I've got too much on, *bella*,' Carlos said. 'A new musician is signing, but maybe next time? What's your trip about?'

Marina slid her arms around Carlos's waist and planted a quick kiss on his lips. *Nosy bastard. There wouldn't be a next time. After this, there would never be a reason to return to England ever again.* 'Oh, it's a friend's wedding, that's all. I'd better go as I don't want to miss my plane. I'll be back in a few days.'

Carlos nodded. 'Okay, *bella*. Enjoy your trip.'

Oh, I will, Marina thought, the manufactured smile sliding from her mouth as she turned and left the apartment.

* * *

'Bloody hell! We have our own offices, yet you still wander into mine like nothing's changed?' Neil muttered, not bothering to look up as Andrew entered.

He was still busy thinking about Seb and his earlier apology over omitting to inform him of his best man choice. He now felt a lot better about everything, therefore felt it important to uphold the usual jokey banter he normally afforded Andrew, rather than the sulky jealous side which had raised its ugly head the other day.

'I have to admit I was surprised to be told you now all have separate offices,' Mal Stoker said, his wife entering the office behind him.

The pen fell from Neil's hand as he recognised the voice he hadn't heard for so long. His head shot up to find the unmistakable form of his parents in his office doorway. 'Dad? Mum?'

Jumping to his feet, he raced over to kiss his mother on the cheek and avidly shake his father's hand. 'You're here! We didn't think you'd make it back in time for the wedding. Seb will be over the moon!' Hugging his mother again, Neil smiled widely.

It hadn't been that many months since his parents had been enjoying their retirement and sailing around the world, but the many lines of worry, the deeply ingrained strain of running the business and all the trouble that went with it, had all but been erased from their faces. It also seemed the pain and sadness so vividly noticeable, especially on his mother's face after the murder of her youngest son, Gary, had also healed.

Not removed. Neil knew nothing would ever remove that permanently. That wouldn't happen for any of them, but it had softened the raw pain of Gary's loss, replaced by a quiet acceptance. 'Wow! You both look so well. So *different.*'

Judith returned Neil's smile, then glanced around. 'Where's Sebastian? And Andrew?'

'Seb's out at the moment,' Neil explained. 'Andrew's about somewhere. He's either in the casino or perhaps in the apartment.' He jerked his head towards the ceiling. 'He's living in Seb's flat now and...'

'Yes, our travels have been most enjoyable,' Mal interrupted, studying his son closely. 'We thought we'd keep our return a surprise.'

'Well, that it certainly has been!' Neil exclaimed. 'Seb will be so pleased that you're here. As will Sam. She's...'

'Probably not quite as surprised as I am to find the casino that was here when I left isn't *this* one.' Mal fixed Neil with an unmoving stare. 'Were any of you planning to tell us what has happened here, or was that your surprise to us?'

Neil blinked. *Fuck.* He'd completely forgotten that neither he, nor *any* of them, had informed their parents of the string of disasters which had befallen them, culminating in the Peacock being burnt to the ground and the firm almost going under.

But judging by the expression on his father's face, this wasn't something that he'd get away with brushing under the carpet. And with Seb and Andrew not being here, it looked like *he* was lumbered with the unenviable task of explaining everything.

Taking a deep breath, Neil gestured to the chairs around his desk. 'You'd better sit down. This will take quite a while.'

With any luck, one of his brothers would shortly appear to give him a bloody hand on this one.

* * *

Making sure to take one of the pool cars, rather than his Audi, Andrew pulled up in the pub car park in Hopwood. It was a palaver not using his own motor, but a top-of-the range one like that would raise flags as to who he really was. Not only with Sophie, but with anyone who happened to look out of the pub window. These people weren't stupid and being as he'd remained under the radar this long, he didn't want to be unmasked now, just when he was on the cusp of coming clean with this woman.

And that would happen as soon as Seb's wedding was over and he got a day or two to devote to Sophie. He'd need time to explain everything because it was unlikely to be a half an hour conversation...

Flicking his cigarette end out the window, Andrew glanced at his watch, hoping Sophie had remembered them arranging to meet today. She didn't have a phone and he'd been reticent to wave around that he'd got one, considering mobiles weren't common-place. Certainly not one like he'd got, anyway.

His story of being 'something to do with the pub trade' wouldn't correspond with the most expensive mobile phone on the market and a top-of-the-range motor, but soon he wouldn't be hiding anything. Soon he'd tell all and just hoped it changed nothing. The concept of losing Sophie wasn't something he wanted to consider a possibility.

Andrew trained his gaze down the road in the hope of seeing a bus or taxi signifying her arrival. He drummed his fingers on the steering wheel, aware he couldn't hang around long because Seb would shortly be at the Peacock.

The shrill ringing of his mobile made Andrew start. He snatched it from the passenger seat, making a mental note to turn the ringer off before Sophie got here.

…Neil calling…

For God's sake. Couldn't Neil leave him alone for a minute?

Buttoning the call, Andrew changed the ringer to silent. He knew there had been no hiccups with disposing of Seb's gun last night, so Neil could bloody wait until he got back.

A taxi pulled into the pub car park before Andrew even clocked it and his heart lurched seeing the woman he wanted to be with.

Hastily shoving his mobile in the glove box, he got out of the Maestro and beamed when Sophie ran into his arms. He kissed her, wishing more than anything he had more time to spend with her.

Andrew brushed a tendril of blonde hair from Sophie's face. 'I'm sorry this can only be a fleeting meeting, but it will be different soon, I promise.'

'That's okay,' Sophie smiled, melting at the sight of those green eyes. She'd have come here just for ten seconds with this man. 'Are we going for a drink?'

'If we go in there, I know I won't be able to leave and unfortunately I have to.' Andrew gestured to his car. 'Let's just sit in here a while.' He laughed hollowly. 'I'm not exactly offering you an exciting or special time, am I, considering I can't see you for a few days?'

'Don't be silly. It's just nice to see you,' Sophie said as she clambered into the Maestro. *It was more than nice...*

Jumping into the driver's seat, Andrew leant over and grabbed a bouquet of flowers. 'These are for you.'

Sophie squealed with delight. *A proper bouquet!* Not that she received flowers often, but the times she had, they were always from garage forecourts with the 'reduced to clear' sticker still in plain sight. 'Oh, Andy, they're gorgeous! Thank you!'

'Not as gorgeous as you!' Andrew's arms slid around Sophie's shoulders. Never could he remember buying flowers for a woman because he'd *wanted* to. Apart from his mother, of course, but that didn't count.

Hearing the distinct buzzing of his mobile from the glove box, he stiffened. *Fuck.* He'd turned the volume off, but not the bloody vibrate function? *Damn it.*

'What's that?' Sophie frowned, reaching towards the glove box. 'It's coming from in here.'

'Don't open it!' Andrew yelped, his hand on hers. 'There's dodgy wiring. The buzzing is the stereo shorting.' He glared at the glove box, betting it was Neil again. 'It's stopped now,' he continued. 'I really must get that fixed.'

Sophie sat back and nestled into Andrew's chest. 'Be careful it doesn't electrocute you!'

Stroking Sophie's hair, Andrew smiled to himself. No, he wouldn't be getting electrocuted, but his brother would if he kept hassling him. 'Once it's less hectic, I want to take you away for a couple of days.'

Sophie tilted her face up, surprise in her big blue eyes. 'Oh, I'd love that! Where?'

'I don't know yet, but somewhere nice,' Andrew said. *There.*

He'd set the timeframe to come clean about everything now. After that, providing Sophie still wanted to be with him, not only would he make their relationship official; tell his family, and everyone else, but he'd ask her to move in with him at the apartment.

And he hoped she agreed because he'd never wanted anything more.

20

'Oh, will you just look at this, Linda!' Vera cooed as she ushered Sophie into her flat. 'Guess where this one's been?'

Linda's eyes danced with delight at the joy on Sophie's face.

'Aren't they gorgeous?' Sophie exclaimed, plonking herself down in Vera's kitchen to gaze at her beautiful bouquet.

'They certainly are!' Linda agreed. 'And you deserve them, too. I take it they're off your man, Andy?'

'It's not like they'd be off anyone else!' Sophie giggled. 'He's so romantic!'

Vera eyed the exquisite flowers. 'By the looks of these, Mr Waterford ain't short of a few quid, my duck. They're from that posh florist in the city centre. They must have set him back a month's bloody wages! I've seen the prices in there!'

'I know the place you mean,' Linda laughed. 'One leaf alone is twenty quid! You've got a good man there, Soph!'

'I don't care about money,' Sophie protested. 'I couldn't care less about that, but I love these! I've never had anything so nice before.' Her eyes lit up with happiness. 'Andy has promised to take me away once his work calms down. He's whisking me away some-where, just the two of us!'

Exchanging glances with Linda, Vera raised an eyebrow. 'You said this Andy works at a pub? How can he afford all of this? Are you sure he's genuine?' If this man wasn't on the level and getting Sophie's hopes up, only to dash them, then she'd make it her busi-ness to have words with the bloke.

Sophie's face fell. *Was Vera insinuating Andy was bullshitting or that he wouldn't take her away?* 'I said he worked in the pub *trade*. I don't know exactly what it is he does.'

Linda shot Vera a warning glance. It achieved nothing to piss on this girl's bonfire. Trashing Sophie's happiness wasn't the way to go. They just needed to keep an eye on this man, if they ever got to meet him, that was, and keep track of what he said. If the worst came to the worst and he was talking out of his arse, which she hoped to fuck he wasn't, then they'd make sure they were here to pick up the pieces.

'Some pub jobs are really well paid, V,' Linda admonished. 'It means owt, so pull your head in!' She patted Sophie's hand. 'Take no notice. Vera's got green-eyed envy syndrome.'

Sophie flushed. Just the mention of green eyes brought Andy's gorgeous face to mind. She couldn't give two hoots if he had a good job in the pub trade or was a broke barman. All she knew was that she loved him.

Her cheeks burnt. *Loved him?* That had come from nowhere, but it was true.

Sophie realised she *did* love Andy Waterford and hoped that he felt the same way about her, but the concept of what Vera had hinted at was depressing.

'One for the road, me thinks!' Linda said, eager to cancel out the awkward atmosphere. She helped herself to a can of cider from

Vera's fridge. 'For fuck's sake, V! Can't you get Strongbow in? This shit tastes like rat's piss!'

Sophie and Vera burst out laughing, the uncomfortable situation defused.

'Are you both sorted for tomorrow?' Linda swigged from the can of cider. 'I've arranged a taxi to collect you at five o'clock. That's what you wanted, wasn't it? To arrive for the evening reception?'

'Yes,' Vera nodded. 'You know why I'm not going to the actual ceremony.'

'Then it's all sorted.' Linda glanced at Sophie, sensing the girl's confusion. 'It's a long story, love. Nothing for you to worry about.'

Sophie continued to admire the beautiful flowers balanced in her lap. She'd like to ask more about why Vera was choosing to miss the wedding itself, but figured it would be rude to pry. She was just happy to be invited, so whatever had gone on in the past with Vera and Linda's daughter wasn't her business.

Scraping her chair across the kitchen floor, Linda jumped up. 'I'm off now. My daughter is staying with me tonight. The night before the wedding and all that gubbins, so a few drinks and an early night for us!'

Tina got herself ready to board the latest plane with the other cleaners. Aside from the unnecessary panic this morning over being spotted by people after her blood, it had been a good day. She'd been stupid to overreact and freak out like she had.

No one was looking for her. She wasn't that important.

She'd apologise to Sam Reynold for her ungrateful behaviour and for any problems she'd caused eventually. Even doing it by means of a letter was better than nothing. She'd just make sure to omit a return address just in case...

Tina smiled with renewed hope for the future after her little wobble.

Regardless of the past history she'd rather forget, Sam Reynold and Seb Stoker would be married tomorrow and she wished them both the very best for the future. But now she had to concentrate on where *she* was going with life.

Spotting another hostess she'd also become friendly with from the British Airways plane just in from Malaga, Tina thought back to the manifest Penny had shown her this morning.

She was yet to see Penny again and suspected she probably wouldn't today. It was already almost six thirty, so there wasn't long left of her shift to go and she wasn't hanging around tonight.

But Tina really wanted to see Penny again. The more she'd thought about those passenger manifests and what had been explained, she now thought she might have got her head around it.

Running over to the hostess, Tina grinned. 'Hi, Becky. I'm due to clean this plane.' She nodded at the paperwork in Becky's hand. 'Is that the passenger list?'

'Yes – the manifest,' Becky answered. 'Why? What's up?'

'Nothing. Penny was explaining to me how these work.' Tina pointed to the sheet.

Becky laughed. 'Penny said you were super enthusiastic about everything.'

Tina beamed. She could do this, she knew she could.

She scanned the list, finding her eyes moving once again to the passenger names. It wasn't like she expected any more Stokers to be on *this* plane, but this morning's paranoia had left a residual urge to check.

Nope. See? No Stokers.

Hang on...

Another name suddenly jumped out from the sheet and Tina forced herself to take a second look to double check she wasn't mistaken.

No, she wasn't...

Becky retrieved the paperwork from Tina's hand and smiled. 'You'll be aircrew sooner rather than later with your attitude, Tina,' she called as she walked away.

Tina returned the smile, but wasn't paying attention. With a thumping heart, she hastened into the staff toilets and locked herself into a cubicle.

She pressed her forehead against the tiled wall to gather her thoughts.

Could it be the same person? It was a bit of a coincidence. A bit *too* much of a coincidence...

Marina Devlin wasn't a common name. It also wasn't a name Tina was likely to forget.

That woman was the ex-girlfriend of the man she'd planned to disappear with away from the trouble. And for that reason alone, the name had been fused in her mind from the off.

Tina closed her eyes and scrabbled in her tabard pocket for the cigarettes she kept for emergencies.

At this particular moment, this felt exactly like an emergency...

Marina wasn't just Dan's ex, but from what he'd told her, a nasty piece of work. She also happened to be Sam Reynold's half-sister. A half-sister who had not only tried to rob her own family, but despised Sam and, according to Dan, wanted to kill her.

Tina felt sick. She had no idea what Marina Devlin looked like or anything about her, but if what Dan had said was right, then wasn't it a little bit suspicious this woman should happen to turn up just before her hated sister's wedding?

Tina chewed the remains of her fingernails.

What should she do?

Perspiration formed across her shoulder blades underneath her white top.

It was nothing to do with her. What Dan said might have been unfounded. This woman might not even be the same person. But why were her instincts screaming that it was?

Tina fanned her sweaty face with her hand.

This woman could be here to cause trouble. She could even be planning to do something to wreck the wedding. Dan said she was unhinged. And if Marina Devlin hated her half-sister that much, she could be planning something *worse*...

But perhaps Sam had invited her and *asked* her to come?

What would Tina look like if that was the case?

She'd look bloody stupid, that's what and it would give Sam and the Stokers even more reason to hate her. *Something else she'd done to cause trouble.*

Tina chewed her lip, tasting the tang of blood.

But then again, what if she said nothing and realised too late that she *should* have acted on her instinct?

Leaning forward, Tina put her head in her hands, panic returning. *What the fuck should she do?*

At the very least, she should discover whether Sam was aware Marina was back in Birmingham. The worst that could happen would be getting sent away with a flea in her ear for being a nosy bitch, wasn't it?

She inhaled deeply. She had to pluck up the courage and make contact with Sam.

Fuck.

So much for letting sleeping dogs lie...

But she'd never forgive herself if this woman *was* a psycho, so checking with Sam was the very *least* she could do after throwing her kindness back in the woman's face.

And it had to happen now, rather than later.

If Marina Devlin was a nutter here to ruin Sam's wedding or worse, then the woman could *not* leave the airport until Tina had contacted Sam to make sure she was aware of this sister's presence.

The only problem was, how the fuck did she do that?

21

'Alan!' Tina waved her arms at the edge of the open-plan Wimpy where she'd not long ago worked. She refrained from stepping over the threshold knowing Amber Davis would go at her for trespassing.

Catching Alan's eye, Tina frantically beckoned him across, glancing over her shoulder as she did so. She hoped Mrs Goldstore wasn't already on the warpath looking for her newest staff member that yesterday she'd had such high hopes for, but had now gone missing whilst on duty.

Alan hurried to the Wimpy's perimeter. 'What on earth's the matter?' he asked Tina, his face full of concern. 'I wondered when you were going to come and see me and let me know how you've been getting on. I'd just about given up, yet now you've turned up looking like you've got a Colombian drug cartel on your case!' He laughed, then stopped as he saw Tina's expression.

Tina would usually scowl at Alan's bad choice of humour, but she was too flustered. 'I don't know what to do, but I'm hoping you will, being as you've worked in the airport for years. I don't want to get things wrong because I'll be in trouble. I'm probably already in the shit because I'm late with my next clean and...'

'Woah! Slow down!' Alan placed his hand on Tina's arm. 'Just tell me what the problem is.'

Tina blinked. That was the point. She didn't know whether there *was* a problem. It wasn't like she could casually explain this in two minutes either. Even if that was possible, she couldn't do it. She didn't want *anyone* knowing one iota of what she'd found herself previously involved in. Her hopes of rebuilding and reinventing her life would be down the toilet if she did, if it wasn't already. She had to hurry. If she was quick, she might be able to sort this and still crack on with the cleaning before anyone noticed her absence.

What could she say to Alan? Quickly, think!

Suddenly, in a flash of inspiration, it came to her. 'I think I've just seen a passenger who's got a gun in their hand luggage,' Tina blurted.

'What?' Alan's eyes widened with shock. 'Who? Where is this person? What did the airport police say?'

'Airport police?' Tina gibbered, thinking perhaps she had just made her situation worse.

'You have told the police, haven't you? Or security?' Alan pressed. 'You raised the alarm?'

'Well, erm... no... I...'

'You have to do that *immediately*!' Alan grabbed Tina's arm. 'I'll come with you. You need to give them a description or point this person out an...'

'I'm getting confused,' Tina gabbled. 'I *did* tell the police. I'm in such a state of shock, I'm not thinking straight.' She flapped her hand. 'They're dealing with it right now.' *Bollocks. How could she give a description of Marina Devlin when she had no idea what the woman looked like?*

Alan stared at Tina curiously. 'Are you sure you've told them? This is mega-important, Tina. If this person has a gun, it's vital they're stopped before leaving the airport.'

'Like I said, I've told them and they're dealing with it,' Tina said quickly. 'I'm just freaked out. I've got to rush now though, otherwise I'll be late for my next job.'

'But...' Alan's words trailed off as Tina disappeared into the crowd.

* * *

'My taxi's here!' Sam called, carting her vanity case and small suitcase down the stairs.

'Don't drag those about!' Seb yelled, snatching the cases out of Sam's hands. 'What have I told you about things like this? No exertion! Get Linda or the taxi driver to carry these when you get there.'

'Seb!' Sam wrapped her arms around Seb's waist. 'I'm pregnant, not made of glass! And if I don't lift a finger as well as not drink, Linda and Gloria will guess.'

Seb laughed. 'They probably already have! Mothers pick up on stuff like that!'

'They'd have asked by now if that was the case. Oh, Seb, I hope we don't get overrun by the bloody press tomorrow. Especially that dreadful man from the *Echo*.' Sam suddenly envisaged the horrible prospect of fighting through throngs of reporters to make her way into the room for the wedding ceremony.

Judging by how pushy that one reporter had been on Monday, she could imagine him inveigling his way into the service to push to the front and interrupting the ceremony to get the scoop on a photograph. She shuddered with the thought.

Seb shrugged. 'I hope not, but what I *do* know is that there won't be further inconvenience from that *Coventry Echo* prick.'

Sam looked at Seb closely. 'You didn't...'

Seeing the familiar spark in Seb's eyes, she sighed with despair. She knew it. She'd just *known* Seb wouldn't leave it. *Fuck.* 'Oh Seb, what did you do?'

'It doesn't matter, but I'm telling you this now – there will be no fallout on me, us or anyone here, okay?' Seb fixed Sam with a look that she knew from old. 'I promised you there would be no secrets and so there aren't, but don't even *think* about giving me grief because it needed to be done.'

Sam pursed her lips. By that statement alone she knew without a doubt Seb had gone the whole hog and offloaded that bloke. It wasn't what she'd wanted, but with Seb, that kind of thing was inevitable. 'That's where you went last night, wasn't it? It wasn't to do with the Irish deals at all!'

'What I said about the Irish deals being arranged is true, but you might be a little bit right about the rest of it...' Seb winked. 'Now, enough questions. It's done. You know the score, so accept it had to happen.' He became serious. 'He nearly hurt you and the baby and no one walks away from that.'

Sam rolled her eyes. 'Like I said, I'm not made of glass!'

'No, you're not.' Seb planted a quick kiss on Sam's lips. 'You're a million times more important!' Bending down, he planted a kiss on her belly. 'See you tomorrow, son or daughter in there! Hey, guess what, I'm marrying your mother and you're invited!'

Sam giggled both from Seb's deep voice vibrating against her, as well as his words. She couldn't be cross with this man of hers. She knew what he was and what he did. If he said there would be no comeback, then that's how it was.

He might be overprotective, go off at the deep end and some-

times infuriate her, but he'd told her the truth and she loved him
unconditionally. 'Don't work too hard tonight.'

Straightening up, Seb folded Sam in his arms. 'I'll try not to...'
Considering the three calls he'd ignored on his mobile from Neil
over the past half an hour, he had the creeping suspicion tonight
would be a busy one. Still, he'd rather that happened now than
once they were on honeymoon.

Nobody would be interrupting the two weeks he'd got with his
wife once they'd flown out of here.

Pressing his lips to Sam's, he kissed her. 'Have you got everything you need?'

'Yes. The dress and everything are already there. Don't forget
your buttonholes are coming to the Peacock in the morning. The
cars are collecting you at one o'clock.'

'I know that, Princess,' Seb laughed. 'I booked them myself,
remember?'

Hearing the taxi honk its horn for the second time, Seb pressed
his lips on Sam's for the final time before she became his wife. 'I
love you and I'll see you tomorrow. Don't be late!'

'Why? It's a woman's prerogative,' Sam winked, following Seb
as he grabbed her bags to load into the waiting taxi.

Waving Sam off as the taxi pulled out of the driveway, Seb
returned to the house and shut the door behind him.

After giving it more thought, levelling with Sam about John
Salter was the right thing to do.

Life was good.

He glanced around the now empty house, all the more quiet
with Sam not being here.

Moving into the living room, he snatched up his mobile. He'd
return Neil's calls to see what he wanted and then get his clobber
together to head over to Andrew's apartment at the Peacock. There
was no point hanging around here. He'd only miss Sam too much.

It was only one night and tomorrow they'd be man and wife at last.

Seb had almost reached the top of the stairs when the doorbell rang. *What had Sam forgotten?*

Loping down the stairs and across the reception hallway, Seb yanked open the door. 'Gone five minutes, yet you missed me so much, you're back alr...'

Stopping mid-sentence, Seb's mouth dropped open at the unexpected figures of his parents on the doorstep. 'Holy shit!' he exclaimed, his face breaking into a wide smile. 'You made it after all. I...'

'I've filled them in on what's been happening,' Neil said, stepping to join his parents in the storm porch. 'I tried to tell them everything. Andrew's on his way over, but th...'

'What Neil's trying to say is that I want your version of events as to who's been trying to destroy our business,' Mal Stoker interrupted. 'Once that's done, we can concentrate on enjoying this wedding. This is only a fleeting visit – we fly back out on Sunday, so we don't want to waste a second of our time here.' He shook Seb's hand. 'It's good to see you, son.'

Seb ushered his parents into his house, thinking it may be a good couple of hours before he got to Andrew's apartment after all.

Tina skittered along the corridor in a state of angst. How could she keep Marina Devlin detained long enough to raise the alarm with Sam Reynold when she didn't know what the bloody woman looked like?

She could only hope Alan believed what she'd said and didn't take it upon himself to inform the police or security about her tall story, otherwise she really would be in the shit. They'd come to find her, expecting a description and she wouldn't be able to give one.

Not knowing what else to do, Tina burst into the British Airways crew room.

The rest of her team were either already or about to start cleaning the Boeing which had come in from Malaga. Mrs Goldstore would not be happy that she'd failed to show up for a job on her schedule, but what else was she supposed to do? She *had* to try and get to the bottom of this.

Everyone looked up as Tina's cleaning caddy bashed loudly against the door.

Becky wasn't in here. Shit.

'Sorry! I thought the room was empty,' Tina blathered, sweat running down her back. Turning on her heels, she raced from the crew room back down the corridor.

Becky had the passenger manifest, which meant she'd be on her way to Operations or the crew room.

Breaking into a run, Tina headed in the direction she hoped Becky had gone. If she didn't stop this before that woman got her bags and left the airport, there was no telling where she would head.

Suddenly glimpsing Becky up ahead, Tina found the energy to run faster, the cleaning caddy smashing painfully against her ankles with each step. 'Becky!' she shouted. 'BECKY!'

Stopping, Becky turned around, a frown on her face. 'Tina? What's up?'

Tina could barely speak she was so out of breath. 'I remembered I spotted a name on your paperwork. I'm sure it's my brother's girlfriend. I don't suppose you can remember what she looked like, do you? I'd love to surprise her!'

Tina frowned. First that bollocks about the gun to Alan and now *this*. She was back to square one – lying all the time. Her plans for her new job and life would be fucked if she carried on like this, but she had to try. She owed Sam Reynold this much.

Tina pointed to the paperwork in Becky's hand. 'It's her – Marina Devlin. What did she look like? I can work out whether she's my brother's missus by your description.' *It also might be enough to give to the police or security...*

Becky stared at the name and frowned. 'Hmm, well, she's blonde, slim and tall. I hope she *isn't* your brother's girlfriend because if she is, he must be a bloody saint! I haven't dealt with such a rude, jumped-up woman in years!'

Tina's stomach lurched with hope. That matched the sort of person Dan had described Marina as. But would that be enough of a description for the police?

Becky nudged Tina. 'There she is, so see for yourself. She's coming out of the baggage hall over there.'

With a thundering heart, Tina craned her neck over the milling crowds to try and focus on who Becky was indicating to.

Spotting a tall, blonde woman strutting across the other side of the room with a case, Tina shook her head. 'Nah, that's not her. It didn't sound like my brother's missus from what you said anyway because his girlfriend is ever so nice. Oh, well. Never mind. Cheers though, Becky.'

Tina rapidly retreated the way she'd come, with one eye still on Marina Devlin. It looked like she was heading to the secure lockers. If she was quick, there was enough time to find security.

She'd use the gun story. She couldn't think of anything else to prompt an immediate response and that was what was required here. She didn't have to go into details – just that she thought she 'may' have seen what 'looked' like a gun as the woman rummaged through her handbag. They'd have to detain her over that, wouldn't they?

Wait!

Frowning, Tina squinted at the sour-faced woman continuing on her mission.

Fuck! That was the same woman she'd worked with at the Sunset Boulevard strip club! Ava! It couldn't be, yet it was. This woman might have blonde hair rather than auburn, but those legs and the eyes...

Tina wouldn't forget those eyes *ever*!

Nausea rolled. Why hadn't she put two and two together before now?

At the time Tina had thought there was something about Ava which rang a bell, but she'd been unable to put her finger on it. Now it was obvious.

Marina Devlin had the *exact* same eyes as Sam Reynold. They were very distinctive. And they were the same because they were *sisters*.

Ava from the Sunset Boulevard was Marina Devlin – Sam Reynold's sister and Dan's ex!

No wonder she'd been so bloody interested in Tina's budding relationship with Dan.

Suddenly, the truth whacked Tina between the eyes.

It was Ava – *Marina* – who'd killed Dan and left his mutilated body in the hallway of her house, *not* Tom Bedworth. It was *Marina* who'd stolen Dan's money and then disappeared – by the looks of it, to Malaga, Marbella or somewhere like that.

Tina's veins pounded with fear and hate. That bitch had killed the man she'd wanted a future with and now she was here – back in Birmingham and across the other side of this hall...

Her legs turned to jelly, yet raw fury filled her veins with the overwhelming urge to race over and kill the woman stone dead.

That bitch had trashed her life.

Tina's hands formed fists; what remained of her chewed nails digging into her palms.

She couldn't kill her. She'd be arrested immediately, her life would be even more screwed and she'd fail to warn Sam Reynold.

There was only one thing to do and that was to find security or the police. She had to ensure this slut was detained long enough for Sam to deal with.

And Tina suspected Seb Stoker wouldn't be far behind on that either...

22

Marina shut the locker door and placed the key card in her handbag, feeling a sense of relief that the metal case containing what was needed was no longer on her person, but also that she'd breezed through customs without a second glance.

Not one person had batted an eyelid, apart from giving her admiring glances of course, but she was used to those.

Although she'd been confident the specially lined compartment in her suitcase would do the business, there had still been a tiny niggle of worry that something would go wrong. But she was through and it was sorted.

Marina wheeled the case onwards. Now to grab a taxi to the hotel and then, as they say, the rest was history.

Or it would be by this time tomorrow...

Having the foresight to arrange the rental of a secure locker this end had been a good idea.

She'd swing by in the morning and collect the gear. She didn't want *that* in her hotel room. In fact, she wanted it near her for as little time as possible, so this was the perfect solution.

Marina smirked. Then, when she'd done what she'd come to this shithole to do, she'd be back on the next plane out of here.

It was all planned to perfect precision.

It wasn't too far from here to the hotel she'd booked or to that Coombe Abbey place either.

Her lips tightened. *Coombe Abbey.* It sounded very impressive.

It was a shame Samantha wouldn't be around long enough to enjoy looking at the photographs of her most special day.

Seb Stoker, meanwhile, would be left only with the haunting reminder that each wedding anniversary from then on would also be the anniversary of the date of his new wife's death.

How utterly tragic...

Marina moved quickly, the exit to the terminal now in view. There would be plenty of cabs outside without having to wait. There always were.

Suddenly getting a strong sense of being watched, Marina bristled. She'd already weighed up the risks of being spotted by Sam or the Stokers, coming to the conclusion that it was unlikely. After all, they'd have better things to do on the eve of the wedding.

But the strong sense of eyes on her continued. The fine blonde hairs on the back of her arms tingled. She wasn't imagining it.

Marina glanced over her shoulder and continued walking, refusing to up her pace or act skittish.

The exit was only a couple of yards away. In a few seconds she'd be out of here, in a taxi and on her way.

She was confident enough of being able to move stealthily and quickly, so would easily lose anyone watching her – if anyone was.

But with a further casual glance around, Marina caught sight of three people that were definitely looking at her. Two men looked like security, but whatever or whoever they were after, it was nothing to do with her. She'd done nothing wrong. And, with a smug smile, she had absolutely *nothing* on her of any interest.

Marina frowned. There was also a woman too. She looked like a cleaner or something. The girl was pointing directly at her and…

Marina overrode the automatic reaction to freeze in her tracks and continued towards the exit, her mind in overdrive.

It was that slut from the Boulevard! Tina!

Her heart clanged inside her chest. Why the fuck was that thick bitch here? She'd have thought the sight of Dan's remains would have been enough to kill the stupid cow stone dead with fright. That or go even more mental.

Shit. Was this about Dan?

No! How could it be? For a start, Tina knew her as a redhead going by the name of Ava. Furthermore, anyone stupid enough to be fooled by Dan's bullshit was hardly likely to work out she was the same person.

Marina frowned, shaking her head at her own silliness.

Think about it – was she *certain* that girl was Tina? She'd only got a quick glance, so it could have been one of many ugly tramps.

Sighing at her overactive imagination, she reached for the exit door, feeling the blast from the air conditioner system above blowing down her neck.

She'd almost passed through and stepped on the pavement when her way was barred.

'Marina Devlin?'

Marina stared at the hand extending out to grip her right arm.

'Would you come with us, please?' one of three large men continued. 'We'd like to ask you a few questions.'

* * *

Tom was checking the equipment he'd earmarked for tomorrow's task. He glared at Potter wedged at the small kitchen table and winced, watching him shovel the contents of a beef and tomato Pot Noodle into his mouth using his hands.

'Mark reckons we'd be better off using cargo straps instead of what you've got there.' Potter nodded towards the crate of bungee straps and heavy-duty carabiner clips.

'Did he?' Tom muttered uninterestedly, supposing there must be a lot of call for cargo straps wherever Mark Ross was now spending eternity? *Amazing what the dead got up to these days...*

But he wouldn't be sarcastic. All he had to do was remember that in a few days from now, he wouldn't have to put up with Potter's ramblings ever again. 'I'll keep his suggestion in mind,' he said pleasantly.

Potter paused from stuffing the string-like noodles into his gob. 'When are you loading the van?'

Tom stared at a clod of noodles dangling from the end of Potter's chin. Or should he say, off the *many* chins Potter possessed. He felt the urge to laugh, but didn't. He'd remain collected and composed. 'I'll load it in a moment.' The sooner Potter quit asking fucking questions and interrupting his train of thought, the quicker things would happen. The man banging on like Tom had no particular urge to get this done in good time was getting right on his tits.

He masked the scowl inching over his face before Potter noticed.

'I also meant to ask, did you find and book a suitable place to keep the bitch in?' Potter continued.

Tom was pretty sure he understood what Potter had said, but now the loser had shoved another mouthful of nuclear waste into his gob, it was tricky to make out. Besides, he'd asked that question before. 'Yeah, that's all done.'

He saw Potter frown into his Pot Noodle. Clearly the fat fuck had finished it. He'd probably start on the plastic next...

Unable to bear the revolting sight any longer, Tom began recounting the items he'd amassed ready for the van. Earlier, he'd been tempted to have a spin down memory lane. Once he'd left this shitehole of a country he wouldn't see any of those places again, so he'd quite fancied a drive past the places that had figured in his life, like a magical mystery tour. All the pubs he'd frequented; the places he'd crashed out at. All of that sort of stuff.

He'd even for a split second contemplated going back along the Hagley Road to see what had become of the Aurora. Something *else* he'd lost thanks to the fucking Stokers and his sad excuse of a daughter.

Being presumed dead, it wasn't like he could casually ask around to see if anyone had heard anything and there was no point asking anyone here. These Telford eejits heard of nothing which happened outside their own backyard.

The Aurora was either sitting derelict or had been bought by a poncey developer with the aim of turning it into a fucking retirement home to fleece cash from trainee corpses with no sense.

No skin off his nose.

Maybe he'd dreamt the horrible shock of seeing Linda posing in the paper? In reality, perhaps she was still mouldering in the Aurora's attic, barely anything left since the maggots had got to work?

Well, fuck Linda. Fuck the Stokers and fuck Samantha!

Although he'd leave that last part to Potter, being as he'd made it clear that particular pastime was on his bucket list. Even if Samantha Reynold wasn't his daughter, Tom would prefer to stick his dick in a pit bull's trap, than in that jumped-up, manipulative greedy bitch.

He closed his eyes, feeling himself beginning to hyperventilate. He'd promised he wouldn't allow any of those fuckfaces to drive him to that any more.

So no, he wouldn't be going to Brum. Aside from still being on the wanted list there, both with the police *and* the Stokers, whilst he was dead, he was safe. He wouldn't risk anything. Not when he was hours away from getting revenge and leaving here for good.

Finally.

Plus, driving past the Orchid and the spangly rebuilt Peacock would only piss him off more than Potter. That alone was a difficult feat to accomplish.

'You're sure there's enough petrol in the van to get us where we need to go and back again?'

Tom's head darted up. Another fucking question?

Slamming the cables and ropes back into the crate, he swung towards Potter, his eyes flashing with rage. 'Shut the fuck up, for Christ's sake, you whingeing bastard! I've lost count again now because of you! Just shut up!' he screamed, his face becoming redder. 'I am not a fucking idiot! We have petrol; we have somewhere to put the bitch; I've worked out the route and the timings. It's all sorted and ready to go, so put a cunting sock in that bleeding hole in your face!'

Turning his back on Potter, Tom snatched up the crate. He'd put this in the van now because if Potter even *thought* about asking one more thing or even *breathed* in his general direction, then he'd sling the fat cunt in the back of the van himself.

Not ideal, but if it meant he didn't have to listen to the man's mental ramblings and stupid fucking questions any more, then it might be worth it. *Almost.*

* * *

Shaking with a mixture of fear and relief watching as Marina Devlin was escorted by security to a room which hopefully also contained police to make things even more time consuming, Tina waited as the call rang out. The money in her hand became slippery from sweat as she waited to insert the coins the second the call connected.

Had Marina spotted her? Realised who she was and what she was doing?

She'd have preferred not to have accompanied security to point out the woman she'd seen with what 'might' have been a gun. But due to time being of the essence to apprehend Marina, Tina knew there was no choice. If she didn't ID the woman, the psycho would walk out of here.

At least she'd been believed when she'd described what she'd 'thought' she'd seen. Security had immediately radioed for assistance, sending men to block all exits, leaving Tina to point the suspect out.

And she *had* pointed Marina out.

But not before the woman had locked eyes with her. Marina had seen and recognised her. She just knew it.

'Come on, come on,' Tina muttered as the call continued ringing out. There had to be staff available to pick up a fucking phone?

'Violet Orchid. Good evening.'

Tina's heart lurched as the call finally connected. Her fumbling fingers attempted to slip the coins into the payphone slot. She glanced over her shoulder, half expecting to see Marina or Ava – whoever she really was, rushing towards her with a knife, ready to slash her face and neck to leave her in a butchered pile like she'd done to Dan.

Instead, she saw the rotund figure of Ruth Goldstore scouring the area. *Shit. She'd probably lost her job now.*

'Hello? Violet Orchid,' the female voice repeated tersely down the line.

'Please don't hang up,' Tina squeaked, finally getting a coin in the slot. 'Hello? Hello? Yes, I'm here... Yes... Can I speak to Samantha Reynold, please?'

'I'm sorry, Ms Reynold is not available.'

'It's really important,' Tina begged. 'I have to speak to her about something th...'

'Can I ask what it's concerning?'

'It's private, but...'

'Ms Reynold isn't here tonight... Could I take your name, madam?'

'Where is she then?' Tina shrieked. 'There must be *someone* I can speak to? I have to speak to Sam or get a message to her. It's vital that I d...'

'I'm sorry. Like I said, there is no one available to speak to you. If you wish to speak to Ms Reynold and she's willing to see you, then I suggest booking an appointment. Her next slot is in two and a half weeks.'

'Two weeks?' Tina cried. 'But I need to speak to her *now*! It's urgent! I...'

Hearing the clear tone down the receiver told her the woman had hung up.

Despair set in.

Now what?

She leant against the payphone, hoping it may shield her from Mrs Goldstore's searching eyes and glanced over her shoulder once more.

Fuck! Mrs Goldstore was making her way over.

'Tina?' Ruth Goldstore called, the expression on her face that of utter frustration. 'TINA!'

Without wasting another moment, Tina dashed away from the payphone and broke into a run straight for the exit doors. She didn't care if she bashed into anyone or if security or the police wanted to speak to her again. Right now neither did she care if she got the sack.

Bursting through the doors into the darkness of the evening, Tina rushed towards the nearest taxi displaying a 'for hire' light. All she could think about was being as far away from the building Marina Devlin was inside and getting a message to Sam.

If the Orchid wouldn't put her through to Sam or let her speak to someone that could help, then she'd go there in person, whatever risks that entailed.

23

'Wakey, wakey!' Andrew nudged his brother in the ribs as he placed a whisky on the coffee table. 'Rise and shine!'

Seb blearily opened one eye, disorientated on seeing the apartment he used to live in. *Why was he here? Shit! The wedding! He was getting married today!*

Pushing himself up off the sofa, he sat bolt upright. 'Fuck! What's the time?' He ran his fingers through his tousled hair, then frantically searched for his mobile phone underneath the cushions. 'I'm not late, am I? If you've allowed me to fucking oversleep, then I'll...'

'Chill out!' Andrew grinned. 'It's only ten thirty. You've got plenty of time. Neil's arrived now, so get your arse into gear!'

'Ten thirty?' Seb roared. 'That's way too late!' He jumped off the sofa. 'I never sleep this late! Why the hell didn't you wake me up? You know I wanted to get up at six. I've got my clothes to press and...'

'Who's having a panic, then?' Neil wandered into the open-plan lounge with two glasses. He handed one to Andrew, then held his own up. 'Now we've all got a drink, I'm raising a toast to our brother's wedding day. Cheers!'

Watching Seb flapping around the room swearing to himself, Andrew grabbed his arm. 'Just stop! Everything's sorted. Your wedding suit, shirt and cravat are freshly pressed.' He nodded to Seb's outfit hanging in a clear plastic suit cover on the curtain rail at the far end of the room. 'Your shoes are polished; your cufflinks and watch are lined up ready and the buttonholes are here. I've got the rings in my pocket, so we're good. That's what the best man's supposed to do, isn't it? Organise everything? There's fuck all for you to do, except for a shit, shower and shave. And *that* I can't do for you!'

Neil laughed as Seb's eyes darted around, clocking everything Andrew said was true. 'Look at the state of him! He hasn't even noticed we're already in our wedding finery!'

Seb blinked. His brothers were indeed suited and booted. Everything was ready. Visibly relaxing, he picked up his whisky. 'Jesus! I thought I'd royally screwed up then.' He swigged the drink. 'Cheers!'

'We thought you could do with a bit of extra kip after last night,' Andrew said. 'Not getting back until 3 a.m. wasn't exactly preferable for the eve of your wedding.'

'Not if you want tonight to be full of action, anyhow!' Neil chuckled.

'I'll have you know my bedroom action *always* runs well, thank you!' Seb grinned. But yes, finally getting back last night, he'd been exhausted. Explaining the long overdue and intricate details to his parents of what had happened to the Peacock, the firm and just about everything else had been hard work.

His unfamiliar nervousness about today was also taking its toll.

He was finally marrying the woman of his dreams. There could never be anyone who could ever come close to Sam and he couldn't believe he was finally making her officially his.

'I think our parents took it well, considering.' Andrew stared at the whisky bottle, wondering whether he could get away with another.

Seb nodded. 'They did. Their main gripe being we hadn't kept them abreast of the disasters. But like I told them, that sort of shit is difficult discussing down the end of a dodgy phone line to someone in the middle of the sea thousands of miles away!'

He chewed his lip thoughtfully. Their parents may have been miffed to have been left out of the loop, but what had been clear was that they were happy with how the situation had been handled and rectified. Proud even. Now everyone could enjoy the wedding in peace.

Seb's eyes narrowed. Unless any fucking reporters overstepped the mark...

'By the way,' Neil said. 'I checked the casino on my way in. The reception said a bird came in last night begging to speak to you.'

Seb frowned. 'Who was it?'

'No idea, but she was a pain in the arse, as well as insistent – coming out with all sorts of bollocks, apparently. She was told to fuck off out in the end.'

'Probably another press hack trying their luck. Trying to catch me shagging a stripper on the eve of my wedding,' Seb muttered.

He and Sam had already compromised by allowing *one* reporter into the wedding for official photographs after the ceremony, but that was it. The press would fail dismally in finding him being unfaithful to Sam because that wasn't something he would *ever* consider.

Nothing would distract or annoy him. Not today. This was the most important day of his life to date and that would not be diluted.

By anyone.

Finishing his whisky, Seb took a deep breath and got to his feet. 'I'm off to get ready. I need to look my best.'

'I hope you believe in miracles,' Neil winked. 'Because you look like utter crap at the moment!'

*   *   *

'Thanks ever so much for this, Alan,' Tina said as she fastened her seat belt. 'I didn't know who else to call.'

Pulling out of the hotel car park, Alan shot a wary glance at Tina. 'What I don't understand is why you're in the centre of Brum on a Saturday morning, still wearing your cleaner's uniform.'

'I didn't have time to go home and change last night,' Tina muttered. 'It was late, so I ended up staying at that hotel.'

And that had been a risk in itself. Not that she'd slept much. There hadn't been much of the night left by the time she had to accept defeat and give up.

But today was a new day and the last chance to get the message to Sam Reynold.

Alan couldn't help but notice the sheer exhaustion on Tina's face. What she was saying worried him. He had a lot of time for her. 'Your boss was going nuts looking for you last night,' he said, not wishing to be the bearer of bad news, but Tina should know what had gone on. 'She even came to the Wimpy looking for you. Word has it that you did a runner...'

Tina stared out of the window, reluctant to answer questions. She knew there would be some, but there were none she was willing to answer. 'I presume I've lost my job?' she muttered. She'd expected it, but now she was finally getting somewhere, the prospect ripped a hole deep within her.

'Is this something to do with that security thing yesterday? I heard a woman was detained. If you explained to your boss that you were late because of what you saw, I'm sure she'd understand?' Alan suggested.

'What's happened to that woman? Is she still being held or did they let her go?'

'By all accounts she was still there when I left at midnight, but I don't know what's happened since.'

Seeing Tina picking at the skin around her fingernails, Alan frowned. '*Is* this something to do with that? How come you ended up in the centre of Birmingham?'

'It's not to do with that!' Tina lied. She'd love to tell Alan everything, but how could she? 'I erm... I just needed to see someone.'

'Oh? Like a boyfriend?' Alan asked, disappointment clear in his voice.

'No, not a boyfriend,' Tina snapped. 'Just leave it, would you!' Immediately feeling guilty, she patted Alan's hand. 'I'm sorry, I'm overtired.'

It had taken a huge amount of courage to go to the Orchid last night, but it turned out to be a wasted journey. The bouncer had point blank refused her entry no matter what she'd said or how much she'd begged. Even saying it could be a life-or-death situation for Samantha Reynold hadn't made a blind bit of difference.

The bouncer had pointedly scrutinised her cleaning uniform, his response merely being, '*Sorry love, you ain't coming in.*'

Yes, Tina knew she wasn't wearing the desired apparel to adhere to the Orchid's dress code, but what she had to say *could* be a matter of life and death and after much thought and walking up and down Broad Street in a state of angst, she'd made the decision to try the Peacock.

An even bigger risk...

This time though, she'd got inside, but that was as far as it had gone. There, she'd hit the same brick wall.

Glancing out of the car window as they exited the Queensway tunnel, Tina clocked the road sign. 'Wait! I don't want to go home, Alan. I need to go to Coventry!'

'Coventry?' Alan hit the brakes, indicating to swap lanes.

'Sorry,' Tina spluttered. 'I thought I'd already said that's where I needed a lift to.' She raked her fingers through her tangled hair. There really was no option but to go to where Sam and Seb were getting married and try her damnedest to relay the message there. It was her last hope of warning them. Her very *last* hope.

That's if she wasn't already too late? Marina Devlin might have already been released...

Tina's heart pounded, her face clammy, not wanting to think about what the repercussions could be for anyone if that had happened. *Herself included...*

Alan remained silent until they cleared spaghetti junction and joined the M6. His forehead furrowed. 'What's going on, Tina? Are you involved in something you shouldn't be? Are you in trouble?'

Tina chewed her lip. *Trouble? Possibly more than Alan could ever imagine.* 'Please don't grill me. I just need a lift, that's all,' she said quietly. 'I don't need you to wait around or anything. I'll make my own way back.'

She'd already taken up enough of Alan's time, plus she didn't want any more questions. Questions, and the answers they spawned, were too dangerous.

24

Looking in the mirror's reflection, Sam could barely contain her excitement as the stylist completed curling her long hair into a mass of tumbling waves.

Her makeup was perfect and Seb's wedding gift of sparkling diamond drop earrings complemented the stunning diamond solitaire necklace her adoptive father had bought her for her birthday not long before he died.

Sam's newly plucked and shaped brows formed a slight frown. It seemed strange referring to her father, as she'd known him, as her *adoptive* father, but that's what Len Reynold was on paper.

In real life, he and Gloria were the only parents she'd known and they had been wonderful ones. That was until Linda's existence had been revealed, blowing Sam's whole identity out of the water.

That's never going to happen to you, baby, Sam thought, her hand moving to rest on the bump underneath her satin robe. Her child would know who its parents were. There would be no secrets on that score, that was for sure.

Despite the bumpy start, having two mothers had turned out to be good. And now having a name for the man who had fathered her meant the end of the book. Today her new chapter started.

Sam watched Linda scrutinising herself in the cheval mirror. 'You look beautiful. That colour really suits you,' she smiled.

'Ta. Gloria looks fab too. We're two very proud mothers of the bride!' Linda straightened the orchid corsage pinned to the lapel of her pastel-green skirt suit. 'This was Gloria's idea.' It was a suitable and fitting tribute to Len Reynold. That man had given Sam a better start in life than she could have ever wished for and she would be eternally grateful to both Gloria and Len for that. 'I see you're wearing one too,' she nodded to the orchid being clipped in Sam's wavy tresses.

'This was the last one Dad got me on my thirtieth,' Sam said fondly. 'Every birthday he bought me a different one.'

'It's beautiful,' Linda smiled. 'The perfect finishing touch.'

Sam looked up as the door suddenly burst open to see an overexcited Tayquan and Shondra racing into the room, followed by a flustered Gloria.

'Sorry!' Gloria gasped. 'I told them to wait until you'd finished getting ready, but they're desperate to show you their posh togs.'

Sam swivelled around to grin at her young brother and sister. 'Well! Don't you two look the best!' She eyed Tayquan's little navy-blue suit and Shondra's calf-length pink dress complete with ruffled hem. 'You both look amazing! Like a prince and princess!'

Beaming from ear to ear with delight, the children raced back off downstairs.

'It's better to let them get their energy out before the wedding, rather than during it, I suppose!' Linda shrugged apologetically. 'Thanks for getting them ready, Gloria. I've done their bags for the next couple of days. I hope they're not going to be too much trouble for their friends' parents.'

'My pleasure,' Gloria said. 'And I'm sure they'll be fine. It's a good idea for them to spend a few days after the wedding with their friends. It will give them a chance to recover from the hectic weekend.' She placed the latest copy of the *Birmingham Mail* on the dressing table. 'By the way, Sam, you'll be glad to know I can't see any articles in here about you or the wedding.'

'That's a relief!' Sam said. 'Let's hope it stays that way. Apart from the one that we've granted, I don't want to be splashed all over the papers.'

'Well, you're not. Not at the moment, anyway.' Gloria smiled. 'However, it seems at least *one* reporter won't be bothering you today...'

Sam looked at the article the paper was left open at.

COVENTRY ECHO REPORTER MISSING

Concerns are growing for the whereabouts of a reporter from the *Coventry Echo*.

John Salter, 45, who has worked tirelessly for the newspaper since 1970 was yesterday reported missing.

His wife, Cindy, stated, 'It's unheard of for John not to let me know if he won't be home. We've been together since 1974 and not once has he not kept me informed, so I'm very worried.'

Mr Salter was last seen leaving the *Coventry Echo* offices on Thursday evening. A colleague stated John left around 10.30 p.m., yet failed to return home. His car remains parked in the car park on Spon Street.

Anyone with information, who knows where John Salter may be, or was in the location on 15 July, please contact...

Sam pushed the newspaper away. 'Maybe he's spent the last two nights camping out at Coombe Abbey to ensure the best position for when we arrive?' She tried to make a joke out of it, but she knew what had happened to John Salter...

Correction. She didn't know *exactly* what had happened, but she *did* know that Seb was behind the man's unexpected disappearance.

The previous desperation she'd experienced when Seb was pulled in for the murders at the Aurora and the hit and run flickered to the surface. The unwanted reminder of how close he'd been to being sent to prison was something she'd not forget.

She shook her thoughts away. Seb had promised there would be no comeback from this, so she must trust that. Furthermore, *nothing* could put a dampener on today of all days.

'Are you almost ready?' Gloria asked. 'The dressmaker is here to help you into your dress.'

'Two minutes,' Sam replied, a wave of nervousness washing over her. Not long now before she would be Seb's wife. *And she couldn't wait.*

Thanking the hairdresser, Sam stared at the beautiful wedding dress hanging on the front of her wardrobe. She inhaled deeply with rising anticipation.

This was it.

* * *

'What do you mean, you can hold me longer?' Marina spat. 'You've already had the audacity to keep me in this dump all night. You had absolutely no grounds to do so. *None!*'

She paced up and down the investigation room. This was ludicrous. A setup.

Samantha was getting married in the space of a few hours and she had to get the stuff out of the locker, get out of here, go to the hotel to get cleaned up and then get to that wedding before it was over, otherwise her plans were in tatters.

That bitch Tina had done this. And for that, she would pay.

Marina glared at the security guard, her eyes like poison darts. 'You know full well I have nothing on me, or in my luggage that matches this gross accusation, so where is your justification for holding me? I'm a British national, not a Congolese drug trafficker!'

Her blood pressure spiked further. 'You're not even the police! Failed at that, did you? Is that why you're a two-bit security guard, you sad pathetic little man? Couldn't get anything else?' she continued, her venomous outrage knowing no bounds. 'I have nothing on me to warrant this treatment. I haven't even been offered legal representation. I'll fucking sue you for this. I'll sue British Airways as well. I'll miss an important function soon if you don't let me out of here and then I'll...'

'We're actually Customs and Excise officers, madam,' the man said, glancing somewhat amusedly at his colleague. 'And we're just completing our checks on you.'

'Checks?' Marina threw her hands in the air, melodrama always being one of her strong points. 'Fucking checks? How long do checks take? And checks on what? I'm not a criminal and I haven't got a gun!' She banged her fist on the table, pausing to check she hadn't damaged her nail extensions. 'You're a joke, the lot of you. Taking the word of some skanky...'

She stopped, suddenly realising that if she continued and labelled Tina as a whore who worked in strip clubs, shagging men for money, then she'd have to explain how she knew that fact.

Going into details about that would do her no favours and would be the cause of getting further detained.

Taking a deep breath, she smiled – a horrible sickening smile that was as fake as it got. 'Look, I understand you're doing your job, but you really must be able to see this is a mix-up?' She sat back down at the wooden table and clasped her hands together. 'I can't miss this function! I've flown here specially. It's extremely important.'

'And what function is that, madam?' the officer asked.

Marina hesitated. She couldn't say that either – not without dropping herself in it when the police found Samantha's body devoid of life. 'That's none of your fucking business,' she snapped, forgetting the nice act. 'I demand a phone call. I'm calling a solic-itor whether you like it or not.' And then she would sue the arse off every single bastard in this stinking place. Yeah, she could afford the best barrister, but not getting out of here in time would screw up everything.

'Just be patient a while longer, madam,' the officer said, smiling coldly. 'We've been informed the checks are almost complete and then you should be able to go on your way.'

Should? Marina thought. She *would* be, he meant.

And if that didn't happen, then make no mistake, she would really lose her temper.

* * *

Keeping his eye firmly on the time, Tom made headway along the M6. The traffic had been shit so far and they were slightly behind schedule. If Potter had got into gear quicker this morning, they wouldn't have been ten minutes late leaving in the first place.

He pulled his eyes from the road to scowl at Potter. He'd made it crystal clear what time they'd needed to be on the road, but Potter wouldn't leave the flat until he'd finished his predictable morning chat with a corpse. Like there was time for that bullshit today of all days.

Stupid bastard.

Then when Tom had finally wrenched Potter from the flat, the dozy twat had gone back in four fucking times, saying he'd forgotten this or forgotten that…

For God's sake!

Tom smiled to himself despite his irritation because last night had been the very last time he'd be lumbered being under the same roof as that mad fool.

His own stuff was safely stashed in the back of the van. There was no way he was coming back to that flat in Telford. There was no need.

Seeing the slip road at the last minute, Tom cut across all three motorway lanes, amidst much blaring of horns and rude hand gestures which he had no problem ignoring. The rest of the traffic could have a pile-up, but he was not missing the exit for anyone.

'What the fuck are you doing?' Potter yelped, the sudden veering of the van causing his head to bounce off the passenger seat window.

'Driving! What does it bloody look like?' Tom spat, thinking if Potter wasn't so invested getting the wrapper off his fourth Twix bar of the journey, then he'd be aware of what was going on.

Taking the first exit off the roundabout, Tom headed down the B4065 towards Anstey. This way, rather than the bypass, was the least likely route to bump into anyone else heading to the venue for the wedding of the year.

Wedding of the year, my arse, Tom thought, his thin mouth twisting into a sneer. It was a fucking joke.

But soon the lives of all the people he hated would be utterly shattered. Including, with any luck, Potter's.

'Not long to go now,' he remarked, doubting whether Potter was even listening, but talking out loud drowned out a percentage of the hideous noise of Potter slurping on his Twix bar.

God, he hated people who ate with their mouths open.

Realistically, he'd hate Potter *whatever* he did, but soon he'd never have to see the bastard again.

Ha ha ha! Hallelujah!

'I'm getting excited now,' Potter said suddenly, making Tom jump. 'I hope we don't have to wait long.'

So do I, Tom thought. 'The ceremony should be underway by now, so with any luck, it will just be a few hours.'

'I think it will be longer than a few hours,' Potter grumbled. 'Good job I have a brain as well as the foresight to think of *this*.'

Tom pushed away the plastic thing Potter waved in his face. 'I can't see where I'm going!' he roared, glaring at the opaque strangely shaped thing Potter clutched in his hand. 'What is it, anyway?'

'It's one of those piss pot things. You know the sort they give those bed-bound old codgers?' Potter examined the large object in his hand. 'Being as we'll both be using it, I bought the biggest one I could find in Boots.'

Tom almost gagged. *Holy fuck!* Just when he'd thought this nightmare was all but over and Potter lands this on him? A piss pot? A fucking *bottle*?

If Potter thought he'd consider sticking his cock into anything that had previously had Potter's dick in it, then the man was even more demented than first presumed.

Tom was so aghast about this, the urge to punch Potter in the face was overwhelming.

He really could only hope and pray that once he'd fucked off with the money away from this reject, that Stoker did what all good Stokers do and blew a hole in Potter's face.

25

The room fell silent as music suddenly filtered in, signifying the important arrival.

'She's here!' Andrew nudged Seb. 'And she looks beautiful!'

Heart lurching, Seb remained facing forward, his eyes fixed on the registrar. *Sam was here? He was getting married!*

He shifted from one foot to the other. Standing at the top of the stunningly decorated room where they were to be married, straight-backed and unmoving, his legs were stiff and, if he was honest, a little shaky.

He hadn't been unduly worried that Sam *wouldn't* turn up, but despite this, he'd still been uncomfortable facing the congregation or chatting with anyone, just in case his very worst fears were realised and she *did* fail to show.

But now she was here...

Taking a deep breath, Seb slowly turned, not only to savour the moment, but so no creases appeared in his wing-collared dress shirt or morning suit. He wanted to look perfect – every inch of what a man Sam was giving herself to should look like.

At the vision moving up the aisle towards him, his breath

caught in his throat. Nowhere in his wildest dreams had he imagined Sam could ever look any more beautiful than she usually did, but she had succeeded.

His eyes roamed over the dress hugging Sam's body – an off-white creation of silk and shimmering crystals which sent dancing rainbows off in every conceivable direction. The sweetheart neckline of the bodice accentuated the new fullness of her breasts and the skirt of the dress followed the line of her hips and legs perfectly to widen out at her feet into a fishtail hem.

Seb couldn't stop his smile from spreading over his entire face. He took a quick glance at his parents in the front row: his father staring at Sam in awe and his mother already dabbing at her eyes.

As she reached Seb, Sam smiled with unfamiliar shyness and took his hand whilst Andrew moved to take his seat.

'You look amazing,' Seb murmured, his lips brushing the side of the veil now fixed perfectly atop Sam's glossy hair. 'Absolutely beautiful.'

Sam's stomach fluttered with nerves and excitement as she stared into the green eyes of the man she was about to pledge the rest of her life to.

And the rest of her life it would be. Never could she imagine looking at anyone aside from Sebastian Stoker. 'You look amazing too,' she whispered.

As the registrar smiled warmly at both Sam and Seb, Sam took the final opportunity to steal a quick glance at Linda and Gloria – both happily sniffling into their handkerchiefs.

Her real mother and her adoptive mother both here to see this most special day – something, not long ago, Sam had believed to be impossible for so many reasons. And the rest of the Stoker family – people, despite the bumpy start, she'd come to love as much as her own.

Things couldn't possibly get any better than this. It would be a day she would remember and cherish for the rest of her life.

Hearing the registrar's voice, Sam grinned at Seb and together they both faced the front as the ceremony began.

* * *

Tina moved as inconspicuously as possible around the grounds of Coombe Abbey pretending to take in the gorgeous gardens, like others were doing.

Seb Stoker and Samantha Reynold were getting married in there...

Her eyes tracked to the part of the majestic building which was clearly holding a massive function. The rest of the grounds and other parts of the hotel were open for guests not associated with the occasion, so no one could stop her from doing this, could they?

She focused on the area festooned with flowers and ribbons, where hordes of press gathered with long-lensed cameras. They waited behind railings, along with a smattering of the public interested to see the spectacle that attracted so much media interest.

The railings hadn't stopped a few reporters from pushing their luck. So far, Tina had already witnessed three escaping their enforced boundaries and approaching the building, hoping for a sneak photograph of the ceremony underway inside.

But within seconds, they'd been stopped.

Tina shuddered, recollecting how Seb Stoker's cleverly concealed security had appeared from nowhere to apprehend the trespassers, who had been promptly and not so gently removed from the vicinity.

She continued walking, becoming more resigned that she would fail in getting near the place where she needed to be.

Lighting a cigarette, Tina stopped in front of a lake running through the grounds and collected her thoughts. How on earth could she do this? If she couldn't get near Sam or anyone connected to her, then it was impossible.

Her only hope was to wander around, hoping no one earmarked her as suspicious and pray that at some point – perhaps during the reception, someone would come out to take a call; grab a breath of fresh air – anything, so she could speak to them and relay the importance of getting a message to Sam or one of the Stokers.

Her heart sank further. But anyone coming out from the reception wouldn't wander around in the space open to the public, would they? If they did, they'd be accosted by the press.

Tina could only presume wherever the reception was being held, it would be in the same part of the building as the ceremony, so there must be a separate exit and grounds away from the masses.

If she could find where that was and how to get to it, then perhaps her chances of coming across someone was higher?

Deciding to walk around the perimeter of the grounds in the opposite direction, Tina kept her eyes peeled for wedding cars or more flowers, ribbons and wedding festivities. *Something* must be visible, even if it was just a hint. From there, she could further weigh up her options.

Tina suddenly noticed a flash of light as sunlight bounced off the roof of a car.

She peered into the distance at a car disappearing up a secluded drive which looked to lead around the side of the building. That drive could be a separate entrance or lead to a car park for private functions. If nothing else, it was worth a try.

With a brightening heart, she hastened along the path and glanced over her shoulder before scurrying across the lawn.

Hoping no one spotted her, Tina then deftly picked her way

through shrubs and foliage. If she followed the main line of the building from a different angle, then...

Bingo!

Another car park opened out in front of her filled with cars – mostly top-of-the- range motors, but also a few vans and trade vehicles. *Caterers and such like?*

Tina's gaze moved to the building which, if her judgement proved correct, mirrored the part of the main building she'd seen from the front – the arrival driveway strewn with flowers and the waiting reporters.

It was here. *This* was the function's private entrance. It had to be because it was also liberally decorated with flowers and ribbons.

Heart hammering, Tina focused on the building, making out movement behind the large windows on the ground floor. She could also see more grounds further along with a grand set of stone steps leading down to what looked like a large ornamental lake. *Perfect for wedding photographs...*

If she could just get closer and further over the other side to wait, she would have to come across someone eventually.

* * *

Hearing a long, drawn-out beep from three storeys below, Vera grabbed her handbag and overnight case. Slamming her front door behind her, she raced along the walkway, her heels clattering on the concrete.

'The cab's here,' she yelled, banging Sophie's door. 'Come on, girl!'

Vera buzzed with excitement, wanting to get to the reception as soon as possible, but as the door opened to reveal Sophie, she gasped, her hands flying to her mouth. 'Bleedin' hell!'

Sophie's smiling face froze in panic. 'What? Do I not look right? Oh no! I knew I'd never be able to pull off wearing something like this.'

She glanced down at the emerald-green evening dress Linda and Vera had sourced for her to wear. It was the most beautiful thing she'd ever seen, let alone worn. But people like *her* never got to wear such exquisite and expensive gowns, let alone go somewhere to wear it!

The fact remained the same – no matter how classy the dress, nothing removed the invisible branding that she'd only ever worn crop tops and skin-tight Lycra miniskirts before. Some things were too ingrained to be completely remodelled, no matter what she did. 'You go, Vera. I can't go looking stupid. I won't make a fool of myself!'

'What are you blathering on about?' Vera snatched up Sophie's overnight bag from the doorway. 'You look amazing! Now get a move on. Taxis around here won't wait about for long in case some fucker pinches their wheels!'

Clattering down the stairwell in her heels, Sophie didn't have time to question whether Vera was being on the level or if she was just trying to make her feel better. Her whole concentration was on staying upright, otherwise she'd break her neck.

Within what seemed like seconds, they reached the pavement outside. Vera steamed ahead waving her hands and screeching for the taxi driver, who started to pull away, to stop. Sophie followed as quickly as possible, her feet already killing.

She clambered gratefully into the back of the taxi and fanned her face. 'You meant what you said?' she whispered. 'That I don't look stupid?'

'Stupid?' Vera gaped. 'You're gorgeous! You look so different! Your hair – *everything*! A true stunner!'

Sophie glowed with a spark of reigniting confidence. 'Do you really think so?'

'I don't think so, I *know* so!' Vera laughed. She poked the taxi driver's shoulder. 'Don't she look the bee's knees?'

'She certainly does,' the taxi driver agreed. 'If I weren't working tonight, I'd be asking you to come for a drink with me!'

'I don't think so, love,' Vera cackled. 'I doubt you'd take her anywhere to justify the getup she's wearing!'

Sophie blushed furiously. It had taken a horribly long time to remove all of the nylon extensions from her hair this evening, sure she'd pulled a considerable amount of her real hair out with them in the process, but she'd achieved a different look – a *very* different look – one which would take a while to get used to, but one that she much preferred.

This was a new look – a new start.

Not so long ago she'd have jumped at the chance for the attention of a man – *any* man. But not now. The only man she was interested in was Andy Waterford.

'Both of you ladies look gorgeous, but you're right, I don't go to places posh enough to warrant the stuff you two have got on, so I guess my luck's not in,' the taxi driver laughed. 'So, where am I driving you to?'

'Coventry, please,' Vera said, her excitement growing once again. 'Coombe Abbey.'

Accelerating away, the driver glanced at Vera and Sophie in his rear-view mirror. 'Blimey! Coombe Abbey? Very nice! Hey, isn't that do on tonight there that was in the papers? You know, that bloke and woman th...'

'I don't know what else is on there, I just know what we're going to,' Vera cut in. 'Now get a move on, mate. We don't want to be late.'

Squeezing Sophie's hand, she began chatting about her dress – anything to stop the taxi driver from opening his gob. He'd been just about to rattle on about Seb and Sam. The last thing she wanted was Sophie finding out exactly whose wedding they were going to.

Luckily, it didn't seem Sophie had cottoned on and Vera wanted it to stay that way. At least until they were ensconced in the reception with drinks in their hands and preferably Linda next to them to soften the shock. And once Sophie had got over the surprise, Vera would take the opportunity to find Sam for a quiet word and smooth things out about the mixed wires over Linda.

'Have you heard from your man today?' she asked.

Sophie shook her head. 'No, but I didn't expect to. He's at that big event he had to go to. I'm sure I'll see him soon.'

'Seems like today is the day for events,' Vera chuckled. 'At least we don't have to worry about getting back later.'

Sophie had almost squealed out loud when Vera told her Linda had booked them a room at the hotel. All expenses paid as well. Linda really was generous. If only she was staying there tonight with Andy too. But then, she could hardly feel deprived being lucky enough to have friends like Vera and Linda in her life. 'It's going to be a fantastic evening,' she beamed. 'I can't wait to meet Linda's daughter and her new husband. I hope they'll like me.'

'Of course they will!' Vera patted Sophie's hand. 'How could they not?' And she'd get the nicest surprise in the world when she realised whose wedding reception she was actually at.

26

Holding Sam in his arms, Seb effortlessly led her around the dance floor to 'Nights in White Satin', his heart feeling like it would burst.

With Sam held so closely, his growing arousal would soon become noticeable if he wasn't careful. 'I can't wait to get you upstairs,' he murmured into Sam's ear.

'I'm afraid you'll have to wait a bit longer for that, being as the reception's only just started,' Sam laughed. 'You never told me you were such an adept dancer!'

'I'm a man of many talents, me,' Seb said. 'Can't we just tell this lot to go home?'

Sam couldn't help but return Seb's smile as his lips pressed into her hair. 'No, not really.' *But she'd love to.* She hadn't thought she could *ever* be this happy, but today it proved anything was possible.

The ceremony had gone without a hitch and to her eternal relief, there were no interruptions from uninvited press. She'd known Seb would succeed keeping them at bay and he had. His men had made sure not *one* reporter or uninvited gatecrasher had sneaked their way in. Plus, they'd got the one agreed photo shoot with the *Birmingham Mail* out of the way too. Even Andrew's best man speech hadn't been too embarrassing.

Catching sight of Tayquan endeavouring to join them on the dance floor only to be sharply pulled back by Linda, Sam chuckled. Her young brother and sister's behaviour had also been exemplary, and Sam couldn't have been more grateful, but she could tell they were itching to let off steam now the evening reception was underway. And they could, once this traditional first dance was done.

It had been a wonderful day so far and tonight promised to be just as good.

Sam pressed herself tighter against Seb, wanting to jump up and down with happiness. Everything was just perfect and tomorrow, as the icing on the cake, they would fly off for two whole uninterrupted weeks together in tropical paradise.

'Just one question,' she whispered as they continued to twirl around to the music. 'Why did you tell that reporter from the *Mail* that we're going on honeymoon to Mauritius, when we're going to the Maldives?'

Seb chuckled. 'Being as the nosy twat kept pushing as to our destination, do you really think I was going to actually tell him? Set ourselves up to be accosted by the press at the bloody airport as well? I think not!'

Sam laughed. 'Ah, so there's method in your madness then?'

As the first dance drew to a close, Seb tilted Sam's face up to his. 'Happy, Mrs Stoker?'

Sam glowed hearing the name she would now use for ever more. 'I've never been happier.'

Seb led Sam from the dance floor to a round of applause from the gathered guests who then wasted no time making their way onto the floor as the disco cranked up the first song of the evening.

Sam craned her neck over the crowd. 'I'm sure I've just spotted Vera,' she said to Seb. 'I'll go and see her now, if you don't mind?'

'I'll leave you to it,' Seb winked, planting a soft kiss on Sam's lips.

Smiling, Sam swished her way across the room in her beautiful dress, knowing it would take time to get through all the people wanting to stop her on route to chat, but she'd get to Vera in the end.

* * *

'I don't believe it,' Tom muttered, not caring if Potter heard. Slamming his can of Coke into the drinks holder, he leant as far forward as possible against the dashboard and focused on the figure.

'What is it?' Potter asked, suddenly coming to life. 'Is it the Reynold bitch?' Receiving no answer, he tugged Tom's sleeve. 'Well, is it? If it is, then I'm not waiting around fo...'

'Get the fuck off!' Tom snarled, snatching his arm away. 'It's not Samantha. Now shut up! I need to concentrate.'

Staring harder at the woman in the distance, Tom's eyes narrowed. *It was that bitch – that skanky whore from the Aurora.*

His blood thickened. So it could have been her at the airport after all?

But why the fuck was she here? And acting furtively too – glancing around and staying close to cover.

What was she up to?

Suddenly, it dawned on him...

'Jesus fucking Christ,' he gibbered, immediately regretting speaking out loud when Potter started nudging him.

There could only be one reason Tina was snooping around.

The lowlife tart must have put two and two together that he'd been the one to kill her mother, Amelia. Okay, even being thick as shit, it wasn't hard for the stupid whore to work out, but she must have stayed around Brum waiting to get her own back all of this time.

Tom then faltered. But she'd have thought him dead, like everyone else did, wouldn't she? She'd have seen the papers? Who hadn't?

Unless she couldn't read?

Tom's brain fell into overdrive. Unable to pull his eyes from Tina, his concentration so channelled, he even filtered out Potter's further questions. *For now.*

If Tina had helped Linda to escape the attic before she'd succumbed to death, then she could also know the crackhead was Samantha's mother.

Tom's blood changed from a thick congealing gloopy mess to a thin icy liquid which threatened to seep out of his very pores.

And if Tina knew Samantha was Linda's daughter, she could have been in contact.

She could have even followed him to the airport the other day, masquerading as a cleaner, to see what he was doing?

Tom's hands clenched into fists. Surely that was absurd? That tramp didn't have the nous to put that kind of thing together.

But she'd played Dan well enough and got the info he'd wanted to enable him to pull off that robbery…

Maybe this wasn't as absurd as he thought?

Tom's breath came in ragged pants, his panic mounting.

If Tina had worked out all of that, then she could have got wind of what they were about to do to Samantha. 'Oh God…' he whispered. He was fucked. His plan was utterly trashed.

'Bedworth!' Potter roared. 'What the bleeding hell is going on? If you don't tell me what the fuck is happening, I swear I'll kill you as well as the Reynold bitch.'

Tom faced Potter. So Potter was having a lucid moment? How convenient... And unhelpful...

But it didn't change that alterations were needed and quickly.

Opening the van door, Tom started to get out. 'What are you doing?' Potter barked, dragging Tom back into the van before his feet hit the tarmac. 'You can't get out here! What's the matter with you? I knew you weren't up to this!'

'Look,' Tom spat, clenching his teeth against the pain from scraping his shin along the car door rim. 'We have a problem. But I have a way to sort it...'

'Problem?' Potter growled. 'What fucking problem?'

'See that woman?' Tom nodded through the dirty windscreen. 'Her – that blonde thing skulking around.' He had to tell Potter the score. Unfortunately, he'd need his help if he was going to pull this bit off. If he was going to pull *any* of it off...

Potter peered into the distance. 'Yeah, what about her?'

'She's on to us,' Tom said. 'We'll have to take her.'

'What?' Potter yelled. 'What do you mean, "take her"? I'm not interested in that thing. You might want to stick your cock in it, but I don't! I want Samantha, no one else. What use is that slag over there in destroying Stoker? Have you lost your fucking mind?'

Tom glowered. If *he'd* lost his mind, then it was undoubtedly in the same place Potter left his the majority of the time.

He knew he'd end up catching Potter's madness eventually.

But no, he wasn't mad. *Yet...*

'I don't mean, instead of! I mean *as well*. We take her *and* Samantha.'

'I don't fucking think so! We'll...'

'We haven't any choice,' Tom snarled. 'Didn't you hear me? The whore is on to us, so if we don't shut her up, then you won't be getting Samantha either because that bitch will tell her we're here. That's what she's waiting to do right now!'

Potter nodded, finally understanding the situation was graver than he'd thought. 'Okay, so when do we do this?'

Tom's eyes narrowed. 'Right fucking now!'

* * *

'This is an amazing place,' Sophie gasped, her eyes still wandering over the many details this building and room offered – from the mediaeval architecture, down to the suits of armour and wrought-iron candelabra. Every time she thought there was nothing left to astound her, she'd spot something else.

It was unbelievable that she'd been invited somewhere like *this*. And to be staying overnight here too?

Her smile was so big it could power the National Grid.

Just wait until she saw Andy and told him. If only she had a camera, then Vera could snap a picture of her in this dress with this magnificent setting as a backdrop. Gosh, it would be like something out of a magazine!

Her face then fell when Vera's words from yesterday flooded back.

As Andy wanted to take her away for the weekend perhaps it would be better not to tell him exactly how special this place was? What if he thought she was hinting at him taking her somewhere like this?

Like Vera said, how could he afford somewhere like this? The last thing she wanted to do was make out she cared about money.

Sophie chewed the corner of her lip. She wouldn't want him to think she wouldn't be happy with wherever he took her. She'd be happy staying in a cardboard box, if it was with him.

'I thought I saw you two arrive.' Linda rushed up to Sophie and Vera to hug them. 'You both look lovely.'

'You don't scrub up too bad yourself for an old bird,' Vera chuckled.

'We haven't been here long,' Sophie said nervously. 'How did the wedding go?'

'It was fantastic!' Linda turned to Vera. 'You should have seen them, V. I blubbed my eyes out!'

'We haven't had a glimpse of the happy couple yet. There are so many people here that even during the first dance I couldn't see over all these fuckers' heads!' Vera said.

Linda laughed. 'There haven't been any reporter problems though, just as we'd all hoped, even though there were hordes outside when we arrived for the ceremony.'

Vera nodded. 'When we arrived I saw a few hangers-on lurking on the main drive. The rest must have given up.'

Sophie looked from Linda to Vera in confusion. *Reporters? Why would there be reporters here?* 'When can I be introduced to your daughter, Linda? I want to thank her for letting me come.'

'If you can get a look in past everyone else waiting to congratulate her, any time you like, bab,' Linda smiled. 'I know she'd love to meet you.'

'I reckon you can do it now then,' Vera grinned. 'Because here she is.'

As Sophie turned to see the bride, Vera pulled Sam into a tight hug. 'Congratulations, sweetheart! You look gorgeous!' Releasing Sam, she grabbed her hand. 'We need to talk, but before we do, let me introduce you to my friend. This is Sophie. She lives in your mum's old flat.' She grinned coyly. 'Sophie, meet Sam. You may recognise her...'

As Vera stepped to one side, Sophie laid eyes on the stunning woman in the wedding dress and her tongue stuck fast to the top of her mouth. 'H-hi,' was all she managed to garble. *Samantha Reynold? Linda's daughter was Samantha Reynold?*

'Hi, Sophie,' Sam smiled. 'Glad you could make it. I hope Vera and my mother are looking after you?'

Feeling like her legs may go from under her, Sophie refrained from collapsing to the floor in shock. 'Y-yes, they are. You... you look beautiful.'

She wanted to make further conversation, but her voice box had given up the ghost and jammed. She wanted to smile – do *anything* other than stand open-mouthed like an idiot, but remained in a state of suspended animation. The only sign of life was her steadily racing heart as she wracked her brain how to get out of here as fast as possible away from this place, this woman and these people.

Sam exchanged concerned glances with Vera and Linda. 'Is she okay?'

Linda laughed. 'I'd say this one is in a state of shock! You see, me and V failed to mention whose wedding this was, other than my daughter's.'

'Yeah, we kind of forgot to mention you were the one and only Sam Reynold, marrying the one and only Sebastian Stoker at the wedding everyone in the world wanted an invite to!' Vera nudged Sophie. 'Sorry about that, chick, but you'd have been too nervous to come if you'd known.'

'Oh, Vera!' Sam scoffed. 'You talk like me and Seb are celebrities!'

'That's because you are!' Linda laughed. 'Around this neck of the woods, anyhow.'

Sam grinned at Sophie. 'Take no notice of these two and grab yourself another drink. Now come on, Vera. Let's go and have that chat.'

Sophie stared after Sam Reynold, resplendent in her wedding dress as she moved with Vera across the floor towards a corridor, and glibly accepted the glass of wine Linda pushed into her hand.

'Bet that was a surprise, wasn't it?'

'You could say that.' Smiling weakly, Sophie sipped at her wine. *Surprise? She'd nearly had a heart attack on the spot.* Not for the reasons Linda and Vera believed though. Although she'd never thought she'd meet someone of such standing and notoriety as Sam Reynold and Seb Stoker, it would have been Linda and Vera who would be surprised if they realised why she was on the cusp of a meltdown.

Sophie knew of Sam Reynold, like everyone else in Birmingham did, but she hadn't known the woman was Marina Devlin's half-sister until the night Marina had dragged her from the Sunset Boulevard to watch Sam knocking on the door of Tina's house.

Whilst Sophie had been pushed face down into the mud to keep her quiet, she'd listened to the torrent of hate spewing from Marina's mouth. She'd then been forced to accompany Marina into the house to recoup the money Marina's ex, Dan, had stolen from the Stokers.

The money robbed from the safes belonging to the man whose wedding reception she was standing in.

She'd also been there when Marina had killed Dan – mutilating him with such viciousness, and worse, enjoyment.

Sophie remembered it well. *How could she forget?*

After fleeing, screaming from the house, she'd laid low in case Marina came looking for her, knowing she and she alone was the only person who knew first-hand what that crazy psycho had done.

Sophie swallowed painfully, convinced she would pass out.

If these people knew that she'd been with Marina, they'd think she was part of stealing the money and killing that Dan person.

But wait! *She'd* seen Sam that night, but Sam hadn't seen *her*. In fact, Sophie was sure Sam had never set eyes on her before now and judging by how the woman had just reacted, she was right.

She could only pray things stayed that way because people like the Stokers would be unlikely to accept she had been unaware of Marina's plans or that she'd had nothing to do with it, despite it being true.

27

Tina had waited patiently for ages – *hours* even. Her legs were aching and she wanted to sit down, eat something and use the toilet, but she could do none of those things. Not until she'd seen someone to get the all-important message to Sam.

Every second that passed mattered. Marina must have been released by now? There was only so long someone could be held. And when it was discovered there was no gun in the luggage, they'd have to let her walk.

Unless, Tina thought with a glimmer of false hope, Marina *had* got a gun somewhere? She certainly wouldn't put it past the psycho.

But even Marina wasn't that nuts to think she'd get something like that through customs.

Tina's eyes darted around, accustomed to the darkness now the evening had closed in. It was late and time was running out, yet there had been no chances to speak to anyone. Only one man had exited the building the entire time and he had been too far away to reach before he'd disappeared back inside.

Plus, there was the security who frequently patrolled the area.

Luckily, they weren't scouring the back end of the car park, otherwise she'd have been spotted a long time ago, but she still needed to watch for them.

What the hell was she going to do?

Almost jumping out of her skin as a van backed into a nearby space, Tina hoped she blended into the bush behind enough not to be spotted. She'd been so focused on how her supposedly well-thought-out plan was unravelling, she hadn't even noticed a vehicle coming. *Stupid, stupid...*

Remaining motionless when a large man lumbered from the van, she held her breath and waited. *He hadn't seen her, thank God.*

Permitting herself to sneak in a small lungful of air, Tina pulled herself to her senses.

Hang on a minute... If this man was in this car park and looked like he would head towards the building with the reception, then he must be something to do with the wedding.

She frowned. From his clothes, he clearly wasn't a guest, but perhaps a tradesman.

Dare she risk it?

Procrastinating, Tina picked her fingers. She had to risk it because there was no one else. She'd have to be quick though because she couldn't step out from behind the parked vehicles where somebody could see her.

Taking a deep breath, Tina inched forward out of the shadows. 'Excuse me. Are you going into that building?'

Level with the van's bonnet, Potter swung around as much as his bulk allowed. *Christ on a bike, this would be easier than he'd supposed.* 'Why are you lurking about there?' he asked gruffly. 'This is a private function.'

Tina's heart leapt. She knew it. This man must be part of the backend organisation of the event. She held her hands up. 'I'm not here to cause trouble. The *opposite* actually.'

'What do you mean by that?'

Tina's eyes moved around the car park. Eager not to put herself in view, she beckoned Potter further back towards the rear of the van. It was a long shot and could blow up in her face, but she had to try. 'I need to get into that building,' she gabbled. 'Or at least get an important message to someone.'

Potter eyed Tina curiously. Not his cup of tea – not even *slightly*, but Bedworth was bang on – this little bitch was here to flap her gums to the Reynold woman, so the dog-rough cow had to be stopped. Nothing could delay him from getting his hands on Samantha Reynold and exacting revenge for Mark.

Potter folded his big arms and stared at Tina. 'Oh yeah? Important message? Who's the message for?'

Tina rapidly weighed up how much to tell this man. There was something unsavoury and a bit strange about him.

Fear glimmered. Had she fucked up?

Before she could analyse this nagging question or decide what to say in response, Tina emitted a small squeak as the back doors of the van flew open.

In a flash of blurred movement, she couldn't register fast enough that the second man appearing to grab her arm was Tom Bedworth. Not that she had time to do anything about it.

As her brain processed what she'd seen and now recognising *exactly* who had hold of her, showing she had indeed utterly fucked up, Tina saw something coming towards her head.

And then it went black.

* * *

'These are my youngest two – Tayquan and Shondra.' Linda ruffled Tayquan's crinkly hair. 'Say hello to the lady.'

'Hi, guys.' Sophie smiled at the two children in front of her. 'You both look great! Have you had a nice day?'

Tayquan nodded shyly, whilst Shondra beamed with pride. 'Yes, we have. My sister looks like a fairy tale queen and is the prettiest woman in the world! Now we have a new uncle! Sebastian runs a casino, just like my sister.' She frowned. 'How do you know them?'

'I... erm... I'm a friend of your mum's,' Sophie blathered.

'That's enough interrogation and showing off, you two,' Linda said, rolling her eyes. 'Now bugger off to dance and leave us grown-ups in peace!'

Sophie smiled, secretly relieved as the children excitedly scurried off back to the dance floor. Talking to children, especially when they asked *those* sort of questions, wasn't a good idea.

Her nerves were in tatters, but she'd reached the conclusion that no one knew of her connection with Marina or what she'd been forced into. Not at the moment. But it was only a matter of time.

Someone somewhere could have seen them together or even that they'd shared a flat for a short time, so all she could do was get through the rest of the evening and then, as much as the thought depressed her, pull back from her friendship with both Vera and Linda.

How could she continue knowing she'd once been shacked up with and shagging Linda's ex-husband? Because, as Marina's father, that's who Mickey Devlin must have been married to – Linda. *The crackhead*, he'd called her.

Sophie thought Linda far from that and one of the nicest people she'd ever met, but it was only a matter of time before one of them discovered the connection – the connection with *everything...*

'Hey!' Linda nudged Sophie. 'I'm talking to you! Are you on Planet Earth or what?'

'Sorry,' Sophie spluttered. 'I still can't quite believe I'm here.' *More so now than ever...*

Linda laughed. 'I'm guessing Sam's still busy putting the world to rights with Vera and will be for a while longer, so why don't we go and see Seb. I haven't introduced you yet.'

Seb Stoker? She might be unrecognised for now, but Sophie didn't want to push her luck. 'What? I... erm... Oh no, I don't want to intrude or...'

'Come on! I insist!' Grabbing Sophie's arm, Linda steered her across the large room.

Internally floundering, Sophie knew she could hardly kick up a fuss. Not only would it be rude, but would also be extremely odd. In normal circumstances, who wouldn't want to meet the groom at a wedding where an invite had been so kindly extended, as well as him being one of the most well-known, infamous men in the West Midlands?

As they neared the bar, Sophie's heart crashed in her chest. The men facing her, all built like brick outhouses, resembled vicious psychopaths and regardless of the smart suits they donned, were the notorious enforcers everyone talked about.

The other three facing away: all tall, dark-haired and equally big built wore morning suits. *They* must be the Stokers.

Meaning one of them was Sebastian Stoker...

Pushing through the invisible wall preventing her from going further, Sophie continued, praying none of these men had ever seen her.

She'd heard the Stokers had come into the Sunset Boulevard once. She'd been working and hadn't personally seen them, but that didn't mean they hadn't seen *her*...

Oh God, God, God!

'Hey, Seb! I've got someone I want you to meet.' Linda's loud voice screeched over the music.

As Seb turned around, Sophie's breath caught in her throat at the amazingly handsome man with eyes that...

'This is Sophie – a friend of mine and Vera's. Soph's living in my old flat, aren't you, duck?'

'Y-yes,' Sophie stammered, not daring to breathe when Seb Stoker grasped her hand and bent to kiss her on the cheek.

'Pleased to meet you, Sophie.'

'Likewise,' Sophie garbled. For a minute there, she thought... It wasn't, but this man looked remarkably similar to...

'Andrew! Neil! Meet Linda's friend, Sophie,' Seb shouted to his brothers.

'Who have we got here then?' Andrew turned to see what Seb was shouting about. 'What th...'

Dizziness rushed from Sophie's brain down to her feet and then back up again. She knew she'd slightly staggered and so did Linda, being as her arm shot out and steadied her.

But Linda wasn't quick enough to catch the fine-stemmed champagne flute which fell from Sophie's fingers to smash on the floor.

What felt like two hundred years of stunned silence followed as everyone in the room turned to see who had been so lax as to smash one of the exquisite goblets.

Sophie dropped to her knees, desperate to retrieve the broken bits of glass, her beautiful dress soaking up the spilt champagne on the floor. 'I'm so sorry,' she gabbled, not knowing what else to say or do.

Anything was better than standing there, seeing those green eyes burning into hers with shock parallel to her own.

Those green eyes that were presently searing a brand into the top of her head were the very same ones she'd seen every night in her dreams since meeting Andy Waterford.

Sophie felt sick. Andy Waterford wasn't Andy Waterford. The man she loved was *Andrew Stoker* – one of the Stoker twins – and Sebastian Stoker's brother.

How could this have happened?

'Leave that, duck. It doesn't matter.' Linda stooped down to pull Sophie from the floor, only to be met with surprisingly strong resistance.

'It's fine,' Sophie blathered. 'I'll get all of this up and obviously I'll pay for the breakages.'

Looking pleadingly at Seb for help with the situation, Linda was relieved when he stepped in.

Suddenly lifted off the floor, Sophie could do little to resist the powerful arms of Seb Stoker as he pulled her to her feet.

'Seriously, leave that, love. It doesn't matter,' Seb said. 'Someone will be over to sweep it up, so don't waste another moment worrying about it.'

'O-okay,' Sophie mumbled. 'Sorry... And thanks...' Now she would have to meet those eyes of Andy's – *Andrew*.

And she had to. She had to know why he'd lied about who he was.

But what did it matter? There was no way she could risk anything with him now. She couldn't wait for him and everyone else to discover she had been involved with that nutter, Marina Devlin.

Braving the inevitable, Sophie raised her eyes, only to find Andrew had disappeared, leaving his virtually identical, but not completely, twin brother next to the place he'd vacated.

Glancing around for any sign of him and finding none, Sophie allowed Linda to lead her away in the direction of a table.

'Let's get you another drink, shall we, chick?' Linda said, a hint of unease on her face.

* * *

'What the fuck do we do with her now?' Potter grumbled. Zipping his jeans up, he placed the urine bottle in the footwell.

'She'll remain in the back until we're ready,' Tom said, eyeing the worryingly full bottle at Potter's feet, betting he trod on it before the night was out. Then he'd be stuck in this tin can, not only with Potter, but stinking of old piss as well.

From what he'd deduced, it looked like he'd been wrong in his assumptions. Potter had been right in thinking Samantha and Stoker were unlikely to leave for their honeymoon tonight and would leave in the morning instead.

People were now leaving the reception. From the blurry memories of the only half-decent wedding he'd ever been invited to, guests didn't tend to leave until either the newlyweds departed for their honeymoon or retired to the bridal chamber.

Stoker and Samantha had definitely not left, so that could only mean they were hunkered down for the night to consummate their pointless marriage.

Tom glowered with pent-up irritation. They'd best put their all into the effort as it would be the last night they got to fuck each other.

So, by the looks of it, he was stuck here with a fat bastard and a piss bottle for the entire night. *Great...*

One good thing though was he'd successfully diverted the additional problem Tina had been about to bring to the table. From what he'd heard the treacherous tart say to Potter, he'd been spot on. The sly little cow had been hoping to get a message to Sam to warn her of his plan.

His mouth curled into a smirk.

It wasn't all doom and gloom for the stupid bitch though. She'd have plenty of time to tell Samantha all about what he was up to once he'd also secured the jumped-up cow in the van. That was if Tina hadn't bled to death by then...

Tom's smirk grew as he replayed the moment he'd cracked Tina's head with a plank of wood. The dull thud as he'd delivered the blow to her skull was pleasing to his ears. Whether she'd regained consciousness yet or not, he didn't know, or care. If she was dead it was of no consequence.

The recognition of it being him attacking had been written all over Tina's face in the split second before her lights went out. And it had been a pleasing sight. It paid dividends allowing folk to know who delivered the last blow. *Cathartic, even.*

He shrugged inwardly. When or *if* Tina re-joined the land of the living, she'd be unable to move a muscle or utter a sound. He'd made sure of that. He'd also made sure to leave adequate provisions in order to gag and bind Samantha up just as tightly when he finally got her.

It was disappointing waiting longer than planned, but it hadn't been a completely wasted journey.

'Had a really good day today, mate,' Potter said. 'Tomorrow will be the best though. You wait until you see what I'm going to do.'

Tom's head snapped up. 'What? What did you say?'

'Shhh!' Potter hissed. 'I'm talking to Mark, so shut up, otherwise I'll lose the connection.'

Sighing, Tom rested his forehead against the driver's side window and prepared to knuckle down and filter Potter's droning voice out for however many hours he had to put up with him talking to his dead brother.

28

Seb took his time undoing the myriad of satin-covered buttons on the back of Sam's bodice.

Finally undoing the last one, he allowed the gorgeous dress to fall to the floor around her ankles and stepped back to admire his stunning wife.

White stockings held from a lacy suspender belt; one leg brandishing a classic ribboned garter; a beautiful V-shaped white thong covering the place he'd been desperate to bury himself in all day and the clear swell of her growing belly, accentuated by the subtle glow of the lighting in this fantastic bridal suite, was just too much to not react to.

Unclipping Sam's white lacy bra, her full breasts spilling out into his hands, Seb groaned with need, his arousal having long since passed the point of being painful. 'God, Sam. I'll burst if I don't have you soon. I've been waiting all fucking day.'

Sweeping her up into his arms, Seb laid Sam gently on the huge four-poster bed surrounded by luxurious velvet drapes.

'What an amazing day,' Sam sighed happily. She'd put everything straight with Vera and everything had run like clockwork.

The only odd thing was on returning from her chat with Vera, she sensed something had happened.

Linda had been sitting with a pale-faced Sophie; Seb was in deep conversation with Neil, and Andrew was nowhere to be seen. But everyone was adamant nothing had happened, short of a spilt drink.

Her first instinct was that something had kicked off or a rogue reporter had finally got in, but apparently not.

'You're sure there wasn't any trouble tonight?' she asked.

Stripping off his shirt and trousers, Seb raised an eyebrow. 'You really think you wouldn't have heard about it if that was the case? Besides, I'd have told you.'

And no, nothing *had* actually happened, but something odd had occurred. Seb didn't know what it was, but he'd seen the reaction on his brother's face on seeing Linda's mate. He'd seen it loud and clear.

He'd also seen that woman – Sophie's reaction.

He shrugged inwardly. Andrew had shrugged it off when asked later about it, so whatever was going on, there wasn't anything he would worry about. Certainly not now, nor when he and Sam were away, either.

'Now, Mrs Stoker,' Seb grinned, clambering onto the bed and pulling Sam down underneath him. 'We'd better get on with doing the honourable and expected thing in making this marriage 100 per cent legal.'

'I completely agree, Mr Stoker,' Sam laughed, wrapping her arms around Seb's neck, eagerly awaiting what she knew would shortly follow.

* * *

'I don't quite know what the fuck we're supposed to do about this, Lin?' Vera exclaimed as she knocked back yet another vodka miniature from the room's mini bar.

'I can't say I do either.' Linda looked between her friend of old and the sweet young thing who had the weight of the world on her shoulders.

One thing was for certain and that was she hadn't expected this girl, who had only recently come out of her shell with Vera's help, and of course, her mystery man to have been dragged into all the shit with that psycho of her other daughter, Marina.

Sophie might have been reluctant to tell them what was really behind her sudden reaction at the reception, but Linda being Linda had shoehorned it out of the girl in the end. Sophie had little choice but to fess up. Especially when both her and Vera knew that as sure as God made little apples, she'd met Andrew Stoker before.

After a bit of working out, they'd put two and two together...

Linda eyed Sophie carefully. 'You genuinely didn't have a clue this man of yours was Andrew Stoker?'

Sophie shook her head, her face puffy from crying, her once perfect makeup ruined. 'No, I had no idea. Had I known, then...'

As much as Linda had been shocked to learn that Sophie had come from London as her ex-husband's bit of fluff and had now fallen in love with none other than Andrew Stoker, she was more shocked to learn that it wasn't Bedworth behind the murder of that one-handed bloke, but her own bloody *daughter*.

Not that it should surprise her. But why the fuck was Andrew Stoker masquerading as someone else?

Linda's brows knitted. Whatever the hell was going on here, she didn't know, but she was damned if she would allow anything to affect Sam and Seb's honeymoon. This knowledge they would have to keep to themselves.

'Tell me this,' Vera mused. 'That day when you freaked out when I banged on your door... It was because you thought it was Marina, wasn't it? It's *her* that you're terrified of running into. It's *her* that you don't want to find out where you are.'

Seeing Sophie's small nod, her body still juddering with the occasional remnants from her sobbing, Linda's lips pursed. She clearly remembered Vera telling her that from Sophie's reaction that day she must have witnessed something dreadful in the past. Vera also believed the girl had been beaten, horribly abused and lived in constant fear of the day when whoever the piece of shit was would catch up with her to ensure her silence.

Linda had also agreed with Vera's opinion that, if it had been on the cards, those sorts of people would have already rooted Sophie out by now. Because they hadn't, it was likely they'd already been offed by someone else. That was the way it worked and she knew this from her own experience.

But that was before she'd realised the person behind it all was her own *daughter*.

Not for the first time did Linda regret Marina taking a breath the day she'd been born. She was also sure Marina wasn't dead either and the horrible woman was *exactly* the sort to harbour a grudge until the end of time.

With Marina's mentality, there were no limits as to the levels the bitch would stoop to for payback.

Linda's face morphed into a scowl. Not only had that evil offspring of hers killed her only son, but she'd tried to kill Sam, shot Seb and killed that Dan bloke. God only knew how many others had been left in her trail of destruction. But to ruin Sophie's life too?

And continuing to ruin it...?

'Andrew doesn't know of any of this, I presume?' she asked.

'No, of course not,' Sophie cried. 'I've told no one about it. No one!' She looked down sadly. 'Not even you two until tonight... I was too scared...'

Wide-eyed, she grabbed Linda's hand. 'I didn't have anything to do with it, I really didn't! I would never... I wouldn't ever go along with something like that. I...'

'But you were willing to lure this Dan into a trap for Marina?' Vera quizzed, raising an eyebrow.

'But not to kill him!' Sophie gasped. 'Marina never said anything about that. She said he owed her money and...' She glanced at Linda in embarrassment. '...and she threatened to ruin things between me and Mickey...'

'It didn't seem like she needed to, considering he ended up battering you to fuck in the end!' Vera added.

'Vera!' Linda warned. 'That's not helpful.'

Vera shook her head in despair. 'I know, I know... I'm just angry how these fuckers trash everyone's lives.'

Linda reached out and grasped Sophie's other trembling hand, holding both tightly in her own. She'd been around too long not to know when someone was telling the truth – the *genuine* truth. And this girl clearly was. 'You must tell Andrew. You said you had a future with him? *Wanted* a future with him?'

Fresh tears cascaded down Sophie's cheeks. 'I haven't got one now... He won't want anything to do with me after this. How can he? He's a Stoker and the Stokers will think I was on side with Marina... They'll think I was in on it from the start!'

'No, they won't!' Linda said. 'I saw how Andrew reacted on seeing you tonight and that he disappeared spoke volumes. It showed he freaked out within his own head. Do you know what else I think?' She looked from Sophie to Vera and then back again. 'I think the reason he hasn't told you who he is, is because he's in love with you and didn't want to put you off when you found out.'

Vera laughed hollowly at the injustice of it all. 'Now they'll both lose out because of Marina?'

'Not if I have anything to do with it,' Linda said sharply. She turned to Sophie. 'I'll go to see Andrew and have it out with him. I want to know why he hid his identity and I'm going to tell him everything you've told me.'

Sophie gasped, her face a picture of horror. 'You can't! You mustn't... He doesn't know about any of this! He'll...'

'There isn't any choice, love,' Vera said. 'It needs to be done before it comes out in the wash. From what I can see, you two have something – something fucking *special*, so if it's meant to be, then things will find a way of coming good.'

'Vera's right,' Linda agreed, seeing Sophie's reluctance.

Sophie shook her head in despair, not daring to hope that might be a possibility. 'It won't work. He'll believe I must have been part of it. He'll never trust me and he'll...'

'Let me worry about that,' Linda barked, her face taut with rage. 'Marina has a lot to answer for and I won't have my bitch of a daughter destroying one more thing for anyone else!'

Sophie faltered, her panic increasing. 'B-but what about Sam and Seb? What will they think...? What will th...?'

'Sam and Seb leave early for their flight and I don't want them getting wind of this before they leave. Nothing can stop them from taking this much-needed honeymoon. Especially something stemming from bloody Marina Devlin!'

'Yes, because they won't go if they know about this,' Vera agreed.

'Exactly! And that isn't happening. Andrew will say nothing either, for the same reasons. There's nothing here that can't be sorted,' Linda said, her mind made up. 'Just leave it with me, okay?'

29

Not bothering with pleasantries, Marina snatched the room key from the receptionist's hand, then stomped up the corridor to her room. She would have been here last night if that wretch of a slut, Tina, hadn't taken it upon herself to trash her well laid-out plans. Now, because of that whore, she'd missed *everything*.

Slamming the door of the hotel room behind her, Marina chucked her suitcase on the bed and stared at it in disgust. Inside was the metal case containing the stuff she'd gone to great lengths to get her hands on in order to do what she'd planned for so long: end Samantha Reynold's miserable, grasping life.

What should have been her sister's happiest day should have ended up as her worst, as well as her last. But now, because of Tina and Customs and bloody Excise, that chance had been snatched away and her plans were in tatters.

Marina breathed heavily, the air hissing through her clenched teeth. *What a bloody waste.*

Hours, she'd been detained in that bloody airport and for what?

Nothing. Nothing at all.

Ridiculous!

She could sue them all she liked, but nothing would bring back this missed opportunity.

Undoing her suitcase, Marina snatched out the metal case and slammed it down on the dressing table. She didn't care if she broke the table or the box. It was no use to her now.

Oh sure, she could have gone straight from the airport to Coombe Abbey the second she was released, but what good would it have done? The wedding reception would have been over and she could hardly sneak her way into the bridal suite to kill her sister whilst Sebastian Stoker casually looked on, could she?

For fuck's sake, what a mess.

She may as well have left this fucking metal case in the locker for all the good it was now. But then, she'd have to pick it up eventually and she wasn't stepping foot in that godforsaken airport until her flight out of here was about to depart. And God knows when that would be now her plans were up the wall.

Those plans would have worked too, had they not been ballsed up by a bleached blonde, ugly tramp with a death wish.

Marina's overplucked brows burrowed deeper towards her nose. When she caught up with Tina over this, the stupid cow would wish she'd been hit by a fucking bus, rather than what was coming for her.

Slapping the lid of her suitcase shut, Marina yanked open the mini bar and grabbed a bottle of wine. Her nose wrinkled in distaste at the presence of a screw top rather than a cork.

Glugging down the sour-tasting wine direct from the bottle, Marina flopped back against the pillows and sighed.

Now she had to think of a new plan – and it would take *weeks*! Time she hadn't got.

Snorting with derision, Marina glanced to the side, doing a

double take at the photograph on the front page of the compli-
mentary copy of the *Birmingham Mail* on her bedside table.

Were they taking the piss?

She scanned for the date. Today – 17 July. The paper was the
second edition.

For God's sake! The final bloody insult!

The bold type of the glaring headline stabbed like needles in
Marina's eyeballs:

IT'S OFFICIAL! THE WEDDING OF THE YEAR!

Those lucky enough to be invited to the wedding of Samantha
Reynold and Sebastian Stoker watched as Birmingham's very
own casino couple tied the knot at the beautiful Coombe Abbey
Hotel in Coventry.

   The *Birmingham Mail* was the only newspaper granted official entry to the coveted ceremony and captured the moment
Samantha and Sebastian became Mr and Mrs Stoker...

Marina didn't want to look at the photograph of the people
who she'd despised for so long, but she couldn't help it; she was
drawn like a moth to a flame out of morbid curiosity, despite
knowing it would inflame her rage past all manageable levels.

Yep, there they were: Seb looking drop-dead handsome in his
made-to-measure morning suit and red cravat. And her most stunning sister looking resplendent in an admittedly gorgeous wedding
dress, which probably cost more than the average three-bed semi.

Marina's eyes narrowed in raw spite. *And there was dearest
Mother.* Even though the photograph only captured a line of the
back of heads in the front row, she'd recognise the skull of her cunt
of a mother anywhere.

She clenched the paper tightly, her fury going past the point of no return. She wanted to rip the whole thing to shreds. Burn it. Burn *them*.

Every. Single. One. Of. Them.

Almost enjoying the sense of self-inflicted pain, Marina continued reading:

> Mr Stoker looked every inch the proud groom as he took his new wife's hand. And who wouldn't? Holding a stunning wedding bouquet of roses, Samantha was the picture of beauty in the gorgeous, fishtailed satin bridal gown, complete with Swarovski crystals.
>
> The ceremony, which took place at 1 p.m. in the mediaeval banqueting hall of the Abbey, was followed by a reception with further guests.
>
> The next adventure for the newlywed Mr and Mrs Stoker is to leave for their honeymoon tomorrow for two weeks of bliss in Mauritius.
>
> We at the *Birmingham Mail* wish the happy couple the very best for the future and for married life...

Marina stared blankly at the photograph, her temples thumping with an approaching migraine. *Stunning wedding bouquet of roses... Swarovski crystals... Blah, blah, fucking blah.*

Yeah, weren't they just so bloody perfect?

Wait a moment...

Focusing on the bouquet her sister clutched demurely at her waist, Marina frowned, a hint of a sneer forming.

If she wasn't mistaken, there was the undeniable hint of something other than the perfectly flat stomach her sister usually possessed. And unless it was an unfortunate camera angle, which she very much doubted, then Samantha had slipped up and failed to hold her cleverly positioned bouquet in the right place for long enough, allowing the camera to capture the unmistakable shape of her pregnancy...

She wasn't too far along, but far along enough to make it out.

And this changed things somewhat...

Marina's mind kickstarted, her eyes flicking back over the article.

Maybe all was not lost?

Her eyes tracked back to the suitcase on the bed.

The paper said they were heading out to Mauritius tomorrow?

Shoving the paper to one side, Marina snatched up the telephone from the bedside table and stabbed in the number for the operator. Her false nails clicked loudly on the plastic dial, but she didn't care if they snapped. This was more important.

'Hello? Yes... Birmingham airport, please. Departures...'

Marina chewed her lip, waiting for the call to connect. The last place she'd wanted to call after her nightmare over the last twenty-four hours was the airport, but needs must.

'Hello? Yes, I'm inquiring what time the flight departs to Mauritius tomorrow. I'm giving my brother a lift to the airport, you see. I can't get hold of him tonight and I've only gone and forgotten what time he's got to be there for...'

Marina laughed – one of those tinkly, giggly laughs people made out of embarrassment. But she wasn't embarrassed – far from it. She was playing a part to get what was needed.

She listened intently. 'The plane departs at four o'clock? So, I'll need to get him to the airport by... erm... around two? Would that be right?'

A wide smile formed on Marina's mouth. 'Great! Thanks so much for your help. Bye.'

Putting the receiver down, she clapped her hands. *Excellent. Plan B now in motion...*

If Sam and Seb had to be at the airport by two, then she would intercept them.

Marina laughed out loud at her mastermind ability in thinking of this plan at last knockings. 'I'll get you still, Samantha,' she said out loud, taking another long swig from the despicable wine.

Her eyes tracked back to the suitcase. This time, she would abandon the plan of money. In reality, she'd got more than enough and the unfortunate changes to her original plan meant that side of things wouldn't be so straightforward. It would also take too long.

This way, she could do things in front of Seb Stoker and it would be so quick, he wouldn't have a hope in hell of stopping it.

It would also leave no trace. No bullets. No blood. Only death...

Result.

And now she suspected the high possibility of there being a secret concealed under Samantha's wedding dress...

Marina raised her eyes to the ceiling and inhaled deeply with renewed conviction.

Two for the price of one was even better!

30

As Tina opened her eyes, she cringed with the pounding pain throbbing mercilessly in her head. The next thing to become apparent was when she attempted to raise her hand to gingerly touch the screaming mass that was her skull, she found that not only could she see nothing, but she was unable to move her arms.

Panic spiralled.

What on earth?

All manner of scenarios flashed through Tina's mind. Was she dead? Had a heart attack? Been run over and now she was paralysed and blind?

Oh God! No, no, no!

Tina started to hyperventilate out of pure desperation, before coming to the conclusion that if any of the nightmarish scenarios she'd just considered were true, then she wouldn't be thrashing about, even if it was getting her precisely nowhere. Neither would she notice or care that what she was lying on was hard and uncomfortable, and that she was chilled to the bone.

Wait! The wedding! That van! The big man she was speaking to...

A vivid flash of recollection answered at least some of her questions.

Bile rose in Tina's throat. *Bedworth.* It was Tom Bedworth. He'd whacked her with something and then... then she didn't know...

And what about that fat bloke? Had he raised the alarm or was he with Tom?

Tina felt the sudden urge to check her clothes to make sure they were still in place, but her arms were tightly bound so she couldn't, but she was fairly sure everything was intact.

But Bedworth was dead! She'd seen it in the paper!

A further rush of ice ran through Tina, chilling her already cold body further.

That man with Bedworth – that was Potter Ross. She'd seen a picture of him in an article about the fire in which he and Bedworth had supposedly died.

But they hadn't, had they? They hadn't fucking died at all!

Christ!

Tina willed her eyes to adjust to the darkness of the back of the van. She held her breath. *Was she even in a van? She must be. But for how long?*

With rising horror, she realised the hard metal floor where she lay was wet and, with building shame, knew it was her own urine. She'd wet herself. When, she didn't know. Neither did she know how long she had been in here for.

Her horror grew. Had she been left to die? Had the van been dumped somewhere?

This had to be because she'd gone to the police and told them Bedworth was behind her mother's murder. He'd waited all of this time for the opportunity to get her.

Remembering where she'd been when she'd been clumped, Tina's eyes widened.

Sam. She remembered now. She'd been attempting to get a message to warn Sam about Marina being back in Birmingham.

Dread deepened. Why had Bedworth been in the car park of Sam's reception?

How Tina wished she'd insisted Alan wait for her after all, rather than begging him to do just the opposite and go.

Digging her teeth into her lip, the pain serving as a reminder that she wasn't dead, Tina instructed herself to remain calm. She couldn't die in the back of a van being gradually starved of oxygen, lying in her own piss. She *wouldn't*.

But if this van had been dumped at the side of a road – abandoned, or worse, hidden in woodland, then it could be days – even *weeks*, before anyone stumbled across it or bothered investigating.

Would Alan report her as missing? No. He wouldn't even *know* she was missing...

Cold sweat poured from Tina's aching head, the pounding from within her skull making her nausea worse.

Suddenly hearing a rumble, her breath caught in her throat as her terror exemplified.

The engine had started.

Continuing to hold her breath for want of not knowing what else to do, Tina couldn't stop from rolling against the side of the van, the metal cold against her arm.

The van was moving. But where to?

* * *

'It was sneaky of us to dash off without seeing if anybody was up!' Sam laughed as she stroked Seb's hand.

'I won't lose any sleep over it,' Seb grinned, checking his mirrors to overtake the slow-moving car in front. 'We'd still be at the hotel trying to get away from everyone wanting to talk to us if we hadn't.' He raised an eyebrow. 'I think I even saw Linda running towards us as we left...'

'You didn't?' Sam gasped. 'Oh Seb! We should have sta...'

'I'm only joking, Princess,' Seb said. 'I didn't really see Linda, but you can imagine what it would have been like if I had. No – we've done the right thing. Now I've got you all to myself for two whole weeks!'

Sam shimmered with pleasure. 'Just think – in a few hours from now we'll be on the other side of the world in a tropical paradise.' She shivered with anticipation. 'I can't wait!' She glanced at her watch. 'We have a while before our plane leaves though. We're really early.'

'Once we've gone through security, we'll get some breakfast and toast the start of our honeymoon.' Moving his hand from the gear stick, Seb traced his fingers across Sam's stomach. 'I can't have my baby getting hungry in there.'

Sam nodded. 'Actually, I am really hungry. I should have had something before we left.'

'Yep, but that's what sneaking off at the crack of dawn does for you. We'll be at the airport soon and after we've eaten, I'll treat you to a new bracelet from duty free. Pick any one you like.'

'You've already bought me lots of beautiful jewellery,' Sam said. 'I really don't need any more.'

'Who said anything about *needing* any more? You're my wife and so therefore I can buy you as much jewellery as I damn well want!' Seb winked.

Sam glowed with happiness. Yes, she was Seb's wife now. *Finally.* Mrs Samantha Stoker – a moniker she was proud to own. 'Well, if you insist... But there is something I would really, *really* like right now...'

'Anything you want, Princess,' Seb said, taking the exit towards Birmingham International.

'Pringles.' Sam's face was a picture of mischief. 'I really need some Pringles. Like, *really* need them.'

'I should have known!' Seb's green eyes twinkled. 'Fuck the offer of a diamond bracelet, the Pringles win hands down every time, right?'

Sam nudged Seb playfully. 'If you have such an issue with Pringles, you shouldn't have got me pregnant! I hated the bloody things before this.'

'Out of all the things I've ever done, getting you pregnant is not something I would change for the world. I'll stop at the next garage. They're bound to have some in there.'

Sam beamed, her mouth already watering with the prospect of an extra-large tube of sour cream and chive Pringles to slake her incessant cravings.

* * *

Tom's concentration was being tested to the limit by tailing Seb Stoker's motor, remaining at least three cars behind so as not to be noticeable. He couldn't lose the bastard now. Not after all of this. But Potter insisting on having a one-sided conversation with a person who only existed in his own head was not doing anything to help the overall situation.

'No, like I've told you, he won't specify how we're taking the Reynold bitch,' Potter said. 'I mean, doing that at the airport will be difficult, but he reckons it will happen... Yeah, I know, I'm beginning to wonder that too... I think you're right... I reckon he's lost it.'

Tom's knuckles whitened against the steering wheel. Talking about him to a ghost and saying *he'd* lost it? He'd have laughed if it wasn't so bloody insulting. Still, they were nearly there now and contrary to Potter's lack of faith, his plan would work.

He *would* get Samantha and he *would* blackmail Stoker for her return. It would happen because it had to, and he'd seize the opportunity when it presented itself.

Tom winced with the resuming thumping from the back of the van which frazzled his already frayed nerves. That slut in the back must have become unsecured from the carabiner clips he'd attached the straps through. How the fuck that had happened he wasn't sure. Potter must have jogged his concentration when he'd been shackling her by wittering on about where the rest of his chocolate had gone. *Had the man not been able to see that he'd been bloody busy?*

Indicating, Tom pulled out into the central lane, his eyes watering from being glued to the car in the distance. For God's sake, he was reticent to even blink in case Stoker suddenly disappeared, taking his chances along with it.

That had very nearly happened already. And would have done, had his spot-on instincts not saved the day.

Around 5 a.m. he'd somehow dropped off. It had only been for about ten seconds, yet something within his brain had jolted him awake. The ten seconds he'd been stupid enough to allow exhaustion to overtake him had been the ten seconds which had almost chucked his chances down the toilet.

Blinking blearily into the coming dawn, Tom had seen a car moving down the secluded lane from the function's car park. It was the one belonging to Seb Stoker. Another couple of seconds and the motor would have gone and the next time he opened his eyes, the car he'd spent most of yesterday and the entire night watching would have disappeared – his plan along with it.

Instead, he'd been just in time to start the van. Ensuring Stoker's motor was out of sight before he followed, Tom's heart had clanged in his chest all the way to the turning from the hotel driveway onto the main road, hoping to fuck he'd correctly guessed the route Stoker would take to the airport.

Flooring it along the main road, Tom had been unable to risk drawing a breath until he'd clocked the sight of Stoker's motor a few cars ahead. Only then could he relax enough to take in oxygen.

And he couldn't give a fuck that Potter had been jerked from his slumber by the erratic driving required to catch up.

'No, we're still following him,' Potter continued, stealing an irritated glance at the side of Tom's head. 'Yeah, I know. He's wasting time. All I want is to fuck that bitch into oblivion and then kill her.'

'Can you tell Mark you'll speak to him later?' Tom barked, coming to a halt at the side of the road.

Potter swung around in surprise. 'What the fuck have you stopped for? Where's Stoker?' Lurching from his seat, he wrapped a meaty hand around Tom's throat. 'You've lost him, haven't you, you cunt? I knew you couldn't manage this, you useless bastard!'

'Get the hell off me,' Tom roared, wrenching Potter's hand away from his neck. With his face a livid shade of red, he straightened his leather jacket. 'Don't ever do that again, you hear me? I've just about had it up to here with you!'

Pretending he hadn't just whacked his knuckles on the roof of the car or that it really bloody hurt, he instead continued shouting at Potter. *One more second in here with him was too long.* 'If you'd bothered fucking watching anything going on, rather than speaking to a part of your bastard imagination, you fucking freak, then you'd have noticed that Stok...'

'My brother is *not* in my imagination!' Spittle flicked from Potter's mouth, his face puce-red. 'I should kill you for insinuating th...'

'Move your fucking head!' Tom screamed, using all his force to push Potter out of his line of sight and back into his seat. 'We have an opportunity and we're taking it.' Releasing his handbrake, he continued up the road, indicating to pull into the petrol station up ahead.

'You're getting petrol? Now? You've lost Stoker and...'

'He's in the petrol station!' Tom hissed. 'If he's left Samantha in the car and no one else is on the forecourt, then we take her. But we have to be quick.'

'What? You mean th...'

'Just do what I tell you, for God's sake!' Tom barked, his pulse hammering in his veins.

Pulling onto the Murco forecourt, he scanned the scene. There was no one else around apart from Stoker's motor. And he could see the outline of a passenger in it. 'I'm going to stop at the pump opposite.'

He peered into the Spar attached to the petrol station. *Stoker wasn't in there, so where the hell was he? Ah, wait! There!* 'He's in the shop browsing for something. When I say, go, then go, okay?'

Taking a final glance around for good measure, Tom pulled the van up next to Seb's car, seeing Sam Reynold glance up and through the window. Meeting eyes with him, she offered a small smile before looking away.

Hello, dear deluded daughter, Tom thought, grateful Samantha didn't have a clue who he was. She didn't even know what he looked like.

This was it. His time to shine. His time to get his dues and get out of here for good. But he had to do this fast with no screw-ups. And with Potter in tow, that was a risk. One that he would have to take.

Grabbing the door handle, Tom took a deep breath. 'NOW!'

31

Seb balanced the fifth tube of sour cream and chive Pringles in his arms, but with the selection of magazines he'd picked out for Sam during the flight, he'd drop everything soon. It would have made more sense buying the stuff from WHSmiths inside the airport, but what if they didn't have this flavour of Pringles? He'd never hear the end of it.

He swallowed his smile. Joking aside, none of it was any trouble. He'd do anything for Sam.

He wedged the fifth tube of Pringles under his chin and edged tentatively towards the till. At least at this time in the morning, being the only one in here he wouldn't have to wait in a queue doing a juggling act.

'Shit!'

Hearing the voice, Seb glanced up at the man behind the till. 'What's up, mate?' he asked, gratefully dumping the Pringles on the counter.

'That van!' the man gasped. 'Two men just dragged a woman from that car. They've put her in the back of that van and are driving off with her!'

'*What?*' Seb peered out of the window, seeing the tail-lights of a white Escort van disappearing out of the garage forecourt onto the main road.

An icy chill flooded him. *That was his car! Sam!*

Bolting from the shop, not caring that the Pringles rolled from the counter onto the floor, Seb raced across the forecourt, chucking the magazines still clutched in his hand in the air to flutter down amongst pools of sand and petrol.

Reaching his motor, he yanked open the driver's door, hoping his worst fears hadn't been realised and that the cashier was referring to another car he'd failed to notice. *But there wasn't another car...* 'Sam?' he bellowed. 'SAM!'

The passenger seat, the space where not five minutes before he'd left his new wife and unborn child, was now empty.

Someone – some fucker had taken Sam!

Filled with both raw fear and rage, Seb threw himself behind the wheel. He fired the engine and handbrake turned the car, not giving a shit if he whacked one of the petrol pumps.

He screeched off in the direction the van had taken, hoping he wasn't too late to catch up with the cunt who thought it clever to take his wife.

Taking one hand off the wheel, Seb pulled his gun from underneath the driver's seat, glad he'd not removed it in preparation for leaving his car in the airport's long-stay car park. Because when he caught up with whoever had done this, he'd empty the entire chamber of bullets into the bastard's face.

* * *

Andrew rubbed his hand over his chin, scowling at the stubbly growth which had appeared during the night. Not that he'd slept... Not a bloody wink.

How could he have?

He'd almost keeled over with shock turning around to find Sophie standing with Linda and Seb last night. She'd been the *last* person he'd expected to see. He'd longed to see her, yes, and thought of little else, but he hadn't wanted Sophie to discover that he hadn't told her about himself like *that*.

If he'd been able to explain why he'd initially hidden his real identity to Sophie during a weekend away, they could have sorted it out. It would have been all right, he was sure of it.

But not now...

Andrew had seen the utter horror on Sophie's face as their eyes had met.

Andrew slugged the neat whisky in his glass. He'd already drunk himself sober so another one wouldn't make any difference. But neither would it change anything. It wouldn't remove his pounding headache either. And having Neil and Linda sitting the other side of his hotel room, staring at him with concern, made things even worse.

Turning to hide the emotions that he was too tired to mask, Andrew stared at the wall instead.

Sophie had looked drop-dead gorgeous too. She'd ditched the hair extensions and false lashes, and without the manufactured look many women sought, her natural beauty was a thousand times more stunning. And that emerald-green dress clinging to her curves had set him on fire. If his jaw hadn't already dropped to see her there in the first place, it would have done from that dress.

Going weak at the knees, he'd been *that* close to pulling her into his arms until he'd remembered his cover was blown when Sophie dropped her champagne glass to the floor in shock.

It was at that point he'd left. He'd had to. Seb and Linda had clocked his reaction. Who hadn't? He wouldn't be responsible for diverting anything away from Seb and Sam's special day. Plus, he hadn't known what else to do, but leave.

All night he'd wracked his brains as to how to explain himself. Where would he even bloody start?

But Neil arriving first thing this morning with Linda in tow had made things more unsavoury in ways he hadn't envisaged.

It wasn't just him harbouring things that should have been shared. What he now knew proved this situation was worse than he'd originally believed.

A lot worse...

Regardless of whatever he did, there could be no relationship with Sophie.

Andrew's clenched jaw ached, waves of anger building to such a degree he felt he may explode. He wanted to smash the hotel room up. He wanted to rip the velvet drapes from the mullioned windows and tear the paintings in their heavy gold frames from the walls to slash the canvases to ribbons.

The first time in his life he'd felt there was an option of a future with a stunning woman that he had feelings for, which he hadn't previously believed existed, had turned into a bag of shite.

'Bruv, I can see this has knocked you for six, but you've got to think logically,' Neil said. 'If you truly love this woman, like I reckon you do, then you should go for it.'

Swinging around, Andrew's eyes glittered with frustration. 'How the fuck can I do that? How can you even *suggest* that after what Linda's just told me?' He punched the wall in frustration. 'You think it's okay to get serious with a woman who was part of that business with that bitch, Marina? Sophie was on side with the person who tried to kill Sam, kill Seb and kill *you*! She was part of butchering that one-handed bloke and taking the money that had already been stolen from our safes!'

And from what Linda had said, this also showed it wasn't

Bedworth behind Dan's murder, but *Marina*. Marina had killed Dan in order to lift the money Bedworth had robbed. It just didn't bear thinking about.

Andrew's hand curled into a fist. 'Was I the next stage of the plan? Was Sophie getting with me in order to rob more? Or set us up, perhaps? Yeah, I see... Sophie plays the pickpocket, whilst Marina plays Fagin?'

Linda placed her hand on Andrew's arm. As well as being mistreated by her own daughter, the fact that Sophie had been in a relationship with her ex-husband was also an unpalatable one for Linda. It made her even more determined to ensure no more damage was accrued by the twisted members of her family, if she could call them that.

'Sophie didn't know anything about any of this. Sophie came to Birmingham with my ex, Mickey. She's been dragged into this, love. She isn't part of anything and never has been. She's been living in fear since escaping from Marina and she's already had several beatings at the hands of my ex and Marina. She's terrified. The girl ain't lying, I know that much.'

Andrew snatched his arm from Linda's grip. 'Sophie lied. She didn't tell me anyth...'

'No,' Linda interrupted. '*You* lied. You made out you were some bloke called Waterford who works in a fucking pub! What the fuck was that all about? Sophie didn't lie – *you* didn't ask the questions.' She softened slightly. 'If you had, I suspect she wouldn't have answered anyway because she hadn't breathed a word about this to me and Vera either until last night. The state she was in after seeing you, she had no choice but to tell us. But she didn't lie. And now she's beside herself because she thinks you won't want anything to do with her.'

'Then she'd be right,' Andrew spat, his face twisting with resentment.

'You're a bloody hypocrite, Andrew Stoker. I'm telling you that Sophie is genuine. *Marina* dragged her into this shit and she's been haunted by what she was forced to witness ever since. But she never lied...' Linda folded her arms and glared at Andrew – the stubborn look of matriarchy clear in her eyes. 'I'll tell you something else for nothing, my son. That girl is desperately in love with you. She doesn't give a rat's arse who you are or whether you're loaded or broke. And from what I can see, you're crazy for her too.'

'*Was* crazy for...' Andrew corrected.

'Bollocks! For fuck's sake, if you're okay throwing away the chance of being happy because of that bitch of a daughter of mine, then you're stupid. It would yet again be something *else* Marina has ruined. Life is too fucking short for regrets, so think about that before getting on your high horse and cutting your nose off to spite your face!'

'She's right, bruv,' Neil said. 'And I'm sure Seb would say the same. If you love the woman, you'll ride the storm.'

Andrew paced the room, raking his fingers through his hair. What should he do? He had to think about this. Was this something that could be worked through? Could he trust Sophie after this? Could she trust him?

He didn't know, but Neil and Linda were right about one thing. He *did* love Sophie. Could he throw that away if what Linda said was true and Sophie hadn't been party to this out of choice?

It went against the grain, but whose grain? His or the firm's? Seb had gone against the grain to be with Sam at first. He'd stood his ground and battled *everyone* to be with her, so was it plausible for him and Sophie?

Yanked from the endless round of torturous questions by his ringing mobile, Andrew pulled it from his pocket.

It was Seb. Maybe if he ran this situation past his brother and if Seb was okay with it, then...

Hang on, hadn't Seb left to go on honeymoon?

Andrew scrabbled to answer the call. 'Seb?' Listening, his face paled. 'What? How? When?' His eyes narrowed. 'Jesus! Where? Okay...'

He scribbled a reg plate on a piece of Coombe Abbey headed notepaper from the desk. 'I'll get the call out to our contacts over in that area whilst we're on our way. We're coming now.'

Sensing something was seriously wrong, Neil was already on his feet. 'What is it?'

Andrew snatched his jacket from the chair and shrugged it on. 'Someone's taken Sam.'

'*What*?' Linda screeched. 'What do you mean, "taken" her?'

'That's all I know,' Andrew said. Grabbing his car keys, he nodded to Neil. 'We've got to get to our lockup over that way. We'll meet Seb there.' He pointed at Linda. 'Not you, though. You're going to go and find Vera, Gloria and my parents right now and tell them to leave here immediately and go home. Then everyone must stay put until further notice. Make sure they all understand. And as for the rest of them in this hotel – act normal. No one else can know about this, okay? *No one*!'

Linda nodded, desperate to accompany the Stokers, but she also knew enough that in instances like this, it was more important to obey orders.

* * *

Eyes wide with fear, Sam placed her arms across her stomach as she swung from one side of the van to the other. Terror raged through her in a way she'd never experienced before.

It had happened so quickly: the car door getting yanked open; being half-dragged/half-lifted out of the passenger seat and thrown in the back of the van. The whole process had taken mere seconds. It hadn't warranted enough time to even open her mouth to scream.

What did these men want? It wasn't to take Seb's car, unless one of the men had taken it, whilst the other drove this van? *There were two men, weren't there?*

There was the man she'd smiled at as the van pulled up next to her, but she was sure there was another. It had all happened in a blur and she was no longer able to separate fact from fiction.

And Seb? How she longed for Seb to stop this.

Feeling her bottom lip quivering, Sam knew she had to quit panicking. She would get nowhere or not be able to weigh anything up by asking herself questions with limitless answers.

Keeping one arm around her belly to protect her baby, Sam used the other to stabilise herself against the erratic swinging motion of the van's movement. She breathed deeply so as not to plummet further into the bottomless pit of despair and panic.

She blinked away the dust thrown up from the base of the van as she'd been launched inside to try and accustom herself to the darkness of her surroundings.

Suddenly she became acutely aware she wasn't the only one in here...

'Who's that?' she hissed, her voice tinged with wariness. *Please don't let it be another one of those men...*

As her eyes adjusted, they widened at the sight of a gagged woman strapped to the side of the van. It was a woman she recognised and one she'd been trying to find. 'Tina?' she gasped.

Seeing the woman nod, Sam shuffled over to the other side of the van, her arms reaching out against the metal to hold herself steady. With fumbling fingers, she picked at the knot securing the filthy rag used as a gag. After several failed attempts, she pulled the material away and out of Tina's mouth.

'Thank you!' Tina cried, spitting the taste from her mouth, still not quite able to believe that Sam Reynold had also been taken and slung in the back of this shed on wheels. 'I'm sorry about...' She stopped. *There was hardly point apologising about the four hundred pounds she'd taken now.* 'Are you okay? I came to the wedding to warn you... but... but they took me. They...'

'Wait! Who? Who are these men?' Sam cried, panic rising. 'They took *you* from my wedding? You were at my wedding? Wh...? And trying to warn me? What do you mean? Did you know these men were going to d...'

'No! I thought it was because I went to the police about my mother. You remember? That thing you asked me to do... I...' Tina struggled to control her breathing. There was so much to say and explain. 'But now they've got you too, I'm thinking maybe Marina is part of this and that they're in it together.'

Sam's mind whirred on ultra-fast speed. 'Marina? Marina is here? And in it with who? Wh...?'

'Bedworth and Ross! It's Tom Bedworth and Potter Ross who have us!' Tina exclaimed, her voice struggling to be heard over the loud growl of the engine. 'Marina came in on a plane from Malaga yesterday. I work at the airport now and I lied to get her detained to give me time to warn you. I worked out she was the one who killed Dan, not Bedworth, but...'

'Holy fuck!' Sam gasped. *Bedworth and Potter Ross?* They were dead! Seb burnt them alive! He burnt the Portakabin himself with them in it, so how could they be here?

Dread avalanched, bile rising up her throat. Dry heaving, Sam wrapped her arms back around herself, fear crashing. Losing her hold on the side of the van's wall, she fell hard against the metal. 'They're going to kill us, aren't they?' she sobbed, finally succumbing to the all-consuming fear of what was to happen.

Not for herself – she'd take that on the chin if she had to, but for the very much wanted baby inside her. A baby that would never grow up, robbing Seb of the chance of being a father, as well as dealing with losing his wife.

Sam had never felt more scared or desperate and it threatened to suffocate her.

'They're not going to kill us. We'll think of something,' Tina said determinedly. She'd never thought she'd ever witness Sam Reynold folding.

But now it was obvious what had changed…

Her eyes fell to Sam's arms protectively wrapped around her middle.

32

With sweat pouring down his face, Seb burst back through the doors of the garage and vaulted the counter. Despite giving chase, he'd failed to find that white van even though he'd turned onto the main road, taking the same direction. He'd scouted the nearby area, but the van had vanished. Continuing to look for it like that was wasting time, so there was no choice but to return to the petrol station.

As Seb pinned the man against the wall by his neck, the phone in the cashier's hand clattered to the floor. He couldn't believe this was happening. Some bastard had Sam? *If she was hurt... If their baby was hurt...*

Adrenaline juddered through his veins. 'Have you called the cops?' he roared. *He* would be getting his hands on whoever had dared to take Sam, not the police. He didn't want the place swarming with the filth because he was ripping those bastards to shreds with his bare hands. *Every. Last. Piece.* 'You had the phone in your hand. Did you call them? I need to know!'

The cashier finally found his voice. 'No, well, yes... I...'

'Which the fuck is it?' Seb spat, inches from the man's terrified face. Applying further pressure, he twisted harder against his windpipe. 'Do I have to shove my gun up your arse to help you answer a simple fucking question?'

'I-I pressed the emergency button,' the man blathered, his frightened eyes darting to the red button visible from this side of the counter. 'They haven't come. I was just about to call again when you came back.'

Seb's eyes darted around the room. 'You got CCTV here or on the forecourt?' For added incentive he slammed the man harder against the wall.

'Y-yes, but it's broken. I kept telling Mr Priora to fix it bu...'

'Good. Now tell me what these fuckers who took my wife look like. I need a description. And a bloody good one,' Seb ranted, his ears open for approaching sirens. He'd got the reg of the van and now he just needed a description of the men.

With Andrew getting their contacts over here to keep watch for white vans, there was a chance they could work out where these tossers were heading. Without that, it was like a needle in a haystack.

But he couldn't think like that. He *couldn't*. It would send him spiralling into panic. He had to get Sam back and fast. Nothing could happen to her. He'd promised nothing bad would *ever* happen to her.

Nothing had better happen either because he didn't have the first clue how he could possibly live without her.

Cold sweat ran between Seb's shoulder blades, drenching the back of his shirt as he listened carefully to the description the cashier squawked through his crushed throat. It was a very clear description of both men. And if it was correct, it matched people it shouldn't.

People who had stopped walking this earth a while ago...

With a loud snarl, Seb released the cashier, leaving him to slide down the wall to his knees, clutching at his throat. 'Cheers for your help,' he muttered. 'If the Old Bill do ever turn up, I never returned here, okay?'

Dashing from the shop, he raced to his car. He had to get out of here, meet his brothers and hunt those fuckers down before the police got to them.

* * *

It had taken some wrangling and a shed load of unnecessary money to arrange a hire car at such short notice, especially getting it delivered to her hotel, but Marina hadn't time to quibble.

Eyes narrowing, she flew up the outside lane of the M42. Undertaking any car hindering her ability to maintain a minimum of ninety-five miles an hour, she swerved back and forth between lanes.

She'd do it this way now or not at all. There was nothing else left.

Fuck the bullshit of upping her bank balance. At the end of the day there was only one thing that mattered and that was removing Samantha Reynold from the picture.

Marina knew Samantha and Stoker were getting to the airport for two o'clock in readiness for their flight, so she would be in situ along the route to intercept them. She'd kill Stoker too if needs be, although what happened to him was nowhere near as vital as removing that thing of a sister of hers.

The target – Samantha.

And this time Samantha would die. What happened after that didn't matter.

Marina smiled sourly. She'd even forgo her own life as long as Samantha's was removed in the process.

That was the driving factor in this entire mission now and she couldn't wait any longer whilst the vermin of the world around her kept screwing up the end result.

Sliding across all three lanes of the motorway, Marina careered up the exit slip road at the last minute at junction six for the NEC and the airport.

Almost there, almost there...

She'd wait for the newlyweds to arrive with their precious cargo within her slut of a sister and then she'd strike.

Game on.

Approaching a collection of flashing blue lights, Marina looked for as long as she could in the direction of the Murco petrol station. Something big must have happened there to command such a turnout of Old Bill.

Always appreciative of learning of others' misfortunes, Marina stabbed the buttons of the car stereo, turning the radio volume up. It was on the hour, so the news should be on. She could do with a laugh.

'...And the incident happened this morning at around 5.40 a.m....'

Yeah, yeah. Which incident? Marina thought. This one?

'Police are continuing to search for the whereabouts of a white van containing two males who snatched a newlywed bride whilst the groom purchased items in the garage shop...'

Giving no warning, Marina swerved to the side of the road and stopped, ignoring the blast of horns from disgusted drivers behind. Her long-nailed fingers fumbled with the radio volume again.

'The terrified petrol cashier told of his horror witnessing Samantha Reynold being dragged from her new husband's car and bundled into the back of a van which then swiftly drove away. The registration number of the van is unknown, but the cashier was able to give the police a detailed description of the attackers. The police are also concerned for the welfare of Samantha's husband, Sebastian Stoker – the owner of the Royal Peacock casino in Birmingham – who hasn't been seen since leaving the garage to try and find his wife. Anyone who may have information, please call us here or get in touch with West Midlands Police, who say it's vital that Mrs Stoker is located unharmed as soon as possible.'

Marina thumped the dashboard of the hire car and then pummelled the leather steering wheel.

'I don't believe this,' she muttered, almost choking with anger. *For Christ's sake! She'd been beaten to the post again?*

Slamming her foot on the accelerator, completely oblivious to the oncoming traffic, Marina U-turned the car and headed back the way she'd come.

Unless Samantha was found pretty damn sharpish, there was no point hanging around here.

But what she *really* wanted to know was which fucker had been thinking along the same lines as her?

* * *

Sam squinted against the unaccustomed brightness of daylight as the back doors of the van opened, her stomach lurching into her throat. She blinked at the two men standing in the opening.

'And here they are! Tweedle Dum and Tweedle Dee!' Tom eyed his long-lost daughter and Tina with distaste. 'Hmm, you don't look so special close up and covered in dust, do you, Samantha?' he sneered. 'I'm surprised Stoker bothered marrying you. There wasn't really any need, being as he must have had you God knows how many times by now.' His eyes glinted with malevolent gratification at the flash of anger in Sam's eyes. 'Ooh! Touched a nerve, have I?'

'Stop wasting time!' Potter yanked Tom to one side. He didn't want to delay getting his end away with Samantha. Bedworth's talk of Stoker rutting on the woman was turning him right off.

He lasciviously pushed the aching bulge in his stained trousers. 'Let's get them out of here.'

Sam instinctively backed away as the man's hand reached out to grasp one of her breasts. 'Don't you dare touch me!' she spat, her hatred overtaking her previous wobble of panic.

So this was Potter Ross? And the other pathetic excuse of a man was Tom Bedworth – the despicable creature who she'd wanted to slowly rip to pieces for so long?

Her lips curled in disgust. This foul individual, this greasy pervert, preyed on people like her mother and Tina, and just look at him!

'Don't freak our captives out, Potter.' Tom pulled Sam to the doors of the van by her arm.

Sam ripped away from Tom's grasp. 'Get your hands off me, you sick bastard!' she screamed. 'I know what you did to my mother. Remember her, do you? I also know what you did to Amelia, and Tina and to lots of other women!'

Her eyes narrowed, the hatred she'd harboured for this grotesque excuse of a human being spewing from her mouth in a long overdue torrent. 'You're a disgusting prick! You'll get yours! I'm going to kill you and make you pay for everyth...'

'Shut the fuck up, you stupid spoilt brat!' Tom belted Sam around the face, the sharp backhander sending her crashing against the metal wall of the van. 'You think your sad little threats bother me?' He chuckled coldly, before turning to Potter. 'Get this one out of this van. And no fucking funny business. I need her in tip-top condition for when husband dearest pays up for her.' He jerked his head in Tina's direction. 'Do what you wish with this other slut though.'

Potter's ugly face morphed into a grimace as he pulled Tom to one side. 'Listen, you cunt! I told you, I ain't interested in money. I just want this bitch!' He groped his groin. 'And after I've had her, I want her dead. An eye for an eye. For Mark, yeah?'

'Fuck Mark!' Tom spat. 'Stop pissing about and drag these two into this place.'

He glanced up at the building that would now be used to hold these daft bints.

It was a bit of a shit having to change the plans and think of something else at last knockings, but being as that silly cow from the Aurora's presence had scuppered his plan of using that grotty B&B to house Potter and Samantha whilst he waited for Stoker to bring the money, he'd had to think of somewhere new.

It had been pure genius remembering the place that bloke who'd solved his passport problem mentioned.

At the time, he'd only half-listened to the bloke's ramblings about his brother being off on the standard two-week factory shut-down summer holiday for all workers of Stonehouse Cement Works. Why the fuck would he care about some bloody factory in Coventry? He'd only been interested in getting his hands on the hallowed passport and the mobile phone which he'd parted with a good chunk of cash for.

But now he was glad he'd caught the general gist of what the bloke had banged on about.

Realising no one in the van had moved, Tom swung back to Potter, ignoring the rabid snarl on the man's face. 'I said to get them the fuck out of there, didn't I? What are you waiting for?'

Tina and Sam both scrabbled as far to the back as possible, but it was to no avail. They could do little to stop it as they were both pulled out of the van by their ankles and dragged along the floor towards what looked like an empty factory.

Humming a cheerful tune, Tom hefted a bag of tools from the

van, leaving Potter to effortlessly drag the two women into the empty factory, whilst he followed behind, triumphant.

He'd done it. He'd only gone and done it. He'd got Samantha and now he would get his money.

Tom dumped the holdall of tools to the ground with a clatter and pulled the mobile from his pocket.

This place was just perfect for keeping these two in. And better still, it was in a convenient area. Having to go back to Telford would have taken ages. Ages, he couldn't afford. And with this place being deserted for at least another week, there wasn't a better place to store them. It was out of the way, with not a soul about – exactly what was required to ensure the final part of this went without a hitch.

And, if things flowed smoothly, he'd barely have to hang around here more than a day.

Stoker would fall over himself packing piles of money into a bag ready to hand over in exchange for the thing that Tom had fathered.

Tom studied Samantha who stared at him with the most vicious expression, whilst Potter secured both her and Tina against the wall, their hands raised over their heads like carcasses on a hook.

What a fitting sight...

That girl had definitely inherited that bitch scowl from her whore of a mother. He could almost sense Linda inside Samantha, waiting to get out.

Potter was another issue. That prick couldn't wait to get in. Tom's face screwed up with revulsion. Just imagining Potter's trousers around his ankles was enough to give him nightmares. And if the fat gimp didn't stop groping himself, then he'd personally chop his cock off before the day was out. It put him right off everything.

Shaking his head with annoyance, Tom tapped in the number for the Royal Peacock. He'd made a point of memorising it by heart. 'Shut it, Potter,' he barked, gesturing to the mobile in his hand. 'I'm about to find out exactly how much Mr Stoker loves his wife...'

And after he'd left a message for Stoker at his shitty casino, he'd sit back and wait for the man himself to return his call. 'We all know Stoker will be up for doing *anything* to get back his most prized possession.'

Sam's heart lurched. *Bedworth was calling Seb?* She glanced at Tina. If Seb knew where they were, they would both get out of here unharmed. If anyone could sort this, Seb could.

With renewed confidence, Sam risked a smile at Tina and set about conserving her energy.

33

'When I find out for sure who is behind this, they are as dead as a fucking doornail,' Seb raged, storming into the back room of the lockup. His hands fumbled with the padlock on a cabinet secured behind a floor-to-ceiling unit filled with tools. 'How long will it be before the scouts in the area get word back?'

He pushed his hair which had fallen loose from its usual slicked-back look out of his eyes. 'Sam could be anywhere by now. Fucking *anywhere!*' And nothing came close to the gut-clenching fear running through every fibre.

All the times he'd been close to death; stared down the barrel of a gun; risked his neck – he'd never, *ever* come close to this abject dread.

But this wasn't about him. This was about Sam – his beautiful wife; the love of his life; his soulmate and the mother of his unborn child.

They were about to become a family – a *real* family.

'Christ!' he roared, driving his fist into the cabinet's metal door, the force leaving a dent. 'Where the fuck have those two cunts taken my wife?'

Andrew and Neil exchanged glances. This was worse than bad. Sam being snatched in broad daylight was one thing, but Bedworth and Ross being behind it when they'd believed them dead, another. And learning that Sam was three months pregnant made this whole situation off the scale.

Things could become disastrous if they couldn't get Sam back and fast before anything happened. Revenge was what this was about and what better way for these people to destroy Seb, than by taking the most important thing in his life, whether they realised Sam held an even more precious member of the family in cargo, or not.

If this went wrong or failed...

'Why the hell has no one called with updates yet?' Seb screamed as he loaded guns into holdalls. 'Someone must have seen the bloody van!'

'It's only been half an hour,' Neil reasoned. 'The van probably laid low somewhere and didn't move for a while to avoid detection.' At least he hoped that was the case because a lot could happen in thirty minutes.

A lot could happen in thirty *seconds*. They more than most had experience of just how much damage could be inflicted in a very short space of time.

'Someone will call soon,' Andrew said, the raw terror on his eldest brother's face instilling him with gnawing dread.

Sam's pregnancy made dealing with this rapidly even more imperative. He couldn't be happier for Seb that Sam was having a baby, but if anything happened to her or that child it would kill his brother.

Andrew shook with rage, only imagining how Seb must feel right now. He was more than furious himself. Not just furious – downright raving. 'Bedworth *again*!' he muttered.

How could this happen? Who the fuck was in that Portakabin if it wasn't Bedworth and that fat cunt, Ross? Whose charred bodies had been dug out instead?

How could this have gone so fucking wrong?

'Let the enforcers at both the casinos know to be on their guard. Tell them to be armed and be within all rooms. They can pull their weapons from the licensed cache on site.' Seb nodded to the holdalls. 'These guns here – get them over to everyone else – Linda, Vera, Gloria. *Everyone!*'

Andrew nodded. 'I'll make sure that's done.'

It was only by sheer good fortune that their parents had already flown out this morning to pick up their next cruise, otherwise they'd have even more people to worry about, as well as more questions to be answered...

But he had to get Sophie covered too. As she'd been involved with this – inadvertently or not, thanks to Marina – who may or may not be associated with Bedworth, it was a must.

Besides, Andrew *wanted* Sophie to be covered. Despite the recent revelation, his feelings for her had not dissipated and the thought that she too might become a target nagged. For all he knew, Bedworth could have been watching him and seen him at the pub in Hopwood with Sophie.

Andrew shuddered. Not knowing where or how the enemy would strike, especially one presumed to no longer be a viable contender, made things difficult.

But he couldn't explain the situation with Sophie to Seb right now. Not whilst this shit with Sam was up in the air. They had to find her and return her unscathed. Any other alternative was not an option.

Flinching at the sudden ringing of his mobile, Andrew answered it before the second ring, praying it was intel on a sighting of Bedworth and Ross. *It was.* 'Yep... okay. Nothing since then...? Okay... Cheers, Baz.'

Ending the call, Andrew looked at his brothers. 'That was one of our contacts. The van was eyeballed a few minutes ago on the Birmingham Road, just past Pickford. It hasn't been seen either end since then, so it's stopped somewhere within that location.'

Seb froze. 'The Birmingham Road? Fuck! They could be anywhere. I've lost her, I've fucking lost her. I should have never got out of the bastard car!'

Giving the cabinet another hefty right hand, Seb dropped onto a plastic chair, blood pouring from his knuckles. 'This is all my fault.'

'Pull yourself together! It's not too late and it's not your fault,' Neil barked. Stomping over, he grabbed Seb's shoulders. 'I know the Pickford and Allesley areas. There's an industrial works there. One place in particular – a big old place that's out of the way, so I'm betting they're in there.'

He yanked Seb to his feet. 'We'll go there now and won't leave until we have Sam, okay?'

* * *

'But how long will it be before we get solid news?' Linda wailed, holding on to Andrew's jacket as she trailed him to Gloria's front door. 'Surely you must have news by now?'

'There's no news to give you at present, but I'll let you know as soon as I have some,' Andrew said curtly, freeing himself from Linda's clutches. Seb's strict instructions not to let Linda or anyone know Bedworth had hold of Sam, he more than agreed with.

He nodded to the gun he'd given to Linda. 'Keep that with you at all times and do not leave this fucking house for any reason.'

His eyes moved back along the hallway to the room where he'd left a shell-shocked Gloria sitting like a statue. 'Keep a close watch on her. She ain't of the same ilk as you and we can't have anyone freaking out. The kids are definitely not here?'

Linda clung to the door jamb in desperation. 'No, they're at their friends' until Tuesday, but...'

'I'll be in touch.'

The door shutting in Linda's face behind Andrew signified she'd get nothing more from him. *If something had happened or if Sam... If Sam had been...*

No! She mustn't think like that. Sam would be fine. Seb would bring her home.

Hatred seared along Linda's scalp like wildfire. Not knowing who had her daughter, or why, was the unknown and dangerous variable. Her heart clamoured, feeling it may jump through her rib cage. Seb had to get Sam back. He *had* to.

Angrily wiping away the tears pushing from her eyes, Linda took a deep breath and stared at the revolver in her hand. Yes, she was of a different ilk to Gloria when it came to things like this. She wouldn't hesitate to blast a hole in anyone's head who came to threaten them. She'd happily do the same to that piece of shit who at this precise moment had Sam.

Jutting out her chin in determination, Linda strode along the hallway to the room where Gloria sat, frozen in shock and terror.

Andrew Stoker was right. She'd need to keep an extra-vigilant eye on Gloria. The woman already appeared close to a total meltdown and that would be detrimental to everybody.

However, Linda would stay up every hour of every day keeping watch until Sam's safe return was confirmed.

Whoever had her daughter would not be coming for anyone here. And not get out alive, anyway.

* * *

It was as Neil and Seb approached the outskirts of Coventry that Seb's mobile rang. Scrambling to answer it, for once he was glad Neil had insisted on driving.

'Yes?' he barked. 'What? When? Okay, hang on...' Scrabbling around the centre console, Seb snatched up a pen. Pulling the top off with his teeth, he spat the lid into the footwell. 'Go on...'

He scrawled the number on his hand. 'Thanks.' Ending the call, he turned to Neil. 'That was the Peacock. Bedworth has called and left a number for me to call back on.'

Neil gritted his teeth. *If ever there was a dead man twice, it was Bedworth.* He waited on tenterhooks, barely able to concentrate on the road as Seb keyed in the number.

'Pull over and do the window up,' Seb muttered. 'I don't want this wanker knowing we're on the road.' Grinding his teeth, he willed himself to remain calm when, in reality, if poisonous thoughts could kill, Bedworth would die on impact the second he answered the call.

That's if he answered the call...

'Come on answer, you cunt!' Seb snarled, his nerves frayed. What could be happening to Sam at this very instant to delay Bedworth from answering this call?

His heart lurched as the call connected, his blood firing with white-hot rage at the sound of Bedworth's gravelly voice. 'Where the fuck is my wife?' Seb's knuckles whitened hearing a distinct chuckle down the end of the line. 'Bedworth,' he spat, 'where have you taken Sam and what do you want with her?'

He'd gladly give anything to ensure the safe return of Sam and his child. *Anything.* 'If it's me you want, then you've got it. Just let Sam go.'

His temples pounded at the silence down the line. This bastard was dragging things out for as long as possible to cause maximum stress.

Seb was about to roar again when Bedworth spoke. He listened carefully, every hair on his body bristling. 'Okay... I'll get that together now. Tell me where to come.' He glanced at Neil, giving him a knowing nod. 'Okay... I'll find it... I'll be about an hour...'

He waved away Neil's confusion. He knew what he was doing. 'What? No! Do I look like I would involve the fucking Old Bill? That's correct... Fine... An hour then...'

Seb's eyes glowed with dark menace. 'Oh, and Bedworth? If one hair on my wife's head is hurt, there will be no money. Understand?'

Ending the call, Seb turned to Neil. 'Drive! I know where they are.'

Firing the engine, Neil pulled swiftly off the kerb, the resounding jolt doing nothing to ease his throbbing headache. 'An hour away? Where the hell are they? What happened to the van being eyeballed at th...'

'Don't worry about that. We're actually ten minutes away.' Seb glanced at his watch. 'They're at the Stonehouse Cement Works. And as for the money Bedworth wants, he won't be needing any.'

Bedworth had best be on the level about where he was, because if he got there and found this to be a wind-up, or Sam was hurt...

Swallowing the rising bile, Seb clenched his jaw and concentrated. Sam's safety first and foremost and then Bedworth and Ross were being blasted to smithereens.

This time, they would not return from the dead.

34

Vera stared aghast at the gun Andrew handed to her. 'Are you going to tell me what the fuck is going on?' she yelled. 'From what Linda told me, I'm well aware Sam's missing. I've come back here like you asked, but now you're giving me this? Who the bloody hell has taken Sam and what does it all mean?'

Andrew sighed. First he'd had the Spanish Inquisition from Linda and now Vera was at it? 'Just take it and use it if needs be. I can't tell you anything more. Now I've got to get back to the Peacock.'

And there he would wait for Neil's call to bring him up to speed. *But there was one thing he needed to broach...*

He glanced around the kitchen and out into the hallway, unsure how to go about this. He could have gone to Sophie's flat himself, but he didn't know what to say. His head was still in a mess and there wasn't time to contemplate what to do about her. Not until things had been sorted with Sam.

In the meantime, part of his duty was to keep everyone protected and safe, which included Sophie.

'You need to give me a better explanation, Andrew!' Vera's

heavily lined face wore a formidable scowl that terrified most people. 'You come in here, hand me a gun with glib instructions to gun down anyone who comes to the door. Does that include the fucking postman? Who? Help me out!'

'Don't be a comedian!' Andrew spat, losing patience. 'I ain't in the mood. And... erm... I need you to get Sophie and keep her here with you.' His lips formed a tight line. 'Being as she was involved with Marina and we don't know exactly how or if that evil cow is linked with this, then Sophie could be a target too. I... I want to make sure she's protected.'

'You think I haven't thought of that?' Vera countered. 'Christ, I may not own a casino, but I do possess a brain! I'll make sure she's covered, of course I will! What do you take me for?' She raised an eyebrow. 'So you *do* still care...?'

'Don't read too much into things,' Andrew said, not appreciating being put on the spot. 'I'm just doing my job.'

'I came back here with Vera from the hotel.' Sophie entered the kitchen, unable to look squarely at the man she loved. 'She insisted.'

Andrew swung around at the voice of the woman haunting his dreams.

'See?' Vera snapped. 'Sophie is staying here with me until we hear otherwise.'

Temporarily knocked off kilter, Andrew stared at Sophie. She was still wearing that beautiful green dress, except now the satin was stained along the hemline and knees. Pieces of her glossy hair had become unclipped from the once perfect upstyle and black trails of makeup tracked her cheeks. She looked like she'd been pulled through a hedge backwards twice over.

A wave of protectiveness and love rushed over Andrew, smothering him to a degree where he could no longer think straight. The decision to step back until deciding whether he should fight to be with this woman or not went straight out of the window.

His immediate and only reaction the second he clapped eyes on her was to wrap her in his arms; protect her from everything that could ever befall her and never let her out of his sight again.

The desperation Seb must feel about Sam's safety resonated and Andrew realised that regardless of anything, he had to be with Sophie. The thought of not seeing her again or something happening to her made him sick to the core.

Before he could question himself he moved towards Sophie, tugged by an invisible magnet.

Without saying a word, he pulled her into his arms and crushed his mouth onto hers. The taste of her lips drawing him past the point of no return.

With the air pushed from her lungs at the unexpected kiss, Sophie swayed when Andrew pulled his mouth away from hers. *Did this mean they still had a chance? Or was this goodbye?*

'I'm sorry...' she whispered, her soul ripping loose with fear over what could happen to Sam, as well as the devastation of losing this beautiful man who had walked into her life.

She buried herself against his shirt, the thundering of his heart loud. Her fingers clutched at the back of his jacket. 'I should have told you about the situation with Marina. I-I didn't know the significance until last night when I realised who you really were.'

'I should have told you about that myself...' Andrew traced his thumb over Sophie's bottom lip, the pain on her face throwing his intentions of pulling away to the bottom of a lift shaft. The pull was too strong to fight logic. His heart told a very different story – a heart which hadn't ever had a say.

Sophie couldn't tear her gaze from Andrew's deep green eyes, even though her shame at the position she'd placed herself and him in burnt brightly. 'B-but what happens now?' She hardly dared ask the question. She wanted to ask it as it had plagued her since the moment he'd turned to face her at the wedding reception, but she was equally scared of the answer. *What if it was one she couldn't live with?* 'What happens with me...? With us...?'

Andrew searched Sophie's face – the truth of Linda's words plain to see. Whether anyone else accepted it, given the circumstances, he didn't know, but he didn't care. What he felt was too powerful not to grab with both hands. 'I don't know what's going to happen,' he said. 'But we'll work it out.'

He was unsure exactly how, but what he *did* know was that he would fight tooth and nail if he had to. But before he could do that, there was a situation which had to be resolved first, come what may. 'I've got to go. Listen to what Vera says. I'll be back as soon as everything's under control, okay?'

Sophie reached after Andrew, but he was already at the door.

Without looking back, knowing if he saw the pleading desperation in Sophie's face for him to remain, then it would be almost impossible to leave. And he had to. *For Sam.*

He nodded to Vera. 'Look after her.'

As the door slammed and Andrew's heavy footsteps resounded along the concrete hallway outside, gradually fading to nothing, Vera inspected the gun in her hand. 'I guess that answers your question? Andrew Stoker ain't going nowhere.'

Sophie leant against the kitchen table, her eyes drawn to the gun in Vera's hand, and only hoped her friend was right on this one.

* * *

'Did you hear what he fucking said, Mark?' Potter raved, stomping around the cavernous expanse of the cement works, his voice and footsteps echoing off the tall walls. 'Bedworth has ruined everything. A bloody hour? That's all I've got?'

Sam and Tina glanced at each other in confusion as Potter continued ranting to someone unknown.

Tom felt his irritation for the imbecile he'd been lumbered with for far too long escalating out of proportion. *Stoker was coming and then he would have his money. End of.*

His eyes glinted. Potter could rant all he liked, but this was happening the way he'd said. And Stoker had best do exactly what he'd stated, otherwise there would be no Samantha to take away with him.

But it wouldn't come to that. Stoker had *far* too much to lose, which is why the demands had been taken up the shitter and the man had jumped straight onto it. Exactly how Tom knew he would.

You see, your patience has finally paid off, he thought. This was working. It really was. Then he'd be free!

Sam watched Potter mumbling and looking up into the darkness towards a ceiling invisible from ground level, so high in order to house a massive vat of continually mixing cement. As he spun on his heels, his beady eyes meeting hers, her stomach lurched with what she saw in them.

Seb was coming. An hour Tom had said. Fear rolled in waves. *An hour was a long time...*

Swallowing the terror stuck in her throat as Potter drew nearer, Sam tugged against her restraints to no avail. She was trussed so tightly to the wall she couldn't move. Couldn't protect herself. *Couldn't protect her baby.*

'Stay away from me!' she shrieked as Potter began undoing his trousers, her fear overflowing. 'I mean it! Stay the fuck away!'

With drool hanging from his mouth, Potter groped inside his

trousers, readying himself. 'What can you do about it, bitch?' he snarled, his arousal overtaking him. 'It's not like you can move!'

Sam glanced at Tina, seeing the same horror and fear reflected back at her. *This beast was going to rape her.*

Turning at the commotion, Tom dragged Potter backwards, the force taking him off guard. 'What have I told you?' he roared. 'I need her in good nick otherwise we won't get the money. Don't be a fucking idiot!'

'Fuck you, Bedworth!' Potter yelled. Regaining his footing, he swung his fist in Tom's direction. 'They was *your* rules, not mine! I'm having revenge for Mark and I'm having it now! I'm fucking her and after that, I'm killing her. Forget what *you* want! And we're not staying here waiting for that wanker to show up either. I'm taking her and keeping her somewhere for a while until I'm done. Do what you like, but she's not going back to Stoker!'

Sam heaved, the prospect of what was set to happen too much to bear. *What about her baby?*

Potter and Tom grappled with each other for control. Potter was bigger than Bedworth, so surely he'd overpower him and then...

'He can have me,' Tina hissed. 'I'll tell him to take me instead.'

With difficulty, Sam twisted her head to face Tina. 'What? You can't! We need to drag things out. Seb will be here soon. He won't let this happen. He'll stop this and then we'll both get out of here and...'

'He won't reach us in time,' Tina said matter-of-factly. There was little point clinging to false hope. 'You heard what was said – he's an hour away, so if this fat bastard wants a shag, then let it be me. I don't care.'

'No!' Sam looked back at the two men rolling on the floor still shouting and wildly throwing punches. Seb had to get here. She couldn't do this. Nor could she let Tina take her place. 'You can't do this!'

'I *can*,' Tina insisted. 'Why not? Think about it. I've lost everything – Dan, my job – the lot! But *you* haven't. There's still a chance for you.'

Sam floundered, her panic mounting. 'It isn't right that y...'

'What's right got to do with it? You're pregnant and don't say you're not because you are, I can tell. Besides, shagging another ugly bastard isn't anything new, so I'll cope with it,' Tina lied.

Having to give herself to men she didn't want had been the main part of her previous job description. That life was supposed to be over, but this was necessary and the only way. 'If he takes me, it will buy us time. Seb will be closer by then.' *At least she hoped that would be the case.*

'But...' Sam's words cut off as Potter lumbered out of nowhere, leaving Bedworth on the floor.

She shrieked in pain as Potter wrenched her head to one side.

'Chat time's over!' Potter snarled, saliva spraying into Sam's face. 'Now I'll show you what a *real* man feels like.' His hand lunged underneath Sam's skirt.

'Have me instead!' Tina shouted. 'You can have me.'

Potter's hand froze midway up Sam's thigh. He laughed loudly. 'You? What the fuck would I want you for?' He eyed Tina with disgust. 'You're an ugly tramp. A whore. I don't want you! I want *her*!'

Sam's legs kicked out as Potter shoved his hand higher, his other hand freeing himself from his trousers.

And then both Potter and his hand disappeared.

'I told you to fucking leave it!' Tom bellowed, standing over Potter who was now lying at Sam's feet.

Momentarily disorientated from whatever he'd been bashed over the head with, Potter looked up. His confusion didn't last long.

Emitting a low growl, he scrabbled on the floor, righting his bulk to get back to his feet. 'I'll kill you, Bedworth. Didn't take you long to jump to her defence! I knew you would in the end, you fucking traitor!'

Dust from Potter's scrabbling feet bloomed in clouds. 'Just because she's your daughter doesn't mean you can change your mind now!'

'Shut it, you retarded lunatic,' Tom snarled.

Sam listened in amazement. *Daughter?* Potter Ross really was insane. He should be in a specialist hospital where he could get help.

All Tom could concentrate on, short of the blood running from the gash on the side of Potter's head to congeal in his thick eyebrows, were pinpoints of white rage dancing behind his eyes. Potter was not ruining this. He'd put up with months of the fat bastard's madness, dragging him down and fucking things up. The cunt wasn't removing his ticket to freedom at last knockings.

Stoker was on route and Tom wasn't so demented not to know that when the man realised his wife had been defiled, the deal would be off. There would be no money and everything would go to shit.

That was not happening.

Potter's madness had driven him to the point of distraction for too long and it stopped now.

Tom glanced around him in desperation before realising what he still had in his hand. He could only hope it still worked after connecting with Potter's lump of a skull.

When Potter got to his knees, emitting a guttural roar as he lunged for Tom's legs, it wasn't a difficult decision to make and Tom wondered why he hadn't done it before.

The only thing spoiling his enjoyment of emptying the industrial nail gun into Potter's face was the earsplitting screeching emanating from the women attached to the wall.

Sam's stomach roiled as tens of long nails blasted into Potter Ross and he keeled over onto the concrete floor. The strange howling coming from his slack mouth turned her blood to ice.

Tina's screaming paled in comparison to the noise clanging inside Sam's own head at the sight of what was going on.

Whooping with joy at Potter looking like something out of a bad spoof of *Hellraiser*, Tom jumped from foot to foot merrily and then stepped forward. *Potter was still trying to get up and fight him, the stupid cunt?* 'You're finished, you fucking loser.' Pressing the nail gun hard against Potter's chest, Tom found it almost orgasmic as nails discharged in their dozens. Potter wasn't going anywhere now.

But the wailing continued. The bitch screeching was making Tom's fucking head bleed. He couldn't think. Couldn't catch his thoughts and he needed to be on the ball for when Stoker arrived.

He feverishly glanced at his watch. Still forty-five minutes to go. More than enough time to get his head straight. But only if this wailing slut shut the fuck up.

Swinging around, he glared at Tina. 'Shut up. Shut the fuck up!' he roared, the volume of his own voice so loud it hurt his throat. *She had to be quiet.* 'Shut. Up. Shut. The. Fuck. Up!'

Tina didn't shut up. She didn't stop at all. The sight of the man blitzed with nails was so revolting, so hideous that the memories of finding Dan's body in her hallway, his head all but decapitated, returned to flash in strobe-like images.

As her screaming raised in pitch, she vaguely noticed Sam out of the corner of her eye, but her vision was tunnelling fast.

Tina didn't even see Tom raise the nail gun. She didn't see it at all.

35

'Just bloody wait!' Neil yelled, reaching over to prevent Seb from opening the passenger door. He'd barely stopped the car before Seb was chomping at the bit to get out. He couldn't blame him, but going in all guns blazing could make things worse.

Seeing the steely glaze of determination in his brother's eyes, Neil knew he had little hope of holding back Seb's formidable strength, especially when fuelled by something so intrinsically personal. 'Seb! Hold off. You must hold off!'

Ripping out of Neil's grip, Seb glared at his brother, his eyes wild. 'How the fuck do you expect me to sit here and wait whilst that pair of cunts do God knows what to my wife and child?'

He lurched back to the door handle, loose hair flopping over his eyes. Neil wanted him to wait? Fuck that! He was going in to rip Bedworth and Ross to shreds with his bare hands. He'd...

'You could be walking into a trap – a fucking setup,' Neil cried, his hand gripping Seb's forearm once again. 'We can't help Sam if we're dead. Think about it! Give me thirty seconds to weigh things up. If it's a trap, then I'll be the one to cop it, but you'll still be alive to deal with them, so just fucking wait!' Sensing a chink of hesitation as his words rang true, he leant over to grab Seb by the shoulders. 'Look at me! Seb, look at me.'

Seb faced Neil, his eyes glittering with rage as well as dread for what he might find inside this cement works. *His worst nightmare? Nothing? What?*

His heart hammered, sweat pouring down his brow. Neil was right. They would be no use to Sam if Bedworth killed them before they could do anything. He jerked his chin, giving the nod to go ahead and scout. 'Thirty seconds, but after that I'm going in.'

Not waiting for Seb to change his mind, Neil jumped from the car and hastened to the building looming in front of him.

With any luck, being as they were over half an hour early, no one would be looking out waiting for their arrival. But he'd have to be quick. Seb would already be counting down the seconds of the allotted thirty.

He glanced around, unsure where to start. They could be anywhere.

He glanced back towards the motor, seeing the outline of his brother still seated inside, then made his way to the biggest and closest, most accessible building. Attempting to put himself in Bedworth's head, he deduced this building was the most likely place where Sam would have been taken. Bedworth wasn't the type to expend more energy than necessary.

Glancing around again for anyone watching and finding no one, he headed towards a long, thin, yet dirty window near the ground floor. If he climbed part of the way up that fire escape, he should be able to see something inside.

Edging his way along the brickwork, keeping as close a profile as possible, Neil flattened himself against the wall and threw his leg over the metal balustrade of the fire exit.

Clambering up three steps, he extended his body as far as he could to the left, which gave him a partial view through the cloudy glass. Closing one eye to block out the reflection from behind, he focused.

Neil almost overbalanced over the metal rail. 'Fuck!' he hissed.

Although his view wasn't great and the cavernous expanse was barely illuminated, he could see a large figure on the floor surrounded by a dark pool of liquid spreading out in a big radius.

Bile rushed up his throat. The guy was a hideous mess, peppered with God knows what. 'Christ!' he muttered, clinging to the metal banister.

But there was more... Someone else...

Someone was attached to the wall – a woman, strung up like a pig – a shock of hair caked in blood hanging down over her face. *Sam?*

Oh God, no!

Neil's hand shot to his mouth, his head turning in the direction of the car only to see Seb striding towards him, shotgun in hand and a murderous expression on his face.

Oh Jesus, this would kill his brother. Torn between intercepting Seb and looking back through the glass, Neil chose the latter, spying something else...

He clambered down from the fire escape and rushed to meet Seb. 'Ross is dead,' Neil panted. 'And there's a woman... She's...'

'Sam?' Seb's face blanched. 'She's fucking dead, isn't she? I can see by your face that she's dead. Where's Bedworth? I'll fucking kill him. I'll...'

'Sam's not dead!' Neil raced after his brother as he stormed towards the door. He grabbed Seb's arm. 'Wait!'

Seb swung around as Neil grabbed his arm, his eyes narrow slits. 'If you don't get the fuck off me, I'll blow you to pieces first!'

Ignoring the threat, Neil pressed on. 'Listen! Sam's alive. It's another woman that's not!' The faceless woman hanging from the wall he *had* thought to be Sam for a few seconds. Those seconds had passed excruciatingly slowly. 'It's someone else, do you hear me? Sam is still alive!'

Seb blinked, his eyes blind with panic. 'You've seen Sam? In there? She's alive?' His pulse raced perilously fast, the blood rushing in his ears.

'Yes, she's alive,' Neil confirmed. 'Bedworth's there too. At least, I presume it's him.'

'Right!' Seb cocked his shotgun and glanced around the outside of the building. 'We're going in and taking that cunt by surprise.'

* * *

Sam couldn't stop shaking – her whole body trembling uncontrollably. Gulping in big lungfuls of air, she fought to calm her panic, but failed as shock, fear and utter devastation washed over her in torrents.

She wanted to scream – scream and scream and scream and never stop, but she couldn't stop her mind from spinning in fast circles from one thing to another.

Her eyes darted to the dead body of Tina suspended from the hook next to her and her heart cracked.

Tina had died to save her. She'd lost her life to buy more time.

This was wrong. So fucking wrong.

Sam pulled against her restraints, but found her arms unresponsive after being tightly bound for so long. Panic swirled higher. *Was her baby okay? Had the shock caused damage?* She longed to touch her bump, but couldn't.

The sudden movement of Tom Bedworth below her snapped Sam back to the stark reality that this was not anywhere near over. *And unless Seb hurried up, it wouldn't be.* She had no idea how much time had passed since that phone call. Time was not moving in a normal way and every second felt like an hour.

Stiffening as Bedworth approached, Sam bristled – every fibre, alert. 'Do not touch me. Don't even...'

'I've no need to lay *that* kind of hand on you, girl,' Tom snarled. 'I'm getting you down off the wall.' He looked impassively into his daughter's face. 'We don't want your husband to get the impression you've been mistreated. Because you haven't...' He nodded to the body of Potter Ross. 'And the reason that didn't happen is because *I* ensured it didn't. You should be grateful.'

'Grateful?' Sam spat. 'You killed Tina, you piece of shit. You...' A quick backhand reminded her that she wasn't the one in control here.

'Shut it, you spoiled bitch, or you'll get another one. Now hold still whilst I get you down,' Tom snarled.

'You lay another hand on her and I'll blow you to fucking smithereens!'

The voice Sam immediately recognised as Seb's by the first syllable echoed around the massive space. Her heart leapt. *Seb! He was here!*

Her stomach lurched with relief, quickly replaced by fear. What if Bedworth attacked Seb like he had Potter Ross? 'Seb! He's got a nail gun.' Her eyes darted around the shadows unable to see her husband. 'Seb?'

Snarling, Tom span about, also looking for his nemesis in the darkness, missing the split-second warning as Neil darted from the other direction to tackle him to the floor.

Sam watched the scene unfold, tears cascading down her cheeks.

Seb stepped forward, his face awash with distress. 'Thank Christ you're okay!' Releasing Sam from her tethers, he lifted her to the ground. Supporting her body, he folded her in his arms. He pressed her against his chest. 'Princess,' he breathed with relief, his lips pressing against her hair. 'You're okay. Thank God you're okay.'

Sam whimpered through her sobs. 'He's killed Tina. He...' Seb couldn't think about Tina, Potter or anyone else. He wouldn't even question where Tina had materialised from and why. She was past help anyway and now Sam was safe, there was only one person he wanted to deal with.

Satisfied that Sam's legs had recovered sufficiently to take her own weight, he gently lowered her into a plastic chair. 'Are you happy for me to deal with this piece of crap?'

His eyes tracked to Bedworth pinned under his brother's weight and jerked his head for Neil to release his prey. 'Get up, Bedworth!'

'Whoa!' Tom scrabbled off the floor. 'We had a deal.' He nodded towards Sam. 'As I promised, you've got her back. You can see she's unharmed.'

'The deal's off,' Seb hissed, as he raised his shotgun. 'It was never on...'

Sam pushed herself out of the chair, hoping her legs would hold. 'I have something to say bef...'

'See? She ain't like you, Stoker. My daughter has morals,' Tom sneered, deciding he had nothing to lose but use the truth Potter had previously uncovered. It just might be enough. He should have realised Stoker would welch out of the deal. 'The girl ain't going to forgive someone who kills their father, so think carefully before you pull that trigger.'

Regardless of the graveness of the situation, Seb couldn't help but laugh. He laughed loudly and coldly, rolling his eyes at Neil for effect. 'Daughter? Is there no part of you, Bedworth, that isn't fucked? I thought Ross was supposed to be the resident crazy, yet you're scraping the barrel coming out with something as ridiculous as that!'

The mirth fell from Seb's face as quickly as it had appeared. He realigned the gun. 'Now, back to where we were...'

Tom caught Sam's eyes before he next spoke. 'Are you sure it's so ridiculous, Stoker? Maybe you should ask my dearest ex-girlfriend?' His voice held that all-knowing sneer he loved to use when he knew was 100 per cent correct. *And on this one, he was.* 'Ever wonder why Linda was kept in the attic at the Aurora? Because she was trying to stiff me, that's why. Trying to keep me away from my daughter.'

That might be the biggest blag in the world, but Stoker would blast that fucker into him any second, sending him to Kingdom Come, so it was worth a try. The wildcard of bargaining chips.

If he convinced Samantha that what he was saying was the truth – the *real* truth, then even if it didn't get him off the hook, it might buy him time to escape.

He had to try something.

Tom glared at Potter's mangled body. This was all *his* fault. If the fat prick hadn't trussed Samantha up, Stoker wouldn't have his knickers in so much of a twist.

Getting to his feet, Tom casually brushed the dust from his jeans like he didn't have a huge problem with the shotgun aimed in his face.

Plastering on a sorrowful face, he met eyes with Sam, bolstered to see her face awash with confusion. 'I only wanted to get to know my daughter, but Linda wouldn't allow it. That's why I tried to get her away from the situation, so I could get to know Sam.'

Seb's mouth twisted with rage. *This prick thought he could mess with Sam's head, the stupid bastard?* 'Nice try, Bedworth. Linda already told us she knew you from years back, but you know as well as I do there's nothing more to it than that. Sam won't buy this. You think talking shit will change what you've done to her; to Linda; to *everyone?*'

'Shit, is it?' Tom raised an eyebrow. 'Really? And Linda's not a liar? She's never lied to *you*? Or to you, Samantha...?'

'For Christ's sake!' Moving behind Tom, Neil grabbed both his arms. 'No one wants to hear any more of this desperate bullshit!'

'Exactly. I for one have more than had enough,' Seb said.

Sam listened to the words issuing back and forth. Linda *had* lied on more than one occasion, but that didn't mean anything in *this* particular situation.

A dull thudding ramped up inside her head as she found herself looking – actually *looking* at Bedworth for similarities to herself.

What was she doing? Why was she even giving his ludicrous statement the time of day?

Linda would have told her if there was any truth to this, regardless of how much Bedworth was her prime and most wanted target.

Giving Neil a knowing look, Seb waited as his brother locked his arms around Tom's neck, then followed up by shoving the barrel of the shotgun in Tom's mouth. 'I wanted to drag this out because you deserve to die slowly like the fucking vermin you are, but now I can't be arsed. You've taken up enough of everyone's time.'

Sam's voice projected calmly and loudly, amazing herself that she was successfully presenting herself as being collected, when inside she was melting. 'Not that it's any of your business, Bedworth, but my mother hasn't lied. I know who my real father is. He's...'

'Don't explain anything to this piece of dirt, Sam,' Seb interjected, yanking the barrel from Tom's mouth.

Sam nodded. She knew that, but wanting to prove the point, continued. 'My real father is a man called Thomas Vaughan.'

Tom laughed, enjoying the surprise reaction on Samantha. He had to give Linda credit for trying to winkle herself out of this one.

'Something fucking funny, Bedworth?' Neil snapped. If Seb didn't hurry up and finish this bastard, then *he'd* do it.

Still chuckling, Tom shook his head. 'Oh, you really are a poor deluded fool, Samantha. But yeah, you're right – Linda didn't lie. *My* name is Thomas Vaughan. Thomas Vaughan Bedworth. I always hated that middle name...'

Sam was about to hit back with a retort, but stopped. Potter had referenced Bedworth being her father too. It couldn't be right?

Seeing Sam floundering, Seb stepped forward and raised the gun once more. He should never have taken it out of this fucker's mouth. 'That's enough bullshit. You're fucking done, Bedworth.'

Through her swirling mind, Sam watched Seb apply pressure to the trigger. 'Stop!'

This was too much. Today had been too much. Tina dying to save her. And Potter...

Her eyes tracked back to the horrific remains of the man near her feet and she gagged. He'd been *that* close to raping her... Her hand fell to her belly. She couldn't take any more. Not today. She had to think of the baby.

Feeling an unwanted rush of tears, Sam knew the last thread of holding herself together had just snapped. 'I said stop!' she screamed.

Seb froze, his eyes darting to Sam. He held the shotgun out to her. 'Sorry, Princess, I thought you'd prefer I finished this bastard after everything you've dealt with today. But I know how much reason you have to be the one to do it because of Linda and...'

'No! Just stop!' Sam fell to her knees, the weight of the last few hours hanging like an unbearable burden around her shoulders that crushed her to the floor. Tears poured down her cheeks.

Was she being weak? Not getting on with what was required?

Probably.

All she knew, was that she couldn't witness any more death today. Not here and not now. The walls and ceilings of this immense building felt like they were closing in, trapping her and sucking the oxygen from her lungs.

'I've got to get out of here!' Her voice raised to fever pitch. 'I want to leave this place!'

Neil exchanged glances with Seb at this unexpected outburst from Sam.

'Hold him,' Seb growled to Neil. He then rushed to Sam and pulled her from the floor. 'I'll sort this, babe. You don't have to look. I...'

'No! I just want to get out of here.' Sam pummelled Seb's chest before flopping against him. 'I can't do this today... I-I can't stand any more...'

Seb tightened his jaw. Regardless of how much he wanted to finish Bedworth and this whole thing right now, he wouldn't have Sam any more distressed. Not with the baby. 'Okay, Princess. Whatever you want.'

'*What*?' Neil shrieked, aware Tom was wearing a look of triumph. 'You're letting this cunt walk?'

'Am I fuck!' Seb spat as he steered Sam towards the door. 'Keep him here whilst I take my pregnant wife home. *Then* we deal with Bedworth.'

36

Making sure he kept one hand firmly clutching Sam's, Seb wedged his mobile phone in his neck and headed as fast as he could from Coventry back to Edgbaston, hoping there was no need to change gear for a while.

He glanced at Sam, concern overtaking the combined exhaustion and relief on his handsome face. 'You're sure you're all right? And the baby?'

Sam managed a small nod, not trusting herself to speak. *Was she okay?* It depended how she looked at it. From what she could tell, physically, yes, but as for mentally... That was different.

Too many things had happened in the space of a few hours and her ability to think straight was stripped bare. She felt naked, exposed, a failure...

If only she'd kept things together just that little bit longer. If she'd controlled the meltdown drowning her at the end and bided her time just a few minutes longer, this would be over. Yet now, because of her, Bedworth was still breathing, whereas Tina, Amelia and all those other people weren't.

Why had she lost it? It wasn't like her.

Perspiration soaked the back of Sam's filthy top, overlying the rest of the sweat that had liberally dripped from her skin these past few hours. She must look a right state, but that was the least of her problems.

It was almost impossible to comprehend that only this morning she'd been set to jet off to a lush tropical paradise with her new husband. Had her wedding only been yesterday? It felt like another lifetime had passed since then.

'You definitely want to go to Gloria's, rather than home?' Seb asked, aware Sam was trapped in a world of her own. Whatever happened, he had to get her somewhere safe. Somewhere where no more harm could come to her.

The memory of thinking her dead still rushed up and down his veins like needles. Once he'd got her safely inside with Gloria and Linda, he'd head straight back to the cement works. Bedworth would die before this day was out.

'Sam? You want to go to Gloria's?' Seb repeated. 'You'll be safe there. I'm about to call Andrew. I need to bring him up to speed.'

'Yes, I want to go to Gloria's.'

Nodding, Seb set his phone to call Andrew who answered before the second ring.

'I've got her. She's safe and unharmed... No, Neil's still with him. Yeah... long story... I'm taking Sam to Gloria's. Listen, I need you to call Baker. I want him to put out a press release.' Seb glanced at Sam. 'Tell him to say the petrol station bloke lied about Sam being taken.'

He gave Sam's hand a quick squeeze. 'Oh, I dunno. Tell him to say the petrol station wanted fame and extra business. Whatever it takes.'

It was the best thing to do. More now than ever, Sam didn't need hounding by the press. Making out the cashier was lying was the perfect solution. It was also the only way he could cover getting rid of Potter Ross's body, as well as Tina's. And of course, Bedworth's, who would join them shortly.

This was Baker's final chance to redeem his previous fuck-ups.

If the police continued investigating and Baker didn't make the rest of the force believe it was a staged stunt, courtesy of a disgruntled petrol cashier, then things would be uncovered which would prove hard to gloss over.

'Is everything okay at the casinos?' Seb nodded, hearing confirmation from his brother. 'Okay, yeah, if you could. I'll see you in a bit.'

Ending the call, Seb squeezed Sam's hand reassuringly. 'Once we're at Gloria's, I'll send guards to police the house and grounds whilst I deal with Bedworth.'

'No!' Sam cried. 'I don't want anyone else there.'

Seb shot Sam a sideways look whilst trying to keep his eyes on the road. 'You must have guards. I need to get back to the cement place and with what you've told me about Marina th...'

'I don't want guards!' Sam shrieked. 'I need some space to process what happened today.' She looked at Seb beseechingly. 'I understand why you want them, but Tina said Marina was detained at the airport. She's probably still there. I know what you've asked Baker to do, but the press could still turn up. They'll see the guards and know that it actually *did* happen.'

She began to shake. 'The last thing I need is them poking their noses in. If people learn someone succeeded in taking me, then it won't be the last time.'

Her hand moved to her belly. 'Any fucker thinking they can take us on will attempt the same thing. How can we let that happen? Our child has to come first.'

She just needed a breather – a bit of undisturbed peace to realign herself and then she could do what was needed.

Even though all she wanted to do was to go to bed and lie

down, her mind would not allow respite. 'Please Seb, I can't have strangers around me at the moment.'

Seb sighed. He wasn't slightly happy not installing his best men to keep watch over Sam, but she had a point.

Even once Baker had put the fake story out, the press was sure to turn up wanting a comment and he didn't want the truth getting out for both of their sakes. Neither did he want to add to Sam's overstressed state of mind. 'I'm not happy about this, but if that's what you want.'

'It is,' Sam mumbled. Next she had to convince Seb to leave Bedworth alone for the time being. There was only one thing in her mind where that bastard was concerned and that was that *she* should be the one removing him from the planet.

And that she would do as soon as her head was straight. A few more hours wouldn't make any difference.

* * *

Hunched over the radio in her hotel room, Marina fiddled impatiently with a false nail gradually working itself loose. Most of the day she'd been stuck here not knowing what else to do, short of waiting for updates on the 'Samantha Reynold Is Missing', headline which had gripped the region.

For Christ's sake, like Samantha needed any help in bolstering her pseudo-celebrity status!

It should have been *her* in the limelight all these years, Marina thought. She naturally emanated that kind of status and positively revelled in attention, whereas Samantha purposely shied away from it.

The stupid cow most likely believed herself above it.

But how pissed off was Marina to think someone else had taken for themselves what she'd spent all this time dreaming of?

No one else had the right to snuff out Samantha's nasty little light, apart from *her*.

She was blood. No one else.

Even acknowledging the bloodline connection made her sick to the end of her toes.

Marina glared at the metal case on her bed. What a waste of time and effort getting that had been.

She half-heartedly poured the remains of a bottle of hotel wine into her glass. She was damned if she would go down to the bar with those sad, lonely businessmen and greasy singletons looking for hook-ups. She had better things to do.

At least she *should* have better things to do...

The question now was how long she waited for Samantha to be found – or for the *body* to be found...

There had been no word from the Stokers via the press: no statement – nothing. The trail was cold, so all she could do was wait.

Marina chewed the inside of her cheek. It was so bloody frustrating. People went missing and didn't turn up for days – weeks even. Samantha might *never* turn up...

Although that thought sat nicely in her mind, it didn't have the same effect of it being *her* behind it. If she had been, she'd be the only person in the world to know what had really happened to wipe Samantha off the face of the earth. Only *she* would have had the joy of witnessing the terror on her sister's face. Only *she* would have been party to Samantha's last words – hearing her sickening voice, begging and pleading for mercy. Saying that she was sorry and wishing she could turn back time...

Well, it was too late, because some other fucker had taken that enjoyment away.

Marina's lips curled into a snarl.

She only realised her hands had turned into fists when her pointed nail extensions dug into her palms.

She couldn't sit in this dump of a hotel for ever. She would have to draw the line at some stage. Every day spent waiting to chase a target which may now be unattainable was a day not living the nice life she'd built for herself in Marbella.

Perhaps she should concentrate on ploughing her energy into what she could take from Carlos instead?

But that wouldn't bring the same gratification from taking Samantha, therefore she'd allow herself another forty-eight hours before making a decision. Whether that resulted in her getting revenge on Samantha or not, before hopping back on the plane to Marbella she'd take a detour and hunt down that bitch, Tina.

That little cow setting the seed, resulting in her missing the wedding in the first place, couldn't go unpunished.

Hearing the jingle signifying the radio news, Marina sat forward, her senses alert. *Come on! There must be an update now?*

She turned up the volume, not caring if the people next door didn't want to listen to it.

'...A statement has just been issued by the West Midlands Police to say Samantha Stoker, owner of the Violet Orchid Casino, has been located safe and well...'

Marina sat bolt upright. What? Samantha was unharmed? What the...?

'...It has been discovered Samantha had not gone missing after all, when it was found that the petrol station cashier responsible for alerting the emergency services fabricated the story in order to drive sales...'

Marina knew the veins in her temples were bulging because she could feel them. *Never gone missing at all? They had to be joking?* All this time she'd been waiting, she could have been intercepting Samantha at the airport as planned?

Had Stoker done this on purpose?

As the news reader continued, Marina wanted to launch the radio at the hotel wall and watch it explode, but continued to listen out of a sense of morbid torture.

She hoped the cashier got banged up for a thousand years for wasting police time and...

'...Mr and Mrs Stoker have decided to delay their honeymoon, opting to spend the start of their married life in peace and quiet locally...'

Marina frowned. *Wait a minute.* They hadn't gone on honeymoon? Something wasn't as it seemed here.

Her mouth slid into a grin. This was bullshit. This was Stoker through and through. Stoker hadn't staged a pretend disappearance as a smokescreen to escape on honeymoon unmolested by the press. *This* was the smokescreen.

Whatever had happened to Samantha, *had* happened and Stoker was pretending it hadn't...

A high-pitched giggle escaped from between Marina's lips.

She rubbed her hands together in glee. Now she could have another stab at her plan. And hers would play out with severer consequences than the inconvenience of a bunch of hack reporters encroaching on their oh-so precious privacy...

She pulled the metal case towards her. No longer was it surplus to requirements. Now it was back in pole position of usefulness.

So, someone had pulled Samantha away from Seb? She'd been taken, but Stoker had succeeded in getting her back.

Marina's mind worked overtime as she raced through plausible scenarios. Stoker would take Sam somewhere safe whilst he dealt with the repercussions. Knowing Stoker, he'd drag out the punishment on the perpetrator for some time – possibly *weeks*. That's why they were delaying their honeymoon.

Revenge.

But where would he take Sam? The Peacock? The Orchid? No – that was too obvious. Their house was a no-no too. There would be too much media interest.

Marina frowned, her mind ticking over at ten to the dozen. Suddenly, her face lit up so brightly that for a moment, the sour hatred that was an inbuilt expression dissolved, revealing below the intrinsic evil usually visible on her face, she was undoubtedly an extremely beautiful woman.

That was it! Seb would take Samantha back to her childhood home – that of Len and Gloria Reynold.

Marina drummed what few nails weren't snapped on the dressing table. *But where was Gloria's house?*

In another fleeting epiphany, she jumped to her feet and shoved them into her stilettos. Grabbing her handbag, she raced out of the door, almost breaking her neck as she hurtled down the stairs. Waiting for the lift would take too long. Providing the traffic wasn't bad, she could get to the library, giving her a good couple of hours to find exactly what she needed.

If Stoker was dealing with whoever snatched Samantha, it meant that bitch was on her own.

37

'I don't know why no one believes me,' Tom whined, determined to push this as far as he possibly could.

The fact that Seb Stoker hadn't shot him already showed there was a chance of this working. It also showed that Samantha must think his words held a grain of truth, otherwise he'd already be dead.

And he wasn't.

But he suspected he soon would be because Stoker wasn't about to walk away and leave this.

Tom glanced around the expanse of the concrete factory – once a good idea, now a prison, his tired brain feverishly searched for a viable plan.

If he could get out of here before Stoker returned…

As it stood, there was only *this* dolt standing between him and freedom.

Neil scrutinised Tom with unconcealed contempt. 'You ask why no one believes you?' He chuckled sourly. 'Hmm, can't imagine…' Neither could he fathom why Seb had taken Sam home, allowing this greasy toad of a wanker to breathe air longer than necessary.

'I'll tell you why.' Tom ignored that he was tightly bound to a chair and his chances of escape were minimal unless the part of the roof above Neil Stoker collapsed. 'Samantha knows I speak the truth. Whether you like it or not, she's my daughter! Linda will fess up, you'll see.'

From what he'd seen, Samantha was a slopy-shouldered slag, like her mother. She'd never have the guts to give the call to kill him. And with Stoker having a thumb print the size of a car on his forehead allowing his wife to tell him what to do, Tom would be home and dry if he played his cards right.

When Samantha finally got the truth from that flea-infested crack-slut, he'd wheedle his way out of this crap.

Neil felt it pointless responding to Tom's deluded rantings. He just wanted Seb to hurry up so they could finish this.

'Your casino looks pretty decent again,' Tom continued, his eyes glinting with malice. 'Shame it got torched...'

If Lady Luck made her usual scheduled appearance, he'd wind this prick up to the point of cardiac arrest and worry about how the fuck he'd untie himself afterwards.

Tom came to the decision too late that it would have been sensible to keep his quips to himself when Neil silenced him with a sharp and effective punch to the jaw.

* * *

The minute Seb left to return to the cement works under the strict promise to hold off Bedworth until she got her head together, Sam knew it was time.

She'd barely spoken a word since getting here, but she'd been pulling her reserves together to get her head into gear.

And now it was.

Sam looked at Linda and Gloria – both their faces drawn with concern as she'd got out of Seb's car.

Oh, Sam had seen that look in Seb's eyes when she'd asked him not to act on Bedworth. She'd seen the anger and frustration over what he perceived as procrastination. But it wasn't that.

She'd never wanted to kill anyone so much in her life as she did Bedworth. What that monster had done to Linda... To her... To *all* of those women...

It was judgement day. And she had to be the one to bring down the final axe.

Linda scrutinised Sam. She didn't think she'd ever experienced so much gratitude than when a dishevelled, but very much alive Sam clambered from Seb's motor.

Linda's whole body throbbed with hatred for the man she'd believed dead. She'd truly thought she'd been hearing things when Seb told her Bedworth was the one behind taking Sam.

But now the scales had tipped. Tom had no control any more. He'd lost his ability to work her like a puppet. Her eyes narrowed. 'I can't understand why you won't let Seb dispatch the piece of shit?' she said, stealing a quick glance at Gloria. It was common knowledge Gloria was uncomfortable with this side of the life. From what had been said, Len always ensured Gloria was never made privy to any of the unsavoury facets of the business.

She knew what went on, but was never *part* of it or *told* of it. Linda, however, had seen enough shit to give a whole continent nightmares, so very little fazed her, short of something happening to Sam.

'I don't want Seb dispatching Bedworth because *I'm* going to do it,' Sam said coldly. She ignored the sharp intake of breath from Gloria. 'It has to be me. This whole thing has centred on me in one way or another. It's affected everybody. And now it stops.'

Saying this out loud had a calming effect on her spinning mind. Concentrating only on the necessary deflected from dwelling on the horror, as well as the desolation as to the events of the day.

It was the only way to stop her mind from imploding.

Sam's hand moved to her belly and gave a silent apology to her unborn child for deciding to commit murder for the second time.

Killing Liam all that time ago had been a necessity borne of self-defence. Tom Bedworth, however, would be premeditated.

But, she reminded herself, *necessary*.

Linda listened to Sam and nodded. 'I understand. Regardless of what you may think, Seb does too. He...' Her eyes fell to Sam's hand caressing her stomach and suddenly things fell into place. *How had she missed this? Sam was pregnant!*

All hateful thoughts and stress flew out of the window at this revelation. *She was going to be a grandmother!*

'Oh my God!' she screamed. 'You're pregnant, aren't you?'

At Sam's blush, Linda jumped to her feet, closely followed by Gloria. 'Oh, love!' she exclaimed. 'This is the best news ever!'

'Why didn't you tell us?' Gloria cried, happiness overflowing. 'I'm so very pleased for you. What wonderful news!'

Linda could jump up and down with joy. No wonder Sam hadn't been drinking. It also explained the revisited questions over who her real father was after all this time.

Gloria dabbed a stray tear from her eye. 'Thank God you weren't hurt today.'

Linda nodded, then froze, her elation replaced with returning rage. Her daughter and grandchild could have been hurt today. Killed... 'You're sure you and that baby in there are okay after... after everything today?'

Sam nodded. 'Yes. I'm shaken up, but otherwise unharmed. I got a couple of backhanders, but thankfully nothing else.'

It could have been very different though. She shuddered with the thought. But now the secret was out about her pregnancy, she was relieved. At least one good thing had come from today.

'Fucking Bedworth!' Linda snarled. 'I hope he rots in hell.'

'He will,' Sam said, her spirit returning. 'Do you know he's that tapped; that *desperate*, he even tried saying he was my real father as a bargaining chip!'

Hearing Gloria inhale with horror, Sam managed a weak smile. 'Don't worry, I put him straight. It would have been funny if it hadn't been such a dreadful day.' She turned to Linda. 'He even tried to make me believe Thomas Vaughan was *his* name.'

Gloria frowned. 'Thomas Vaughan? Who's Thomas Vaughan?'

'My real father's name.' Sam nodded to Linda. 'We had a conversation only recently and...' Her voice trailed off at the blanched face of her mother. 'What? What is it? Shouldn't I have...'

Linda sagged into the chair. 'Did you believe what he said?'

'Don't be silly! Why would I?' A prickle of fear unfurled and gradually gained strength in Sam's mind. *No.* She could barely bring herself to utter the words. Bedworth's words were absurd. *Weren't they?* 'It's... it's not him, is it?'

She despised herself for asking. Why would she bother? It was ridiculous!

Realising Linda hadn't answered, cold rushed through Sam's body. *Why hadn't she said anything?* 'Mum...?'

Linda didn't have to answer. Her face said it all.

'Oh my God!' Gloria squeaked, her hand flew to her mouth, unsure how this could happen. 'It's not? It can't be?' Tom Bedworth – that evil bastard was Samantha's father? Len had paid that lowlife for their beautiful child? And that beautiful child had been Bedworth's?

Sam blinked in disbelief. The world stopped turning and strange flashing lights dotted in kaleidoscopic patterns appeared behind her eyes. She clutched at the side of the chair and fleetingly wondered whether the howling noise she heard was coming from her own mouth.

'I-I'm sorry,' Linda whispered hollowly, her face wet with tears. 'I didn't want you to know that he... That... I tried to shield you from it... I'm so sorry, Sam...'

Sam heard the words. She could see Linda's lips moving, but nothing made sense. That creature was her *father*?

It was his blood coursing around inside her?

Linda leant forward. 'Please, sweetheart. I'm sorry, I...'

Sam tried to hold it in, but she could do nothing to stop the projectile surge of vomit as it sprayed out over Gloria's armchair and the sheepskin rug.

With a tremendous amount of effort, Seb and Andrew manoeuvred Potter up the metal stairs to the top of the cement vat. A huge structure, it wasn't an easy task – made even harder with the immense weight, not to mention the sight of hundreds of nails wedged deep all over this man's flesh. Despite having the constitution of an ox when it came to butchered or dismembered bodies, it made Seb's stomach turn.

It had taken hours to get this lump of lard this far and Seb was knackered. But it wasn't over yet.

Puffing with exertion, they propped Potter's body up against the chute and Seb kept him upright with the help of his shoulder.

'Fuck's sake,' Andrew muttered, sweat running freely down his face.

'Let's just get him in this bloody thing and then we'll get the girl.' Seb wasn't looking forward to going back down to the area housing Tom Bedworth. Even dragging this fat fuck around and sweating his nuts off was preferable to breathing the same air as the creature he wanted to destroy. He knew he'd struggle not unleashing his uncontrollable rage if he spent more than ten seconds in the same vicinity. But he had to keep control because this was Sam's call.

A nerve twitched in his neck. It still didn't stop him wanting to torture the bastard.

With a grunt, Andrew lifted Potter's feet, whilst Seb fed the man's head and neck into the massive chute used for adding the aggregate to the churning vat.

'No one will find him in here,' he grinned, attempting to make light of the situation. 'Sam *will* follow through with Bedworth, won't she?'

Seb nodded. 'I reckon it would take wild horses to stop her. She's dead set on doing it herself, despite what she's been through.'

'But she's okay, right?'

'She says so,' Seb said. *And she'd better be.* Because if she wasn't, there was only one person to blame.

His teeth clenched. If Sam wasn't up to finishing Bedworth like she insisted on, then he would.

And it *would* happen this time. He'd make sure the fucker was definitely Bedworth until the cunt took his last breath. It would happen in front of him this time, rather than from behind an inferno inside a Portakabin.

'By the way, there's been no sign of that Marina bitch anywhere,' Andrew said. 'I alerted all the staff.'

Andrew's thoughts tracked, not for the first time, back to how Sophie was faring, consoling himself with the knowledge that, however abrasive Vera was when he'd handed her that gun, the woman had Sophie's back more than most.

His throat constricted with thoughts of Sophie. Something else to broach with Seb, but certainly not now. Would there ever be a good time?

Whichever way he looked at it, he'd made up his mind.

He loved Sophie and wanted a future with her.

Glad to see the back of Potter Ross disappearing into the void of mixing concrete, Seb knew it would be a long time, possibly never, before the bodies were discovered.

Two more to go...

Seb wiped the glistening sweat from his brow with the back of his arm. He wouldn't lay his hand anywhere after handling Potter's ruined corpse. Even sandblasting wouldn't rid him of the pervading stench of death and metal cloying the air. 'Let's go and get the woman, then.'

Tina's death was unfortunate. Sam was upset about it, he could tell. She'd always had a soft spot for the girl and despite him less than trusting Tina after pulling that stunt at the Orchid, she didn't deserve this.

The girl had more than paid back her dues by buying Sam extra time.

Seb's eyes narrowed, thinking on what *could* have happened.

Death was too good for these bastards.

He squinted down to the ground many metres below at Bedworth. Just looking at the man filled him with murderous rage.

Seb was descending the steps at the side of the mixing vat, when the shrill ring of Andrew's mobile rang out into the echoey expanse.

He stiffened. There would only be a certain amount of people who would call his brother right now, which meant this was unlikely to be good news.

Answering, Andrew listened and frowned, his gaze darting to Seb. 'What? She said, *what*?'

38

At the crack of dawn, Seb rushed through the door the second Gloria opened it, stopping himself from embedding the poor woman into the wall in his haste to reach Sam.

Aware he was still covered in dust and mottled with specks of dried blood over his arms and shirt from handling the bodies at the cement works, he ignored Gloria's horrified expression and grabbed her. 'What the fuck is this about?' he hissed. 'Surely it's not true?'

'I'm afraid it is. I can hardly believe it either,' Gloria stammered, her nerves in shreds. 'I didn't know what else to do but call the first number to hand where I thought you could be reached. I had to get hold of you.'

Seb grimaced. *Didn't he just know it!* Andrew could barely bring himself to relay what he'd learnt from that short phone call.

For God's sake, if this *was* true, it would push Sam over the edge. It would *crucify* her. More than that – it changed *everything*.

'You did the right thing.' Seb's gaze moved around the eerily quiet house. 'Where is she?'

Gloria nodded towards the back reception room. 'In there. With Linda...'

Seb's eyes narrowed. Linda. How could she have not said anything all of this time?

He began to storm down the corridor, but Gloria grabbed his arm. 'Don't be too hard on Linda,' she whispered. 'I know what you're thinking. I thought the same until I heard her reasoning. She was desperate to shield Sam from this and whilst she believed Bedworth to be dead, she felt there was no point in throwing this bombshell into the works.'

She shrugged. 'People do anything to protect their children, including living with the guilt of hiding the truth.' She fidgeted uncomfortably. 'I should know. Look what I kept from Sam.'

Keeping the secret that she and Len weren't Sam's biological parents for thirty years had almost cost her entire relationship with Sam. Gloria only hoped that wouldn't happen for Linda. 'Linda's reasonings were unselfish, Seb. It might not seem that way, but they were. No doubt you'll find that out yourself soon as I hear congratulations are in order?'

Seb didn't ask how Sam's pregnancy was now known. People knowing about it mattered less now *this* was on the cards.

But did Gloria have a point? Would he rush to tell his son or daughter the ins and outs – warts and all about everything *he'd* done at the first opportunity?

Probably not.

But this? *Jesus!*

Continuing down the hallway with Gloria on his heels, Seb burst into the back reception room. Shooting Linda a harsh look, he pulled Sam into his arms.

Just by the haunted look in her eyes, he knew things weren't good. 'It's okay, Princess,' he said softly.

'Okay? How can this be okay?' Sam yelped.

Initially, she'd remained silent for quite some time. Despite Linda begging and pleading for her to say something, she'd been unable to do anything but remain locked inside her own head from this unexpected and horrific revelation.

She'd cycled through everything: questioning her own identity more than ever before; questioning how she could continue *being* anything, let alone entertain the prospect of bringing a child into the world, knowing she would inflict a percentage of the poisonous blood coursing through her own veins into the body of her very much wanted baby.

There were no answers...

But it was that last question which pushed her from numb desolation into becoming derailed.

She'd lurched from silence into screaming accusations at Linda. The truth had been hidden – *again*. She'd been purposely kept in the dark over something so important – *again*. She'd been put in an untenable position. *Again...*

Her out-of-control rant had prompted Gloria's desperate call to bring Seb to her side, but what could he do? What could he do to fix this and put it right? Or change it?

Nothing.

The truth was, Seb had married and created a child with someone who should never have been born.

'Sam.' Seb tilted Sam's face to look into his eyes. 'This changes nothing. I love you and that will never differ.'

'You're happy with my tainted blood being part of your own child? Forever looking at him or her for resemblance of the bastard who trashed our lives?' Sam spat. 'And being with me, knowing I was created by that monster?'

Seb didn't acknowledge the sob coming from Linda's direction. He couldn't look at her right now. Yeah, she may have wanted to protect Sam from this, but what had it achieved, aside from blowing everyone's world apart?

He clutched Sam's shoulders. 'When I look at you, I only see what I've only ever seen. What I'll *always* see – a woman I love. Our child will remind me of *you* – no one else! That I can promise.'

Sam shook her head in disbelief. 'I don't see how you can promise that. You don't know it will be like that.' She laid her hand on her bump. 'How can I have this baby knowing its cursed bloodline?'

Seb's eyes narrowed. 'Don't ever say that again, do you hear?'

He'd kill Bedworth twice over for this if Sam didn't.

His thoughts suddenly paused. As if Sam's spirit being shattered into pieces wasn't bad enough, where did that leave the current situation with that wanker trussed up at the cement works? Sam was in no fit state even to walk around the house right now, let alone kill someone. Especially when that someone happened to be her own bloody father.

Seb's jaw clenched. He had no doubt Sam would get through this disastrous revelation in time. He'd help her every step of the way on that, but how could she take on the added burden of dispatching that man?

There was no way she could successfully deal with that with her head in this state. But if he took over and did the job, then she'd hate that too. She might even hate him for killing her own father down the line – bastard or not.

Seb's teeth grated. That wasn't a conversation which could be had at the moment, so what the hell should he do?

Sam was his priority, but Bedworth also had to go quickly. The longer that waster remained in the cement works, the higher the percentage was of him being discovered. And that would ruin even more things. *For everyone.*

* * *

Even being mid-July didn't stop the damp dew of the early morning from gradually seeping into Marina's bones. But it was of no consequence. Sitting in a car all night was a doddle and more than worth it. She wasn't even tired. Sleep was irrelevant when there were things of greater magnitude to deal with.

Her theory of going to Birmingham Library yesterday had proved a good one. She'd even swallowed her irritation at the slow response of the librarians acting on her enquiries. She expected nothing less from people who spent their lives cooped up with a bunch of old books and antiquated newspapers. But them having a different concept of time to the rest of mankind didn't help her overall frustration. *She* had things to do.

As it turned out, the dusty collection of microfilm reels containing past copies of the *Birmingham Mail* was worth the hour spent with her arse turning to cement from perching on a hard chair, peering through the viewing lens of the microfilm machine.

She'd got exactly what she'd gone for. And it had brought her *here*.

Marina glanced up at the silent frontage of the house in Edgbaston and a small smile slithered across her face. She'd been correct.

Samantha was in this very house.

And soon she'd deliver the final card in the deck, which would undoubtedly be an ace.

It hadn't been difficult to find articles about the Violet Orchid in the annals of the library's collection of newspapers. Everyone knew how much people like the Reynold and Stoker families loved bigging up their casinos. This, of course, meant there were plenty of articles to choose from – ranging from Len Reynold's business partner being 'tragically' killed in 1983; countless stories of dear little Samantha's birthday celebrations throughout the years; Malcolm Stoker's retirement and Linda Matthews being reunited with her long-lost daughter...

Marina's bitterness grew. Yeah, there was tons of stuff, but there was only *one* she really wanted to get her hands on.

And finally she had.

Len Reynold, 68, the well-known founder and owner of the Violet Orchid casino on Broad Street, was found dead at the scene after a head-on collision with a tree, yards from his home...

And that was how she'd known where to come last night.

Marina's eyes flicked back to the house near where she'd parked. Her hire car was out of view enough not to be obvious, but the house was still within her sights to see who came in. And, more importantly, who went out.

But her assumptions of this being where Seb would bring Samantha could have been wrong. The first worrying hint was the lack of Stoker's thugs patrolling the grounds.

But Marina was glad she hadn't jumped to conclusions and left, because Stoker had finally arrived. His car had screeched up the driveway of Samantha's childhood home. He'd been on his own, which meant only one thing: Samantha was already inside.

And when Stoker left, not ten minutes ago, he'd *still* been alone. All that was needed now was her crackhead of a mother to disappear.

Marina's face screwed into a scowl.

Yeah, Linda was in there, but she needed to be *out* of there. Marina didn't give a shit if Gloria happened to still be lurking about after that. That ditsy old bat could easily be dispatched.

Linda, however, was a different kettle of fish. She was too much of a hellcat to die slowly. She'd already proved that more than once, so she had to be absent before a move could be made.

And then, with Stoker and Linda out of the picture, it would be all systems go.

Marina's eyes tracked to the Holy Grail sitting on the back seat of her car in the shape of a metal case. It would be difficult to decide which one of the delightful samples to pick to rid the world of her dear sister.

Maybe a concoction of several would be best? She didn't want any miraculous recoveries.

There was only one shot at this and it had to be infallible.

Sensing movement, Marina's focus darted to the black cab pulling up at the end of the Reynolds' driveway. Senses alert, she waited, her skin tingling. *Who was arriving now? Or who was leaving?*

Watching a figure emerge from the driveway into the purple dawn, Marina beamed. 'Hello, Mother,' she snarled, her voice loud in the confines of the car. 'Are you leaving? How very unfortunate...'

Grabbing the metal case from the back seat, Marina pulled it onto her lap. Her heart thumped with rising anticipation as Linda got into the waiting taxi and it pulled away.

Now she'd give it five minutes before starting the party.

Jerked from her doze, Vera jumped from the armchair, the gun still firmly clutched in her hand like it had been since Andrew Stoker left yesterday.

It was early – *really* early. Not even 6 a.m. and for all her bravado, she was more on edge than she'd allow anyone to realise.

'Who's that?' Sophie hissed, uncurling from the uncomfortable ball she'd formed herself into during the small hours.

'I don't know, do I?' Vera snapped. 'Just keep quiet!'

Sophie watched in horror as Vera tentatively edged towards the hallway, the front door continuing to hammer relentlessly. 'Don't open it! Don't even look! Just stay h...'

'I've got to see who it is!' But Vera had no intention of opening the door. If it was Marina Devlin, she certainly wasn't giving that bitch an easy passage into her home.

But it could be Seb with news or even the police...

Nearing the rickety front door, her throat constricted, with growing trepidation that the old wood wouldn't hold should a forced entrance be attempted.

Her clammy fingers tightened on the gun, the metal heavy and cold in her hand. Remembering what she'd been shown, Vera flicked off the safety catch and with her back against the wall, slid along the wallpaper towards the door.

She'd glimpse who was the other side through the peephole without being sensed.

A new barrage of banging made her jump out of her skin. 'Christ!' Vera muttered under her breath, her heart thrashing.

Reaching the peephole, she squinted through. 'Fuck!'

Quickly unbolting the door, she removed the chains. Taking a quick glance around outside, she yanked Linda inside and shut the door with a loud slam. 'You shouldn't be here. Where's Sam?'

'Gloria's with her,' Linda gabbled.

Shooting the bolts back home, Vera clocked the tear-stained face of her friend and her stomach fell to her feet. 'What the fuck's happened?'

'I just had to get out. I needed air.'

Sophie darted from the sitting room. 'Linda! Are you all right?

Sam? What about Andrew?' *Please don't let anything have happened to Andrew...*

'How can anyone be all right?' Linda snapped. Moving into the sitting room, she fell into a chair and wrapped her arms around herself, like it would prevent the truth from causing further hurt. 'Everything's my fault... Sam will never forgive me.'

'For what? What's your fault?' Vera pushed. 'You're making no sense. Pull yourself together, woman, and tell me what the hell is going on!'

'Tom Bedworth is Sam's real father.' Linda's voice was barely audible. 'And now Sam knows...'

Vera felt like she'd been whacked in the face with a frying pan. She was about to scold Linda for playing stupid jokes, until the clear dread on her friend's face underlined this was no joke.

Fuck.

'Tom Bedworth is Sam's *father*?' Vera repeated, her voice like an automaton. 'You never told me! You said that it...'

'I never told anyone!' Linda screamed. 'How could I? I had to shield Sam from that reality. Tom was supposed to be dead, so no one needed to know!'

Vera blinked and then blinked again. This man from the past who had returned to Linda's life – the one she said she knew from old, and the one who got her to fall for him all over again had treated her like shit; robbed her and then who tortured and drugged her up, was the very same bastard that had abandoned her as a pregnant fifteen-year-old.

He'd sold Linda's child!

Samantha.

'But you denied Bedworth was anything to do with Sam,' Vera cried, knowing she'd asked Linda at the time whether this 'man from her past' was anything to do with her firstborn. She'd hated

Bedworth from the off, and now it seemed there was more reason for this than she'd realised.

'I know, I know,' Linda sobbed. 'I didn't want to ruin things. To my shame, I loved him, but when I finally saw the light after he turned me over for the second time, how could I tell my beautiful daughter or *anyone* that she was fathered by that pimp; that bastard?'

Her tears dried up to be replaced with raw fury. 'I *hate* him!' she hissed, venom spewing from her words. 'He could have killed Sam yesterday. Killed his own daughter! And she's pregnant... He'd have killed both of them...'

'Jesus!' Vera's anger at being omitted from Linda's truth dissipated. 'Sam's pregnant? How has she taken it about Bedworth?'

Linda shook her head sadly. 'How the hell do you think?'

39

'I know this must be dreadful for you, sweetheart, but things will seem better once you've had some rest,' Gloria said, absentmindedly playing with Sam's hair.

Sam tried to smile, but failed. No amount of rest could make Bedworth being her father better. *Ever.*

And now Linda had gone out, going God only knew where.

As much as she tried not to let it, Gloria fussing her hair the very way she used to do no longer worked in comforting her. Instead, it made her bristle with hundreds of painful needles.

Her body was oversensitive; alert and wired. She just wanted to be on her own.

Sam had heard everything Linda said: the reasoning behind why she hadn't been told the truth. She'd also heard Gloria say not to be too hard on Linda – several times, but even though deep down, she understood her mother's motives, Sam couldn't help rage from festering within her soul.

She felt lost, naked and blitzed.

Sam wanted to believe Seb's words too. She wanted to truly

believe this would change nothing between them, but no one could see into the future, could they?

What if it did?

Words were merely words – they meant nothing unless they became reality.

Plus, through the murky sludge of the mass crowding her brain there was the added pressure of needing to deal with Bedworth. The narrowing window of time ticked like a time bomb, pulsing in a never-ending reminder that although her world had ground to a halt, everything else must continue with or without her.

Despite the events of the past twenty-four hours crushing her to a pulp, *she'd* demanded to be the one to dispatch Bedworth. She'd waited too long to personally finish that man for anyone else to take the spoils.

But *insisting* that was the only way it could happen, had been before her bloodline to Tom Bedworth was uncovered.

And now...

Now, she had to summon the energy to pull herself from this oblivion and push through the invisible web of strangulating wires pinning her to the floor and honour what she'd said.

Sam genuinely didn't know how she would do it. She didn't want to ever see that man again and although she more than wanted to kill him, Bedworth was her father, therefore doing this went against all instincts.

Sam started shaking once again, resenting herself further.

Suddenly feeling a strange sensation, her hand shot to the hard swell of her belly. *There it was again. She hadn't imagined it.*

It was only slight – barely anything. Certainly not enough to see or feel from the outside, but she'd felt it from the *inside*.

Butterfly flutters – the first time she'd felt her baby move.

Unshed tears glistened, giving her the push she needed. This was *her* baby! Nothing to do with who had or hadn't fathered her. Her child was nothing to do with Tom fucking Bedworth.

A flicker of resolve sparked deep and with renewed strength, Sam smiled. She got to her feet. 'I'm going to have a shower. I need to sort myself out.'

'Okay, sweetheart,' Gloria said. 'Use the downstairs guest room. There's fresh towels in there. I'll leave you in peace for a while. Just shout if you need anything.'

Leaving the room, Sam walked down the corridor.

She'd do it. She'd kill Bedworth, just like she'd promised. But she didn't yet have the first clue where to find the strength from, nor how the act would leave her afterwards, but providing she kept her resolve in place, then she'd deal with it.

* * *

At first it was cathartic taking turns with Neil and Andrew to punch Bedworth in the face. But now it was becoming difficult, as well as dangerous.

The close proximity to this piece of shit was fast pushing Seb over the edge. Although each time his fist connected with Bedworth's jaw was enjoyable, every second being around the man fuelled his rage and Seb knew he risked losing control. Unable to stop himself from letting rip, he would soon beat the man to death. It was what he wanted to do more than anything.

Seeing Andrew line up for another turn at the bleeding man strapped to the chair, Seb held his hand up, his index finger indicating his brothers should follow. 'Let's leave this cunt to his own devices for a while,' he said, motioning to a separate room at the rear of the building. 'He ain't going anywhere.'

Tom gibbered something unintelligible which Seb ignored,

finding it impossible to look at the creature any longer. He'd already caught himself looking for resemblances to Sam in Bedworth's face and that could not happen. It would be the last time he would allow himself to even *think* about that.

He pulled his gaze from Tom's pale blue stare and the smashed and bloodied nose on his face, as well as the rapidly swelling mess of his jaw line.

'How long have we got to put up with him?' Andrew entered the small side room. 'There's only so long we can do this.'

Seb shut the door behind him and mulled over the question he'd asked himself countless times already. 'I'm giving Sam until this afternoon to act.' He glanced between his brothers, recognising the same lack of belief in his words that he held himself. 'As you know, she's not in a good way and I can't see that changing.' He shrugged miserably. 'Whether she'll forgive me for pulling rank and taking over, I don't know, but there's not much I can do about that.'

Neil nodded sagely. 'It's got to be done. There isn't time to play the waiting game.'

'I agree. Enough time has passed as it is. Look, I can do it if that would be better?' Andrew added. Sam could hate *him* if she wanted. There was little more he wanted than to remove Bedworth, short of not being here at all and being with Sophie instead...

Seb flexed his knuckles, the gravity of the situation becoming heavier by the minute. 'Sam was adamant she was doing it, so in her absence, it must be me.'

'It must be hard for her. He's her father,' Neil frowned.

'But she insisted on doing the job *before* she knew that.' Seb rubbed his hand over his jaw. 'Oh Christ, I don't know. All I *do* know is this whole thing has knocked her for fucking six. She may end up resenting me, but I have to act on what's best for her in *here.*' He thumped his chest. 'And then there's the baby. This stress isn't good for either of them.'

Andrew paced the room like a caged tiger. 'So what happens in the meantime?'

'We wait,' Seb said. 'I have to give Sam those few more hours. If you can stay here, I'll go to the Peacock and have a shower. I need to clear my head before the shit starts.'

* * *

Aware of every rustling leaf and movement the breeze made on her surroundings, Marina's breath was loud, her anticipation levels growing to fever pitch.

She remained motionless against the back wall of the property, catching enough glimpses through the cracks of the slatted blinds of the ground floor room to know Samantha was in there. There was no sign of Gloria, so this was the perfect opportunity. It was the best she was going to get, anyway, because she couldn't wait around indefinitely. Seb and Linda would return at some point and when that happened, she'd be outnumbered.

Spotting Samantha coming out of another door within the room, Marina stiffened. Water was running – she could hear it. The nasty cow was about to have a shower.

But how did she get into this room without alerting the bitch?

Marina ran her nails along the length of the window frame, looking for a weak spot to force the window open. If she waited till the cow got in the shower, the noise of the water would cancel out any racket she made whilst getting into Fort Knox.

Her anticipation rose further as Sam slipped off her fluffy robe, revealing what Marina suspected. Her eyes roamed over the swell of her sister's belly and a slow smile cracked over her lips.

Voila! She knew it.

'At least you won't have to worry about your husband going off you in a couple of months when you're the size of a cow,' she whispered with raw hatred. 'Because you won't get that far...'

Sam moved out of view into the adjoining room, the door closing behind her and Marina's heart leapt, feeling a gap in the window. The window had been left ajar.

Twisting her fingers, Marina pushed the gold metal stay and fully opened the window.

Samantha thought herself so infallible that she could do away with security guards and sense?

'You deserve everything you get,' she sniggered, pleased the maintenance of the house was up to par. The window hadn't emitted even a squeak.

Perfect.

Grabbing the metal case from her feet, Marina pushed to her tiptoes, leant through the window and deposited the case into the room.

Following suit, she hoisted herself up on the windowsill, priding herself on her ability to remain supple.

Dropping to the floor, she scowled at the room. How positively divine – a floral bedspread, matching curtains and strategically placed cushions on the double bed. How delightfully predictable...

With the water from the en suite shower room still in full force, Marina laid the metal case on the bed and flipped the catches open.

She had to be ready.

Pulling a vial from the padded compartment of the metal case, Marina checked the labels. She'd grouped her favourite ones together and this one would do nicely.

Rapidly assembling the hypodermic needle provided, she plunged it through the lid of the vial and pulled the liquid into the syringe. This was enough to quickly finish off both Sam and her horrible heir. Then she'd be out of here before anyone noticed something was amiss. And by that point it would be too late.

Startled by a tap on the door, Marina stiffened.

Shit.

'Sam? Do you need anything?'

Fuck! Gloria. The old cow would bring Sam running from the bathroom if she kept on.

Marina darted to the side of the bedroom door, hearing a tune hummed over the gush of the shower.

That's it, Sam. Keep singing stupid songs, then you won't hear this.

Marina's eyes locked on the slowly turning doorknob. She leapt over to the bed, slung down the syringe and snatched up the metal case.

'Sam? Are you still in the shower? Can I come in?'

Knowing she must act immediately, Marina flung the door open.

'Ah, there you a... Oh!' Gloria's mouth froze into a shocked 'O'. 'Who are y...?'

Seeing the murderous rage in the strangely familiar eyes of the stranger in her guest room, Gloria took a step back. Unfortunately, she didn't get chance to raise her hands to defend herself from the blow of the metal object which connected with her left temple.

Standing over the prone woman, Marina heard the shower stop.

Shit! Samantha was coming out of the shower.

Her eyes darted back to Gloria unconscious in the corridor, a thin trail of blood seeping from the cut on her head. She'd be out for the count for a while and could be finished off later easily enough. For now, the priority was Samantha. If she wasn't ready to pounce when the bitch exited the en suite, then things would be a lot harder.

Shutting the bedroom door to block Gloria from sight as well as mind, Marina placed the case back on the bed and snatched up the syringe. Then she silently moved into position and took her place to wait at the side of the en suite door.

40

Leaving the en suite, the hairbrush fell from Sam's hand as she was grabbed around the throat and pushed face first into the wall. 'What the...?'

Her arms flailed, failing to strike the perpetrator. She hadn't even caught a glimpse of who was behind it. *Had Bedworth escaped? He couldn't have... Oh God, where was Gloria?*

'I doubt you expected to find me here?' Marina's voice was loud in Sam's ear.

Sam felt sick to the marrow of her bones.

Marina Devlin.

The only time she'd heard that voice before was ingrained in her memory: the night in her office at the Orchid when her half-sister had attempted to kill her and had shot Seb instead.

That split second of believing the man she loved had been killed was impossible to remove from her brain.

From the recess of somewhere inside, Sam pulled on every reserve of fake bravado.

It was better to act unfazed, rather than give this psychotic woman hints that she was terrified. People like that got off on instilling fear and Sam wouldn't give this evil piece of work any additional enjoyment.

She willed the tremoring travelling through her body to remain undetected. 'I presumed you'd returned to London,' she lied, her voice muffled as her mouth was pushed into the wallpaper.

Marina laughed, the screeching noise hurting Sam's ears. 'Presumed wrong then, didn't you?'

'Or Marbella perhaps...?' Sam countered, remembering Tina's words. She promptly wished she'd said nothing when the atmosphere changed from charged to cloying and loaded with ice.

'It's not difficult to guess how you found *that* out.' Marina pushed Sam harder into the wall. 'In it together, you and that Tina slut? Keeping tabs on me all this time and getting me arrested at the airport? Well, your fun is over.'

Grabbing a fistful of Sam's hair, Marina twisted it and yanked, gratified to hear a yelp. 'You've been very stupid. You pull shit like that, yet think you can waltz around playing happy families?'

'And I'm thinking you hate that because you don't have one,' Sam spat. 'Maybe because you felt the need to kill your own brother. *Our* brother! You've alienated everybody.'

'Don't you dare associate yourself with *my* brother! You had nothing to do with Grant. Nothing!' Marina screeched.

Growing anger overtook Sam's shock of finding this woman in the house. To think, when first learning of Marina, that she'd believed, with some work, they may become close. It was laughable. *How wrong she'd been.* 'You're evil, Marina. Evil!'

Marina's high cackle filled the room. 'And you're not?' She twisted Sam's hair harder. 'You think it's okay to take everything? Leaving nothing for anyone else?' Her eyes gleamed with malevolence. 'Well, it's not. None of it is okay and you'll soon learn that.'

Marina started humming a tune Sam half-recognised, but

couldn't quite place. Fear shimmered and began to overtake her anger. *The tune was a hymn – one common at funerals...*

'How did you get in here?' Sam cried, dread mounting. 'Where's Gloria? What have you done to her?'

'Dead, but that's the least of your problems,' Marina laughed. Whether the old cow was dead or not, she would be as soon as this bitch was dealt with. *Oh, this was all too easy. Dearest Samantha was playing right into her hands.*

'You've got nothing now, you whore!' she screamed, pulling Sam forward. 'Your new husband will be condemned to hell – forever trapped with memories of what should have been.'

Sam's slippered feet skidded on the parquet flooring, fighting to keep her balance against Marina's extraordinary force.

Dead? Gloria was dead? No!

Marina slammed her knee into the small of Sam's back and pushed her into the dressing table. 'Yeah, Gloria is no more. Shame that... The same will be said for your baby – the child who won't get to exist.' Gripping the syringe, she smiled. 'Didn't think I knew about that either, did you?' *It was time for the finale.*

Taking the full brunt of the edge of the dressing table in her belly brought the return of Sam's white fear.

Marina knew about the baby! She was going to hurt it. No!

Sam's eyes suddenly narrowed as rage overtook her internal battle with fear.

Fighting the suffocating urge to curl into a ball to protect her unborn child, Sam pulled on a previously unknown reserve of force and swung around, pushing Marina with all her might.

She had to take control otherwise this would not stop. If she could overbalance this woman...

Taken off guard, shock fleetingly passed over Marina's face. She staggered backwards, seeing a blur as Sam lunged towards her.

With a sick smile, it took very little effort to raise the syringe in her hand, stopping Sam in her tracks. 'Attempt to hit me all you like, but I'm stronger than you. And see?' She eyed the syringe gleefully. 'This will take no effort to administer. Bang! A split second and you, as well at that creature spawning inside you, will be done!'

Sam's eyes remained glued to the hypodermic needle in Marina's hand. *What the fuck?*

Panic picked up an incessant rhythm. She had no idea what was in that thing, but had no doubt that whatever it was, it would kill her and her baby. Only Marina could pull something like this.

Bile threatened to rush into her mouth. What if she could overpower Marina and turn the syringe on her?

As Marina moved towards her, Sam lunged forward only to be met with what felt like a punch to her stomach. *Or was it the syringe?*

Winded, she fell to her knees, pain tearing through her. *Her baby!* 'Don't hurt my baby!'

'Beg all you like, bitch!' Marina screamed. 'It matters not. Words won't fucking help you now! It's amusing how much your alien foetus has become your Achilles heel. It's made you weak!'

Pushing Sam onto her back, Marina jumped astride, the needle a millimetre from her neck. 'Time to go, Samantha. Say thank you, then, dear sister. Say fucking thank you!'

'I'm sick of this,' Andrew muttered. Glaring at Tom, he cracked his knuckles. 'How long will Seb be?'

'He'll be here,' Neil replied. 'You heard what he said. He's got to give Sam a few hours to decide whether she's doing the job. It must be her call.'

Andrew glared at his brother. 'Why? We all know she's not in a fit state at the moment, so why don't we just get on with it?' His eyes gleamed with the promise. 'If we carry on, then it will be done and the problem solved. I'm happy to take the fallout.'

Neil sighed. 'In some respects I agree, but I also hear where Seb's coming from. It has to be his judgement. Sam's his wife.'

Andrew booted a large metal barrel across the room in frustration. Would he feel the same if Sophie was in this position?

Probably, but that was something he hoped he'd never have to deal with.

Stomping over to a semiconscious Tom, he yanked his head back. 'I'm bored of doing nothing but looking at this dribbling cunt.'

Hearing the groan from Tom's smashed mouth, a trail of vomit trickling from one side, Neil stepped forward. 'We've already given him a hell of a pasting. He won't withstand much more.' He stared at the pitifully bashed creature who had been behind so much destruction, knowing Andrew would kill the fucker, then pass it off as an accident.

'You lot love being the big "I ams".' Tom's voice came as a surprise to Neil and Andrew. 'Still following big brother's orders? Pathetic!'

Andrew's face creased into a snarl. 'See? This wanker ain't nowhere near finished!' Delivering a hefty boot to Tom's chest which tipped the chair and its contents backwards, he stood over the upturned body, relishing the spluttering yelps. 'Reckon you know it all, do you, Bedworth? You abject cu...'

'Hang on!' Neil grabbed Andrew's arm. 'I've got a better idea – one which will pass the time *and* prove a source of enjoyment.'

Stooping over, he undid Tom's jeans and yanked them down to reveal a pair of rather unpleasant stained underpants, which he also tugged down around the man's ankles.

'What the fuck are you doing?' Andrew yelled. 'I don't want to see his fucking cock!' He snatched up a pair of bolt cutters. 'I'll cut the bastard thing off though!'

'What?' Tom spluttered, barely able to pull air into his crushed lungs. 'You can't do that. I'll...'

'You'll what? Cry? Be sarcastic?' Andrew raged. 'Fuck off, Bedworth. Your time's up.'

Neil leant over Tom. 'I thought you should experience a little of what you put all those girls and women through during your distinguished career...' He grinned savagely. 'We'll give you a dose of humiliation like you've never experienced before. See how you get on with it.'

'W-what?' Tom struggled to focus on the two lunatics standing over him and suddenly, not that it was possible, a further month cooped up with Potter Ross was preferable. 'I was just making money. You lot do things to make money and...'

'We don't abuse women and young girls! That's reserved for filth like you,' Andrew snarled. He glanced around the enormous space, already having earmarked some things that could be utilised to help Bedworth's final humiliation before he met his end.

He winked at Neil. This wasn't a bad idea. Not a bad idea at all. It would make spending the next hour or so with this worthless piece of dirt more palatable. 'Do you fancy going first, Neil, or shall I?'

* * *

Knowing she had to take the bull by the horns, Linda was on the way home. She could only hope Vera was right when she'd said by leaving and giving Sam space the way she had, she'd have now calmed down and be seeing things differently.

She dragged her hand under her nose to wipe away the snot,

courtesy of the many tears she'd shed over the course of the last hour and a half.

She'd have loved to seek refuge at Vera's a while longer. Even the disappointment and contempt clear on her oldest friend's face since the truth had emerged was preferable to seeing the hatred on Sam's every time she looked at her.

Linda felt like screaming from years of pain and bitterness. Could she ever put this right? Was her relationship with Sam now destroyed forever?

'We're in Edgbaston now, so where to from here, love?' The taxi driver eyed Linda curiously in his rear-view mirror.

Snapped from her thoughts, Linda blinked into the bright sunlight of her surroundings. *They were almost back already?* 'Oh, erm... next left please. Then it's halfway down on the right.'

As they turned into the road, Linda wondered whether Seb had returned to the house yet. With the state she was in, Sam couldn't finish Tom off – that much was clear. But *she* could.

She could, and she *would*.

After all, no one would be in this fucking mess if it hadn't been for her shitty decisions.

41

Through a swirling mist of pain, the screaming and shouting filtered into Gloria's mind. Blinking to clear her swimming vision, she found herself staring at the hallway ceiling and her brain scrambled to work out why she was lying here.

Had she fainted? Had a funny turn? What about the blinding pain in her head?

She gingerly reached up to touch her temple, wincing as the pain ricocheted deeper. She frowned, seeing blood on her fingers.

Wait! Whose were those voices?

The recall of what prompted her to be lying on the floor in her own house suddenly returned with a cold rush.

The stranger in her guest room...

Gloria's eyes darted to the bedroom door, hearing the voice of someone unfamiliar shouting a venomous diatribe audible to all.

She might not have seen that woman before, but she'd recognised the eyes. They were the same as Samantha's – as *Linda's*.

It was Marina Devlin – Linda's other daughter. The woman who had tried to kill Samantha and then escaped. It had to be.

Overriding the crushing pain in her head, Gloria scrambled to her feet. Being as Linda had gone to Vera's and Seb had left, there was no one here to do anything, apart from *her*.

Hearing a loud scream which Gloria knew belonged to Sam, she realised she had to act. She could hear what Marina Devlin was saying, God knows what she was doing, but it wasn't good.

Samantha was pregnant, remember?

With her breath reduced to shallow gasps, Gloria lurched towards the door of the bedroom and frantically looked around. She couldn't take on a young woman like Marina Devlin without help. She'd never raised a fist to anyone in her life before. It had not been necessary.

Oh, she knew what her husband's business had involved; what he'd been party to and capable of, but he'd always kept her away from that and Gloria was incessantly grateful about it.

But this was *now*. Len was no longer here and neither was anyone else. *It had to be her.*

It was a life-or-death situation and she would not allow Samantha and her baby to be hurt.

Barely able to believe what was happening, Gloria continued scanning for something to help her. She snatched her favourite ornament from the hallway windowsill.

Do whatever you need to do, Gloria thought, Sam's pregnancy giving her the impetus she required.

Not sparing a second, she barged into the room, her eyes widening at the woman sitting astride Samantha with a needle in her hand.

The woman hadn't seen her. Neither had Samantha.

Go, go, go!

With courage she hadn't believed she possessed, Gloria raised the heavy ornament and brought it swiftly down onto the back of the stranger's head.

Marina fell forward onto Sam, before swinging around wearing the most vicious snarl Gloria had ever seen on a woman before. 'You old cunt!' she roared.

Almost in slow motion, Gloria watched the woman scrambling to get off Samantha, the needle still in her hand.

Do it again, Gloria. Do it again.

So she did...

Swinging wildly, her best brass ornament collided with the side of Marina Devlin's face, giving Gloria the chance to raise it again and again. She heard a high-pitched scream coming from her own mouth which hurt her ears.

The splattering blood sprayed over both her and Sam, but she didn't stop. And she wouldn't until this woman no longer moved.

* * *

'It's this one just here, mate.' Linda flapped her hand in the direction of the house.

As the taxi pulled up, Linda frowned at a blue car parked further along the road, sure that was there when she'd left earlier. One of the neighbours must have a new motor? Why didn't they park on the drive? Everyone round here knew the traffic wardens gave short shrift to anyone who parked on the road.

Still, not her problem.

Shrugging, Linda slipped a tenner into the driver's hand, got out and hurried into the house.

Wariness crept along her spine from the moment she shut the front door. It was too quiet. *Far* too quiet.

Where was everyone?

Sam wouldn't have gone before sorting this mess out between them, would she?

Despair bloomed. Linda desperately wanted to properly

explain and make Sam understand that she'd never intended to hide things, but a case of...

What the fuck?

Stopping halfway down the hallway, Linda happened to glance along the corridor to the right leading to the guest room.

What was that on the floor?

She squinted harder. It looked like a small pool of blood.

It was!

Gloria's white and light grey floor tiles made something like blood stand out a mile.

Horror grew.

What had happened in her absence?

'Sam? Gloria?' Linda screeched, her shaky legs propelling her along the corridor. 'Hello? Where are you?'

Shit! Had Tom escaped the Stokers? No, surely he couldn't have?

'Sam?' Linda's voice was now quiet as she gingerly pushed open the door to the guest bedroom. 'Are you in h...?'

Freezing in the doorway, her hand flew to her mouth with the sight. Sam was curled into a ball on the bed, her face whiter than snow, and Gloria stood in the corner with the telephone in her hand.

Both of them were splattered with blood.

Lots of it.

Linda then focused on someone lying on the floor surrounded by a pool of blood.

Her other daughter...

She gagged. Half of Marina's skull was caved in; chunks of flesh and bits of bone covered with clumps of bloodied blonde hair lay nearby. 'Oh my God!' she murmured. That nutter of a daughter of hers had returned to finish what she'd started and Sam had been forced to kill her?

Linda should be horrified and devastated that her own daughter had been bludgeoned to death.

But she wasn't.

She felt only relief that Marina could no longer destroy anyone.

Remembering the situation, Linda rushed over to the bed and pulled Sam into her arms, glad that despite the circumstances, there was no resistance. Sam didn't pull away. She'd done the opposite. Her daughter clung to her in a way, thanks to being absent most of her life, she'd never experienced. 'Oh my God! Are you okay?'

Sam shook her head and the sobs came thick and fast. 'She's dead. She's my sister and she's dead and now I've got to kill my own father...'

Linda pulled Sam close, her own tears dropping into Sam's hair. 'I'm so sorry you have had to go through all of this. I should have told you everything from the start. If I hadn't been such a fuck-up in the first place, then none of this – none of *any* of what's happened, would have.'

'That doesn't matter now,' Sam hiccupped. 'But what am I going to do? How am I...?'

Linda's gaze tracked back to Marina, whose glassy eyes stared unseeing to the ceiling. 'How did she get in? How did you kill her?'

'Sam didn't do it,' Gloria said, her voice strange. 'It was me...'

'*You?*' Linda gasped. '*You* killed Marina?'

Gloria placed the receiver down with shaking hands. 'I know she's your daughter, Linda, but I had no choice. She was about to inject Samantha with something.'

'W-what? Inject her? What with?' Linda cried. Was there no end to her middle daughter's wickedness?

Gloria shook her head, wincing as the movement intensified

her raging headache. 'I don't know what it was, but she was going to kill both Sam and the baby...'

A stray tear rolled down her cheek, the base knowledge that she, Gloria Reynold, had killed somebody, prodding relentlessly. 'I hit her with that.' She nodded to a brass shire horse. 'It was all I had to hand.'

Linda stared at the large ornament, ever grateful it had been there. She then pointed at the dried blood on Gloria's face. 'She hit you?'

Gloria gently touched the painful cut on her temple. 'Yes, with something metal.' She glanced at Sam. 'When I came to, I heard the commotion and came into the room.' Her eyes filled with tears. 'She had Sam on the floor with a syringe to her neck...'

'Fuck!' Linda hissed. She clutched Sam's hand. 'The baby? Is the baby okay? Did she get you with the syringe?'

'I-I think I'm okay,' Sam said hollowly, averting her eyes from Marina's body.

'But the syringe? Did it go in you?' Linda screamed, panic rising with the implications.

Sam shook her head. 'No. I'm sure it didn't.'

'Maybe you should go to the hospital and get checked out?'

'I really don't need to. I think I'm fine – just shaken up.' Sam couldn't bring herself to mention the glancing blow Marina had landed to her belly or being slammed into the edge of the dressing table. If she referenced it, then it was almost inviting something to happen. Her baby had to be okay. It just had to.

She caressed her bump. It still hurt and she had strange pains, but surely that was normal with what had happened?

'What am I going to do about Bedworth?' she sobbed, desperate to put her mind on something else. The time had ticked on even further now. 'I can't let him get away with everything he's done.'

'Don't worry about that right now,' Linda said, pulling herself into gear. 'We need to sort this out first.'

She eyed the gruesome scene once more, suddenly having a horrible thought. 'Gloria, you haven't called the police and admitted this, have you?' Her head jerked in the direction of Marina's body.

Gloria smiled weakly. 'Actually, I was about to call Andrew. I know he'll come and sort the... erm... the mess out.'

Linda stared at Gloria in amazement, hardly able to believe she had stepped up like this. This kind of thing was so far out of her orbit, it was a different galaxy, but she'd done the lot.

But if she hadn't...

Shuddering with the thought of what could have been, her eyes fixed on the liquid-filled syringe lying on the floor which had rolled from Marina's dead hand.

'Phoning Andrew or Neil is a good idea,' Linda agreed. 'And, by the way, I'll probably go to hell for saying this, but I'm glad Marina is dead. Either way, it's true. I didn't think you had it in you, Glor, but well done.'

She pulled Sam back in for a hug. She would put this right somehow.

Frowning, she spotted a strange metal case on the bed and tugged it towards her. She opened it.

What was this then?

Eyeing the contents, nausea rose. *This had to be Marina's.*

One good thing had come from this and that was that Linda now knew exactly how she could put this right. She didn't have all the answers as to how yet, but she would. And this was a good starting point.

But she'd keep her plan to herself.

* * *

Vera had paced around enough to wear out the soles of her shoes. Moving across the room, she looked out of the kitchen window for the hundredth time seeing nothing, aside from the usual collection of no hopers wandering past her flat, swearing and mumbling.

Staring at the gun still clutched in her hand, she harrumphed loudly. 'I've had enough of this!'

Sophie looked up from the patch of lino she'd focused on for the past hour to see Vera stuffing the gun into her handbag. 'What are you doing?' she cried, on edge with this sudden change of direction.

'I can't bear waiting around any longer,' Vera scowled. 'We've had no news for *hours*. Andrew promised he'd keep us updated, yet I've heard fuck all and I'm not having it.' She zipped up her bag. 'We're going to Gloria's ourselves to find out what's going on.'

'What?' Sophie gasped, wide-eyed. 'We can't! We were told to stay here and go nowhere until w...'

'Yeah, until we heard otherwise, but being as we've heard nothing, we're going!' Vera grabbed her jacket. 'Come on!'

Sophie swallowed nervously. And that was a major part of what was bothering her, grating on her nerve endings consistently. Because they hadn't heard a thing, what did that signify? Did it mean something else had happened? That Andrew was hurt?

Her teeth cut into her bottom lip. Had they heard nothing because no one was available to tell them? Because everyone was dead...? 'What if we go and Andrew comes here? What if we put the others at risk by going out? Someone could be watching us.'

Vera tugged Sophie from the chair by her arm. 'Bollocks to that! I ain't waiting no more. If something's happened, then I need to know about it. Linda's my best pal and Sam's like a daughter to me, so I'm finding out what's going on.'

Sophie's pulse ramped up as she was frogmarched to the hallway, the terror of whoever was behind this growing tenfold. She had no choice but to accompany Vera though. She could hardly stay here on her own. She'd heard Andrew say she could also be a target.

Shoving her feet into her shoes, Sophie reluctantly followed Vera to the front door, hoping they weren't about to step into a minefield.

42

Andrew hadn't believed anything about this entire situation could prove to be amusing, but this threw his theory out of the water. He wished he had a camera. The only depressing thing was that they had now run out of things to use.

'Looks a picture, doesn't he?' Neil chuckled, his eyes twinkling as he stared at Tom Bedworth.

'That he does! But we've omitted something...' Andrew fished a foil wrap from his pocket and unwrapped it. Quickly cutting the cocaine on the table with his credit card, he pushed it into a thin copper pipe.

Glancing at the muttering mess which was Bedworth, his head lolling on his bare chest, Andrew grinned. 'The silly fucker's away with the fairies, so he needs waking up a bit. We don't want him missing out on how his new look feels...'

Keeping his thumb over the bottom of the thin pipe to ensure the cocaine remained inside, he nodded to Neil. 'Tip his head up.'

Neil grabbed Tom's hair and yanked his head up. 'Wakey, wakey!'

Squatting down, making doubly sure not to stand in the

spreading pool of urine under Tom, Andrew shoved the end of the pipe into one of Tom's nostrils and blew hard on the other end whilst Neil pinched Tom's lips together with his thumb and forefinger.

Jerked from his stupor, Tom flailed around pointlessly, crying and spluttering as he was forced to sniff back the cocaine. His bloodshot eyes flickered open, a low moan coming from his mouth.

'Do you reckon he's now aware of the full extent of his costume?' Neil laughed, stepping back for another view at their artwork. What a fantastic job they'd made.

Tom's face twisted into a grimace as the cocaine reached his brain, kickstarting and accelerating the awareness he'd been desperate to keep switched off.

Stripped naked, he'd been powerless to stop the Stoker lunatics from unstrapping him from the chair. His arms and legs were barely functional they'd stiffened up to such a degree. He'd been too focused on not getting his cock burnt off with the blow torch one of the Stokers had made a big deal of lighting to worry about being hoisted into a harness to suspend him horizontally.

Half curled up, he'd tried in vain to straighten out, but he just didn't have the strength.

Yes, his full focus had been on that blow torch until a very painful and thoroughly different situation unfolded.

Although Tom was never usually known to turn down a blast of the white powder, now was not the time to be alert. He clenched his teeth with the renewal of pain and humiliation, jerking his body to expel some of these bloody things out of him.

Andrew laughed louder as Tom thrashed about in his bindings. 'You look like a maggot on a hook, Bedworth.'

'Our additional decorations don't half suit you,' Neil added. 'Your arse looks like a porcupine. How we got so many of those tubes up there is a miracle. You must have an arsehole the size of the Dartford tunnel!'

Andrew admired Neil's handiwork. There was no way *he* was going near Bedworth's stinking arsehole. His part in this was to attach bulldog clips, the sort with serrated edges, along the man's cock, on his nipples, earlobes, the side of his nose, eyebrows – anywhere really. It was fucking hilarious and the best laugh he'd had in days.

Watching this abject tosser relive the attack on his nerve endings was priceless. And the plastic tubes poking out of Tom's backside – some long, some short, was a top idea. 'Wouldn't it be a travesty if the harness broke and he fell, pushing those things right up inside? Maybe that's something we could arrange for later?'

'I wonder if there's anything else we can add?' Neil mused, eyeing Tom malevolently.

'No! Please! Come on!' Tom screamed. 'You've had your fucking fun.'

'Fun?' Andrew snarled. 'We haven't even started yet!' Spying something feasible, he went to grab it when the loud ring of his mobile interrupted him.

His amusement waning, he searched his pocket for the phone. *It must be Seb.* 'Are you on your way? Oh!' Catching Neil's eye, he raised his eyebrows. 'What? She did wh...? Okay, okay, stop! Say no more over the phone. We'll come and deal with it. Sam okay...? Good, good. No, he's not here... He's at the Peacock but will be back here shortly... Okay, one of us will be with you as soon as we can.'

'What's going on?' Neil asked impatiently when Andrew ended the call.

His expression grim, Andrew beckoned Neil away from Tom's earshot. 'That was Gloria. We have a problem...'

* * *

Linda made good time in heading to Broad Street. Luckily, there was an abundance of cabs on call and she'd only had to wait a few minutes before one arrived at the house.

Grinding to a halt at Five Ways, she willed the lights to change. 'As quick as you can, please,' she muttered to the driver. 'Anywhere near the Peacock will be fine.'

'Feeling lucky tonight, love,' the driver asked, grinning in his rear-view mirror. 'Is it poker you play or roulette?'

'Whichever,' Linda mumbled, not in the mood for conversation. She had to get to the Peacock before Seb left. That's if he hadn't already.

Linda picked her fingers. If Seb had left, then she'd be too late. Without him, she hadn't a clue where Bedworth was. If this one and only opportunity was missed, then it would be too late.

But now she knew for definite Bedworth was firmly under lock and Marina was dead, it was safe to leave Sam for a while. Although her instinct was to remain with her daughter whilst she was in such a state of shock, the fact remained that there was no choice but to take the opportunity to put at least one thing right whilst she still could.

Linda glanced from the taxi window as the car began moving again, hoping the one chance to take added pressure from Sam wouldn't be wasted.

And she knew exactly what she was going to do.

'Just here will be fine,' Linda said as they turned into Broad Street seeing the usual snarl of queuing traffic snaking ahead of them. 'I'll walk the rest of the way.' It would be quicker than inching along behind this lot. She wasn't so decrepit that she couldn't leg it a hundred yards or so. *Fuck, she'd take her shoes off, if needs be.*

'Here you go.' Slapping a twenty-pound note into the driver's hand, aware it was way over the fare even including a hefty tip, Linda didn't care. There wasn't time to ponce about waiting for change.

Opening the car door before the taxi had fully stopped, she grabbed the metal case from the seat and hurried down the road. Clattering along in her heels, Linda gave up apologising for barging into people after she'd knocked or elbowed the fifth person.

Clearing the Peacock's steps, Linda waved away the doorman, daring his chances of refusing her entry, should he fail to recognise her.

She reached the reception desk, sweating and out of breath. Leaning on the counter, she forced air into her tortured lungs. 'Seb Stoker,' Linda gasped. 'I need to see Seb Stoker.'

The receptionist eyed Linda curiously. 'Mr Stoker isn't available at the moment.'

Linda gave the woman one of her best scowls. 'Considering I'm his fucking mother-in-law, I think you'll find he is. I'll make my own way to his office, shall I?'

Without waiting for a reply, Linda turned her back on the receptionist and slammed through the double doors leading to the Stoker brothers' offices, hoping Seb was still on site.

Come on, come on, she thought, her heels clicking on the shiny floor.

Reaching Seb's office, Linda didn't see the point in knocking and slammed straight into the room.

Seb swung away from the gun cabinet at the far end of his office, his anger evident at the unexpected intrusion.

'I expect I'm not your favourite person at the moment with what's happened.' Linda wasn't about to give Seb the chance to launch into her about what her decision had caused this time.

What she had to do was too important, and given time, everybody would realise that.

Seeing Linda, rather than a member of staff, Seb fell into panic mode. 'Is Sam okay? The baby? Is the baby okay?' Darting over, he grabbed Linda, a shotgun still in one hand.

'Sam's fine.' Eyeing the shotgun uncomfortably, Linda pushed the barrel in the opposite direction. 'Put that bloody thing down. Look, you need to tell me where you're holding Bedworth.'

Seb stared at the shotgun, almost surprised to see it. Placing it on the desk, he indicated for Linda to take a seat. 'Why would I do that?'

'I'm aware you're going to finish this prick behind Sam's back.' Linda held her hand up at the flash of anger on Seb's face. 'I don't blame you. With the new developments, Sam's in no fit state to do it and...' She looked down at her hands uncomfortably, 'I'm not entirely sure she knows what she wants to do. But before you do anything...'

'Yes?' Seb impatiently crossed his ankle over one knee and steepled his fingers under his chin. 'What is it?'

'I want to confront him,' Linda said. 'I know he'll soon be dead, so I want to be able to look my daughter in the eye and tell her that I've given the man who ruined everyone's lives a piece of my mind. I want Bedworth to know what he's done to both me and to his daughter.'

After all these years, saying out loud to another person that Tom Bedworth was Sam's father was strange. Three decades she'd maintained a different story. Admitting she'd borne that monster's child was hard, but she in no way regretted the beautiful daughter she had in Sam. She just wished she could say *anyone* other than Bedworth had fathered her. 'I want that bastard to know how much he's impacted everyone.'

Seb raised an eyebrow. 'You do realise he'll get off on that, knowing just how much he's hurt you all?'

'That's as maybe.' Linda's eyes narrowed. 'But he can think what he likes. This is what Sam would do and I owe her. You can take away her decision to finish this herself all you like, but she's going to know that I've said my piece first.'

She glanced at the metal case belonging to Marina which sat at her feet. She had worked out what she would do and exactly what she would utilise to accomplish it. She just needed in and once she had that, *she'd* be dispatching Tom Bedworth.

She'd brought him into everyone's lives, so it was right she should be the one to remove him. And, if this went to plan, Seb would unknowingly make that possible.

Seb mulled over Linda's words. Although he had to give her credit for being hard-headed with good intentions, he didn't want to muddy the waters. Taking her to Bedworth would slow things up and he had to get this finished as quickly as possible. 'I'm not sure, Linda. I was just about to call Gloria to check on Sam. I take it she's still not in a good state?'

'Andrew hasn't called you yet about what's happened?' Linda asked.

Seb frowned. He'd had a missed call from Andrew not long ago, but had stalled on returning it, presuming it was about when he was returning. 'What you do you mean?'

Linda tensed. *Shit!* She'd presumed Andrew had informed his brother. Now she had no choice but to tell him. 'Well, I... erm...' Saved by the ringing of his mobile, she exhaled with relief.

'I told you I'll be there, Andrew,' Seb barked. 'It's just... *What?*' His eyes swung accusingly in Linda's direction. 'Marina? And Gloria did this?'

Linda watched a nerve in Seb's neck twitch. She thought she'd been saved by the bell and that the phone call would buy her some time then, but maybe not...

'And Sam?' Seb roared, getting to his feet. 'Is she okay...? And you're sure?'

When Seb shrugged on his jacket, Linda leapt from her chair. 'Sam's fine. I've seen myself that she's fine!'

Swinging around, Seb glared at Linda. 'Why the fuck didn't *you* tell me about this?'

'I thought you'd been already told.'

'I'll have to go round there now and... No, I was talking to Linda. Yeah, she's here... Listen, Andrew... No way! It has to be me who does it. I'm coming now!'

Linda jumped back in the minute Seb ended the call. 'I mean it! Sam is fine. Honestly, she is. Do you think I would have left the house if she wasn't?'

Gritting his teeth, Seb snatched up his car keys. 'I'm doing Bedworth now. I'll call Gloria on the way and speak to Sam. If she's not fine, then everyone's head will be on the fucking chopping block and Bedworth will have to wait!'

'I'm coming with you.' Linda grabbed the metal case and followed Seb out of the door.

Seb strode down the corridor towards the underground car park where his motor waited. *Gloria had removed Marina Devlin from the picture?* He didn't think the old girl had it in her, but was glad she had.

He barged through the double doors to the steps, not caring if they rebounded in Linda's face. There wasn't a moment to lose and he didn't have time to argue any more as to whether she was coming or not.

* * *

Sam was aware Gloria was watching her every move, but there were only two things she could concentrate on: willing the stomach cramps to subside and scraping together the resolve to deal with Tom Bedworth.

She still hadn't mentioned the nagging pains in her belly, and instead, convinced herself they weren't worsening.

Sam chewed her lip to hide the wince as pain shot through her once again. It wasn't getting worse. It was only because she couldn't stop thinking about it, terrified something unbearable was happening to her baby.

But she had to stop concentrating on them. It solved nothing. Neither did tying herself in knots about whether Marina had succeeded in jabbing that syringe into her without her noticing. The more she thought about it; the more she wracked her brains to piece together every movement; every word and every expression that occurred during the short time she'd been cornered by the woman sharing half her blood, the more confused she became.

Her eyes tracked once again to the lump of Marina's body on the floor, shrouded in a bedspread Linda had thrown over her.

Sam shuddered. She'd done the same thing with Dan to prevent Tina from fixating on his body, but hadn't realised it made no difference. She knew *exactly* what lay underneath that bedspread – the dark red seeping through the material an unnecessary reminder.

'Andrew or Neil will be here soon...' Gloria said, seeing where Sam's focus lay. 'It won't be long now.'

'Has Seb called?' Sam asked, her voice croaky.

'Not yet,' Gloria answered nonchalantly, but her nerves were fluttering in the breeze. She'd held it together this long, promising Linda she'd keep things calm here and that, she intended to do.

Sam frowned. She'd to'd and fro'd with the impossible decision she had to make for what seemed like forever. Now she'd reached a conclusion. Nothing else, no matter what, could take precedence in front of her baby.

Keeping her child safe was tantamount. It always had been, but now more than ever. She could and *would* not entertain anything else to up the stress levels. In body or mind.

'I need to speak to Seb.' Sam took a deep breath, unsure whether she felt a failure or the opposite for reaching her decision. 'Under the circumstances, I think Seb should deal with that man, rather than me.'

And that's who he was – 'that man'. The name 'Tom Bedworth' had stuck in her throat long before this, but now, uttering those words out loud made his very essence hang like a miasma.

Gloria nodded, hiding her relief. 'I think that's a good decision.'

'Can you call him?' Sam pushed, eager to set her decision in stone before her exhausted brain backtracked. The circling arguments in her head were driving her to distraction.

'I'm sure he'll call us soon.' Gloria played down the worry of being party to keeping Sam in the dark over something else. Linda had already told her that being as Sam was okay, she'd play down the extent of what Marina had attempted to do. Seb would be over like a shot otherwise.

But Gloria had her suspicions of what Linda was planning. She too had seen the contents of Marina's metal case and when Linda had said she'd be back shortly, taking the case with her, it was fairly clear what was going through her mind.

She'd opened her mouth to speak, only to be silenced by Linda's slight nod to keep schtum.

Whether she was correct with her theory hardly mattered. What mattered was that this ended with everyone intact.

'Gloria, can you *please* call Seb?' Sam repeated, this time unable to hide the wince as another pain crunched through her body.

Gloria tensed. 'Is something hurting you? Is there something you haven't told us? Something that we should know in case we need t...'

'No, I'm fine,' Sam said hastily. 'I just want to speak to my husband and get this nightmare wrapped up.'

'Okay.' Gloria hesitatingly got up from the chair. 'I'll just give it a few more minutes and then I'll call.'

43

Andrew slammed the door behind him to drown out the noise of Tom's wailing and ranting. 'It won't be long before Seb's here, so give me a hand finding stuff for the clean-up at Gloria's. There's bound to be things here I can use.'

'What? I'm staying here with this goon again?' Neil spat. 'For Christ's sake, Andrew!'

'I can't leave Sam and Gloria with a body longer than necessary,' Andrew shrugged. 'I'll take the van, but I'll be back as soon as I can. Personally, I'd prefer to watch Bedworth taking his final breath, but shit happens.'

Neil rummaged around a store cupboard for heavy-duty bleach and cloths, whilst Andrew grappled with a tarpaulin. 'I presume you're bringing the body back for it to join the others?' He nodded to the concrete mixer vat.

'Might as well. A couple more won't hurt, as long as they don't block the ducts up. By the way, I've untied that fuckwit. He's supported only by the harness now so Seb can crack straight on with offloading him and won't have to mess about afterwards.' Andrew bundled the materials up in his arms – the only thing stopping him from giving Bedworth a punch in the trap for luck on his way out.

Instead he consoled himself with a quick boot to the ribs. 'Enjoy your death!' he snarled. 'This prick's finally run out of steam, so I doubt whether Seb will need to do much more than blow on him to send him on his merry way!'

Glancing in Bedworth's direction, Neil couldn't disagree. But Seb wouldn't be pleased arriving to find the life all but ebbed from the man. Their brother found it important for targets to be fully aware how they died and by whom.

Watching Andrew slam the van door, clamber in and set off, Neil returned to the shop floor of the cement works. Perhaps Bedworth could use a bit more coke to put a spring back in his step?

'What is this place?' As they approached the industrial site, Linda craned her neck to peer up at the towering building.

'A cement works,' Seb muttered. 'Not our choice. It's where Bedworth and Potter brought Sam and that other woman.' The thought of Sam being here, strung up against the wall like an animal, still burnt the very fibres of his soul. The vivid image of his beautiful, pregnant wife in this dump pushed his simmering rage up several notches to boiling point.

'Are you happy now you've spoken to Sam yourself?' Linda asked, cringing with the intensity of anger flowing from Seb.

'Happy is the wrong word.'

Linda kept the metal case safely wedged between her feet in the footwell and continued chatting brightly. 'At least now you can do what's needed with a clean conscience.'

Having heard Sam's voice down the phone on the way over

here had been a salve. It had put Seb's mind at rest that Sam was safe. It had also been a reminder of what that cunt, Bedworth, had done.

He smiled wryly. And yes, Sam's decision made things easier, but a clean conscience was not something usually attached to someone about to take another's life.

'I have to say, I'm surprised she changed her tune and wants you to do Bedworth,' Linda continued. *Not that Seb would be doing it, but he didn't know that yet...*

'Stop prattling on, for God's sake!' Seb snapped. 'I just want to get this done.'

Stopping the car, he got out. Sam may have given him the all-clear to finish the man and he was happy to comply. He'd have done so anyway, but he couldn't help but think that at some point down the line, she would come to resent him for it. It was something he'd have to risk regardless.

Seb banged on the door of the building and within ten seconds the grinding noise of metal filled the air as the heavy door was dragged open.

'What's she doing here?' Neil cried, spotting Linda standing behind Seb.

Seb indicated for Linda to follow. 'She wants to talk to Bedworth.'

'Seriously?' Neil frowned. His eyes flickered to Linda. 'We can't waste any more time.'

'It's not a waste!' Linda snapped, walking into the expanse of the large building. 'I've got every right to say what I need before that cunt departs this earth. He's Sam's father and needs to know the countless problems he's caused.'

'You don't have to remind us of that unpleasant fact,' Neil muttered, his resentment clear. He was still unable to get his head around the fact that Sam was physically related to that bastard.

'I've said she can have a few minutes,' Seb barked, his patience too frayed to discuss his decision. Allowing Linda to get what she wanted off her chest was better than putting up with her fucking nagging.

'She'd best hurry up, then,' Neil sniped. 'He ain't got long left.'

Seb's eyes flashed. 'What have you done? I told both you and Andrew not to go over the top or fuck him up past all help. That's *my* job!'

MY job, Linda thought, itching to get to Tom. She eyed the high-ceilinged space, then frowned at the immense vat in the distance. The place was creepy. *Horrible.* Her insides churned. The thought of Sam being kept in this awful place for even a few hours made her skin crawl. 'Where is he?'

'Over there. Behind that partition.' Seb grabbed Linda's arm as she hurried forward. 'Wait! I need to sort my stuff out first.'

Shaking her arm from Seb's grip, Linda pursed her lips, chomping at the bit to do what was necessary to the bastard who had usurped her life, ruined her daughter's and almost killed her grandchild.

She would finish Tom Bedworth all right, but to do that, she needed to be on her own, otherwise Seb would step in. 'I'll be fine alone with him.'

'Don't be stupid,' Seb growled. 'You think I'll risk you being alone with that tosser? He could attack you.'

'Fat chance of that!' Neil shrugged his large shoulders. 'He's not in a state to do shag all!'

Ignoring Seb's irritation at Neil's remark, Linda took the opportunity to press on. 'Look, I only want to say my piece, but I need space to do that. There are things I need to say... personal things that I'm not discussing with an audience. My prior decisions are humiliating enough as it is.'

She looked straight at Seb. 'What I want to do will only take a few minutes. Get your stuff ready and then he's all yours.' *Even though there will be nothing left for you to do...*

Seb cracked his knuckles. Bedworth was trussed up and secure and being as his brothers had taken it upon themselves to go over the top, the man sounded incapable of attacking Linda. He didn't want to be explaining to Sam that he'd given the go-ahead for her mother to walk into a trap, so he'd check for himself. 'One minute,' he muttered.

He walked in the direction of where Bedworth was held. If the cunt was as fubared as Neil said, Linda could have her time.

He could do without this. He'd told himself the next time he laid eyes on this bastard would be the last, but now he'd have to look at him twice.

Rounding the corner, nausea flooded through him at the sight of the man he despised with every cell of his body. 'Fucking hell,' he hissed. *Neil wasn't lying. It would take no time to finish this cunt off.*

He would normally be aggrieved by this, but in this scenario, he wasn't. Now he just wanted it over with. *Done.*

Moving closer, Seb watched Tom's eyes darting around all over the place. He booted him in his ribs, adding another bruise to the blue and purple ones covering his torso. 'Hey, tosser! You have a visitor.'

'Visitor?' Tom squawked. 'Samantha? Is she here?' He *knew* Sam would come through for him in the end. She'd come to rescue him, hadn't she? 'Let me see my daughter then, you bastard!'

Seb controlled his raw need to bin Linda's wishes off and stab this prick in the throat here and now. The wanker was wired to fuck, the stupid cunt. He hoped minimum coke had been wasted on the prick.

'Well?' Tom screeched, his voice high-pitched. 'Bring me my daughter, Stoker!'

Seb turned on his heels, leaving Bedworth to continue ranting his demands. He'd suddenly found the energy for that, hadn't he? But judging by the state of his body, he was no threat to Linda.

Shaking his head with half-amusement at the twisted spectacle his brothers had made Tom Bedworth into, he moved back around the corner and nodded at his mother-in-law. Bedworth wouldn't be expecting Linda to turn up to give him a round of fucks. 'You've got two minutes.'

Then it was *his* turn.

Watching Linda rush in Tom's direction, Seb turned to Neil. 'Get yourself over to Gloria's and give Andrew a hand in sorting out that body.'

'But I wanted to see wh...'

'Just go, Neil! It doesn't need two of us to finish this. From what I can see, you've already had your turn, so get over there, help Andrew and double check my wife is all right!'

'You don't need to see this, love.' Gloria held her hand out for Sam to take.

'I'll be as quick as I can,' Andrew said, uncomfortably aware of Sam watching intently as he unravelled the tarpaulin next to the lump on the floor. Shocked and pale she may be, but she was physically okay, which was the main thing.

Sam refused Gloria's offer of being steered from the room like a child at an unsuitable movie. 'I'm staying where I am,' she said firmly, wanting to witness for herself that her sister – the one who hated her enough to kill her and her child, was truly dead.

Her initial shocked guilt had now dissipated – an out of place and unnecessary reaction to one more thing in a chain of mind-fuck events.

She was thinking clearly now. Seb was dealing with Tom

Bedworth and it would soon be done, if it wasn't already. And that's who he was – *Tom Bedworth* – not her father. Her father – the one which counted, was Len Reynold – the man who had brought her up.

And *that* was what she would concentrate on remembering from now on.

44

'I knew it.' Vera rushed up the driveway. 'There's a van here! I told you there must have been developments!'

Sophie flung a tenner at the bemused taxi driver and hurried after Vera, cursing as her foot went over on the gravel. She could see the van, but whose was it? 'Vera, wait! That could belong to anybody! It could be someone who...'

'If you think I'm waiting, then you're nuts, girl!' Vera bent over, her ample backside taking centre stage. She scrabbled behind a stone urn. 'I reckon, if we're lucky, this should still be here.'

Lucky? If what was there? Whatever Vera was doing, Sophie didn't like the look of it one bit. She nervously clocked the substantial property that looked to be in darkness.

'A-ha!' Vera cried triumphantly, holding up a gold-coloured Yale key. 'Linda's a creature of habit. She told me ages ago she'd left a spare somewhere around here in case of emergencies. And if this isn't one, I don't know what is!'

Sophie almost choked. 'We can't just let ourselves in! This isn't our house. I...'

'We can and we fucking well shall!' Vera pulled Sophie forward so she had no choice but to follow up the steps to the door.

With a thumping heart, Sophie watched Vera shove the key into the lock. 'But what if...'

'My friends could be in trouble. Sam could be in trouble!' Vera hissed as the door opened. 'Now shut the hell up and get inside.'

Sophie moved reluctantly behind Vera into the large hallway illuminated only by a table lamp in the corner. 'I don't like this. It's too quiet. Maybe we...'

'Shh!' Vera held up her hand for silence. 'I can hear something. It's coming from down there.'

As Vera walked away, Sophie glanced around, unwilling to be left standing alone in a stranger's house when people intent on causing damage could be on the loose. Feeling she may pass out with fright, she followed into the shadows of the long hallway.

'There! It's coming from up there!' Vera gestured towards where the hallway spliced off to a further corridor on the right-hand side.

Sophie tentatively edged into the darkness, sure the noise of her banging heart would alert anyone who might be in this place. But she *could* hear something – a rustling sound combined with dragging. 'What is it?'

Vera put her fingers to Sophie's lips and mouthed the word 'quiet', then turned back to the closed door in front of her. Her stomach lurched with what she may find. A torrent of worst-case scenarios flashed through her mind.

Apart from this strange noise, the house *was* too quiet; too still. Where were Gloria and Sam? And Linda? Her best friend had the voice of a foghorn, not leaving any doubt as to her presence, so why could she hear nothing apart from that odd noise?

Holding her breath, Vera pressed herself closer to the door. The noise was definitely coming from this room. There was nothing else for it. She'd have to burst in. If there was someone in there, she'd have to pray the element of surprise was enough to get a head start.

Taking a deep breath, Vera turned the doorknob and quickly shouldered the door open.

Momentarily blinded with the bright light after the contrast of the darkened hallway, it took a couple of seconds before she registered what was inside. 'Fuck!' she shrieked.

'What the hell are you doing here?' Andrew roared at the unexpected intrusion, further surprised to see it was Vera. It was only then he saw she wasn't alone as Sophie came into view, an expression of unparalleled horror across her face.

He glanced down at the sight visible to these two women: the lifeless and staring face of Marina Devlin with large parts of her face and skull missing; the rest of her body wrapped in the tarpaulin.

Shit, shit, shit! Sophie wasn't supposed to see this. She. Wasn't. Supposed. To. See. This...

Unable to move her eyes from the battered remains of the woman who had once been Marina Devlin, a scream wedged in Sophie's throat.

She hated Marina. The woman terrified her, but killing her like that?

Her eyelids fluttered, her head spinning. Reaching out, she steadied herself against the wall. The man she loved had battered a woman to death so viciously that half of her skull was missing?

Her hand flew to her mouth as vomit threatened to lurch from the pit of her stomach across the nicely decorated bedroom.

Or what once *had* been nicely decorated, if it wasn't peppered with blood...

The minute Sophie realised the man she'd fallen so hard for was a Stoker, knowing what he and the rest of his family were involved with, it had crossed her mind what she would see or be aware of if she pursued a relationship with him. But *this* underlined it in a no-holds-barred technicolour image.

Her heart raced. She loved Andrew and the thought of not being with him was intolerable, but how could she truly love a man who could kill a woman – kill *anyone*, in cold blood like this? And blatantly getting rid of the evidence – acting like cleaning up the mess was as simple as making a cup of tea?

Could anyone else have killed Marina, apart from him?

Her eyes flicked around the room, seeing only Sam and an older woman who didn't look like she'd say boo to a goose.

Sophie shook uncontrollably, guilt raging that she felt nothing but relief that the woman who had terrorised her could no longer do so. It also clawed deep that no matter what Andrew Stoker had done or continued to do, she couldn't walk away. Her feelings ran too deep.

Her thoughts froze as Andrew moved towards her, his outstretched hands covered in blood. *Marina's blood.*

'Sophie,' Andrew said quietly. 'You weren't supposed to see this. I never wanted you to see anything like th...'

'Forget that shit!' Vera yelled. 'Are you all right, Sam? And you, Gloria? Did this bitch attack either of you? Where the fuck is Linda?' Her eyes flickered around the room. 'Don't tell me Marina got Linda? Where is she?'

'We're okay, Vera. But Linda?' Sam sat up, a new trace of worry flickering across her face. 'I thought she went back to yours again?' She turned to Gloria. 'You said she went back to Vera's.' She jumped from the seat in panic. 'If she's not there, where has she gone?'

Sophie allowed herself to be enveloped in Andrew's powerful arms. She couldn't stop her feelings. She loved him no matter what and would have to learn to adapt to this gruesome life of his. *Somehow...*

Andrew pulled Sophie close, aware his hands were caked with blood, but all he knew was that Sophie had accepted him. But he could almost taste the assumptions speeding through her mind. He'd never wanted her to witness something like this. Not ever. Thanks to Marina, she'd already seen enough to haunt her for life and this would only add to her horror and unease. 'Sophie... I...'

'Will someone tell me where Linda is?' Sam repeated, her voice tinged with rising panic. 'Gloria, you said th...'

'I-I think she went looking for Seb so she could see Tom Bedworth,' Gloria blurted.

'What?' Sam cried. 'Why? How?'

'I don't know for certain, but she took the case – the case that... that woman brought and...'

'Oh my God!' Sam gasped, the truth dawning. 'She's gone to kill Bedworth herself! She's going to inject him, like Marina tried to do to me!' Feeling another twinge, her hands fell to her belly. 'But how does she know where he is? I didn't tell her! Oh God! Bedworth will kill her... He'll...'

'Inject you?' Andrew interrupted. 'What do you mean, "inject you"?' He swung towards Gloria. 'What the bloody hell is this? You never mentioned anything about that!'

'Do you want random people wandering in here? The fucking front door's wide open!' Neil moved into the room, stopping on seeing Sophie and Vera. 'What's going on?'

'Why aren't you at the cement works?' Andrew yelled. 'Is Seb with Bedworth?'

'Yes. I left him with Linda. Seb decided to let her talk to the prick before he...' He glanced between the women... 'erm... before he finishes the job.'

'*What*?' Sam shrieked.

'Seb will make sure she comes to no harm,' Andrew said, determined to calm this shit down. 'And that's good he's there because even though Bedworth's fucked out of his mind, I still wouldn't want her too close being as I untied him ready for death.'

'Fuck! I forgot to mention that. Seb agreed to let Linda see Bedworth alone!' Neil raked his hand through his hair. *How could he have forgot?* 'Fuck!'

'Fuck' didn't even half sum it up, Andrew thought. Fumbling for his phone, he was halfway through dialling Seb when Sam falling to her knees clutching her stomach stopped him in his tracks.

45

'This is probably the most fitting thing for you to look like at the end, you piece of shit,' Linda spat. She knew she was limited in doing what was needed before Seb said her time was up, but it was impossible not to have a dig at Tom over the Stokers' brilliant masterpiece.

How she loved the Stokers. She couldn't have dreamt up a better tribute to this amoeba if she'd tried.

If she wasn't so strapped for time, she could spend hours ridiculing him, knowing the prick resented humiliation more than losing at cards, the shallow bastard.

Tom's disappointment when Linda, rather than his daughter, moved into the room had merged into something slightly different. Neil Stoker giving him that extra blast of coke may have had sinister intentions, but unbeknownst to the dolt, it had worked in *his* favour.

He couldn't escape from here – not now Sam coming to his aid was not happening. He should have known the spoilt bitch wouldn't come through for him. But his arsehole was now so numb, he'd almost forgotten the collection of stupid fucking pipes rammed up there. Or the clips over the rest of him, which was one benefit.

Yeah, the Stokers had had their fun.

Tom smiled with what was left of his teeth. He was going to die and he wasn't happy about it. To be honest, he'd teetered between hysteria and true panic, sprinkled with hope on hearing he'd got a visitor, but now that hope was dead.

And soon, so would he.

But whichever stupid thick fuck had allowed the witch who had screwed up his life for decades in here to have one last pop at him had overlooked something. And that gave him the drive to keep his heart beating and override the pain coursing through his body. The Stokers had let this slut from hell in here – *alone*, whilst leaving him untied. 'Still an ugly fucking old cunt, then Linda?' he sneered. 'Oh well. No amount of makeup could ever help you!'

Cheap insults, but the stupid cow had a complex and every last dig he could get, counted.

He may be battered to a pulp, but decades of resentment worked wonders in scraping that last miniscule piece of resolve to ensure that being as he was fucked, so would *she* be.

Because his slag of a greedy daughter had clearly authorised this, it was fitting Samantha should pay. She'd officially be an orphan after today and forever have to live with that being *her* fault.

'I've always been good at biding my time.' Tom's smashed mouth curled into his trademark smirk that he knew Linda hated. He'd do it all the more even though it hurt like fuck.

Linda placed the metal case on the table and flicked open the catches. 'Say what you like. Sam deserves better than you for a father. She always did.'

'That's why I sold her. Not because I didn't think myself worthy,' Tom sneered. 'But because I didn't want her. I still don't. I *never* wanted her. Like I never wanted *you*. You were a bad shag, stupid enough to get knocked up.'

Linda burnt with rage, but controlled her desire to smash Tom's sneering face. 'You're disgusting.'

'Ah, but you loved me long enough despite it all. You probably still do,' Tom laughed. It hurt his raw throat, but the added pain seeing the humiliation burning on Linda's face was worth it. The bitch knew every word was true.

'I'm supposed to take you seriously when you have tubes coming out of your arse?' Linda snapped. A pathetic thing to say, but that his comment had got to her, was worse.

Time was running out. She mustn't rise to Tom's barbs. *Nothing* this despicable man said must rile her enough to deflect from her aim.

Peering into the case, she fished out a vial. She unscrewed the top. This was the one she would use. It was lethal, plus it was the only one out of all of them that she'd ever heard of.

She hadn't a clue how to administer it and could only hope this would work. It had to.

She involuntarily shuddered as she wondered which of these things Marina had planned to inject into Sam. It wasn't the one she'd chosen for Tom because this one was bitty, not liquid, but she guessed that whatever Marina had picked, its effects would have been equally detrimental.

Christ, Marina had been a sick fuck. *Had* being the operative word, thank God.

But what did that make her?

Linda's mouth flattened into a thin, straight line.

It made her a woman; a mother – repaying the beast who had

used and abused her, sold her daughter and trashed everything around him.

And to do that, she would live with the guilt.

Taking the opportunity of Linda's distraction, Tom's exhausted, wired mind decided to quit the insults and take his chance to strike whilst the chance afforded him.

Clenching his jaw, he steeled himself against the pain and gingerly readjusted himself in the harness, willing it not to squeak. Or worse, give way.

He couldn't alert Linda to the fact that he was about to finish her before she had the chance to do whatever *she'd* got planned.

Oh God, he'd waited years for this. Yeah, it was a tad depressing he was set to shortly lose his place on earth, but at least he could go to his death knowing that Linda fucking Matthews had gone to hers first.

And that was worth everything.

His own death wouldn't be too bad. Stoker was too much of a hot-tempered cunt to drag his demise out for long. As much as the wanker wanted to, Tom knew all he had to do was say enough to blow the freak's temper and he'd lose it.

He smiled. Even in death he'd get at least one last laugh on Sebastian Stoker.

But... His eyes swivelled to concentrate on Linda's back as she busied herself at the table with whatever she was doing. He'd deal with *her* first.

Gratified the harness hadn't squeaked, Tom rolled his hips to one side, making sure he didn't push any tubes up to where the sun didn't shine. He snaked one hand around to his backside and gingerly felt for an end. Sickness rolled as he touched it – even light pressure shot weird sensations in places he'd rather not dwell on.

Bastard Stokers.

Tom slowly pulled one of the plastic tubes out and lowered it to the floor. Holding his breath, he dropped it, hoping the noise would go unnoticed.

It did.

He repeated this several times. How many of these bloody things had those wankers shoved up there?

Satisfied he'd removed them all, he inched forward and turned, ready to pounce. Letting his backside take the weight to swing his stiff legs down to the ground, Tom made an unearthly sound as a bolt of pain shot high in his rectum.

Fuck! He'd missed one.

Swinging around, Linda yelped as Tom flew forward from the harness to land face down on the floor. *He wasn't secured? How the hell could he not have been secured?*

Tom scrabbled around, willing his arms to push himself to his knees and Linda knew she had to act fast.

Like *now*.

Dashing over, she snatched one of the plastic tubes from the floor.

Shoving it into the vial, she hoped enough of the contents remained stuck to the unmentionable slime on the tube to have an effect.

Shoving this stuff up Tom's arse hadn't been the way she planned to do this, but she'd take whatever she could get now.

She moved towards Tom, his arse still up in the air as he regained his footing, offering her an opportunity, and cringing with revulsion, Linda slammed the tube in the general area of the one already poking from his backside, not caring if it ripped his arsehole to shreds.

From Tom's guttural roar and the tube half-disappearing, Linda thought she'd hit the mark. But would it be enough to do the job? She didn't know.

Tom lurched to get to his knees, his expression feral as he lunged towards Linda. 'You raddled fucking sow!'

Holding the half-empty vial out of reach, Linda shoved her thumb nail into Tom's right eyeball.

Screaming, Tom raised his hand to his eye. Tipping backwards, he only succeeded in pushing the wedged pipes up further.

With Tom lying on the floor screaming blue murder, Linda tipped the remains of the vial into his gaping mouth.

'What the hell?' Tom spluttered, spitting to rid his mouth of whatever was in there. Any more fucking coke and he'd have a heart attack.

Deciding he had little to lose, he reached around and yanked the plastic tubes from his backside and tossed them across the room and then went for Linda.

Linda leapt backwards towards the door. It hadn't worked! It wasn't going to work! He wasn't dead! Shit!

* * *

'It's got really bad,' Sam panted, her face twisting with pain. 'I thought it was getting better.'

'Why the fuck didn't you tell us about this earlier, duck?' Vera soothed. Squatting down, she stroked Sam's hair. 'Try and keep calm. Panic will only make things worse.'

'Am I losing the baby?' Sam cried, her panic intensifying. These days, not much in life bothered her, but this... this was different. 'Please tell me – am I losing my child?'

'No!' Vera said, hoping her words proved true. 'I won't let that happen.'

'I thought it was subsiding. I thought it... Aaargh!'

Vera looked to Gloria, then Andrew and Neil. 'This isn't right. We need to get her to hospital.'

'No!' Sam shrieked. 'I can't! What about...' Her eyes darted to the now fully wrapped tarpaulin on the floor.

'Don't worry about that. This pair will sort it. Just concentrate on yourself,' Vera said, then mouthed to Andrew to phone for an ambulance.

Feeling utterly impotent to help, Andrew dialled 999 and looked on in horror as Sam winced with another stomach cramp. Why hadn't she told anyone she'd been kicked in the stomach and hit the dressing table before? *Shit – if she lost this baby...* 'Hello? Yes, ambulance, please.'

Turning his back in the hope of shielding the words he was reluctant to utter, he gritted his teeth. 'It looks like it may be a miscarriage... About twelve weeks, I think. No, not me. I'm her husband's brother. Yes... okay.'

Sophie locked eyes with Andrew, seeing his worry and was unable to stop a tear from sliding down her cheek. Sam couldn't lose this baby. Not after getting through all of this. It wasn't fair.

'The ambulance is on its way.' Andrew stared at the mobile in his hand. 'I need to call Seb and let him know what's happening.' *And it would floor his brother.*

Rounding the corner at the sudden noise, only to see Linda pinned to the floor by her throat, the naked Bedworth astride her, Seb launched into damage limitation mode. *How the fuck was Bedworth out of his tethers?*

'Get your hands off her!' he roared, ripping Tom off Linda by the back of his neck.

'I'll kill the bitch!' Tom screamed, his arms and legs flailing wildly in the air as Seb launched him across the other side of the room.

Hearing Bedworth's skull crack against the brickwork was gratifying, but nowhere near as pleasant as when the bastard stopped breathing.

'What the hell happened?' Seb growled as Linda scrabbled off the floor, angry red welts already visible on her neck.

'He just went for me! I didn't realise he was loose. I...'

Seb grimaced. *He hadn't realised Bedworth was loose either.* Christ, he knew leaving Linda alone with this tosser was a bad move. He should have stuck to his guns.

He focused back on the horrible sight of Tom getting up from the floor. This one should be in no fit state to fight back after what his brothers had unleashed, but it seemed the man had more stamina than he'd given credit for.

Or his hate overrode even death.

Seb rolled up his sleeves, not having the time to spend removing jackets. He'd finish this now, come what may.

'I thought it would work,' Linda babbled, horrified that her plan had gone so horribly wrong. 'I really thought it would work.'

Taking no notice of Linda's senseless chatter, Seb moved towards Tom. Because of this unexpected change, he had no tools; no weapons; no nothing. He'd do it with his bare hands.

Tom was almost on his feet, his face twisted with hatred when something changed. Freezing mid-grimace, his expression morphed into something completely different.

Fear.

Tom clutched his throat. 'Aaargh!' he screamed. 'It's fucking burning me. I can't... I can't swallow. I...'

Seb grabbed a fistful of Tom's hair. 'Shame about that, Bedworth. Saves me having to strangle you, but I'll do it anyway.'

'It's like needles! I'm on fucking fire.' Tom batted his hands around, his eyes building with panic. 'I can't... I can't swallow. You've got to help me!'

Seb braced himself to lay his hands on this creature. Taking a deep breath, he slammed Tom up against the wall, his eyes narrowing to menacing slits.

'Wait!' Linda cried, a glimmer of hope resurfacing. 'Wait just a second! It might be working after all!'

Seb swung around, confusion mixing with his anger. 'What?'

'The poison!' Linda cried, not taking her eyes off Tom. 'I think it's working!'

'Poison? Christ, I haven't got time for this.'

'Arsenic! I gave him arsenic!' Linda's face broke into a smile seeing Tom clutch his stomach and retch. 'Get back, Seb! Quickly!'

Seb jumped back just in time to avoid being hit full on by a shower of projectile vomit. 'Oh fuck,' he muttered. *Arsenic? Linda had poisoned Bedworth with fucking arsenic?* 'What the...'

'It was Marina's.' Linda pointed to the metal case on the side, her eyes dancing with glee.

'Somebody... somebody help!' Tom wailed, his voice shredded like he'd swallowed broken glass. More vomit sprayed from his mouth and he fell to his knees, his hand darting between his throat and his stomach. 'Oh no! Oh...'

Seb grimaced with disgust as Tom's bowels emptied onto the floor with the same urgency as the vomit. His hand flew to cover his mouth and nose, the stench appalling. 'Jesus Christ.'

'See! It's working!' Linda exclaimed. 'Brilliant! Ha ha ha! I hope you're enjoying yourself, Tom!'

Seb staggered against the wall, his eyes watering from the over-powering foetid smell. He could stomach most things, but this was bloody hideous and the noise coming from Tom's mouth – the strange screaming coupled with grunting, made his skin crawl.

It took a few seconds before he realised his mobile was ringing.

He tugged it from his pocket and stared at the screen:

...Andrew calling...

Seb's stomach lurched. *Shit.* Something had better not have gone pear-shaped. He'd have thought they'd have returned by now with the body. 'Andrew, I'm a bit busy at the mo... What?'

Linda's heart dropped into her shoes as the colour drained from Seb's face. Her fear intensified when he steadied himself using one arm against the wall. 'What's happened? It's not Sam, is it? Is it Sam?'

Seb batted Linda's questions away, desperate to hear everything Andrew said. 'Fuck, bruv. Okay, yes.'

Ending the call, all thoughts of Bedworth on the backburner, he blanked out the animalistic screeching and the smell and turned to Linda.

'Seb?' Linda was barely able to ask the question which she knew must contain an answer which was not good. Seb looked haunted. *Destroyed.* 'W-what's happened? Tell me what's hap...'

'Sam's been taken to hospital in an ambulance.' Seb's voice was low and quiet. He dragged his arm across his eyes to remove the brewing tears. 'They think she's having a miscarriage.'

'Oh Christ!' Linda's hand flew to her mouth. *No! Not that!* She gulped air into her lungs. 'You must go. Go now!'

Seeing Seb's gaze move to Bedworth, she steered him towards the door. 'He's not important compared to this. I'll oversee it. He won't get out of this now, so go! Sam needs you.'

Linda wanted to be by her daughter's side too, but this was between husband and wife. All she could do was wrap things up here.

Pushing a stunned and panic-stricken Seb out of the door, Linda stared at Tom with renewed hatred at a level she hadn't believed possible to experience. 'See what your actions have caused?' she screamed, as his writhing body purged its contents. 'See what you've done to your own daughter?'

It was the stress that had brought this on. It had to be. Now Sam was losing her much longed for baby and it was *his* fault.

Dying like this was too good for him.

46

Seb crashed through the double doors of the hospital, his face ashen. He rushed up to the reception desk. 'My wife, Samantha Stoker, was brought in by ambulance. Can you tell me what's going on, please?'

As the woman painstakingly tapped the details in her computer, he felt like grabbing her around the neck to hurry her up. 'Come on!'

The receptionist eyed Seb curiously. 'Mr...?'

'Stoker. Seb Stoker,' Seb barked. 'I'm her husband. Just tell me what the fuck is going on with my wife!'

'Please calm down, Mr Stoker,' the receptionist said. 'I'm locating your wife's details now.'

'I need to see her!' Seb's fist crashed onto the counter, making the receptionist recoil in shock as well as gathering the attention of every pair of eyes in the overcrowded A&E waiting room. 'She came in by ambulance, for Christ's sake! She's pregnant! Surely someone knows what's going on?'

'I thought I could hear you!' Andrew entered through a set of double doors off to the left and placed his hand on Seb's shoulder. 'We're waiting through here. Come through.' He smiled thinly at the shaking receptionist. 'He's a bit stressed, that's all.'

Seb glared at Andrew. *A bit stressed?* His wife and child could be dead for the second time in as many days; his nemesis was in the death throes of arsenic poisoning, courtesy of his mother-in-law and his brother was driving around with the corpse of his wife's sister in the back of one of the Peacock's vans somewhere...

Stressed? No, he was having a cracking day.

Entering a large room full of people who looked like they were about to be condemned to death, Seb's resolve finally cracked.

He sagged into a plastic chair, his huge shoulders jerking with violent sobs. 'I can't lose her. I can't lose Sam or my child. Can't someone tell me what the fuck is going on?'

'Sam's in theatre,' Andrew said, never gladder than to see a pale-faced Gloria heading their way with two cups of plastic-tasting tea.

Sitting down next to Seb, Gloria placed her hand on his.

Seb looked between Gloria and his brother. 'Has she lost the baby? The stomach cramps? What were they? What?'

'That's what they're trying to find out,' Gloria said, her voice inexplicably soothing Seb's fractured mind. 'She's in the best place, dear. They'll find out what the problem is.'

'I can't stand this! Sam's my life. The baby – they mean every-thing to me. *Everything!*' Seb barked, his nerves unable to take much more. 'When will we be told?'

Andrew dug his nails into his palms to stop himself from losing it. He'd seen his big brother upset like this fewer times than he could count on one hand and each time ripped the soul from his body. 'I don't know how long it will be. As soon as they have some-thing to tell us, I guess.'

'But I need to know what's happening *now*!' Seb swiped his tears away and jumped to his feet. 'Fuck this! I'll find out myself if they...'

'Wait! Someone's coming now.' Gloria nodded towards the approaching man. 'Not sure whether it's for us.'

Seb swung around to see a grim-faced man in surgical scrubs heading in their direction. Judging by the look on the man's face, whoever he was heading for was unlikely to get good news.

His breath stuck halfway from his lungs as the doctor looked at him. 'Mr Stoker?'

* * *

'I-I wish there was something we could do,' Sophie sniffed, her puffy eyes sore from crying. She barely knew Sam Stoker, yet the anguish on the woman's face had ripped her heart clean in two.

Sam couldn't lose that baby. It was too cruel.

She knew she was trembling. She'd been trembling for the majority of the time these past few months and the last couple of days had pushed her to the edge.

Her gaze moved to the spot where the body of Marina Devlin had lain. Now nothing but a stained rug remained in that place. But the smashed skull of that woman; the staring eyes; the blood... *they* remained shining brightly in her mind and she suspected they would do so for some time, if not forever.

That was two gruesome deaths she'd seen now. By remaining with Andrew, Sophie suspected she would see many more...

'I think I've got most of it out now,' Vera said, her knees aching from kneeling to scrub the carpet. She was getting too old for this, but at least it kept her mind occupied, otherwise she'd be pacing the room until news got back to them.

Her bottom lip quivered as she muttered a silent prayer for Sam and the baby. *Please let them be safe.*

Vera would have gladly accompanied Sam in the ambulance. She'd wanted to, but it was only right that Gloria and Andrew should go. Gloria had been Sam's mother all those years in Linda's absence and Andrew would meet Seb at the hospital.

That there had been still no word of Linda played on her mind too. If Linda had been with Seb wherever Bedworth was held, then she'd already know about this nightmare and be at the hospital, but if Seb hadn't reached Linda in time and Bedworth had...

Vera shook her head to rid her brain of these fast-appearing scenarios. She was driving herself crazy with the what-ifs.

Surely someone had news by now?

'I hope Sam will be okay,' Sophie repeated for the fifteenth time.

Remembering the girl was still sitting in a chair like a spare thumb, Vera frowned. The poor girl had just undertaken a baptism of fire – one she could have done without.

She studied Sophie's elf-like face that bore the weight of the world. She'd need to toughen up if she were to survive a life with Andrew Stoker. As decent as the man was, this life was not for the faint of heart.

Vera's mouth formed a wry smile. She may not be doing shag all, short of waiting for news and scrubbing some slut's blood from Gloria's beige rug, but there was *one* thing she could say to lift a small amount of mental overload from this girl's brain.

'Sophie?' Vera waited until Sophie looked up and gave her full attention. 'I'm not sure which thing is the worst in your mind right now, but I think knowing this may help a little...'

Sophie's eyebrows raised, unsure whether *anything* could neutralise her inner turmoil.

'Andrew didn't kill Marina Devlin,' Vera said, slowly and clearly. 'It was Gloria.'

'G-Gloria?' Sophie blinked, unsure she'd heard correctly.

Vera couldn't help but chuckle. 'I know the old girl dresses well, has a posh gaff and looks more like she belongs in a Women's Institute meeting than in a life like this, but she knows what goes on. And no, murder is not something she usually partakes in, but it's amazing what people can do when push comes to shove to protect the people they love.'

Relief poured from Sophie. *Andrew hadn't done it after all?* But from what had been said previously, there was no choice but to kill Marina. What else could anyone have done?

Vera frowned at Sophie's obvious relief. 'Don't think this won't be something you won't need to deal with in the future if you remain by Andrew's side, my girl.' She cocked an eyebrow. 'And from what I've seen, you *will* remain with him.'

'I know and you're right.' Sophie accepted this as the truth on both counts. She'd already decided she would live with whatever Andrew was involved in. At least now she didn't have such an uncomfortable starting point. 'I guess looking at things that way is something I'll have to get used to.'

Both women jumped when Gloria's home phone rang.

Vera scrambled up from her knees in a rush to reach it, the bloodied cloth in her hand falling to the floor. *Was it Linda or one of the Stokers ringing from the hospital with news?*

She snatched up the receiver. 'Yes? Yes, it's me... Andrew? You're still at the hospital? With Seb? Yes? Have you any... She's what?'

Sophie moved to the edge of her chair seeing Vera sag against the wall.

'Yes, I understand...' Vera continued. 'Linda must be still over there. Neil's on his way now, taking... erm... you know...' She grabbed a pen and notepad. 'Give me Neil's mobile number and I'll call him to let him know so he can pass the news on to Linda.'

She shakily replaced the receiver and met eyes with Sophie before bursting into tears.

47

It was quiet in the concrete works. So quiet that Linda's breathing sounded as loud as an industrial air conditioning unit.

Her backside had long since gone to sleep from sitting on the hard plastic chair and although she'd raised her feet so they were out of touching distance of the river of grotesque fluid Tom had expelled from all orifices which relentlessly kept coming, she was unable to pull her eyes from the stenching liquid covering the floor.

She could leave. She could have left some time ago, but the unearthly smell no longer assaulted her nostrils.

It had taken ages for Tom to die – or it might have been quick. Linda wasn't sure. Time ran in a strange continuum. But she did know it was a horrible way to go. One which when the end finally came, Tom would have been grateful for.

Even then, just before he'd passed into the fiery pits of hell, Linda hadn't been able to refrain from bracing the foul, almost luminous bile and blood dripping from Tom's mouth and nose and the blood-stained clear liquid still emptying from somewhere within his bowels and intestines to stand over him.

She'd laughed.

Forcing his pain-wracked, terrified eyes to meet hers, she'd let him beg and plead for the final time for her to save him and do something. Her response?

She'd laughed again.

Linda had laughed and laughed and laughed as Tom left this earth.

He hadn't even had the energy to utter one last abusive comment...

But neither had he apologised for what he'd done. Not for a single thing.

For the first time, Linda noticed her hands were covered in blood. And it wasn't Tom's – it was her *own*.

She numbly eyed the gouges her fingernails had cut into the soft flesh of her palms, unaware she'd done it. She hadn't felt the pain.

She hadn't felt anything.

So why were tears coursing down her cheeks?

Linda shuddered, her laboured breathing coming in fast hiccupping sobs as she raised her eyes once more to look at the empty grey shell which had once been Tom Bedworth.

Why was she even upset?

Was she upset?

How could she possibly be upset that this monster had died such a fitting death?

Slightly panicking, Linda analysed her strange reaction. Surely she couldn't be sad or regret what she'd done? What she'd both wanted and *needed* to do?

Was she crying for herself? For Tom? For Sam?

Suddenly the fog lifted and her reasoning became crystal clear.

With a jolt, Linda suddenly realised her tears were for what Tom had done – to her, to Sam; to all those women and faceless, nameless people he'd hurt and destroyed... Then there was the Stokers; the Reynold family – *everyone*...

The tears were also for what *could* have been.

Once she'd been that fifteen-year-old girl who had fallen madly in love. She'd given herself to this man and him alone. They had created a child.

They *could* have been happy. They *could* have had a nice life together. They may not have had much, but that would have been okay. They could have made it work and got by with each other and their little family, like countless others.

But *he'd* decided that wasn't going to happen. Tom had thrown it all away.

And now he was dead.

Dead by her own hand.

Linda put her head in her hands and sobbed harder, thirty years of anguish and sadness finally releasing in a loud wailing from a heart which had been broken too many times.

She fought to breathe through her heaving lungs, gasping in the foetid air around her in a mixture of crushing sadness as well as relief.

It didn't have to end like this, but it had.

'Why did you have to be like that, Tom?' Linda said out loud. 'You threw everything away.'

Wrapping her arms around her knees, Linda curled into a ball and rocked backwards and forwards on the chair, pretending she was being comforted by unknown arms.

It was over.

She'd lost the only man she'd ever loved, yet the only one she hated so much to murder in a way so horribly agonising, she wouldn't inflict on a rabid animal. She'd lost a daughter as well as a son.

And she might have lost her grandchild by now...

Linda suddenly sat bolt upright and put her feet firmly on the ground, not caring if her shoes touched the filth coating the floor.

It wasn't over.

Of *course* it wasn't over.

She still had Sam. Hopefully a grandchild too. She still had Tayquan and Shondra, as well as her dear friend, Vera.

No, it wasn't over.

Linda's mouth set resolutely. 'Pull yourself together,' she snapped. 'You've done what was needed and now you must sort yourself out!'

She needed to get to the hospital. There was no reason to stay here. Her daughter needed her. If the worst had happened, then Sam would need her to be strong now more than ever, not a self-pitying mess over what she 'could' have had.

Taking one final glance at the shrivelled remains of Tom Bedworth, Linda darted towards the door. She'd run to the main road and flag down a cab to take her to the hospital.

With an immense amount of effort, she dragged open the heavy metal door, only to freeze in her tracks as a car screeched to a halt outside.

Neil. It was Neil Stoker.

Clinging to the door frame, Linda's heart picked up a strange off-beat rhythm as Neil got out of the car, his face drawn.

Neil wouldn't have been sent here when he was busy dealing with the mess at Gloria's.

Unless...

'Linda,' Neil shouted. 'I've had news from the hospital.'

Linda didn't want to hear it.

Putting her hands over her ears, she slid down the doorjamb to land on concrete which sliced into her knees.

Her ear-piercing screams echoed around the deserted yard.

EPILOGUE

SIX MONTHS LATER

Seb supposed he should make the effort to be pleased, but in all truth, a celebration, even if his family and everyone important to him was here, was the last thing he wanted.

He'd just wanted time alone to gather his thoughts, but that wasn't going to happen.

Did everyone think he couldn't cope?

Because he could.

He'd coped with a hell of a lot of stuff that had been thrown at him. Far too much, in fact. But he would continue to cope, regardless and would manage with *this* too. And, well too, he hoped.

'You could at least look happy!' Andrew said, digging Seb in the ribs as he handed him a large whisky.

'I'm trying...' Seb muttered, eyeing the decorations strewn around his kitchen, a bit like the rest of the house.

Gloria and Linda's doing, no doubt. He suspected his mother had also had a hand in it.

Now his parents had decided, under the circumstances, to return to Birmingham several months early, it meant there were even more people fussing about and Seb had never been a fan of fuss.

'It will be fine, you know.' Andrew slapped Seb on the back. 'It really will.'

Seb looked thoughtfully at his brother. 'Yeah, I know. I know. It's just... well, it's all a bit...'

Andrew nodded. 'You don't need to explain.'

He understood. He understood why Seb was so edgy. Everyone did. He'd be the same himself.

As Tayquan and Shondra suddenly raced through the kitchen and out the other side, Andrew tensed when they almost ran slap bang into Sophie making her way in.

It was true he'd become more overprotective than he should after what happened to Sam. Who could blame him?

He slipped his arm around Sophie's waist and kissed her as she approached.

When he'd finally felt able to approach Seb about his wanting a relationship with Sophie, things had gone easier than he'd expected. And for his brother's acceptance, he was thankful.

Seb kissed Sophie on the cheek. 'All right, love? You're managing to keep him under control for the special occasion, then? Kept an eye on his spirit intake?'

He knew he needed to make the effort to not act like a slapped haddock about this rather unwanted intrusion into his house. Furthermore, he was glad for Andrew.

Like he'd said, when Andrew first came to him, explaining the woman he loved had prior involvement with Marina Devlin, that if his brother believed Sophie wasn't knowingly involved with that whore, then Seb would take his lead. As would the rest of the family. And they had. It had been easy, really.

For fuck's sake, Seb more than most knew life was too short not to grab happiness when the chance arose. He shuddered, forcing away the unwanted thoughts spilling into his head.

Now Andrew and Sophie were engaged. Even Neil had managed to bag himself a girlfriend.

'Don't look now,' Andrew hissed, 'but you can guess who are on their way in here...'

Inwardly groaning, Seb steeled himself for the onslaught. Plastering on a smile, he turned just as Linda, Gloria and his mother descended.

Oh, wait – Vera too! *Super...*

'What are you doing hiding in here?' Linda cried. 'When are you coming to join the celebrations?'

'Yes, come on, Sebastian,' Gloria smiled. 'You should be in the sitting room with everyone else, not hiding in here!'

'Everyone's waiting, son,' Judith added.

Vera eyed the whisky in Seb's hand. 'He's busy having a couple of swiftys on the quiet whilst he still can!'

'I'll be in soon. I'm just having a breather,' Seb sighed, hoping someone would get the hint. He *would* join in with everyone soon.

Soon, but not quite yet...

'Come on,' Gloria said, pulling the women back towards the sitting room. 'Let's give him a bit of space.' She knew how necessary that was sometimes. It had been the same for her. For instance, it had taken some time to get her head around what she'd done to Marina Devlin.

It had been extremely difficult to accept that her actions went against her principles, but eventually, with everyone else's help, Gloria had reached the conclusion that she'd done the right thing.

And she *had*. She didn't regret what she'd done. It was the best and the *only* thing to do under those circumstances. Okay, so *this* situation wasn't the same, but everything took time.

Flashing Seb an understanding smile, Gloria led the other women out of the kitchen.

Andrew studied the stress on his brother's face. 'You know, you really should go and see if... Ah-ha!'

The worry and stress mounting in Seb's mind immediately melted away as he turned around, a wide grin forming on his face. 'You look perfect!' he smiled, moving forward.

Sam gazed at their newborn son in her arms, her heart swelling with more love than she'd ever believed possible to exist. 'I told you I just needed half an hour to tidy myself up and get the smell of delivery rooms off me. We're downstairs now and ready, so let's do this.'

Supporting his child's head with a big hand, Seb carefully lifted his baby son from Sam's arms and gazed into his little face.

The perfect child – the one who, not many months ago, he'd thought he'd never have.

That day the doctor had appeared, Seb had truly thought he'd lost both of them, but a ruptured appendix had been the culprit of Sam's excruciating stomach cramps.

Undergoing emergency surgery to deal with the appendix, which was risky whilst pregnant, Sam had then been monitored to ensure the blow which had ruptured the appendix hadn't damaged the baby. It had been a fraught time.

She'd finally been given the all clear, but even with this reassurance, both he and Sam had tiptoed on eggshells for the remainder of the pregnancy, unable to fully presume their baby would be born healthy.

And that stress and worry had continued. Until yesterday.

But, Seb stared transfixed into the face of his son, they now knew without a doubt that Joseph Leonard Stoker was 100 per cent healthy and perfect.

Seb's relief was astronomical. But along with relief, it had uncovered a new set of fears. He'd never had anything to do with babies before and he wanted to make sure he did everything perfectly. How did he even change a nappy, for God's sake?

'Oh my God! He's adorable!' Sophie squealed. 'Oh, Sam, you've done fantastic! You look amazing too!'

'Keep your voice down,' Andrew said. 'They'll all come running in otherwise.'

'We've kept them waiting long enough!' Sam smiled. 'So, let's go and do the big reveal!'

She knew Seb was overcome. She was too.

She also knew that Seb would have preferred to spend the first night as a family on their own, but these people were part of what had enabled them to *become* a family. Every single one of them had played their part in different ways. If it hadn't been for the things these people had done, then...

Sam pushed the thoughts away. Just like she was slowly successfully managing with the other things plaguing her.

Like Seb said, it was over. *Really* over.

And yes, it would take a long time to get her head around who her father really had been, but with Seb on her side, her beautiful child healthy and this family around her, she'd get through it.

Seb delicately handed their newborn back to Sam, who planted a kiss on her baby's tiny forehead and drank in the beautiful smell that only babies had. 'Let's do it, then.'

On top of the world now Sam and his child were at his side, Seb flung open the sitting room door. 'Ladies and gentlemen, please meet our gorgeous son, Joseph Leonard Stoker!'

Amidst the shrieks, cheers and gasps of delight, Seb placed his arm around the shoulders of his wife and thanked his lucky stars once again for his good fortune.

He had no problem knowing what his remit was: that he would ensure these two had everything they wished for and needed. And that, he would deliver 100 per cent.

His family would be festooned with his love until the day he died.

ACKNOWLEDGMENTS

It has been a pleasure writing this series set in the city that was my home for so many years. Now the series has come to an end I will miss absorbing myself in the sights, smells and places of Birmingham that I remember so very well.

I will also miss Seb and Sam and even Tom Bedworth (even though he was a thoroughly despicable bloke and a character I had to force myself not to kill off since book one!).

My thanks go to my lovely editor Emily Ruston and the whole team at Boldwood, as well as Annie Aldington, who is deservedly so well-renowned for doing a fantastic job in bringing characters of gangland fiction to life. She certainly got all of the characters in the Allegiance series down to a tee!

Again, huge thanks to all the readers who enjoy my books and without whom I would have no one to write for. I hope that you will step into more of my books and find further characters both to love and hate.

Finally love to my husband and son, family and friends.

Much love to you all.

Edie x

MORE FROM EDIE BAYLIS

We hope you enjoyed reading *Judgement*. If you did, please leave a review.

If you'd like to gift a copy, this book is also available as an ebook, large print, hardback, digital audio download and audiobook CD.

Sign up to Edie Baylis's mailing list for news, competitions and updates on future books.

https://bit.ly/EdieBaylisnews

Explore the rest of the Allegiance series now...

ABOUT THE AUTHOR

Edie Baylis is a successful self-published author of dark gritty thrillers with violent background settings. She lives in Worcestershire, has a history of owning daft cars and several motorbikes and is licensed to run a pub.

Visit Edie's website: http://www.ediebaylis.co.uk/

Follow Edie on social media:

twitter.com/ediebaylis
facebook.com/downfallseries
instagram.com/ediebaylis

PEAKY READERS

GANG LOYALTIES. DARK SECRETS.
BLOODY REVENGE.

A READER COMMUNITY FOR
GANGLAND CRIME THRILLER FANS!

DISCOVER PAGE-TURNING NOVELS
FROM YOUR FAVOURITE AUTHORS
AND MEET NEW FRIENDS.

JOIN OUR BOOK CLUB
FACEBOOK GROUP

BIT.LY/PEAKYREADERSFB

SIGN UP TO OUR
NEWSLETTER

BIT.LY/PEAKYREADERSNEWS

Boldwood

Boldwood Books is an award-winning fiction publishing company seeking out the best stories from around the world.

Find out more at www.boldwoodbooks.com

Join our reader community for brilliant books, competitions and offers!

Follow us
@BoldwoodBooks
@BookandTonic

Sign up to our weekly deals newsletter

https://bit.ly/BookandTonicNews